COLD BLOOD

DIRTY BLOOD SERIES

BOOK TWO

HEATHER HILDENBRAND

Cold Blood

Dirty Blood Series Book 2

Jacket Design by Malice & Mayhem Book Covers

Edge Design & Character Art by Samaiya

Hard Case Cover Design by We Got You Covered Book Designs

www.heatherhildenbrand.com

CHAPTER ONE

"I can't believe this. You punched her in the face? Twice?!" My mother's voice rose to a shriek.

"Um." There wasn't anything I could say to make this one go down easier, so I stayed wisely silent and stared down at my hands propped on the faux marble of the island countertop. We were facing off in the kitchen. Two days had passed since … well, since I'd almost died. And Mom, too.

Grandma was rummaging around upstairs, probably rearranging my mother's furniture in the guest room. Again. Which I knew added to my mother's stress level and left me taking the heat.

In the aftermath of that day, I'd forgotten all about the incident at school. Only now did I realize how little the office had told my mother during that initial phone call before she'd gone and tried to sacrifice herself to Leo, my evil uncle.

I'd somehow dodged it again when she'd called to withdraw me from my high school, giving them the address at Wood Point to send my transcripts. Whichever clueless old lady she'd talked to at reception hadn't even mentioned the suspension. But then today, she'd received the letter, and the explanation it contained from Principal Sellers that cleared it all up. In detail.

My mother blew out a breath and a stray piece of hair flew off her forehead and then back down again. I think she would've paced, but then she wouldn't have been able to hold the icy glare she was using on me. I shifted my weight, wondering if it would be a mistake to make a break for the stairs. Probably.

My mother waved the letter from Principal Sellers in my face, as if I might not remember whatever it said happened.

"I can't believe this," she repeated. "Suspended. For fighting. This goes on your permanent record, you know. Colleges will see it. If you make it that far. And at this rate, you might not. We're lucky Grandma secured your spot at Wood Point already."

Wood Point. Yeah, lucky. I hung onto my silence, but it was getting harder. I wanted to say that if I'd known it would get me out of boarding school, I'd happily punch Cindy Adams all over again. I had a feeling that was not something I should say out loud.

The oven timer dinged, signaling the self-cleaning was done. My mother broke her gaze and glanced at the appliance like it was calling to her. "We'll talk about this later."

I scurried out before she'd finished pulling on her yellow cleaning gloves.

I thought about going back to my room to hide out, while my mother worked her frustrations out on the oven, but it was depressing in there. All of my clothes were packed and ready to go for the trip to Wood Point tomorrow. So were most of my books, bedding, and anything else remotely important to me. Everything except Wes.

I hovered outside my room, leaning against the wall, and trying to ignore the dull pang that arose from thinking his name. He'd been by every day, under the watchful and disapproving eyes of my mother. He was slow to convince that I really was recovering. At least, that's why he claimed to be checking on me. He hadn't said much about anything else, including us, or school, or how we were supposed to be 'us' with me at school. I was afraid to ask because I wasn't sure what his answer would be.

I was still hung up on the whole magnetic pull between us. The more time that passed, the more it bothered me. What if that was the only reason I was attracted to him? Or him, to me? What if we only wanted to be together because of some strange chemical reaction in our blood? It was hard to believe, because just thinking about him made me ache and yearn in ways I'd never thought possible. But, I couldn't shake the doubts and wondering…

And then there was his completely annoying over protectiveness that fell somewhere between macho extreme and unnecessary. I was trying to be understanding and let it go. I was the first to jump on the protective bandwagon when it came to someone I loved, but every time he made a decision about what was best for me, without actually consulting me, it grated.

"There you are." Grandma poked her head out of the guest room next to mine. She glanced behind me, probably making sure my mother hadn't followed me up. When she saw I was alone, her gaze darted back to me and she relaxed. "Come in here, will you?"

I pushed off from the wall and followed her through her open door. Sure enough, the furniture was set up totally different than before. The bed was pushed against the far right wall, instead of centered between the windows, and the dresser was pushed up against the window, so that the mirror and frame blocked the view outside.

"Love what you've done with the place," I said, crossing to a blue cushioned chair, next to the narrow bookshelf she was using to block the opposite window.

"Your mother is naïve and careless." She took a seat on the edge of her bed, looking so normal in her elastic waist jeans and 'Number One Grandma' sweatshirt. But I could still picture her back in the warehouse, cutting a path of dead Werewolves with the speed of someone a third her age. I no longer let her unassuming air fool me. "She forgets we're fighting a war and need to operate accordingly. This house is a painted target after what happened with Leo, and she leaves it wide open. Like 'Come and get me.'"

She clucked her tongue and pulled open her nightstand drawer. I waited; I knew better than to get in the middle of anything to do with her and my mother. She reached in and pulled out a thick, leather-bound volume and held it out to me.

"What's this?" I asked. I took the book, staring at the cover. The symbols on the front looked familiar, and I remembered where I'd seen it. The book Fee had let me borrow. The one that had eventually led to my mother discovering what I knew. But this one looked a little different, and it felt older, more used somehow. "The Draven?"

"Our Draven. The one you had was borrowed. I gave it back to Fee. This one is yours. And the rest of the family's. Traditionally, it should go to your mother next, but I don't think she'll accept it. Besides, what with school and all, I think you should have it."

"Thanks, Grandma." I paged through it and eyed the familiar drawings depicting battles and weapons. "I already read a lot of this, though."

She shook her head. "Turn to the back."

I flipped to somewhere near the end. The last few pages, which should've been blank, had some sort of chart drawn in with handwritten names on each connecting line. All of it was interconnected with lines joining certain branches together. I spotted Grandma's name on the last page, along with my grandfather and the dates of his life span underneath. My name was somewhere near the bottom, underneath my mother and father.

"It's our family tree," I said.

"Hunters take pride in their lineage and knowing where they came from. So should you. You come from the best Hunter stock there is. You'll learn all about it at Wood Point. Lineage is very important there." She shifted her attention back to me. "Now, tell me about this girl you punched."

I made a face and let the book fall closed. "It was a bad idea. I didn't mean to, but that girl's been pushing my buttons for way too long. She went too far, and I realized how much stronger than her I was and…" I broke off, my shoulders slumping when I saw that Grandma was frowning at me. "Yeah, I shouldn't have done it."

"I expected more, Tara."

"I know."

"No, I mean, literally, I expected her to have provoked you, thrown the first punch, something. I didn't think you'd attack an innocent human without provocation."

"It's been a long time coming. And I wouldn't have done it if I'd known I'd hurt her that bad," I said, which was a total lie. I'd been hoping to damage Cindy at the time; I just hated disappointing Grandma. It was worse than my mother being angry, because Grandma had a way of piling on the guilt through disappointment. I sighed.

"You have a responsibility to protect those weaker than you, not use your strength against them," Grandma said. "You need to remember that."

"I know. I guess I…lost control."

Grandma didn't answer. When I looked up, she was studying me with a more serious expression than I'd seen her wear in a long time. It made me feel even worse.

"Sorry," I said. "Go ahead and lecture me."

"I'm not going to lecture you. You already know it was wrong and that you need to work on keeping a hold of your temper. You're just new and haven't had time to learn. If anything, I blame your mother."

"Blame me for what?" My mother stood in the doorway, yellow-gloved hands on her hips. "Everything's my fault, right?"

Crap. I really didn't want to get caught in the crossfire when this one blew up.

Before Grandma could answer, my mother looked at me and said, "Angela and Sam are here to say goodbye. They're downstairs waiting for you."

"Thanks." I got up and hurried out, ducking past my mother and heading for the stairs.

Angela and Sam were in the den. The room had been put back together since Leo's intrusion, minus several pieces of furniture that were too broken to salvage. The couch was saved, along with the coffee table. A spare TV from the garage had been set up on a bookshelf and a brand new marbled glass globe covered the light fixture on the ceiling. Other than that, the room was pretty empty. It was the room that had seen the most destruction from Leo's goons. Grandma said it was because the den was the first room I would've seen when I came home that day, and Leo knew that. He'd trashed the house even after my mother had agreed to go with him, all to get a reaction out of me and send me running after him. It had worked.

Sam was watching E! News and twirling a lock of silky hair between her fingers. Angela flipped through one of my mother's gardening magazines. They both looked up when I came in.

"Hey, stranger," Sam said, raising the remote to click the TV off.

"You should leave it on." I sent a pointed look at the ceiling where muffled voices could be heard rising with each comment. "It'll drown out the static." I sank onto the couch, next to Angela. She gave me a sorrowful look.

"How are you?" she asked. "I mean, really?"

"Miserable," I admitted. Though they only knew half of it, or maybe less than half. As far as they knew, I'd punched Cindy, my mother flipped out, and now I was being shipped off to boarding school. That, in itself, was enough to make a girl miserable, so I figured it was fine to admit.

"Yeah, I'd be miserable, too. But I mean, at least its co-ed," Sam said. Angela shot Sam a look. "What? I'm trying to help her look at the bright side."

"She's with Wes, remember?" Angela whispered. They also both knew that my mother was not a fan of Wes.

"A girl can window shop," Sam hissed back.

Angela turned to me, rolling her eyes. "You have to email us every day, okay? And call whenever you can. They will let you call, right?"

"I don't really know. I'll call as much as I can."

"Oh, and we're supposed to give you this." Angela reached into her pocket and handed me a folded up piece of notebook paper, flattened out from all the handling. "It's from George. You can read it later."

"Oh, no way, she reads it now. I've got to hear this." Sam shifted like she was getting comfortable and waited expectantly.

I unfolded the paper and silently scanned the words. Oh geez. I looked up. Sam – and even Angela – was still waiting. Sam had the ghost of a grin on her lips. Judging by her smile, there was a good chance she already knew what it said. Making me read it out loud was icing on the cake. I cleared my throat and read the words in a low voice. Words about Romeo bleeding and love that lasts forever, always.

When I was done–and completely red faced–I lowered the paper and looked at the girls.

“Wow. That was…” Angela began.

“Hot,” Sam finished. “Who knew the boy had it in him? Do you think he got it off the internet?”

“No, he didn’t get it off the internet,” Angela argued.

Sam shrugged. “He could’ve. We should google it.”

"You guys? It's Bon Jovi." I folded the letter and shoved it into my jeans pocket. "It was our song. It doesn’t matter, anyway. I’m leaving, remember?”

“And you have Wes,” Angela put in.

“Who is way hotter than George,” Sam added.

I grinned; I couldn’t help it. “I’m going to miss you guys.”

Sam and I threw our arms around Angela and brought it in for a group hug that had us giggling until the doorbell rang. All three of us eyed each other with raised brows.

“Five bucks on George,” Sam said.

I arrived at the door at the same time as my mother. She stepped in front of me and eyed the peephole before pulling it open. She frowned, which didn’t give away all that much since she'd been doing a lot of that lately, but then she stepped back, and I saw who it was.

“Hey,” Wes said. His eyes locked on to mine.

“Hey,” I answered, staring back.

“Dinner’s in an hour.” My mother held onto her frown, but she wandered back towards the kitchen, leaving us alone.

Sam and Angela slipped past me, knowing smiles pasted on their faces.

“We’d better get going,” said Angela.

She stepped forward and hugged me tightly. When she pulled away, Sam threw an arm around my neck and squeezed. “Yum,” she whispered.

“Call us when you get settled in,” Angela reminded me.

Sam turned and winked. "Don't do anything I would."

I rolled my eyes and waved goodbye. When they were gone, Wes stepped inside and shoved his hands into his jean pockets. He looked wound up, rolling back and forth from his heels to his toes.

"Everything okay?" I asked.

"Can we take a walk?" he asked, glancing towards the kitchen–and the sound of a spray bottle at work.

"Um, how about the backyard?" A knot of anxiety pinched my gut.

He nodded, and I led him through the sunroom and out the sliding door. The sun was bright and cheery; hinting at warmer days to come but with enough of a chill in the air to remind you it was still technically winter.

The branches were still bare, dead leaves covering the ground. It had rained during the night and the smell of wet grass and mud covered everything, permeating every breath until you could taste spring trying to emerge. Somewhere deep in the trees, a single bird called intermittently. It all felt entirely too lonely.

I wrapped my sweatshirt around myself and crossed my arms. We walked to the edge of the yard and stepped into the covered gazebo, sitting on the small bench that faced the woods.

The silence ran on, and I felt my stomach tighten. Was this him being reluctant to say goodbye, or was it something more?

"How's Jack?" I finally asked.

"He's better, I guess. Still in bed, though. Fee won't let him up and he's going a little crazy." A ghost of a smile appeared and then faded again. "You can hear them picking at each other in every room of the house. I was glad for the chance to get away."

"At least you can go home at night," I said.

He shook his head. "I've moved some stuff over. I'm going to stay with them for a while. With Jack out of commission and Miles still out there, I don't want to leave Fee."

"That makes sense." I tried to read into his responses and figure out what he wasn't saying. He seemed tense, fidgeting with his pants, and shoes, and whatever else was close. "Wes. What's wrong?"

Wes' eyes flickered to mine and away again, never really settling on any particular spot. A nervous pang went through my gut. "Wes?"

"Jack pulled me aside yesterday. He said he knows he can't handle things himself with The Cause." He paused. "He wants me to step up, help run things." He finally looked up and met my eyes. "He wants me to lead."

I blinked back at him, relieved to hear what was behind his mood and glad it wasn't something… well, bad. Or maybe it was, for him at least. He didn't exactly look thrilled. "But what's so bad about that?"

Without a word, he grabbed my wrist and pulled me off the bench, half dragging me into the woods. He ducked behind a massive oak and pulled me behind it with him, wrapping his arms around me and burying his face in my hair. My surprise at his sudden affection eased, and I pressed closer and let him hold me.

Until this moment, he'd been so careful with me, as if I'd break from any physical contact rougher than hand holding or lips grazing. This was so much better.

When he pulled away, his expression was halfway between pained and hungry. "I was going to come with you," he said.

I pulled back. "To school? Really?"

He nodded. "But now, with everything happening with Jack, I can't. I have to stay." He didn't give me a chance to answer, instead pressing his lips to mine in short, hungry kisses that left me dizzy and breathless. The pull between us sprang to life, and my body ached to be closer, a part of him.

"You can come visit me," I said, between kisses.

His lips slowed and stilled against mine, and then he pulled away. His eyes were sad. "No, I can't. At least not for a while. Jack wants me to take over immediately. I'm moving in to help until he's up and around, and then I have to start travelling. He needs to introduce me to all of the allies we have left, so they'll trust me enough to work with me when he hands the reigns over. It's a full time job. I'm sorry."

"I understand," I said. And suddenly I did. Vera's vision sprang to mind – a picture of Wes and me leading The Cause–and I wondered if this was the first step towards making it true. I shook that off, not wanting to make this bigger than it already was. I focused on the fact that Wes had wanted to come in the first place. His reluctance at talking to me wasn't about not wanting to be with me, or worrying about the long distance part of our relationship; it was about his responsibility to The Cause. That made me feel better. "It's okay," I assured him. "I'll be home for the summer. We'll see each other in a few months."

"I know," he whispered, still gazing at me with a mournful expression.

"So what's the problem? You don't want to take over?"

"It's not that. I...." He stepped away and began to pace in front of me. "I don't know. My father was in charge, and look what it got him. An early grave. It's not like I care about my own life, but–" He broke off and looked up at me. "What if something happens to you, up at that school? And I wasn't there to stop it, because I put business before you? My father put business before family, and it got him and my mother killed. I won't let that happen." He walked over to me, running his hand through my hair.

"Wes, you are not your father. And nothing is going to happen to me." I slipped my hands inside his jacket, running my palms over his chest. I wanted to comfort him, but I didn't know what to say. I thought of Vera's vision again, wondering if he even realized what his taking over meant.

He leaned over, pressing his lips to my forehead, then my temple, then my cheek; I held on to him as his lips trailed along my jaw and then found my mouth. "You have to promise to be careful," he whispered, between kisses. "Stay on school property. Don't go anywhere alone."

All I could do was mumble a noise that resembled, "Okay."

He finally pulled away, on a long, almost painful exhale and cupped my face in his hands. "I'm going to find Miles and end him. And then you're going to come home to me, okay?"

I smiled crookedly, too caught up in the moment to mind his protective demands. "And if my mom still hates you?"

His lips curved. "I have three months until summer break to wear her down with my charm. Piece of cake."

My laughter was interrupted by my mother's shrill voice cutting across the yard. "Tara, time's up. Get inside!"

"Coming!" I stayed wedged between the tree and Wes, waiting for him to move and let me free.

"Don't forget about me up there," he whispered.

"Never," I whispered back, already missing him.

CHAPTER TWO

"Elizabeth, let's get a move on," Grandma called from the open doorway.

The sky was beginning to lighten from black to gray– the sun hadn't yet made its appearance – and in the dim light of morning, the black Hummer parked at the curb looked more like an army tank. A very shiny army tank.

"Coming," my mother called, hauling the last of the bags from my room and maneuvering carefully down the stairs under their weight. She'd made it clear she wasn't excited about taking the Hummer, but I suspected she dreaded the ride home alone with Grandma.

I stood, bleary eyed on the porch, with my duffel bag slung over my shoulder, a pillow in one hand and a travel coffee mug in the other. I was as ready as I would ever be, especially at five thirty in the morning.

"We've gotta roll if we want to make it out of town before rush hour," Grandma said.

My mother glared at Grandma as she shuffled past her with the bags, arms straining under the weight. "We'd already be on our way if you'd help carry something."

Grandma held up her quilted purse that was the size of a small suitcase. “I have this, don’t I? It’s got snacks for the car.”

My mother muttered something under her breath that she’d once told me a lady should never say and heaved the last bag into the back of the Hummer with a thunk.

Grandma closed and locked the front door, and I slid into the cold backseat of the car/truck/weapon of mass destruction. It had a leathery new car smell that I didn’t remember from the first time I’d ridden in it; then again, I’d been barely conscious and clinging to life, so a smell going unnoticed was to be expected.

Grandma and my mother climbed into the front seats, and I do mean climbed. Grandma had to use the metal bar hanging below her open door, like a step ladder, and then another above her head to pull herself up. The massive front seat seemed to swallow her. My mother didn’t notice the extra step or the pull-bar, so she gripped the corners of the seat and climbed in like a toddler. I muffled a laugh, and she glared at me.

At the turn of the key the engine roared to life, and Grandma eased us out of the neighborhood. I turned back once before we rounded the corner at the stop sign and watched my house disappear from view. I couldn’t help but feel a certain finality to it all, like home would never feel the same again.

Grandma and my mother were quiet on the drive out of Frederick Falls, and I forced myself to sleep. The only other choice would’ve been to stare out the window and watch everything that was familiar fade away, until nothing was recognizable.

I AWOKE TO THE TIRES BUMPING OVER THE LIP OF THE ASPHALT; Grandma was pulling into a Burger King. We were off the highway, though there wasn't much to see. A lonely looking Burger King sat beside an Exxon. Both were surrounded by trees in all directions. The only interruption was the two lane road we had turned off of. State route something-or-other.

Grandma parked the Hummer beside a faded blue Camry and cut the engine. She glanced back and smiled when she saw that I was awake.

"Pit stop," Grandma said. "You gotta go?"

I shook my head, still a little dazed from the nap, and rubbed my eyes. "No, I'm good. What time is it?"

"Around seven. You want coffee?"

I nodded. "Please." The reality hit me that I was closer to Wood Point than home, and I knew I wouldn't be able to sleep now.

My mom hopped out and turned back to me. "I'll bring you a coffee and a breakfast sandwich," she said.

"Back in a flash," Grandma called.

Their doors slammed shut at the same time, and I watched them disappear into the building. When they were gone, I reached over and rummaged inside my backpack for my cell phone. I was hoping my mother wouldn't notice it was gone until it was too late to get it back from me, like after she'd left me at school. She must've known by now that I'd swiped it back since she tried confiscating it, but she hadn't said anything yet.

I powered it on and waited for the screen to light up with any new calls. A new text flashed first, and I clicked it open, hoping it was Wes. I still wanted to find something to say to make him feel better, but it was from George.

Did u get my note? I'll miss u. Call me.

Crap. I'd almost forgotten about the song lyrics he'd sent through Angela. It was a sweet gesture, but I wasn't sure what to say to him. "Thanks" didn't seem like enough. He'd be expecting more than that. I just didn't have more than that to say right now. I missed his friendship, but I didn't really know how to get that back when he was still so focused on a relationship. I closed the text. I'd figure something out later.

The screen beeped with a new voice mail. I punched the call button and listened. The voice that reached my ears was not at all the one I'd been expecting. I froze.

"Tara, darling. I heard the good news. You survived, Jack survived;

we all survived. Oh wait, not all of us. Dear old Dad didn't make it. Pity. I guess the burden of world domination falls to me. Or should I say, to us. I'm sure by now there are search parties out looking for me. Wes, Cord, Derek, Jack. Maybe not Jack. No matter. They won't find me. But don't worry; you and I aren't finished yet. We're connected in a way that no one else can touch. And I'll find you, when I'm ready. I have a project to complete first, but I'll see you soon. Ciao."

I sat there, still as a statue, until the recorded voice had asked me three times whether I wanted to save or delete the message. I hit the button to end the call and let the phone fall to my lap. I stared blankly out the windshield, trying to decide whether I was actually even surprised by Miles' call. Not really. I guess I'd known he would contact me when he found out his shot had missed the mark. The thing that bothered me was the way he spoke. He sounded so much like Leo; smooth charm with a layer of psycho and a dash of sarcasm.

I shuddered. Movement outside caught my eye, and I looked up. Grandma held the door for my mother, who had a drink tray in one hand and a bag of greasy breakfast sandwiches in the other. Grandma let go of the door and took the bag from my mother before they started towards the car. If I wasn't freaking out, I might've been able to appreciate the fact that they were being nice to each other.

Instead, I punched the power button on my phone and shoved it back into my backpack just as they reached the car. In that split second, I decided not to tell my mom. I didn't even have time to second guess it before she opened her car door and hauled herself inside.

"Sausage biscuit?" she asked, handing a wrapped sandwich over her shoulder.

I mumbled a "thanks" and took it as Grandma settled in the driver's seat and passed me a paper coffee cup. Steam rose through the tiny hole in the lid. I set the food aside and wrapped both hands around it, enjoying the emanating warmth. Grandma turned the key and the Hummer roared to life. In no time, we were back on the highway.

I ate my sandwich, or what little of it I could manage to get down. The voice mail had pretty much killed my appetite. All I could think about was Leo, and how truly crazy he'd been. Not only because he was willing to kill his own flesh and blood, but he'd made sure to instill the same kind of narcissistic hate in his own son. I still didn't understand why, completely, but I was pretty sure I knew who had answers.

"Mom, can I ask you something?"

"Sure," she answered, without turning. "What's up?"

"I was thinking about Leo. I mean, what happened to make him hate us so much?"

My mother sighed, and Grandma glanced over at her, like she was wondering if my mother was even going to answer.

A minute passed.

“Mom?”

“Tara, can we talk about this some other time?”

“You said that last time.” Even though she couldn't see me, I crossed my arms over my chest, defiantly. She wouldn't put me off again. “When you told me about being related to him, and I asked why that would make him want to kill me, you said, 'There's a lot you don't understand and I can't take the time to explain it all right now', remember?”

My mother’s shoulders rose and fell like she was sighing again, but no sound came out. “You're right. I did.”

“And you also said you'd stop treating me like I'm helpless,” I pointed out. Saying the words made me grit my teeth. If she'd really meant them, she wouldn't be about to drop me off at a boarding school in the middle of nowhere.

“You're right,” she said, “I did say that.” She paused for so long I wondered if she was ignoring me. Finally, she glanced over at Grandma and spoke. "I met Leo through your father. There was enough of an age gap that Leo was already living on his own by then, but I'd gone over for dinner one night and he was there, too. He was charming and outgoing and made people laugh, though I could see there was something else lurking underneath, even then.

“Your father was trying to talk him into joining the Cause but Leo wouldn’t commit. He and I spent a lot of time together, just the two of us, while your father was gone on missions. Looking back, I think Leo never intended to join us. He only wanted to spend time with me. I–”

she broke off and then continued after a beat. “I never realized what was happening…"

Her voice drifted off, leaving a tense silence. Grandma said nothing. We both waited to hear the rest; I wondered how much of this Grandma had even heard.

"He came to me one night. Your father was away, and I was alone. He brought flowers and dinner, and I let him because we were friends, and I was naïve. I thought I might be able to use it to convince him to join The Cause. He kissed me, or tried to, and I pushed him away. Then he brought out a ring. Said he would never love anyone else, ever, so I had to say yes. Of course, I didn't. I loved your father, and I told him that.

“I don't think I've ever seen eyes that hard in my entire life. It was as if all the light went out of them in that instant. Then he left. By the time your father got back, Leo had disappeared."

My heart ached, though I wasn't sure for whom. My mother had lost a friend, my father his brother, and Leo his mind – all in one night. "Where did he go?"

"I don't know. By the time he came back a few years later, your father and I were married and you were on the way. He came to the front door and stood there, staring at my belly. Then he turned on his heel and walked away. I never saw him after that but I heard rumors. I think seeing me like that sent him over the edge. I never imagined–" She broke off and pressed her fingers over her lips, staring out the window while winter-dead trees rushed by in a blur.

Grandma sent me a look in the rearview mirror.

“After that, Leo started campaigning against the Cause,” my mother went on. “Gathering Werewolves to his side to fight against us. When you were born, I got a card from him. I thought it was a 'Congratulations' card, like the others, but it wasn't. It said: I'm sorry for your loss. I didn't really know what it meant until the attack happened. That’s when I knew he'd kill you. That's why I ran."

"Wow, Mom. I'm sorry," I said.

"No, I'm sorry." She shook her head. "He did all of this because I rejected him."

I wanted to say something to make her feel better, because it's not like any of it was her fault, but I had absolutely no idea what to say. Something about her explanation confused me. Leo's comments had all been about me being a dirty blood, but if he'd done it all because my mother had rejected him, then why did he care about me being a product of both races?

My Grandma spoke up, throwing fiery glances at my mother. "Elizabeth, he was a grown man. None of this is your fault, so let's not even go down that road. You have nothin' to apologize for. Leo was plain nuts, and that's that."

My mom blinked and then nodded. "Thanks, Mom," she said.

I smiled. I loved my Grandma.

CHAPTER THREE

It wasn't long before Grandma steered the Hummer off the highway, onto what the sign referred to as Rural Route 3. Thick woods bordered both sides of the two lane road. Through the bare branches, I could just barely make out the purple haze of mountains in the distance. When Grandma slowed and turned onto a newly paved drive that was blocked by wrought iron gates, my stomach clenched.

Grandma pulled to a stop in front of the gates, and I stared. It was like something out of an old movie. The gates were made of thick, black iron and swirled and curled together in intricate designs. Each one was attached to an iron fence, at least ten feet tall, that disappeared to my right and left into the trees that bordered the property on each side. Beyond the gate, the asphalt driveway disappeared around a hill of perfectly manicured grass that was somehow lush and green despite the season.

Grandma rolled down her window.

"Hello," she called.

I searched for some sort of intercom, but I didn't see anything and no one answered her. A mechanical buzzing sounded, and I saw a tiny black camera mounted to the side of the gate. Grandma waited while it whirred and swiveled, and then the gate swung open on silent hinges. When the opening was wide enough for the Hummer to pass through, Grandma eased us forward. I stared out the window, feeling suddenly edgy and nervous. We were finally here.

The driveway wound through grassy hills bordered by rows of perfectly groomed trees. It looked like the setting to a country club or golf course, not a hidden boarding school for supernaturals. Then again, how many hidden boarding schools had I actually been to?

“Looks the same,” my mother murmured to her window.

“You went here?” I asked.

Grandma nodded. “Everyone in your family has gone to Wood Point. It’s the best Hunter school in the country.”

She sounded so proud that I clamped down my complaints and we rode on in silence.

Grandma rounded another curve, and the school came into view. It was... massive. And rigidly beautiful. The walls were a smooth, cream-colored stone that rose higher and higher, interrupted by wide balconies that opened up from third and fourth floor doorways. Long, narrow windows all displayed white curtains which clashed sharply with the dark trim that matched the wrought iron of the gates. Large columns on either side of the entrance ran all the way to the roof, ending in what looked like small turrets. It struck me as a cross between a military school and Buckingham Palace.

Grandma made the turn into the parking lot, and I caught a glimpse of another building behind this one. It was the same chalky stone without the fancy details. Grandma pulled in, double parking so the Hummer had room to spare on either side, should someone take the chance of parking next to us. Not likely.

"Looks like they got that foundational issue taken care of," Grandma said, looking critically at the far corner of the building. “I wasn’t sure if Vernon would be able to deal with the contractor after that screw-up with the permits.”

My mother muttered a response that made it sound like she knew what Grandma was referring to but didn’t really care enough to respond. I, on the other hand, had no idea. Before I could even ask her about it, she cut the engine and turned back to me.

“You ready?" Her eyes were soft and understanding.

I was tempted to stick my chin out and say, “No, I most certainly am not ready” and let Grandma take me in her arms and hug me like I was five again, but my mother was looking at me, too, and the softness wasn't nearly as evident in her gaze. I sighed.

"Yeah, let's go," I said. I grabbed my backpack and we piled out. I blinked, adjusting to the brightness of the sun after sitting behind tinted windows all morning.

I gazed up at the building in front of me, charmed despite my reservations. Up close, I could see the stone was dotted with pale green ivy that twisted and turned its way up the walls. The ivy looked faded and reckless in its half-dead state, and I wondered what it would look like in spring, when everything was bright and alive.

“Tara, come on,” my mother called.

I shifted my gaze from the view above and rounded the hood of the Hummer, hurrying to catch up, and collided with someone. I steadied myself and stepped back.

"Sorry," a male voice muttered.

I opened my mouth to brush it off as my fault and stopped, my eyes locked onto his. The dark hair and tanned skin might have been hard to place, but the striking green eyes were not. This was the boy I'd seen at Leo's warehouse, the one who'd saved me.

He stared back at me without speaking, his expression one of disdain.

"Tara?" Grandma's voice came from somewhere behind him.

Again, I opened my mouth to say something, but he gave a curt nod and stepped around me, disappearing around the corner of the building. I stared after him, wondering what had caused him to look at me like that. Surely, he’d recognized me.

When he was gone, I joined Grandma and my mother; neither of which commented on the boy I’d seen. Then again, he’d darted away so quickly they probably hadn’t recognized him from that far away.

As Grandma reached for the door, it swung open and a short, stocky man stepped out, holding it ajar with his backside. He smiled expectantly at Grandma–an action that pushed his round glasses further up his nose–and crinkled his eyes so his irises disappeared behind tiny slits.

"Edie, it's good to see you," he said, holding his hand out towards her.

"Vernon." Grandma took his hand and then leaned in to kiss the man's cheek. His already flushed cheeks flamed a little brighter from her attention, and his eyes flicked to my mother.

"Hello, Elizabeth," he said shyly.

My mother smiled back at him, a gesture that was more genuine than I'd expected. "Vern, how are you?" She, too, leaned down and kissed his cheeks before passing through the doors.

Vernon reddened again and then looked back at me. "Miss Godfrey. I'm Headmaster Whitfield. Welcome." He waved me inside with a polite gesture.

"Thanks," I mumbled. Headmaster? Was this place above using the word "principal?"

I heard the door close behind me, and the robust headmaster stepped around me, heading for Grandma.

"You made good time," he said as they took up the lead and drifted towards a side hallway.

Grandma responded with something about traffic and the Hummer being a smoother ride than you'd think. I tuned it out and stared at the lobby. The walls next to me were covered with long tapestries colored to look like foreign flags and interspersed with large oil paintings of some alumni or another from decades past. Bronzed plaques hung underneath the paintings, giving names and dates. Again, I was struck by how little this felt like a normal school; College, maybe. More like the UN, though.

And what was that boy doing here? Did he go to school here? Grandma would know, since she'd brought him with her that day as part of her team, but I couldn't ask her now. She was still locked in conversation with my new principal. Sorry, Headmaster.

"Tara." I turned at the sound of my mother's voice. She'd paused at the edge of a hallway where Grandma and Headmaster had disappeared. Her foot tapped a harsh beat against the gleaming floor.

"Coming," I said.

The hallway we turned down felt much more like a school office. Flyers for various protocols and procedures were stuck to the walls or hung on bulletin boards. I passed a few doors, mostly open, and was greeted with polite smiles from secretary-looking women who looked up at me over the rim of their reading glasses before going back to the click-click of their computer keyboards.

At the end of the hall, I followed my mother into an office and found Grandma already sitting in a leather chair across from Headmaster, who sat behind the biggest desk I'd ever seen. Despite his roundness, he looked tiny behind that desk; or maybe his chair was too low to the ground. I couldn't decide. He and Grandma were still talking and laughing, but grew quiet when my mother shut the door behind me with a click. Grandma gestured for me to join her.

I sat in the chair next to her, while my mother lowered herself onto the sofa that lined the wall behind us. There were more framed portraits in here, with more names I'd never heard of, and a dark green tapestry covered the wall behind Vernon's desk with some sort of seal on it that depicted an eagle with a sword in its beak.

"Tara, this is Headmaster Whitfield. He runs Wood Point Academy," Grandma said, calling me back to the moment.

My eyes flicked from hers to his and I managed a polite smile. "Nice to meet you," I said.

Headmaster Whitfield, on the other hand, was grinning widely at the mention of his proper title and responsibility. His chest puffed out as he spoke. "And you, Tara. It's a privilege to have a Godfrey at our school again. We're very excited to have you. Do you have any questions for me?" I shook my head and he went on. "I know, due to your, er, circumstances this is a bit rushed. There isn't much time to do anything but jump in. Then again, from what your Grandma tells me, you're making up for lost time in your combat capabilities with raw talent. Still, we need to get you caught up. I've arranged for a tutor to help with that. If you work hard, you should have no trouble catching up in time to graduate next year."

"Sounds great," I said, wondering if he could hear the absolute lack of energy in my words. If he did, he ignored it.

"Here is your schedule." He handed me a sheet of paper. "We used your previous school's records to determine placement in English and Math. The rest is pretty standard here, but if you have any questions or concerns, don't hesitate to voice them. We want this transition to be as seamless as possible. Oh, and there's a map of the property, and I've marked your room number and building so you can find it later."

Headmaster Whitfield handed me everything across the desk and glanced at Grandma, looking very much like a schoolboy seeking his teacher's approval. She rewarded him with a smile and a nod that I took to mean she was satisfied. Headmaster Whitfield beamed.

I skimmed the schedule, trying to figure out what the names of the classes meant. I recognized English, and Algebra II, and American History, but the rest were foreign to me. There were classes like 'Hunter History' and 'Defensive Maneuvers 2'. Those actually sounded interesting. Then my eyes caught on a class called 'Lineage', and I remembered what Grandma had said about Hunters family lines being a source of pride here. So, I had to study genealogy? I'd rather do math.

"Oh, honey, I'm so excited for you," Grandma said. I looked up and saw that she was smiling at me, her face shining with pride.

"Thanks, Grandma." I held up my schedule. "Everything looks really, uh, interesting."

Headmaster Whitfield cleared his throat. "Well, I think you belong in Defensive Maneuvers 2 right now."

"Right, we should let you get settled," Grandma said. She turned to Headmaster. "Oh, Vernon, her bags are still in the truck."

He waved his hands. "I'll have a student aide take them to her room for her. She can get right to class and unpack later."

"Thank you." Grandma rose, and I followed her lead.

From the back of the room, my mother did the same and held the door open for us again. Grandma put her arm around me and guided me out.

"Let us know if you need anything, okay? And we'll visit in a few weeks." She pulled me into a hug before I could respond, which was good because words caught in my throat. A few weeks? I was stuck here for a few weeks before they'd be back to check on me?

I blinked the tears back, not wanting to show how upset I was. It wasn't like I'd never been away from home. I'd done summer camps before and this wasn't much different, but it felt so foreign…and final. There was all this unspoken pressure for me to live up to a family legacy that I didn't even know existed until now.

Grandma stepped back, holding me at arm's length for a long look before finally letting me go. My mother stepped up and reached out for me. Behind her tight frown, her eyes were sad and, as usual, worried.

"You be careful, okay? Stay on school grounds. Don't leave at all," she said, into my ear.

"Oh, don't worry, Elizabeth. Students aren't allowed to leave school grounds at all," Headmaster Whitfield said.

My mother gave me a look that said "never stopped her before" and shook her head. Then they were walking away, down the long hall towards the lobby. At the end, they waved once, and then they were gone. I stared after them, feeling empty.

The sound of Headmaster's voice made me jump. I'd almost forgotten I wasn't alone.

"If you'll wait in the lobby, your tutor will be along in a few minutes to show you to your class," said Headmaster Whitfield.

I nodded, and he disappeared back into his office.

I made my way back to the lobby and wandered along the wall, pretending to study the portraits I'd seen earlier. A few kids came and went; most of them didn't even bother to hide the fact that they were staring at me. I assumed they were trying to figure out who the new kid was, until I heard one of them whisper, "That's her," as they passed by.

"What a freak," said the other one. Both of them looked at me like I was day old seafood.

I watched them walk away, feeling confused more than offended. I did a quick outfit check. I knew I didn't look runway ready in my jeans and hoodie, but I hadn't had time to change after the trip. And now, with my bags being sent to my room, I guess I wouldn't. I ran a hand through my hair and used the tie on my wrist to pull it up into a quick ponytail. Maybe that would help.

A couple more students passed through the lobby, and I got funny looks again, but they weren't close enough for me to hear what they were saying. I was getting paranoid. I wandered towards the wall where the polished plaques of dead alumni hung and used the reflective glass as a mirror. I pulled a lip gloss out of my backpack and slid some over my lips.

Someone cleared their throat behind me. I turned and found myself face to face with the same green eyed boy from the parking lot – and the warehouse.

"I know you," I blurted, finally managing words this time. He looked back at me with lifted brows. "I mean, I saw you. In the warehouse. You saved me. Thanks." My words were rushed partly because I was afraid he was going to bolt again and partly because my nerves were starting to get to me.

He shrugged like he wanted to be done with it, and when he spoke, his words were fast and clipped. "No biggie. I'm Alex."

"I'm Tara."

"You ready to go?"

"Go?" I blinked at him. "You're my tutor?"

"Apparently. Is that a problem?"

"Well, I mean, you're a kid. I guess I expected a teacher or something."

A hint of a smile appeared, but it was rough at the edges and sarcastic, like his words. "We'll make do." He gestured to the schedule I held. "Is that your class list?"

I nodded and handed it over. He skimmed it and handed it back.

"Defensive Maneuvers Two, huh? They must think you're capable enough. Hopefully they're right and training will be easier than I thought." He headed for the doors without waiting to see if I was following, or noticing that I was now glaring. "Coming?"

I rolled my eyes and followed him out.

CHAPTER FOUR

Alex led me around the side of the building where he'd disappeared earlier. As soon as we turned, several more buildings became visible. Apparently, the main building was so enormous it hid the rest of the campus from view. The buildings behind it were set up across from each other, two on each side, forming a large square, with a grassy courtyard in the middle.

Each one was made of the same stone material, worn smooth and half hidden by layers of moss and climbing vines that made them seem to spring up from the ground like a part of the forest; especially since that's what closed us in on all sides. Despite the season, there was green in every direction. A fair amount of them were fir and pine trees so the ground was littered with needles and small twigs but it was packed tight from years of foot traffic (or an expensive landscape company), creating a narrow path that led straight into the center of the square. There was even a small garden with a fountain in the center of the courtyard, lined with decorative trees and marble benches. I breathed in the crisp smell of bark and dirt and stared. It looked like the secret woodland home of garden fairies.

All around us, kids were milling around; some standing in small groups to whisper to each other, some sitting in pairs hovering over their open books, or horsing around in the courtyard. I resisted the urge to stare, to look for differences between these kids and the kids at my school back home. I knew there shouldn't be, but I'd never actually seen this many Hunters up close, especially my own age. A part of me was excited by it.

Someone laughed, though the sound was soft, somewhere closer to bells tinkling, and I looked up to locate the source. It was a girl my age, with flowing blond hair that reached past her shoulder blades standing with her back to me, near a bench in the center of the courtyard. Even though I couldn't see her eyes, I knew they'd be a perfect blue. I knew it in the way you just know when you've seen the most popular kid in school.

A group of girls stood in a circle around her. One of them broke eye contact with her long enough to glance over and spot me walking by. Then the girl, a skinny brunette with lashes that seemed to hold an entire bottle of mascara on them, turned back and said something to the blond, too low for me to hear. She began to turn, flipping her hair over her shoulder as her neck swiveled. Our eyes met and held for only a second before I glanced away. I immediately cursed myself for being the one to look away first. That is not how you were supposed to overcome "new kid syndrome".

A couple of snickers went up, and out of the corner of my eye, I caught a glimpse of her smirking at me with a curled lip and a manicured hand on her hip before she turned back to the group and her jaw began moving again. Something about the way she smirked made me think of Cindy Adams, and I felt my hands close into fists automatically. My tension must've shown because I felt Alex glance over at me, one eyebrow raised. I forced a smile, eased my hands open, and willed myself to relax.

As if the rest of the student body was taking their cue from the blond, more heads began to turn in my direction. When they did, it was like a domino effect. One alerted another, who alerted another, and another. Soon, everyone was pointing at me and whispering. None of them looked outright hateful, but none of them looked particularly friendly either. It was the same expression I'd seen from those first two kids, in the lobby. The ones who'd called me a freak. I was beginning to realize there was something going on here; something bigger than rumpled clothes and smudged makeup. It was starting to get to me.

I kept my face carefully blank and my eyes averted, making it a point to notice the scenery above their heads, instead of their faces. I stared purposefully at the bright green ivy that covered the front of the building we approached. It wasn't entirely difficult to be distracted by it. The shade of green was mesmerizing. It wasn't like I hadn't seen ivy before, or woods, but the colors here were so vibrant; brighter than the woods at home.

Somewhere nearby whispered voices drifted over.

"She's the one I was telling you about. The wolf chic," whispered a girl's voice.

"No way. Eww," was the response. "Why did they let Kane's crew help her anyway?"

"I don't know. She's not one of us."

Beside me, I felt Alex stiffen and then relax again. He said nothing but he picked up the pace and we hurried on. We'd almost made it to the doors of the building when I heard it.

"Hey, look. That's the dirty blood."

This time, I was sure Alex noticed–in the way that people try to politely ignore an uncomfortable situation. He kept his eyes forward and his expression neutral, but again, he picked up the pace. When we reached the doors, Alex stepped over and opened one, holding it wide for me to pass through. When we were both inside and the door had clicked shut behind us, I sighed. Alex made no move to continue. He stood, staring at me with a curious look on his face.

"What?" I asked bracing myself because I wasn't really sure I wanted to know what. Crossing the courtyard had been a combination of being the raggedy new kid in a school full of rich kids, and doing the walk of shame after prom and being caught by your mother. Horrible.

"Nothing," he said after a pause. "C'mon."

We started walking again, bypassing a grand staircase wide enough for an eighteen wheeler to come down – sideways, down a long narrow hallway to our left. The scent of bleach and floor wax mixed with the smell that was inherent to any learning institution. The halls were empty, thank goodness, but every few steps I passed a flyer advertising some student club or event. I saw one for a “Fight Club”–yes that’s what it was called–and stopped to read it.

Three spots available in the junior class Fight Club. Tryouts held every Monday and Wednesday after last bell. Not responsible for injuries sustained. Medical team on standby. Come on out if you think you’ve got what it takes.

There was more about waiving liability for possible injuries and I probably would’ve kept reading, but Alex waited with arms crossed over his chest and a scowl at the end of the hall. I hurried to catch up and we took a right down another hallway.

"Why is everyone staring at me?" I asked.

“What do you mean?”

I looked at him with narrowed eyes. “You know what I mean. I know you heard some of the comments being made outside.”

The muscles in his jaw tightened. “Most of the kids here have been together since they were kids. Same school, same social circles. You know how it is. Not everyone is so quick to adjust to a new face.”

I shook my head, not willing to accept such an easy answer. “No, it’s more than that. I heard what they were saying about me. They know that I’m – you know, mixed or whatever. And they have a problem with that.”

“Of course they do,” he snapped. “Do you think any of us want a Werewolf–even a half-ass one–at our school? Learning our moves? Fighting with us?”

I hadn’t been prepared for that; I had no idea what to say. I blinked up at him, mortified by the tears I could feel forming, and looked away while I tried to get myself together. Underneath the urge to cry, I was mad. So I clung to that and grit my teeth before glaring back at him.

“I see,” I said. “Well thanks for the heads up. In the meantime I’ll need a new tutor. One who isn’t a bigoted asshole.”

Alex exhaled, and some of the fire went out of his eyes, leaving them pale and apologetic. “Look, I’m sorry.” His shoulders relaxed and he was running a hand over his buzzed hair like he didn't know what to do next. "I didn't mean to – I don't feel that way. I've known your Grandma for a long time. She was good to me and I intend to return the favor, so I'll tutor you, and I'm sorry for what I said. The truth is the warehouse fight still has me wound up. That's what the kids are still talking about and none of them have all the right details, which is probably why you've been labeled the enemy. Give it a few days and it'll pass."

I purposely held back from answering for a few seconds. It wasn't that I didn't believe him. I wanted to; but the look he'd given me when he'd talked about having a Werewolf in their midst – something told me he'd meant it. Even if he was trying not to. Finally, I nodded. "Okay, fine. Apology accepted."

Alex looked relieved, and we started walking again. I thought about the warehouse fight. It made sense something like that would've been passed through the halls of a Hunter school, especially since Grandma's rescue team apparently went to school here. I'd have to ask her about that. Between that, and how well she seemed to know Headmaster Whitfield, it seemed Grandma was more involved–or at least connected–than I knew.

"Here we are," said Alex, swinging to a stop outside the last door on the left.

Through the small window, I caught a glimpse of desks filled with students. Posters with various fighting stances hung on the walls.

"So here's how this is going to work," he said, pulling my attention back. "I'll meet you after last bell to show you the way to where we'll train." He glanced down at my jeans and hoodie. "You might want to change into more suitable clothes."

I looked down at myself and then back at him. "More suitable how? We're just studying?"

"No, we're training," he said. He raised an eyebrow at my blank look. "Combat? Fighting?"

"Oh. I didn't know. They said tutor and I thought... my bags are being sent to my room for me. I didn't have time to change."

"No biggie, today will be a light day. Starting tomorrow, though, you'll want to be comfortable."

Something about the way he'd said light day made me defensive; like he expected me to suck or something.

The door opened and a petite red head appeared. "Mr. Channing. What can I do for you?" she asked Alex, and I realized she was the teacher.

"Professor Flaherty, this is Tara Godfrey."

The woman turned to me and smiled. "Miss Godfrey, it's nice to meet you." I took the hand she offered and shook it, trying to figure out where I'd seen her before. She wore black pants that molded to her and had a mass of red hair secured in a haphazard bun high on her head.

"Nice to meet you, too," I said. "Do I know you?"

"We've never been introduced. I know your grandmother. You might have seen me at the warehouse incident a few days back."

"Oh, right." I remembered the tiny red head, but I hadn't been close enough to make out facial features – and I'd assumed based on her size that she was a student.

Professor Flaherty looked at Alex. "It was nice of you to show our new student to her class. I'll take it from here."

"I'll see you at three," he said, nodding to me as he retreated down the hall.

Professor Flaherty turned to me with a knowing look. "Not what you expected for a combat teacher am I right?"

For a second I thought she was talking about Alex and I didn't know what to say, but then I realized she was gesturing to herself. "Oh, no, I guess not," I admitted.

She smiled wider, which lit her face and hair, making it all seem to glow. It helped soften the sharp glint that she wore in her eyes. "Then again, if we're being honest, you're not what I pictured either, for the daughter of a legend."

I opened my mouth to ask her what she'd meant, but a movement behind her cut me off. An object was sailing through the air, heading straight for the back of Professor Flaherty's head. I opened my mouth to yell a warning but there wasn't time.

Professor Flaherty twisted and her hand shot out, grabbing the object out of the air just before it made impact against her skull. She held it up and frowned. It was a rock the size of my fist. Her smile disappeared, replaced by a scowl that intimidated me far more than any other teacher I'd ever had, and turned back to the rest of the class.

"Who did this?" she snapped.

"Sorry Professor Flaherty. I was aiming for Justin," called a male voice from a few rows back. I caught a glimpse of a jock-looking guy with messy brown hair, smiling apologetically.

"Your aim is atrocious, Levi," Professor Flaherty responded.

She stepped further into the room, motioning for me to join her, and set the rock on her desk, the incident already forgotten. I stared, trying to understand how almost getting your skull bashed in was no big deal.

"Class, this is Tara Godfrey," Professor Flaherty said, placing a small hand on my shoulder. "She's new here, and I expect every single one of you to treat her like you would anyone else."

Quiet snickers and mumbled words followed as I shuffled to my seat. A foot shot out a few rows in, and I barely missed face-planting in the aisle as I stumbled and slid into the empty desk. I got another round of snickers and laughter. If Professor Flaherty noticed, she didn't comment. I glared at the kids around me until they looked away.

Up front, Professor Flaherty gathered papers and files while she talked. "We'll be working outside today, so go ahead and assemble on the lawn. I'll meet you out there in a couple of minutes."

Smiles appeared and a couple of whoops went up around the room as kids jumped up and began filing out a side door. I took a step in that direction, but Professor Flaherty's voice stopped me. She was bent over her desk, rummaging through its drawers as if she'd lost something.

"Tara, hang on, and I'll walk with you," she said without looking up.

"Oh, I'll walk her, Professor Flaherty." A boy hung back in the doorway, a baseball cap pulled low over his eyes. He wore old jeans – not ratty, but worn and comfortable, and a shirt that said something about the 17th annual science fair scrawled on it. His backpack was filled to overflowing and looked like it weighed more than he did.

“Mr. Sandefur,” Professor Flaherty said, barely glancing over before going back to her search. "That’s fine. I’ll be there in a minute.”

I followed the boy out but kept my distance, unsure why he was being so nice after the way the rest of the kids had acted.

“Hey, I’m Logan,” he said, extending his hand.

I shook it, still skeptical. “Tara.”

“I know. The battle grounds are this way,” he said, setting off on a narrow path that led into the trees.

I hesitated.

He stopped and walked back over to me. “If I’m lying, you could probably take me in a fight,” he said. “I’m just saying, if that makes you feel better.”

I considered that. “Okay, let’s go.”

He smiled, and a tiny dimple appeared in his cheek above his lip. I smiled back, an automatic gesture, and let Logan lead the way down the narrow path. I was half tempted to turn and look for Professor Flaherty behind us, just to be sure, but I didn’t. I’d made the decision to trust someone on the basis of a dimple, and I couldn’t turn back now.

The air was cooler in the cover of the trees. I was glad I still had my hoodie and pulled it tighter across my abdomen and zipped it up. I glanced up at the thick green canopy of leaves – mostly pine needles – and branches that dimmed the sunlight. The contrast of the rich green against the brown bark was mesmerizing. I breathed in deeply, and the scent of dirt and moss filled my head. It made me think of Wes and the goodbye we’d had in the trees behind my house.

Wanting to push the image away, I turned my attention back to the path in front of me and saw that the trees were breaking up ahead. Logan stepped off the path and pushed his way through light bushes, into a clearing. I stepped through behind him and saw that he hadn’t deceived me after all. The rest of the class was all assembled, broken into little groups and talking and laughing.

“Thanks,” I said.

"Don't mention it. Sucks being the new kid," said Logan.

"How do you know?"

"I was it last year. Not fun. I had to buy new underwear five times. Eventually I just carried it in my backpack so they couldn't get to it."

I looked at him with wide eyes, unable to bring myself to ask why he'd needed new underwear. Maybe I didn't want to know.

Behind us, Professor Flaherty appeared with an armload of files and notebooks. She dropped it all onto the ground with a thud and picked up the stopwatch lying on the top of the pile.

"All right, everyone. Find your sparring partners," she called.

The cliques broke up and everyone lined up, pairing up in a way that let me know they'd done this before. Logan moved away and went to stand in front of a boy with skinny jeans and a purple tee shirt with a picture of black piano keys trailing diagonally across the fabric. He looked bored, but Logan shot me a dimpled grin and crouched into a ready position. I stood back near the edge of the clearing, waiting to see what would happen next. Professor Flaherty came up beside me.

"Tara, I understand you've never had any proper combat or self-defense training, so for today, I will allow you to observe. By Monday I expect you to be ready to join the class." She turned to face the rest of the class without waiting for an answer. "Jeremy, you can call it today."

A blond boy with big arms stepped forward and then turned to face the rest of his classmates. Geez, was everyone here pretty? Professor Flaherty waited until Jeremy was in place and then called out, "Warm ups. Begin."

I started to argue and tell her that I didn't need to watch; that despite my lack of training, I could handle myself just fine. That I'd had proper training, because Jack was a better fighter than half the people here, probably. Then I saw the rest of the class begin to move, and I realized how petty and dumb I would've sounded.

Instead of ripping into each other in mock combat, they stood facing front and in perfect harmony began moving their bodies. Jeremy called out various poses or positions and everyone responded by throwing their bodies that way. It looked like a combination of kung-fu and power yoga. I'd never seen anything like it. I clamped my mouth closed and watched.

"Forward thrust," called Jeremy.

In response, the entire class' right fists shot out. Only, it wasn't a normal punch. It looked graceful and powerful. Even their legs moved in sync as one came forward to balance the other, their knees bending in exactly the same place.

"Back block," Jeremy called.

Everyone's hands thrust backward, bent at the elbows, accompanied by a collective grunt at the force put into the move. All I could do was stare, in fascination and dread. There was no way I'd be able to learn this crap in three days. They looked like the karate kid army.

When the warm ups were over – and I knew they were because all movement ceased, and Jeremy stepped back in a stiff military march – Professor Flaherty addressed the class.

"It looks good, guys. We're going to use the rest of the class for one-on-one practice. I want you to find a way to use as many of the warm ups as you can, in your defensive moves. Give each other breaks as needed and go easy. I do not want any more strained backs, like last week." A few chuckles went around but they faded quickly as everyone readied themselves. "Begin."

It was a blur of blocked punches and deflected kicks. No one wasted time in pretending to attack each other, and from where I stood, no one held back, either. There were grunts and hard breaths, evidence of the fact that full force was given to every attempted attack. I glanced over at Logan and his music-loving partner. Whatever expression of boredom the kid had worn before was gone, replaced by grim concentration as he managed to duck and block Logan's attack. From what I could tell, blocking was about all he had time for; Logan was a blur of hands and feet.

A hand pressed lightly on my arm, and I looked up. Professor Flaherty was watching me, a glint in her green eyes. "A lot to take in. Then again, from what I saw, you'll pick it up in no time."

"You mean at the warehouse? Thanks, but this is something different. This is more… controlled," I finally said, still watching the fights.

"Control is learned over time, with practice. You seem to have the talent you need to get there."

"Maybe." I looked back at her. "Not like you, though. You were amazing. I couldn't believe how fast you moved."

She smiled. "It was refreshing to be able to get out there and practice what I preach. Good exercise. You weren't so bad yourself."

"I don't know. Alex had to save my butt in there. If he hadn't…"

"Everyone needs a wingman once in a while. You're lucky to have Alex as a trainer. He's one of the best at this school."

"Is that why he got stuck training me?"

She smiled, but her eyes were hard and no longer on me. "Being the best has its price."

CHAPTER FIVE

When class ended, Logan appeared at my side looking winded and happy with himself. He slung his bag over his shoulders and let it settle into place before attempting to walk with it. "So what did you think? Are we any match for you?"

It took me a second to realize he was teasing. Before I could answer, his partner trudged past, shooting him a dirty look.

"What happened to going easy, Sandefur?"

Logan shrugged, which seemed difficult under the weight he carried. "Guess I was in a mood."

The kid stalked off, but not before turning his glare on me. I did my best to ignore it and followed Logan onto the path, relieved he'd waited until the rest of the class had gone ahead to head back.

"You were really good," I said as we walked.

He laughed. "Justin spends too much time reading comics and not enough time in the gym. Besides, this class is pretty easy. Wait until we get to Combat Strategy next year. I hear that one's pretty tough."

"How is that one different?"

"This one is basically hand to hand wrestling. Straightforward attack and defend. Combat Strategy gives you situations where you have to plan and strategize how to get your enemy where you want them, for the easiest kill or best outcome. I hear there's a lot of one-on-three and stuff like that."

"Wow," I said, shaking my head and feeling completely out of my league. I should've realized it would be like this, a sort of military feel to the way they did things, what with a Hunter's basic life goal being to learn to kill, but I hadn't expected to feel so… inadequate. I thought I'd reached a point where my fighting skills were decent enough. Apparently, I was still a beginner.

The greens of the leaves began to lighten and the filtering sunlight shown through more and more, signaling that we were getting closer to school. It still felt cool, but I could feel my body already acclimating. I didn't need the hoodie wrapped quite so tight anymore. The cool felt good. The air was refreshing against my skin. One thing to like so far, compared to home: class outside. Not a very long list.

"You okay?" Logan asked, pulling me out of my thoughts as we stepped clear of the trees. Someone had left the classroom door propped open, and I concentrated on that instead of meeting his eyes.

"Yeah, I'm fine. Just hungry." Half-truth. I really was starving. That greasy breakfast sandwich I'd eaten earlier was long gone.

"Well, then, you're in for a treat. One thing I can say for Wood Point: the food is the best."

We passed through the now empty classroom and out into the hall. The press of bodies, and the buzz of voices, animated now that there was a break in class, reminded me of my high school back home; or any high school for that matter.

A shoulder slammed into mine, jarring me. I backed up a step from the impact and looked up into a blond halo of hair and a sugary smile that dripped acid. It was the girl from the courtyard. A couple of her brunette followers flanked her. None of them looked sorry, or surprised, that she'd run into me.

"Oops, I didn't see you there," she said, her smile pasted on. She moved away, but not before I heard her turn to her minions and say, "you know dogs, always underfoot."

My jaw fell open in surprise. For a moment, I was too stunned to react. Despite everything I'd already seen and heard that morning, no one had said anything to my face. Until now. I bit back on my temper as I watched her fade into the throng of moving bodies and disappear down the hall.

"Who was that?" I asked, concentrating on Logan's face, and trying to resist the urge to run after the blond and take a chunk of that pretty hair out of her head. I balled my hands into fists and squeezed.

"Victoria Lexington," said Logan in a tight voice. "Her father is on the Board for the school and a member of the Commission. Her mother does charity work for Hunter organizations."

"Commission?" The words weren't making sense, maybe because I wanted to take a bite out of Victoria Lexington's face.

Logan raised an eyebrow underneath his baseball cap. "The Commission of Hunter Affairs and Security." He spoke slowly, like he was speaking to a toddler. "You've seriously never heard of it?"

I shook my head.

"Wow. So you really weren't told anything?"

"How do you know what I was told?"

Logan ducked his head, looking guilty. "It's hard not to hear things." He gestured at the bodies around us.

I nodded. I could understand that.

We made our way past the large entrance doors and up the wide set of stairs I'd seen earlier. At the top was another hallway and in front of us, a set of heavy double doors, propped open. Through them I could see a large, open room with tables set in loose rows. Kids talked and laughed, their voices drifting out in a collective boom. Running the length of one wall sat a long counter lined with various food choices and kids browsing the entrée selections as they slid trays along towards the end.

"Come on," said Logan, stepping through the doors and veering off to the right to join the buffet line.

I followed and fell in line behind him, taking the empty tray he offered. I pushed forward and stopped again, eyeing a steaming bin of chicken Alfredo that smelled as good as it looked. Next to it stood a simmering pot of vegetable soup, with rolls that looked shiny and freshly baked, instead of dull and browned, like my old high school's version. The smell alone was enough to convince me that it was edible. I hesitated, craning my neck to see what was up ahead. My stomach growled.

A tray bumped into mine and I noticed a tanned arm holding the tray next to mine. My eyes traveled up, following the arm to the body it belonged to. It was the brown haired jock from my Defensive Maneuvers class; the one who'd thrown the rock. He was wearing a dark green jacket that was definitely school issued, for sports, and had that permanent wet-hair look you got from wearing too much gel.

"Hey," he said, leaning towards me with a too-wide smile.

"Hi."

"Tara, right? I'm Levi." He didn't offer his hand, just leaned in closer and leered at me.

"Nice to meet you," I mumbled.

"So, listen. My friends over there." He pointed behind him to a table by the window where a group of look-alike jocks were watching and listening. "We're a little confused about something and wondering if you could help us out."

"Okaay," I said, drawing out the word.

"So, you're like half-Werewolf right?"

"Yeah." I didn't see a point in denying it. Everyone already knew.

He leaned closer. "Well, my friend Dave says that wolves are in the dog family or whatever. So what we want to know is, does that mean you do it doggy style?"

The entire table erupted in hoots and laughter while I stood there, glaring back at jock boy and gripping my tray with white knuckles. I could feel the burn in my cheeks, and I knew he could see it, but he kept playing into it. He gave an overly dramatic shrug, for the benefit of our audience, and then looked back at his friends. Hot tears blurred my vision and I blinked them back. I bit my lip until I tasted blood; I refused to give them a reaction.

"She's pleading the fifth I guess," he called.

When it was clear I wasn't going to be any more fun for him, he picked up his tray and went around me to pay for his food before heading for his table. A few more kids copied and darted around me to get through the line. I didn't move until a hand fell over my arm; I jolted even though the touch was light and the hand jerked away. I looked up at Logan.

He didn't say anything, and I was grateful for the silence. We started moving towards the cashier and paid for our meals. I kept my back to the rest of the cafeteria as we inched forward, unsure who else might've witnessed the side show I'd become. I managed to get myself composed enough that I was almost sure I wouldn't have a break down until we found a place to sit, and turned to follow Logan to a table. Some kids at a nearby table stared at me and whispered, but I forced myself to ignore them and scanned for a seat. A body stepped in front of me, blocking my view of the room and cutting me off from Logan. I looked up and focused on an already sickeningly familiar face.

Victoria Lexington stood in my path.

"We don't serve doggie biscuits so you might as well stop looking," she said.

Something tenuous snapped inside me and I felt the humiliation give way to anger, hot and liquid in my veins. I was not going down like this, not on my first day.

"You would know. I hear you answer to bitch," I snapped at her. I gripped my tray with both hands and tried not to shake.

Victoria's eyes narrowed at my words and she glanced around before focusing even more intently on me. She was clearly unaccustomed to being challenged. "You might be half-Werewolf, but you are not the alpha here," she said, taking a step closer.

"What is your problem? You don't even know me."

"You are the problem. You think a little bit of palm greasing can open any door. As if having money gives you the right to be here. While I can admire that trait, there are limits to where you're power can reach. "

"What are you talking about?"

"Don't play dumb. You think you're so much better than everyone here, but you're not. You're a dirty blood and should be banned from school and from… life." Without waiting for a response, she turned on her heel and stalked off – towards the table at the window.

My eyes began to blur and I blinked back tears, mortified that they were there in the first place. I was not that girl; the girl that cried in the lunch room in front of the whole school. I blinked faster. I didn't even have to look around to know that every single face in the room was fastened on me.

A tense few seconds passed with no sound, and then gradually the background noise returned and people went back to their conversations. The faces closest to me looked disappointed that nothing more had happened than words exchanged.

"Rough day?"

The tears cleared, and my eyes focused on a girl. She had midnight black hair that was all swept up in a messy-but-chic bun except for her bangs which hung down on one side of her face, completely covering one eye. The exposed eye was darkly lined and had a thin splash of glitter underneath. She wore the strappiest heels I'd ever seen that laced all the way up to just below her knees, and her arms were covered in some sort of lacy material that stopped a few inches above her elbow. The whole thing should have been Goth, but on her it was exotic–and hip. Sam would've loved it.

"Um, you could say that," I said, realizing she was still waiting for an answer. I probably should've been suspicious that she was even talking to me, but I was too exhausted to be on my guard right now. It would've been the perfect time to finish taking me down.

The dark haired girl nodded and eyed me. She brought a hand up and swept her long bangs out of her eyes in a careless gesture that made me think she'd done it a million times. Within seconds her bangs had reverted right back, concealing her forehead and almost all of one eye. She ignored it and nodded for me join her.

"Come on. You can sit with me," she said.

"Oh, uh, thanks, but I think I'm sitting with Logan," I said. I gestured to Logan, who'd all but disappeared into the background during my face off with Victoria and was now inching his way back to this side of the salad bar.

"Hey Logan. You wanna break bread together with new girl?"

Logan shrugged. "Sure."

The girl beamed at me. "I vote for a picnic. You?"

"Sounds amazing," I agreed. I readjusted my backpack higher on my shoulder and followed her out the door.

We were halfway to the stairs when, without warning, she stopped and turned to face me. I tensed at her sudden movement, but her expression was friendly and easy. "Geez, how rude am I? Not even intro'ing myself properly. I'm Cambria."

"I'm–"

"Tara, I know. Oh, sorry I interrupted. I'm horrible about that. But I know who you are. Everyone knows who you are. Dude, you killed like a hundred Werewolves AND that Leo guy."

I shifted my tray, unsure how to respond, especially after all of the comments I'd heard so far. "I'm sure I didn't kill a hundred–"

"Okay, maybe it was like twenty, but that's what kids are saying. Doesn't matter. Still badass. Especially since you've never trained. Which, by the way, is lucky. I mean, do you know how early we have to get up?"

When she stopped, I wasn't sure if it was to let me answer her question or to take a breath. Before I could figure her out, she cocked her head to the side, letting her bangs fall away from her face, and stared at me quizzically.

"You should eat," she said firmly, like that was her official diagnosis.

We headed down the stairs and out the front door, ending up in the courtyard I'd come through that morning with Alex. There were a few groups of kids scattered around, eating and hanging out. I got stares and dirty looks but not all of them were aimed at me. Some were aimed at Cambria and Logan.

We sat on the grass, under the cover of a hedge trimmed to look like a bear, and I popped the top on my soda. The ground was cold, but not uncomfortable, and the grass was dry, at least. Either way, it was a million times better than eating in the cafeteria.

"You're not eating?" Logan asked Cambria.

"Hmm? Of course I am." She reached into her backpack and pulled out a bag of peanut M&M's and a soda and held it up. "See? Lunch is served."

Logan shook his head. "You're going to clog your arteries and die."

"But not today," she said. "And by then, you'll be some famous scientist and discover a cure to heal me."

"You can't heal gluttony."

Cambria stared at an M&M and sighed. "Too bad I can't charm the chocolate into not attaching itself to my hips. That would make a great weight loss plan. I'd be rich." She popped the candy into her mouth and chewed.

"Charm the candy?" I repeated, raising my eyebrows.

"Oh, yeah," said Logan, and then stopped. He looked at Cambria nervously like they'd spilled something important.

"No worries. Tara and I are going to be besties so she has a right to know. Besides, it's not a secret around here," Cambria said, rolling her eyes.

Logan didn't look as convinced. I wasn't sure if it had something to do with a lack of trust in me or something else.

"So, you've heard that some of our kind have extra abilities, right?" Cambria asked.

I thought of Fee, with her healing ability, but she was a Werewolf. I thought of Vera instead, with her ability to locate people, and I nodded.

"Well, I have the ability to charm," she said.

"Charm," I repeated.

Cambria nodded but didn't elaborate; like that one word was enough of an explanation.

"And how does that work exactly?" I asked.

"Cambria can convince people to do whatever she wants," explained Logan.

"Like compel them? Against their will?" I probably sounded more horrified than impressed, but I couldn't help it. For the past few weeks, I'd seen way more evil than good, and I could only imagine what sort of destruction and mayhem you could cause with a power like that.

"If she wanted to," Logan said. "But she can't. Not here, anyway. Wood Point has very strict rules about the use of extra abilities."

"Yeah, numero uno being don't use them – ever," said Cambria. She popped another M&M into her mouth. "And it's not like I'm evil or something so don't worry. I've never harmed someone with my ability."

Logan gave her a look and she scowled at him.

"That had nothing to do with my ability, Logan, so stuff it. Besides he was an ass, so I kicked it," she said.

Logan shook his head and chuckled.

"What are you talking about?" I asked, still contemplating the possibilities of Cambria's gift.

"Logan hooked me up with his friend Chris last year," Cambria began.

"Hey, you made me. And he was not my friend," he argued.

"I made you a deal," she said. "I'd get him off your back if he was distracted." Cambria looked at me. "Chris was sort of the ringleader of Logan's little welcoming committee. Made sure he never had clean, wearable underwear. Anyway, if he had a girlfriend he'd be too busy to torture Logan."

"And we all know how well that turned out," Logan muttered.

Cambria shot him a look but otherwise ignored him. "Sadly, it didn't work out. I found him in bed with his lab partner." She glanced at Logan.

"His lab partner wasn't a chic," Logan finished.

"Oh," was all I could say.

"I still say you got the better end of that deal," Cambria told Logan. "Chris got sent home, and you haven't had to buy new underwear since."

Logan laughed and stretched out on his side on the grass. Cambria eyed me.

"Are you okay?" she asked, looking genuinely concerned. "You look… lost."

I let out a heavy breath and tried for a smile. "Yeah, I'm okay. I think."

"Being the new kid sucks," Cambria said.

It wasn't a question, but I agreed with a shake of my head.

"Victoria," Logan explained when I didn't answer.

She scowled. "Enough said." Then she cocked her head, and looked at me with one brow raised. "What are you going to do?"

I sighed. "Nothing. Ignore her."

Logan nodded, as if he agreed this was a wise decision.

Cambria's eyes widened. "Seriously? Nothing?"

"I can't," I said. "I would get into a lot of trouble if I did and not from school. I – well, I – sort of got kicked out of my last school for fighting."

"You got expelled?" Logan's eyes were wide in disbelief.

Cambria laughed, eyes dancing in amusement. "I knew we were meant to be best friends. You're already my kind of girl."

"And what kind of girl is that? Violent?" Logan asked.

"Not boring," Cambria shot back. "Go on," she said, looking at me.

"My mom would kill me. Trust me, she's waiting for a good reason. And worse, Grandma would be disappointed. And I don't think I could go home anyway. They'd just ship me off somewhere else."

Logan and Cambria both nodded in understanding and let the subject drop.

I picked at my food until I was sure I wouldn't be able to force anything else down. "Can I ask you guys something?"

They nodded.

"Why are you being nice to me? Everyone else here hates me and has no problem letting me know it. And I've already seen them looking at you the same way for being with me. I'm not saying I don't appreciate it, but why bother?"

"You don't strike me as the type who cares what other people think," Cambria said.

"I'm not," I said. "But I'd hate to see you guys getting dumped on for being seen with me. I would understand if you want to walk away."

Cambria shook her head. "And where would the fun in that be? Logan?"

"No fun at all," he agreed, smiling.

Cambria glanced at him and then back at me, smiling. "If you haven't noticed already, Logan and I are officially what you would call misfits. Logan doesn't fit in anywhere. He's too much of a hottie to blend with the geeks and the cool kids all figured out that he's too smart to sink to their shallow standards. So he's got nowhere to go. And me, well, I'm too stubborn to conform. Or at least that's what my transcript says. They don't know I read that, though."

She winked at me, and I couldn't help but laugh. It wasn't loud or long but it was still laughter and it felt good to let it out.

"Don't let her noble speech fool you," Logan said. "Cambria likes to stir the pot, and you being here has already kicked it up a notch. Besides, anything that pisses off Victoria is right up her alley."

Cambria shrugged, neither confirming nor denying Logan's words, and looked back at me. "And the way it's looking, you're no better off than we are, socially speaking. So, you're stuck with us. Might as well make the best of it."

CHAPTER SIX

The bell rang, and everyone gathered up their trash and headed for the doors. I noticed not all of the kids were heading for our building.

"Where are they going?" I asked, pointing to two girls walking in the opposite direction we were.

"Sophomores are in Ashton Hall, over there," said Cambria, pointing. "Freshman are there, and those two are senior buildings. They get so much more room than we do." She sounded wistful, and I wondered what could possibly make a school building so much nicer by having fewer kids to fill it up.

"So all the junior classes are in this building?" I asked.

Cambria nodded. "Lexington Hall."

I stopped walking. "Wait, what?" I knew that name. It was Victoria's name.

"You heard me right. Named after Victoria's great-great somebody." Cambria shook her head. "You'd think with all that dough they could get that girl some class – or some sense."

I didn't say anything. I was thinking about the comment Victoria had made in the lunch room, about having money. But she obviously had money, and I didn't, so what was she talking about.

I hooked my bag over my shoulder, dumped my trash into a receptacle cleverly hidden between shrubs, and fell into step between Logan and Cambria.

"What class do you have next?" Logan asked.

I dug my schedule out of my back pocket and smoothed it open as we headed back inside. "Lineage, Professor Lopez."

"Eww. Boring." Cambria wrinkled her nose. "I can't believe they're making you take that."

"Why?"

"It's a freshman class," she said.

"But it's a requirement if she's going to graduate," said Logan.

"Sucks to be you," Cambria said. "But it's on the way to my class so I'll walk you there."

Logan checked his watch. "I better get going. Calculus is at the other end. I'll see you guys later." He shuffled away with his bulging backpack and disappeared into the crowd.

I turned and followed Cambria down a different hallway that led behind the staircase. While we walked, she peered over my shoulder at my classes.

"Looks like we have math and history together, so I'll meet you after and we can go there together," she said.

"What class do you have now?" I asked.

"PT. Physical Training," she said. "The rest of us have more physical training than you do. I guess they're letting you get caught up in all the classes you missed."

"I'm sure I'll make up for it with Alex," I said.

Cambria shot me a sideways look, letting her bangs fall away from her eyes, and stared at me. "Alex Channing?"

"I think so. He's going to be my tutor. Headmaster Whitfield said I need to work with him to get caught up."

"Oh em gee. That boy is magically delicious." Cambria sighed and leaned against the wall behind her, a faraway look in her eyes.

"He's okay," I said. I didn't want to admit she was right, that Alex was definitely easy on the eyes, especially after how crappy he'd been this morning.

She snapped her gaze back to mine. “Okay? He is more than okay and you get to work with him every day. I officially feel no sympathy for you. I wish I was the new kid.”

She leaned against the wall again, pretending to swoon, and I laughed. Then the bell rang and she straightened. “You better get in there. I’ll see you after. Time to go run off all this tension you’ve given me. Later,” she called, as she jogged down the hallway.

I slipped into the classroom as the teacher reached over to close the door. A short, balding man with a paisley tie and thick glasses peered at me. His lips were so thin they all but disappeared, but he managed to purse them in annoyance.

“You must be Miss Godfrey." His voice was surprisingly deep for such a small man.

“Yes, sir. Sorry I’m late.”

“You weren’t. If you were, I’d have already closed the door and you wouldn’t be permitted inside.”

I didn’t really know what to say to that so I nodded and waited while the teacher drifted back towards his desk. Behind me, I could hear a few quiet snickers, but I didn’t turn. I didn’t want to see it.

The teacher turned back to me and held out a thick red textbook. “I’m Professor Lopez. Here’s your book. You may take a seat and follow along.”

I nodded and turned to scan for an empty seat. It wasn’t hard to find one. Most of the seats were empty. Only about six were filled. Unfortunately, one of the six was a brunette I’d seen shadowing Victoria. The one with lashes that drooped under the weight of her mascara.

I took the empty desk furthest from her and turned to the page Professor Lopez called out.

“Today we are reviewing the Wilhelm line, starting with Jacob Aster. Can anyone tell me what he is known for?” Professor Lopez asked.

A single hand went up.

“Miss Lawler,” Professor Lopez called.

A petite brunette with a French braid spoke up. “Jacob Wilhelm is responsible for coordinating and executing the Boston cleanup of 1868."

"Correct," Professor Lopez said, turning to make notes on the board.

When his back was turned, a small folded piece of paper landed on my desk. I grabbed it and looked around but no one was looking at me. I unfolded the piece of paper, careful to keep my eyes on Professor Lopez. I had a feeling that passing notes didn't go over well with him. When the paper was laid open, I slid my book over it and then glanced down, peeking underneath the book to read the words.

'Dogs should be kept on a short leash. Watch your step.'

I let the book fall back into place and pressed my lips together. I looked up as Professor Lopez turned around again and resisted the urge to scan the room a second time. My money was on the trampy looking minion, but who knew for sure. The entire school felt this way; it could be anyone. I studied the backs of the heads around me, until I was certain I hadn't had a direct encounter with any of them – yet. Again, that didn't mean anything.

When no more notes came, and no one went out of their way to shoot me a dirty look, I tried to tune back into whatever lecture the teacher was giving–something about Boston and cleaning up the streets–but I couldn't concentrate.

Instead, I let my thoughts drift to home. I'd only been here for a few hours, but it felt like I'd already been gone for days. Did anyone at school notice I was gone? Were Sam and Angela telling people I'd left? Were they still going to the mall for girl's night without me? I remembered the phone in my bag, still powered off, and was glad I'd thought to bring it. First chance I got, I'd call them, and gossip for as long as the battery lasted. Once I'd promised myself to call, I felt better, and my thoughts drifted to Wes.

What was he doing right now? Was he thinking of me? The big question was whether I should tell him about the message from Miles. I knew if I did, he'd freak out and maybe even insist on coming up here to be nearby, to protect me. But as much as I missed him and wanted to see him, I didn't want him out there, roaming the woods day after day, either. The balance between boyfriend and protector still felt off to me and I wasn't quite sure how to fix it yet.

Besides, I wasn't convinced Miles' message was that threatening. I mean, he didn't even know where I was. And he'd made it sound like coming to get me was on the back burner until he'd finished doing other things. Who knew how long that would take? For now, I decided to let it go, and not freak anyone out. We all deserved a break after the chaos of the last few weeks.

The bell rang, jolting me back, and the few kids in the room pushed and moved, heading for the door. Professor Lopez ignored everyone by going back to his desk and burying his face in a paperback with the picture of a cowboy on the front.

I packed up my stuff, including the anonymous note, and shuffled towards the door.

"Miss Godfrey." Professor Lopez looked up from his novel and frowned, like I was the one interrupting him. "You're coming in late, so there will be a lot of lost time to make up for. Everyone in this class is making up the work so we are on an accelerated schedule as it is, but I will need you to complete some extra credit in order to pass the class and not return to me in the fall."

I nodded, already deciding I didn't want to return to him.

"You will need to complete a family tree project and hand it in to me by the end of the year. Here are the details." He shuffled some papers around, and handed me a flyer with instructions.

"Thanks," I said.

"Don't thank me yet. You have a lot of work to do and I won't be giving you a free pass just because you're a Godfrey, either."

"Okay." I stuffed the paper in my bag, trying to figure out what he meant. This was the second time today I'd been targeted based on my family name.

Professor Lopez went back to reading his book, signaling our conversation was over, and I decided to let it go, with him at least. I'd get my answers someplace else.

Cambria was waiting for me in the hall. "Hey," she said, pushing off from the wall and falling into step beside me. "How did it go with Loco Lopez?"

"Is that what they call him?"

"That and Lonely Lopez, Loony Lopez. There's a bunch. He's not really loony… I think. He's really into the past, so he takes his job way serious."

"So, Lineage is all about the history of famous Hunters and stuff?" I asked. I was letting Cambria lead the way, since I had no idea where I was going, and I had to dodge bodies to keep up with her.

"Basically. You also learn about your own family line. Is he making you do a research paper?"

"Yeah, some kind of family tree thing."

"Snooze. You should ask Logan to help you. He's a pro at that sort of thing."

"Writing research papers?"

"Getting A's."

MATH AND HISTORY WERE UNEVENTFUL. CAMBRIA FELL ASLEEP IN History, while Professor Hugo – who looked like he'd be more comfortable fighting wars than talking about them–lectured about the Cold War. I guess human history was still relevant, after all. I tried taking notes, so I could figure out what I missed, and find a way to get caught up, but I was distracted; either by thoughts of home or of everything that had already happened here. Thankfully, I didn't get any more hate mail.

When class ended for the day, Cambria and I were the last ones out. She waited near the door while Professor Hugo gave me a long list of chapters to read and a list of essays due on each one. Apparently, he wasn't cutting me any slack, either. His thick brows knitted together and became one as he squinted down at me, but I wasn't sure if it was something he always did, or if he already didn't like me. I took the handouts from him and assured him I would get to work as soon as possible.

"So do you want to hang out?" asked Cambria.

"Sure, I–" I stopped outside the door at the sight of Alex leaning against the wall, arms crossed in a look of impatience. "Hey," I said to him.

"Finally. You ready?" he asked, pushing away from the concrete.

"Yeah," I said, trying not to sound like I'd forgotten –which I had.

He started down the hall. I looked at Cambria apologetically, who was grinning like a moron at the back of Alex's head, and then hurried to catch up.

"How long is this going to take exactly?" I asked.

"We'll train until dinner and then you can eat and have free time." He didn't even look over at me as he talked, but stared straight ahead at the almost empty hallway, and kept walking.

"Until dinner? Every day?" I repeated his words because I wasn't sure what else to say. If I thought I had a choice at all, I would have argued, but I knew that I didn't. Just like I had no choice about anything else that was required here, just like I'd had no choice in coming here in the first place. "What about weekends?"

"I'll let you know once I've seen you in action."

I gritted my teeth, determined to be good enough to get the weekends off.

I expected Alex to lead me out the front doors and back across the courtyard we'd crossed earlier, but he didn't. Instead, he turned right and took a door that let us out in the back of the building, on the opposite end as my Defensive Maneuvers class. The door clicked closed behind us, and Alex turned and headed into the trees. There was no sign of a trail or path, and I had no choice but to trust Alex knew where he was going.

We walked for several minutes, dodging branches and stepping over low bushes, until we finally emerged onto a wide trail and turned right, following it further away from the school. Even on the trail, Alex walked fast enough that he stayed a few steps ahead of me, instead of walking beside me.

"Where are we going?" I asked.

"Almost there," was all he said.

A few minutes later, the path opened up and the trees disappeared and we stood at the edge of a large clearing, bordered by tall pines and oaks. The grass was cropped short, like it had been mowed recently but it was still nice and green.

"This is where we're going to train?" I asked.

Alex walked further out into the field and turned to face me, his expression unreadable. "Yes."

I wandered out to where he stood. "What do you want me to do?"

"Touch your toes."

I blinked. "What?"

"Touch your toes. You need to stretch out before we start," he explained.

"Oh, right," I mumbled.

I dropped my bag and bent down and touched my fingertips to my sneakers, holding them there until I felt the pull in the muscles behind my knees. Alex did the same.

I followed him through a few more stretching exercises and then straightened, waiting to begin.

For a long moment, Alex looked at me. His head was tilted to one side and even though his eyes never left my face, I had the feeling he was taking in my entire body, down to each individual muscle. When he spoke, his voice was brusque, and I wondered if maybe he didn't like what he saw.

"Before we can get into technique or positions, I need to see you move," he said.

"Move how?"

"Attack me."

"Seriously?" I stared at him. "Are you sure?"

"I'm sure. Come on."

I took a slow step forward, unsure what to do. Alex watched me, his expression teetering on boredom.

That did it. I might not be able to move like the kids here, with all their power yoga and kung-fu kicks, but I'd taken down more than one Werewolf in my time. He didn't have the right to look bored.

I squared my shoulders, bent my knees, and ran at him. The moment my body was in motion, Alex tensed. Not nervously, but in a way that said he was readying his muscles for action. He didn't move forward to meet me, though; instead choosing to wait and let me come to him. When I was two steps away, I leapt, closing the distance in the air, with my arms extended in front of me.

I swept out with a fist, knowing he'd swerve to miss it, and came around quickly with the other.

He was fast. He managed to swerve and duck out of both punches.

I fell on him, the impact sending us both to the ground.

He tried to roll away from me, but I pushed hard against his shoulders and let myself become dead weight against him, pinning him momentarily in place. I raised my fist, ready to bring it down on his jaw, but out of the corner of my eye, I could see his free hand already coming around to knock me loose.

So I did the only thing I could to win.

I brought my knee up as hard as I could–into his groin.

His eyes rolled back, and he let out a guttural groan.

I rolled off, knowing the fight was over, and sat up, feeling incredibly guilty for the low blow. I wasn't even sure why I'd resorted to it except that I'd needed to prove I wasn't completely useless, and I knew if I'd lost the fight, it would permanently ingrain me as a loser in Alex's mind. My self-respect–or temper–wouldn't allow that.

Alex rolled away from me and writhed on the ground. He was groaning and making me feel even worse. "I'm really sorry," I said.

No answer.

After a minute, he finally rolled back over and managed to sit up. He was breathing heavily and glaring at me. A vein in his temple stood out against his sun-tanned skin and it made me think of a cartoon character whose eyes were drawn like they would bulge out of their sockets at any moment. The image was enough to make me smile but I held it back, knowing that would be a mistake.

"I'm sorry. I shouldn't have done that. Are you okay?" I asked.

"I'm fine," he said, through gritted teeth.

"Are you sure? I couldn't think of any other way to avoid your fist."

His eyes narrowed, but some of the heat in his expression diminished. "You saw that?"

"Your hand coming up? Yeah, why?"

He sighed, seeming to come to some internal decision, and slowly got to his feet. "I can't fault you for doing whatever you could to win. And your instincts and awareness under pressure are good if you saw my hand coming up. Most people wouldn't have from that angle. I know from personal experience. Let's agree that from now on, a hit like that is off limits. Deal?"

I scrambled to my feet and faced him, relieved at how easy that had been. "Deal," I agreed before he could change his mind.

We got to our feet, and Alex walked a few steps away, stretching his leg muscles carefully. I waited, not wanting to make it worse by asking if he was okay again. It was probably best not to bring it up anymore. And I was still distracted by his sort-of compliment about my fighting skills. He didn't seem like the type to dish out praise very often.

"Okay, I think we should work on technique," Alex said, returning to the center of the clearing. He looked ready to go again which was kind of impressive. I knew my strength was more than that of a normal seventeen year old and he had to still be feeling the effects of my knee. But he didn't show it. "You're attack was basically head on, which is okay. I mean, it tells me a lot about you."

"Like what?" I asked, not quite sure I was going to like the answer.

"Like the fact that you're impulsive. You like to act first and think later. And you're slightly overconfident. You don't really care if I see it coming, because you're convinced you can win."

My chin came up, and the glow of his compliments faded. "But I did win," I pointed out.

"Which is why I said slightly and not completely overconfident. Your reflexes are good, though, and so are your instincts. We can build on that. And from what I've been told, that warehouse fight wasn't your first encounter with Werewolves, and you managed to not get killed up 'til now, so I have to assume there's some raw talent there."

He paused, eyeing me in a way that seemed to suggest he was planning what to do with me next. A ripple of excitement shot up my back under his gaze, and I clamped down on my muscles, mortified that he'd somehow see it and say something.

I mean, I wasn't blind or dead, so I couldn't help but notice that Alex wasn't entirely disgusting to look at–okay he was drill sergeant hot–but I had a boyfriend. A boyfriend that I was in love with. But you couldn't simply shut off your body; it reacted with a mind of its own. Still, I didn't want or need that kind of distraction. Especially when I was here to learn about fighting and killing and how to fit in with all these crazy yoga kids. I was determined not to let anything get in the way of my goal.

"Anyway, you're not the worst I've seen," Alex finished. He was, thankfully, oblivious to my silent argument with myself.

"Thanks," I muttered, pretty sure that most of what he'd said in the last five minutes had fully negated his earlier compliment.

"Let's start with the basics. You can't win if your enemy is in better shape than you. But if you can outlast them in endurance and energy, you can find a way to outmaneuver them as well, even if they're stronger and faster."

"Endurance," I repeated, not sure if I liked where this was going. "How do we train for endurance?"

Alex's lips parted in the first genuine smile I'd seen on him, so far. "We run."

I ignored the way his smile lit up his eyes and grumbled incoherently. "Run? Seriously? I hate running."

His smile twisted at the corners, and I realized the mistake I'd made in complaining. Maybe he wasn't going to forgive me so easily after all. "Then this is going to be a long semester because my trainees run. A lot."

"Your trainees? So I'm not the first student you've trained?"

"No. But you are the last." He spun as he talked, and kicked off, jogging towards the clearing head, where the trees parted to reveal rolling green hills. "Talk and run. Come on," he called out.

"What about my bag?" I called back.

"You better carry it," he yelled, obviously not caring what happened to it.

I rolled my eyes and slung my backpack onto my shoulders. I caught up to him as he broke free of the trees, and we headed into the open space that made up the endless front lawn of the grounds. We were climbing up, coming closer to the top of a hill that would take us down towards the front gates. I was already winded by the time I matched my pace to his.

"So why am I the last?" I asked.

"Because I'm graduating at the end of the year, and with any luck, I'll get placed on a strike team and won't have to train anymore. Unless it's in the field, of course."

"What's a strike team?"

He glanced sideways at me and then shook his head. "I keep forgetting you don't know anything. A strike team is assigned a specific area or region of the country. They are paid by the Hunter community to do nothing but search for Werewolf packs and take them out. Sort of like a SWAT team on a police force."

"So you just go in and kill them all?" I asked, shocked enough that I stilled my body, and stood staring after him. A rush of unexpected anger washed over me at the thought. It was barbaric. Inhuman. Genocide. At least it would be, if humans knew about it and labeled it. Apparently for Hunters, it was all in a day's work.

Alex finally noticed I wasn't beside him, anymore, and jogged back. He came to a stop in front of me, his eyes on mine in an expression of curiosity and something else…accusation? "If we determine they are a threat, yes, we kill them. If we find they are aligned with your little Cause group, then we leave them alone. If they are peaceable, we can't touch them."

I narrowed my eyes at his tone. "You say it like it's a bad thing."

"The concept of peace is not possible for a Werewolf. It never was and it never will be. They were born monsters. We were born to eradicate them."

"You can't be born a monster," I said, in a low voice. I was tempted to be angry but I wasn't sure what to think anymore. Alex was the epitome of a true Hunter to me. Strong, powerful, and obviously, completely prejudiced against Werewolves. If that was how they all were, who was I to try and change it, or judge it. Then again, where did that leave me? Did he think I was a monster?

"Monsters are made through outside influences in their environment," I said. "By definition, you could be labeled a monster, for hating someone because of their DNA."

"You really believe that?" He continued to stare me down, challenging me to continue the argument. A vein bulged in his temple, and we both breathed heavily, but I was pretty sure it wasn't from the short run.

"You're relieved of your trainer duties," I said. "I'll speak with Headmaster and find someone else. I can only hope that all Hunters aren't as prejudiced and close minded as you are." Without waiting for an answer, I pushed past him and strode quickly across the lawn, heading for the main building that loomed up at the bottom of the hill.

I hadn't gone far when a hand clamped down on my shoulder and spun me around. Alex's eyes were no longer quietly angry, but blazing with fury. I opened my mouth to cut him off, to yell about equality and acceptance, but something made me stop.

"What?" I demanded.

"You think you've got me all figured out. You think you've got all of us all figured out. You don't know anything about me."

"I could say the same about you," I shot back. "You think I don't see the disgust when you look at me?"

"We all have our reasons," he said, not even trying to deny it. "But this is what we were born to do."

"That may be true, for you. I'm not so sure I can fit into that mold. Either way, we definitely should not be working together. How can you possibly trust me, knowing that I'm half monster? That must bother you."

"It's not the same. I won't be going into battle with you."

My eyebrows shot up, and I had to hold my hands behind my back to keep from hitting him. "That's why it's not the same? Because you don't have to fight me? Aren't you afraid I'll turn on you in a training session and kill you?"

He shrugged. "Maybe. If you were capable."

That did it. Maybe it was the events of the day, as a whole, that snapped my temper–the dog comments, and the note, and the threats. Maybe it was that Alex was way too cocky and condescending for his own good. Either way, I'd had enough.

I brought my fist around and connected with Alex's jaw. His neck snapped sideways and from his profile, I could see the momentary shock on his face. I knew enough to take advantage of that, and that it wouldn't last much longer, and I swung my other fist out, and smashed it into his gut.

Alex doubled over, clutching his stomach with one arm, and scrambled back a few steps, putting some distance between us. I didn't try to close it. Not yet. I knew he was ready for it, now. It wouldn't be that easy. Still, I was mad enough that I wasn't finished.

"What the hell was that for?" he growled.

"To show you I'm capable."

"Message received."

I took a step forward, eyes narrowed, hands fisted, letting all the tension and stress rise to the surface and boil over. "It's clear we are too different to work together, much less be friends. I am half Werewolf, after all."

Alex winced a little at the word Werewolf, as I expected he would. Then he planted his feet and his eyes hardened. "Fine," he said. "You're right. You're a dirty blood. But you fight like a human."

With a hiss, I launched myself at him. When I landed on him, we went down, and I had the satisfaction of hearing the breath whoosh out of him as his back thudded against the dirt. Before I could do anything more, his fist came up and landed hard against my rib cage. I felt my body curl in on itself, but I resisted the urge to roll off. Instead, I let myself go limp, becoming dead weight against him, pinning him down.

He was wriggling and writhing under me, and I knew that any second, he'd land a second rib punch and be out from under me. I knew I had to keep him there, because if I ended up on the bottom, I was dead meat.

So, I resorted to fighting dirty – again.

I found a bare patch of skin where his neck and shoulder met, and I bit down. There was a yell and then a grunt in my ear, and then his hands came up to pull me off. When they did, I cocked my fists back, and brought both of them into the side of his stomach as hard as I could. They landed right where I wanted them to; in that small unprotected space of flesh between his ribs and his hips. I felt his body jerk under me and I pulled my teeth away from the flesh I'd torn underneath his collarbone.

I caught a glimpse of blood trickling out of the wound and then his hands were pinning mine out of the way and a knee came up, driving into my ribs where the first hit had landed. The already bruising skin was too sensitive and I jerked sideways.

I could feel myself falling off and Alex's hands pushing me, but I knew if I lost the advantage, it was over. I grabbed his shirt and curled my fingers against the fabric and then jerked hard to the side. For a second, I felt only my body falling away from his, but just before my back hit the dirt, I felt his body give and pull towards me, landing with a thump on top of mine. I wrapped my legs around his, pinning his feet, and then tried doing the same with his hands, but he was already wriggling against it. The movement of our bodies, trying to writhe free of the other must have been too much because, then, we were rolling.

I thought we'd only roll a few times and then stop again, but after the first couple of disorienting turns, I realized we were picking up speed. We must've been closer to the edge of the hill than I thought because it felt steep underneath my overturning limbs. The ground was turning over and over beneath me at a dizzying rate, with no sign of slowing.

My legs were still wrapped around Alex's, pinning him against me. If I let go, I'd be able to roll free of him, and stop myself, but that felt too much like losing. I couldn't lose.

Instead, I clamped tighter to his legs and, ignoring the bumps and jerks caused by our bodies tumbling over each other, brought my fist out and then into his ribs. He grunted; it sounded like it was more out of frustration than pain. He stopped trying to break free and started fighting back. After that, it was all knees and fists and teeth. I think I even felt my hair being pulled once or twice.

We finally rolled to a stop, and it took me a minute to notice, I was so busy protecting my face from Alex's fists. What eventually got my attention was the clapping–and the whistles.

CHAPTER SEVEN

"Woot Woot!"

"Is that a new tactical maneuver, Channing?"

"Wow. New girl doesn't waste any time."

Alex jerked away from me, and I did the same, pulling my hands free like they'd been burned.

I felt heat rise to my face and throat.

Alex stood up and stared down at me, offering his hand, and effectively ignoring the calls and whistles from the gathering crowd. I wished I could ignore them as well as he could, but the catcalls and innuendos traveled to my eardrum and then seeped into my brain, burrowing, and making my humiliation that much sharper. I glanced up into the faces that crowded around and stood smirking at us. I recognized several of them from my classes, though most were strangers. Every one of them stared at us in a way that let me know this moment would be the topic of conversation for days to come.

I ignored Alex's outstretched hand and got to my feet on my own. Pain shot through my left foot, but I kept my face blank. I wasn't about to show weakness in front of this crowd, or Alex. The anger was gone–at least the attacking kind–especially after rolling right into half the student body, but my chin jutted with a stubbornness that wouldn't allow me to admit any sort of defeat.

"All right, ladies and gentlemen, clear the area."

A man appeared from behind the crowd of kids, his booming voice cutting a path between the bodies. Kids backed further out of the way as he approached.

"Unless you all want to explain to me what you're doing allowing a fight on school grounds, I suggest you move on," he said.

Great. Not only did the entire student body think Alex and I had been caught in some sort of a dirty make out session, a teacher was going to bust us for fighting. I glanced over at Alex, not sure who I blamed more for this, him or myself. I caught him watching me, and was surprised to see his expression was friendly and open; I could've sworn there was actually laughter in his eyes.

Did he think this was funny?

I scowled at him as the rest of the kids scurried off, leaving us alone with the teacher who'd found us. I looked up at the man for the first time and stared. He was tall and broad shouldered, with shaggy hair that hung in his face, almost obscuring deep set eyes. The way he moved spoke of confidence and power, and I knew instinctively he wasn't someone you disobeyed; no wonder kids moved out of his way at the sound of his voice.

The man came closer and shook his hair out of his eyes, and I caught sight of his face. My feet automatically took a step back. The right side was completely normal while the left was marred from eyebrow to jawbone with jagged lines so deep that the insides were marred with a ghostly white line where the skin had scarred and toughened around the wounds.

"Miss Godfrey," he said, nodding at me in that way some people can do without moving their heads.

"Sir," I said, unsure what else to call him at this point.

The man turned and regarded Alex. "Mr. Channing, what's going on here?"

"Hi, Professor Kane," Alex said. "Sorry about the disruption. Tara and I were training up on the hill and must've got too close to the edge. We took a tumble."

Alex gestured to the hill we'd come down and Professor Kane nodded. "Understandable. In the future, let's be a little more careful. The student body doesn't need any more fuel for gossip than they already have. Agreed?"

Alex shrugged. "Agreed."

Professor Kane looked over at me, obviously wanting a response.

"Agreed," I mumbled.

He raised an eyebrow, causing the scars on his face to elongate, and something glinted in his eyes. He walked over to me and lifted his hand, pausing when I flinched. His lips twitched in amusement and he plucked something out of my hair and held it out to me. A clump of moss and dirt fell to the ground between us.

"I don't think we've been properly introduced," he said. "I'm Professor Jonah Kane. I teach Offensive Tactics."

He extended his hand and I took it, both of us noticing the dirt crusted around my knuckles, mixed with a little blood.

Professor Kane released my hand and stepped back, eyeing me with an interest that sent a chill through me. I wasn't scared, exactly, but I knew not to piss him off, either.

"You obviously have some skill if you were able to take Alex for a roll down the hill. With any luck, you'll catch up enough to be in my class next year." He looked over at Alex again, who was trying to examine the bite wound I'd given him on his shoulder. "She's one to watch. You should get that looked at," he told him, already turning and leaving the way he'd come.

Alex grunted something unintelligible and kept straining to see the wound that was just out of reach of his eyes. I watched Professor Kane disappear around the stone building and then looked back at Alex, finally noticing the full state of his appearance.

The bite wound was jagged and ugly. Even though it wasn't very big, dried blood caked the skin around it, and his shirt had been stretched out so that it hung loosely off his shoulder. His jeans had a rip in one knee all the way to his ankle and the fabric was frayed and covered in grass stains. I caught a glimpse of dirt and blood on his exposed knee. I looked back up at his face, beginning to feel a stab of guilt over attacking him. There was a scratch on his cheek with a thin line of blood trailing down to his chin, where it had dried. A thin layer of dirt and sweat covered his face and neck.

"I'm sorry for attacking you," I said.

At my words, he stopped messing with the bite wound and looked over at me with raised brows. "Are you really?"

For some reason, it bothered me that he didn't even look upset about the fact that we'd rolled down the hill, trying to kill each other. If anything, he looked happy about it. I could feel my temper being pricked and struggled to push it down. "What does that mean? Of course I'm sorry. I said I was."

"Right. You said it, but I'm not sure you mean it. You don't look very sorry. And you definitely weren't sorry at the time."

I clenched my teeth and prepared to fire off a nasty comment.

"If it helps, I'm not sorry, either," he said.

"What?"

"Well, I'm not, if I'm being honest. Now we know not to press each other's buttons, and I think the fact that we don't really like each other will make you a better fighter."

"Didn't you hear what I said up there? I'm not working with you."

"Give it a rest, Godfrey." The lightness was gone from his eyes, replaced with determination. His tone was matter of fact as he closed the distance between us. "You're not nearly as warm and fuzzy about Werewolves as you'd like me to think. Just like I'm not all warm and fuzzy about a lot of Hunters, either. I'm not a bigot or prejudiced, and you're not a Werewolf-rights activist. Both of us are entitled to an opinion, though, and that's fine. It doesn't prevent us from working together."

He was standing in front of me, close, with arms crossed loosely, waiting for me to argue. Probably hoping I would, since at this point, if I tried, I would look like the prejudiced one, the one who couldn't handle letting someone else have an opinion that was different than mine.

I sucked in a breath. Fine. But there was one other problem he hadn't addressed. "That doesn't change the fact that I'm half Were," I pointed out.

"No, it doesn't. Is that a problem for you?"

"I'm not the one with the problem here."

"Good. Then it's settled. Training again tomorrow, after last bell. Might as well meet me on the hill." He paused and let the hint of a smile creep onto his face. "I'm sure you'll remember how to get there now."

He walked away, and I felt my hands curl into fists at my sides as I watched him go.

I thought about going to talk to Headmaster about getting a different trainer but I dismissed the idea. Instead, I turned and jogged back up the hill for my bag. It dawned on me that Alex hadn't really denied having a problem with me being half Were. In a way, though, it made me want to work with him. If only to be able to beat the crap out of him day after day until he admitted he was wrong.

Or I killed him.

I retrieved my bag and hurried back down the hill, cutting through the trees as I made my way back to the junior's building, otherwise known as Lexington Hall. I found a narrow path that led me straight there while keeping under the cover of the trees, and realized I wasn't the first to avoid the crowded courtyard. I had a feeling I'd be taking this path a lot in the coming months. I made it back without running into anyone and hurried inside.

I didn't remember seeing any dorm rooms here, but I figured I could wander around until I found someone worth asking, or better yet, someone worth following. In all the stress of the day, I'd forgotten to ask Cambria where my room might be and I certainly didn't want to ask anyone now.

I thought about the layout of the campus and counted buildings in my head, matching them up to what Cambria had told me at lunch. Besides the main admin building, there was one for the freshman, one for the sophomores, one for the juniors, and two for the seniors. But these were all for classes, so where were the dorm buildings?

The halls were mostly empty when I got inside, with most of the traffic going up and down the stairs towards the cafeteria where dinner was being served. I definitely didn't want to go up there. I had a feeling I looked as bad as Alex. I pulled a loose blade of grass from my shirt as proof; definitely not going up there. Instead, I leaned against the wall near the front doors and waited.

Several kids wandered down the stairs, some in pairs and some alone. They all turned to wander down the hall that led to classrooms, though, so I didn't bother to follow. Another few minutes passed and a group of girls came down. One of them mentioned heading back to her room but she must've left something in her class because she, too, turned down the hall instead of going outside. I waited, but they didn't reappear. I thought about walking that way, to see if they'd taken another exit, but then a familiar face caught my eye. A slight brunette with a French braid that I remembered from my Lineage class. Nina something.

"Hey, Nina, right?" I called out to her and stepped away from the wall.

The girl caught sight of me, and her eyes widened. She didn't respond, and I remembered what I must look like.

"I know, I uh, had training earlier. With Alex Channing? He's a difficult teacher." I smiled, hoping to reassure her.

"Um, okay." She finally managed to pull her jaw closed and took a step, then stopped again, glancing around. She still looked scared, and I didn't think it had to do with my appearance. "Do you need medical help?"

"Oh, no. I was hoping you could show me where the dorms are. I haven't seen them anywhere."

"No one showed you yet?" she asked, brows furrowing.

I shrugged. "No, I guess everyone thought someone else would do it."

Nina bit her lip and looked over her shoulder, obviously not wanting to be seen with me. She looked me over again and sighed. "Yeah, come on."

I fell into step beside her and was surprised when she turned down the same hallway the others had walked down, towards the classrooms. Maybe there was a shortcut this way. Neither of us spoke as we walked, and Nina kept looking around, like any minute she'd be spotted consorting with the enemy.

At end of the hall, Nina stopped in front of a thick wooden door and pushed it open. I was about to ask what we were doing back in a classroom, but I closed my mouth as I passed into a stairwell. The stairs wound downward, only I couldn't imagine to where since we were already on the ground floor.

The door closed behind me with a thud. I jumped, feeling claustrophobic in the musty space. Then I realized the door was attached to an iron rod at the top that made it swing closed automatically. The touch of modern calmed me, and I was able to convince myself I wasn't spiraling down towards a dungeon or torture chamber.

"Where are we going?" I asked. My voice echoed off the empty stone walls as we wound down another flight. We had to be passing below ground level now.

"To the dorms," she answered, as if it were obvious.

"The dorms are in the basement?"

Nina slowed enough to glance back at me and then resumed her steady pace. "No, underground. Didn't anyone explain this to you?"

"Um, no. I think I would remember that little detail. How far underground?" The walls were changing, becoming less like the smooth stone surfaces of the school and more like hand-packed cement. It smelled like wet dirt.

"Three stories," Nina answered.

I stopped on the landing that led to yet another flight of winding stairs and stared at Nina's braid. "Seriously? Three stories? Why? Was there no money for dorm room buildings? They had to tunnel underneath the classrooms like gophers?"

Nina turned to face me. "It's a security measure," she explained. "We're most vulnerable at night, when everything's closed down, and we're all sleeping. So, the dorms are fortified by layers of concrete and hidden underground. Trust me, no expense was spared on the accommodations themselves. I'm sure you'll be comfortable."

"Vulnerable to what?"

"To attack," she said, drawing out the words like she was speaking to a toddler.

"Does that happen?"

"Not in a long time, but they don't like to take chances here." She eyed me. "Can we go now? I've got homework."

"Oh, yeah," I said, distracted. I started walking again, remembering the story Wes had told me of the way Werewolves had attacked Hunters years ago. They'd gone for the kids first, which meant places like this had been attacked and destroyed at some point. Remembering that made underground dorms seem a little less extreme.

We reached the bottom and the floor leveled out, leaving the stairs in a winding loop behind us. In front of me, a brightly lit hallway extended in three directions, each lined by colored doors on both sides. The walls were covered with flyers for various activities or dry erase boards with personal messages scrawled. Scattered between the paper signs were wall mounted candelabras that glowed dim and yellow and were drowned out by the fluorescent overhead lighting. I had the impression they weren't so much functional as decoration. Girls loitered in open doorways and music drifted out of rooms and mingled together, creating an unintelligible buzz of sound. It all seemed very college dorm-ish.

A few girls looked up from their conversations and sent me unfriendly looks. Nina turned to me, looking uneasy again.

"So, which one do you think is mine?" I asked, as eager to escape the spotlight as she was.

She shifted her weight from one foot to the other, not meeting my eyes. "Um, I don't know. I heard there was an available bed in a room down the left hallway, though. You could try there."

"Okay, thanks. I guess I can ask around down there…"

I stopped talking because Nina was already walking away, taking the hallway to the right, before I could answer further.

A couple of girls from the hall in front of me were still eyeing me, and with Nina gone, I felt really exposed, standing there all dirty and grass stained. One of them pushed off from her spot against the wall, heading for me. I hooked a left, hoping she wouldn't follow, and made my way down a short hallway before turning right again, onto the main corridor that held dorm rooms on this side. I passed what looked like an office but the door was closed and a 'Do Not Disturb' sign hung on the window, covering it up. I kept going.

A couple of girls stood talking near the end of the hall so I wandered towards them. One had a shower bag in her hand. That worked out perfectly. I could get her to help me find my room and then she could tell me where I could shower. As long as they didn't try to kill me first.

They looked up as I got close, and I could see their faces change the moment they saw me. They were quicker to hide it than the girls in the last hallway, but I still saw it. I took a deep breath and prayed one of them would answer me.

"Excuse me," I said.

They frowned at me. "Can we help you?" The girl with the shower bag was the one who spoke.

"I'm looking for my room. I heard there was an empty bed in one of these rooms. Do you know if any luggage has been dropped off to a room on this hall?"

"I think–"

The other girl started to speak but was cut off by a look from the shower bag girl. "No luggage here," she said, in a tone that was way too nice for me to believe.

"Huh. I guess they forgot to bring it. I'll have to go room by room, then." I stepped up to the first door, closest to shower bag girl, and turned the knob, yanking the door open. I stepped inside and looked around.

Shower bag girl flew in behind me. "Hey! What the hell? Get out of my room!"

I caught sight of two twin beds on opposite walls, both decked out with the frilliest pink and purple bedspread I had ever seen. Two desks separated the spaces and both had pens with feathers attached, all stuffed into cups decorated with glitter. Wow. It was like a bedazzler had vomited. I was glad this wasn't my room.

But I wasn't done. I walked to the middle of the room and shook myself so that pieces of grass and dirt fell to the carpet around me. Shower bag girl screamed.

"Fine! Whatever! Its number sixteen. Just get out!"

"Thanks," I said, smiling brightly at her.

I turned and walked out, to room sixteen. I was annoyed enough that I didn't bother knocking first. I mean, if this was my room, then I shouldn't have to knock. I pushed the door open and stepped in. The first thing I noticed were my bags, pushed all the way against the far wall and lying on their sides, like they'd been shoved or kicked. The second thing I noticed was that the other bed–the one closest to the door–was occupied.

By two people.

They had their arms wrapped around each other and their lips firmly locked. Their bodies writhed in tandem, and I coughed. They broke abruptly apart and sat up so I was able to see their faces.

Levi, the guy who'd come onto me at lunch – and Victoria.

My new roommate.

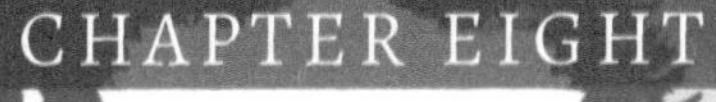

CHAPTER EIGHT

I groaned. "No way."

Victoria shrieked and threw Levi off of her. He rolled to the side, a cocky half-grin on his face as he took in the situation. He obviously didn't mind getting caught. Knowing that grossed me out even more.

"Get out!" Victoria yelled and looked wildly around the room. I think she might have been looking for something to throw.

Despite my urge to gag and run away, I planted my feet and crossed my arms. "No," I said. "This is apparently my room, too. I'm not leaving, so wrap it up."

"What? That's your crap in the corner?" Victoria gestured to my bags. "What the…?" She rubbed her temples. "This is not happening."

Someone came up behind me in the open doorway and stopped short of running me over. "Oh, wow."

I turned at the sound of Cambria's voice and caught her grinning at the scene in front of us.

"Shut up, Cambria," Victoria snapped.

Cambria grinned wider.

I turned back to Victoria and waited. She looked down at Levi, who was still lying where she'd thrown him, on the edge of the bed propped up on his elbow. He smiled up at her, and she narrowed her eyes at him and pointed.

"Get out," she said.

Levi sat up, still smiling. "Aw, come on Vic. It's a party now." He wiggled his eyebrows.

"Get. Out." She continued to glare at him, and in that moment, I didn't doubt Victoria could easily take him out in a fight.

Levi finally slid off the bed and planted a loud kiss on her cheek. Victoria didn't move or react; just waited for him to leave.

"I'll call you later," he said.

Maybe he was used to her ignoring him because he didn't seem bothered at all by her lack of reaction. He turned and walked towards the door, which Cambria and I still blocked. I felt Cambria move over, to allow him to pass, but looking at the challenge in Victoria's expression, I couldn't allow myself to move aside. So I kept my feet planted and made him move around me to get by.

His body brushed against mine, a lot more than was needed for him to fit through the gap, and he stopped next to me, leaning down to speak into my ear. "We'll all party next time."

His breath tickled my ear, but I didn't look away from Victoria. Finally, I felt him leave. Cambria came around to stand beside me, and I felt her eyes on me.

"Well, I can see you two have a lot to discuss. So, I'll leave you to it," Cambria said, heading for the door.

"No. Wait," I said. "I need a shower. Can you show me where it is?"

"Yeah."

"I'll get my stuff." I broke eye contact with Victoria and moved past her. I grabbed the bag that I knew held a couple of changes of clothes and my shower stuff and threw it on what was now my bed and zipped it open. I rummaged around until I found what I needed. No one spoke while I did all of that. I could still feel Victoria's eyes boring into my back.

I gathered everything I needed and tucked the pile of clothes under my arm, trying not to let it rub on the dirt that still covered my clothes. I ignored Victoria and looked at Cambria.

"Ready," I said.

"Let's go."

I followed her out and closed the door behind me with a harsh thud.

"Oh, wow," Cambria said when we were alone in the hall.

"I know."

She shook her head, tossing her hair in and out of her eyes. "I don't know where to start. The fact that your roommate is Satan's spawn, or that you look like you got mauled by a tree-hugging hippie."

"Not a hippie. Alex."

Cambria shot me a look, eyebrows raised. "Did you two train in a mud bath? Because that actually sounds kind of hot."

I sighed. She'd hear about it soon enough. "No. Actually, I sort of attacked him."

She snorted a laugh as we passed through the door at the end of the hall. "Explain."

We were in what resembled a large gym locker now. Bathroom stalls lined one wall, with a line of sinks to match. A dividing wall separated that from the changing areas where I could see curtained stalls with benches, and the metal glint of shower heads tucked further inside the stalls.

I walked that way. The air felt moist and warm, and I followed the sound of running water to the showers. I chose one at the end, farthest away from the already running shower near the front.

I still hadn't answered Cambria's question, but she wasn't deterred. She followed me into the changing stall and sat down on the bench. "Go ahead." She gestured to the attached shower stall I was already standing in. "Talk and shower."

I shook my head and gave into her demands. While I showered, I filled her in on my wreck of a training session.

"He told me to attack him, so I did," I said.

"Holy hotness, you touched his body, didn't you?"

I laughed as I rubbed shampoo through my grimy hair. I was already glad for Cambria's friendship. It helped lighten the mood after the most stressful day I could remember. The feeling of finally being clean helped, too.

"Yes, I guess I touched his body. If kicking him in the groin counts."

Cambria gasped. "You didn't."

"It was the only way to win. He had me pinned."

"Oh, wow. That was low, Tara." Cambria laughed. "So how did you get dirty? Did he literally drag you through the mud after that?"

"No. He said he understood why I did it, to win the fight. But then… he said some things, about Werewolves." I could feel my muscles tensing at the memory of the conversation.

"Like what?" Cambria asked. She no longer sounded amused.

I repeated the conversation that had led up to me tackling him.

"That sucks," Cambria said when I was done. "I mean, it's basically what we're all taught, though."

"That doesn't make it right."

Cambria didn't respond, and I finished my shower in silence. When I pulled the curtain open and stepped back into the changing area, Cambria was gone. I pulled on fresh jeans and an old tee shirt with a picture of roller-skating penguins and stepped out. Cambria was at the sink waiting for me.

"Are you pissed at me, now?" I asked.

Cambria shook her head. "Of course not, but you have to understand something, Tara. While most Hunters are taught to hate Werewolves from birth, Alex has his own reasons for doing things. He's had it rough, and it's because of Werewolves. He's probably a little harder than the rest of us because of it."

"What happened?"

"The way I hear it, his dad was an elite member of a strike group that worked directly for the Committee. He made a lot of enemies. One day, a Werewolf pack tracked him back to his house. They waited until Alex's dad left and went in and killed Alex's mother. They made Alex watch and held him hostage, and when his dad was coming home, they bit Alex. Just enough to make it hurt like hell until his dad found him and got him to a healer. By the time his dad was able to go out and look for the pack, they were gone. Alex didn't know who they were, and they were never identified. After that, his dad quit the strike team and started drinking really bad."

"Geez. That sucks," I said. "How old was Alex?"

"Like, twelve, I think? I don't know. Most of it is passed around like gossip since he won't talk about it to anyone."

I didn't know what to say, so I picked up a comb and ran it through my wet hair, staring at my reflection without really seeing it.

"I'm not saying you should feel sorry for him," said Cambria. "But I thought you should know he's not a complete asshole. Well, not without reason, anyway." She grinned, and just like that, I felt the mood lighten. "So, you never finished telling me. What happened after he talked all that crap to you?"

"I tackled him," I said, cringing. Despite Cambria telling me not to, I couldn't help but feel bad after everything she'd told me. "And then we rolled down the hill, fighting."

Cambria grinned. "Yeah, I know. I heard. I just wanted to hear it from you."

"Oh, crap. Already?"

"It's already everywhere. Sorry. According to the story, you and Alex were caught making out at the edge of the woods by Griffin Hall."

My eyes widened. "What? Crap. That is not what happened!"

"Obviously. But it sounds way better than you attacking your trainer in a rage and rolling down a hill."

"I did more damage than that," I said, knowing I sounded pathetically defensive. "He was just as messed up as me at the bottom. Worse, actually. I bit him."

"You... bit him?" Cambria's eyes were wide with surprise and then her expression changed and she burst out laughing.

"It's not funny. He was bleeding," I said, still feeling guilty.

Cambria was shaking and gripping the sink for support. A girl at the other end of the stalls peeked out and scurried towards the door, sending us odd looks. Cambria finally got a hold of herself by sucking in deep breaths that sounded like hyperventilating.

"So, look," she began. "You probably shouldn't tell people about the whole biting thing if you want them to believe it was a raging fight instead of a quickie in the grass." She muffled a giggle again. "Especially with the whole 'dog' persona you've got going on."

I shot Cambria a look. "Whatever," I muttered.

Cambria snorted another laugh, and I ignored her and finished combing my hair. I twisted it up behind me to get it out of the way and a grumbling noise echoed out around me.

"What was that?" Cambria asked.

"My stomach. I'm starved. Can we eat now?"

"Sure thing."

We left the bathroom, and I slowed when we got close to my door. I really didn't want to go back in there.

"Can I put my stuff in your room 'til we get back?" I asked.

"No prob."

She stopped in front of a door only a few up from mine. It was black with glow in the dark stars stuck on it and a brassy sign with 'Number Eleven' engraved on the front. The inside smelled like musky incense and expensive perfume. One bed was covered in clothes and magazines and the other was made up neatly like it hadn't been used recently.

"I bet your roommate doesn't suck," I said, dropping my bag onto the messy bed. I didn't have to ask to know that one was Cambria's.

"No, she's never here. I like that about her."

We headed for the stairs that would take us back up to ground level. On our way out, we passed by the office door I'd seen earlier, and I slowed.

"Whose room is this?" I asked, trying to see inside around the Do Not Disturb sign that still covered the window.

"Un-uh. Come on." Cambria grabbed my wrist and pulled me towards the stairs. "That's Ms. Fincham's room. She's what you would call a dorm mother." Cambria snorted. "Except crazier."

"What do you mean?"

"Cambria Hebert?" a shrill voice called out from behind us. "Is that you? Is that my new student you've got with you?"

Cambria cringed and stopped. "Come on. Get it over with," she whispered.

We turned, and I saw a willowy woman with frizzy brown hair standing near the office doorway. She had on a flower print robe over dingy sweatpants and bunny slippers on her feet.

"Hey, Ms. Fincham," Cambria said.

"Hey, yourself. Is this my new girl?" Ms. Fincham squinted at me even though I was standing right in front of her. She smelled like bread dough and hand sanitizer.

"Her name's Tara Godfrey, Ms. Fincham."

"Huh. Nice to meet you. Be sure you follow my rules," she said, frowning at me.

"What are the rules?" I asked.

Ms. Fincham thrust a piece of paper at me. "These are the rules. Sign them and drop them into the slot in my doorway after dinner."

Somewhere inside the office, a timer dinged. Ms. Fincham whirled and disappeared inside, slamming the door behind her.

"That was interesting," I said.

"Actually, that was pretty calm," said Cambria. "Baking does that, even though you couldn't pay me to eat whatever it is she's making. Come on."

We went through the line and sat at a small table in the corner, tucked out of the way of the group by the window. Victoria wasn't there, but the brunette I'd seen this morning was; the one who had more mascara than eyelashes. And she was clearly holding court in Victoria's absence. Her smile was wide enough – and fake enough – to swallow whole some of the jocks she was trying to charm, and it curved into something edgy and mean when she spotted us. I held her gaze for as long as she stared back at me and even a few seconds after, just to prove a point. I wasn't sure what that point was, but it made me feel slightly more confident.

"Who's the brunette at Victoria's table?" I asked Cambria.

Cambria glanced behind her and then twisted her lip into a snarl. "Demi Johanssen. Second in command, wants to be first. She follows Victoria around like a slave, waiting for the moment Victoria is gone long enough so she can steal the spotlight for a little while."

A shadow fell over our table, and we looked up. Logan stood there, minus the baseball cap for the first time all day. His hair was wet from the shower and he had on fresh clothes.

"Hey," he said, smiling and sliding onto a chair next to Cambria. His tray was loaded down, and he dug in like he hadn't eaten in a week.

"Hey," Cambria mumbled around a mouthful of cheesy fries.

"Do you have a trainer, too?" I asked.

"What?" He blinked at me, his face blank for a second, and then he seemed to realize what I'd meant. "Oh. No. I got caught up on a project I'm working on and then I spilled some solution on myself and had to shower."

Cambria stopped, a french fry halfway to her mouth. "Eww. It wasn't formaldehyde again was it?"

"No. Saline, but I was working with blood, and I didn't want to take the chance."

"Why blood?" I asked, before Cambria could voice her disgust again. She went back to her fries.

He shrugged. "It's extra credit. I'm studying the differences between Hunter DNA and human DNA. White blood cell count, immune system, that sort of thing."

Cambria rolled her eyes. "Logan, don't lie to sound cooler. It's not extra credit. You do this crap for fun."

Logan's cheeks reddened a little and he shot Cambria a look. "There's nothing wrong with being smart, Cam."

"I think it's pretty interesting. What have you found?" I asked.

"It's still in the beginning stages," he said. "Not a lot of collected data. But from what we can tell, Hunter blood has all the same DNA make up as humans plus some extras.

"Like what?"

"Think of our DNA like a human's on steroids. Stronger immune system, even to long-term diseases like cancer. And we don't get colds or the flu as often. There's a lot of speculation as to exactly how or why that is. Hunters haven't had the access or funding we've needed in the past to really get these kinds of answers. So this sort of project is really exciting."

Cambria snorted, but I smiled. "Sounds like it." It made me wonder what my DNA would look like, with traces of human, Hunter, and Werewolf blood all mixed together. I was kind of afraid to ask.

Victoria breezed through the doors as we finished up and dumped our trays. She had a mini entourage behind her, which included Levi, and I tensed. I hadn't really figured out how I was going to handle the roommate thing. Part of me wanted to march down to Griffin Hall and demand to be moved. The other part of me felt like a coward for even considering it.

"I think I'm going to get some air," I said, staying clear until they'd passed. Victoria didn't even turn to glare at me. Maybe we'd moved on to ignoring. One could hope.

"You want some company?" Cambria asked, scrutinizing me.

I shook my head. "No thanks. It's been a long day. I want a few minutes to unwind."

Some of the intensity and worry left her face. "No worries. I need to charm Logan here into finishing some homework for me, anyway."

Logan glared at her. "You try to compel me–"

"See you later," she called, cutting him off and yanking him down the hall.

I smiled. "See you later."

I went down the stairs and out the back set of doors; the ones that opened up almost straight into the woods. The sun had set enough to cast deep shadows on everything, leaving all the colors washed in a gray undertone. I leaned against the stone building, reached in my bag, and pulled out my phone.

I held my breath while the screen loaded, waiting to see if there would be any messages. After today, I wasn't sure if I could handle any more out of Miles. The screen lit up with a missed call, but it was my home number. Probably safe to assume my mom had realized I'd swiped the phone. No message. I decided not to call back yet. See how long she'd let it go.

I scrolled through my address book and found Wes' number. I punched it and waited while it rang. Around me, the sound of cicadas grew loud and steady with nightfall. The warmth of the sun had faded into a chill that grew heavier as it grew darker, made worse by the cold damp stone at my back. I wished I'd brought a jacket out.

"Hello?"

My breath caught at the sudden emotion that came from simply hearing the sound of his voice. "Hey," I managed. Hot tears filled my eyes, and I blinked them back, hugging my arms around myself and wishing they were his.

"Tara? Is everything okay?" Wes' tone changed immediately–to one of alert. He was already assuming danger.

I sniffled. "Yeah, it's fine," I lied, putting a huge amount of false cheer into my answer.

"Is it that bad?"

"Yes." I sighed. "No. Maybe. First days are always the worst, right?"

"Tell me what happened."

There it was again. That soft, deep tone he had that made my eyes burn because I couldn't see the face that went with it. So, I told him. All about Victoria, and the threats, and Alex, who may or may not already hate me but definitely didn't like me simply because my DNA made us enemies. I even told him about the humiliating tumble down the hill and getting caught by half the student body at the bottom.

Wes laughed out loud at that, but cut off abruptly when he remembered my mood. "I'm sorry, not funny." I could hear him smiling. "Do you want me to talk to him?"

"No, I can handle it." I was already feeling a tiny bit better for being able to tell him about it all, and I was feeling more like a drama queen every second, especially when I remembered everything he had to deal with. "How are things there? How's Jack?"

"Jack's good. He's getting around a little more. Still on Fee's nerves, though. She's threatened to put evil ingredients into his dinner."

I had to laugh at that. Something told me it could be scary being on Fee's bad side. Static filled the line, and we waited for it to pass. I repositioned myself, hoping to find a clear spot. "What about you?" I asked when it cleared.

"I'm good," he said. His voice had gotten quieter, though, and strained. "I miss you already."

I kicked at some rocks at my feet, sending them rolling into the trees where they disappeared in the darkness. "I still think this is a dumb idea. I should be home."

"No!" He stopped and took a deep breath. "Tara, I want you to be careful. Don't go anywhere alone, okay? And stay on school grounds."

"Why? Did something happen?" Something about his tone was too edgy for vague worrying, but it had smoothed out by the time he spoke again, and I wasn't sure if I'd imagined it. Or maybe my own stress was making me paranoid.

"I want to know your safe. It's not easy being so far away from you."

Static broke into the connection again. I waited, debating whether or not to say anything about the message from Miles. I knew I should, but I also knew that if I did, I'd never hear the end of it about being safe and never alone and blah blah blah. So when the static cleared, I stayed silent.

"Edie says there's a visitation day next month. I'm going to try and drive up."

"You talked to Grandma?"

"Yeah she's talking about coming to the next Cause meeting."

"Seriously?"

"Yeah, your mom's not happy, but what can she do, right? I hope she does. Maybe it'll distract Jack long enough to give me a break. All he does is quiz me on names and pack locations. He's talking about sending me out to meet another group of them, but I don't think it'll happen for a while."

"Why not? If you're going to take over The Cause you need to know these people. They need to know you."

"They do know me. That's the problem."

"What do you mean?"

He sighed and went quiet. "It's not going over well with the other packs, Tara."

It took me a minute to realize what he meant, but the tone of his voice was clear. It was the same self-deprecating way he talked whenever his mixed blood came up.

"That's stupid," I said. "Your parents helped found The Cause. They should be glad you have both of their blood in you."

"It's not that simple, Tara. You know that."

I kicked another rock, harder than the others, and sent it flying. "It's still stupid."

The static chimed in after that, louder than before, and with no sign of diminishing. A minute passed. I looked at the readout on my phone. It said Call Lost. I tried dialing again, but now there was a blinking message that said No Signal. I sighed and pocketed the phone.

Somewhere in the trees a branch snapped, and I jerked my head towards the sound. Darkness shrouded the wooded area in front of me and I couldn't make out anything. Then, further in, I saw movement. I shrank back into the heavy shadows of the building and held my breath. A moment later, a figure appeared on the path. I waited as it emerged from the thick trees, and I saw who it was.

He saw me at the same time and stopped.

"What are you doing out here?" Alex asked. He wasn't accusing, but he didn't sound very friendly, either.

I stepped away from the building, pretending I wasn't cowering against the wall. "Um, making a call." I bit my lip as soon as I said it, hoping I wasn't breaking some rule and he wouldn't run off and rat me out.

He nodded, like he really couldn't care one way or another.

His shirt was soaked with sweat, and he was wiping his neck and head with a towel. A white bandage was taped to his shoulder and poked out from underneath his collar. He walked over to a large tree and pulled something out of the hollow created between two roots protruding from the moss. A water bottle. He lifted it to his lips and drank without stopping. I tried to ignore the way he looked so approachable when he wasn't staring at me with those accusing eyes – or that I could see what Cambria meant about the hotness, when he wasn't so focused on hating me. He finished drinking and turned, catching me staring. I looked away quickly and then felt like an idiot for it.

"Who were you talking to?" he asked, wiping his face with the towel again.

"Oh, it was my um, Wes." For some reason, I hadn't wanted to say 'my boyfriend' which made me angry at myself, so I'd finished it with his name instead.

"Your Wes?" Even without enough light to see his expression, I could visualize the raised eyebrow – and the smirk.

It grated on me. "Whatever. I'm going in now."

Alex didn't answer, and I slid through the door and hurried down the hall, putting distance between us. How did that boy have the power to make me so mad with only two words.

CHAPTER NINE

I opened my eyes and groaned. Even before I moved, I could feel the stiff pain of my muscles. My little roll down the hill had cost me. The only thing that gave me the motivation to get up was the hope that Alex felt the same way. I stumbled to the shower, grateful that Victoria was already gone from the room. I hadn't felt this sore since the morning after my fight with Liliana; the day I'd learned what I was. It seemed like a lifetime ago, now. So much had happened since then; so many things had changed.

I ran the shower as hot as it would go and stood under it with my eyes squeezed shut. The burning it caused was a small price to pay while I waited for my muscles to unclench. It happened slowly, and I leaned against the wall, enjoying the inch by inch release I could feel inside me. The water, combined with my body's natural ability to heal fast, went a long way towards giving me the energy not to crawl back into bed. And geez, that sounded like a good idea.

"Hey, Tara, is that you in there?" Cambria sounded wide awake and way too cheerful from the other side of the curtain.

"Yeah, it's me," I called. I poked my head out of the stall as Cambria slid inside the changing room and sat on the bench. Her cheeks were flushed.

"How was waking up with Sleeping Beauty this morning?" she asked.

"Great, actually," I answered. "She was already gone when I got up."

"Huh. Maybe she relocated."

"You think she'll change rooms?" I asked.

Cambria snorted. "Only if they start allowing co-ed rooms. She probably snuck over to Levi's."

"Oh. Yeah, he's um…"

"Full of himself? An asshat? All of the above? I agree. Perfect for Victoria."

"I was going to say gross."

"That too. Like I said, perfect for each other."

I shut the water off and towel dried before pulling the curtain aside. Cambria stepped out while I changed, and I joined her at the mirror when I was done. "Why is Victoria such a–"

"Bitch?" Cambria finished for me. She shrugged. "Good question. Some people have had tragedies or negative circumstances. And some people have no excuse. That would be Victoria." She leaned forward, swiping at the line of black eyeliner under her eyes. She had to pull her bangs out of the way to swipe at the other eye.

I took a closer look at her and saw that she was practically jumping up and down in her black leggings and boots. Her off-the-shoulder shirt was a bright, energetic yellow, which matched perfectly with her mood. Something was up.

"What's up with you?" I asked, seeing the way she was messing with her hair and jewelry.

She turned to me and grinned. "You wouldn't believe what happened to me after you left last night."

"I'm guessing this doesn't have anything to do with getting Logan to do your homework," I said. She shook her head, and I leaned against the sink and crossed my arms. "What's his name?"

"Phillipe. He's Italian. Sexy, right?" She grinned. "Anyway, he's new on Kane's security detail, and he is total hot sauce."

"What security detail?"

"Oh, Kane is in charge of school security and uses mostly seniors to head it up, with a couple adults to run things. Phillipe just got hired this week, so I haven't seen him before. Trust me, I'd remember."

"Kane's the one with the scar on his face, right?"

"Hmm? Oh, yeah." Cambria was distracted again, swiping at her makeup and examining her reflection. "Werewolf attack, pretty effed up looking, isn't it?"

"He seems pretty scary even without the scars," I said.

"He's tough, from what I hear. We'll have him next year, and he doesn't mess around with combat training. Sends kids out on their own, and they can't come back until they've downed a Were."

I frowned and finished with the nonexistent amount of makeup I bothered with. "That's crazy."

Cambria nodded, but she was smiling. Like 'crazy' was a compliment. "I know. So you can imagine what kinds of standards he must set for his employees. Which means Phillipe must be bad ass in a fight." She sighed. "It's the older ones from now on. No more high school guys for me."

I didn't say anything; Instead, I listened to Cambria make up new words to describe this Phillipe guy and thought about Wes.

"I'm ready," I said, eventually gathering up my stuff and turning to Cambria.

Her face fell. "Oh, honey, no you're not."

"What do you mean?"

Cambria stared at me with something resembling sympathy. "I know the lighting in here sucks, but you should take a closer look at your face."

I looked from her to the mirror and leaned in. Then I saw it. A large patch of skin near my eye was yellow with the first stages of a bruise, courtesy of Alex. "Crap."

"Here." Cambria handed me a bottle of foundation, and I got to work. The bruise hurt a little to touch, but I managed to pat enough cover-up on to mostly blot it out. I think. It was hard to tell in the dim, yellowish light of the bathroom.

"What do you think?" I asked, turning to Cambria.

She shrugged. "It could be worse."

I promised myself I'd make Alex pay in my next training session. I dropped my stuff off in my room and grabbed my backpack before following Cambria up to ground level for breakfast. The glares and comments didn't affect me today as much as they had yesterday, and I wasn't sure whether I should be happy or depressed about that. I could still hear the same derogatory references being used to identify me as I passed.

"Dogs…"

"Mutt."

"Dirty Blood."

I didn't catch the rest of the comments but those few words were enough to figure out the overall message wasn't a nice one. One kid even put his foot out as I passed, not even trying to be slick in his effort to trip me. When I stopped and eyed him, he just pulled his foot back and snickered. Cambria stayed close beside me, giving out as many dirty looks as I got. Maybe having a friend beside me made the walk easier.

We reached the cafeteria door at the same time as Logan. He sported a backwards hat, same as yesterday, and his overflowing backpack hung off one shoulder.

"Hey," I said, happy to see another familiar face, even if my current limit was only two.

"Hey." He started to smile and then made a face as he caught sight of my cheek. "Ooh. Are you okay?"

I sighed. "I'm fine. And no, we're not talking about it."

He shrugged, like he was fine with that answer. "Let's eat."

We filled our trays and ended up at the same table as the day before, tucked in the corner and away from the crowds. Today I made sure to sit facing the wall, so I didn't have to pretend to ignore all the glares and whispers. I dug into my muffin, picking pieces off it and chewing slowly. Although the rest of my muscles had loosened, the soreness behind the bruise was just warming up and moving my jaw to chew sent painful jabs up to my temple.

Across the table, Cambria's eyes focused on something behind me. "Don't look now, but I think you've reached celebrity status."

"I know, they're all looking at me," I said, refusing to turn.

"You're tumble is big news," said Logan, looking sympathetic.

"How'd you even know about that?" I asked.

Logan had the grace to look guilty. "Like I said big news…"

"Putting the moves on an upperclassman on your first day is pretty major," added Cambria.

I didn't answer.

"Uh-oh," said Cambria. "Enemy approaching."

Victoria had entered and was scanning the room. Her eyes lit on mine and she smiled the most perfect evil smile I'd ever seen. She headed our way, two minions trailing behind her.

"What do you want?" I asked when she stopped at our table.

"Is that any way to talk to your roommate?" Victoria's voice was so syrupy fake that it hurt my teeth. "I brought you a present. Sort of a house warming thing. Here." She held out a plain paper bag and set it on the table.

I stared at her, unwilling to take the bait and open the bag. God knows what was in there. Apparently, this didn't work for Victoria because she leaned forward, acidic smile frozen in place, and shoved it towards me. "Open it, silly."

I looked over at Logan, who was staring down at his tray, pushing his scrambled eggs around with his fork. His face was beet red. No help there. I caught Cambria's eye and she stared back at me with one eyebrow raised. What was that supposed to mean? I took the bag.

"Thanks. Bye now," I said, hoping she'd take the hint.

Thankfully, she did. Either that or she realized I wasn't going to open her stupid bag until she left. She deepened the smile for a split second, revealing teeth that I had no doubt wanted to tear me to shreds.

"See you later, roomie," she called.

Then she spun and headed for her table by the window. The two girls trailing after her were the same girls I'd met in the hallway when I'd been looking for my room. I waited until they were across the cafeteria and seated at their window table.

"Are you going to open it?" Cambria asked.

Logan looked up at me again, waiting for me to answer. His color was returning to normal.

"Later," I said, picking up the bag and setting it under the table at my feet. "It's going to be either hideous or embarrassing. I'm not going to fall for her BS and open it in here in front of everyone."

We emptied our trays and headed out. I'd flipped through the stack of papers given to me by Headmaster the day before and found my locker number and combination, so I headed there first, even though it was a Saturday. I wanted to drop my backpack there for safe keeping – nothing felt safe in my room and my phone was in there. Cambria and Logan stuck with me, probably too curious to know what was in the paper bag to do anything else.

I found my locker, which was only a few doors down from Logan's, and slid the dial back and forth until it popped open. I hung my backpack inside and then shifted the paper bag so I was holding it from underneath. Logan and Cambria didn't say anything, just watched me and waited. A few kids passed us on the way to breakfast.

"Here goes," I muttered. I pulled open the bag flap and leaned forward to peek inside.

BAM!

It blew up in my face. I jerked backwards and dropped the bag, wiping crud out of my eyes and trying to figure out what had happened. My hands came away covered in soggy brown goo. I stared at it in shock and then looked at Logan. His eyes were round and his lips formed a wide 'O'. I looked back down at the muddy-looking goo that caked my hands–and the rest of my upper body–still trying to figure out what it was. Then I caught a whiff of something. No way. It couldn't be. Slowly, I brought my hand to my nose and inhaled.

Eww.

I jerked my hand away. There was only one answer for that smell.

"Dog food!" I slammed my locker shut with a bang. "Dog food!" I couldn't do anything but repeat myself. Okay, well I could do something else, but I was trying to decide what to do first. Shower (again) or find Victoria.

"Tara…" Logan trailed off, and I could only assume it was because he had no idea what else to say. He glanced away, to something behind and beside me. I followed the direction of his eyes, and then turned away again. I was gaining an audience and it was getting bigger the longer I stood here.

Beside him, Cambria hadn't said a word. She gaped at me like she couldn't believe what she saw. Then she seemed to snap back to reality, and her jaw tensed and she whirled on our little audience, eyes blazing.

"I know you have somewhere to be," she said, advancing on them until they began to scatter. There were a couple of stragglers, who apparently didn't know enough to be afraid of Cambria. She rounded on them and her voice changed as she approached. "You two need to get to the library and check out some gay romance novels right now. Forget what you saw and get reading," she said. Her voice was low and crooning, and the boys stared at her for a second before snapping up straight and walking off without another word.

When they were gone, Cambria walked back to me, looking satisfied. "You need to shower. Again," she said. "Come on."

I clenched my jaw tight and let her take the paper bag and lead me away.

"We'll catch up with you later, Logan," Cambria called. I didn't hear him respond as we hurried for the dorms.

The entire way to the shower, and all the way through it, I entertained myself with thoughts of maiming Victoria. It helped a little.

Cambria disposed of the paper bag in the trash can in the bathroom and I bagged up and dropped off my soiled clothes in the chute next to Ms. Fincham's door marked 'Laundry,' which according to Cambria was run by any student bad enough to get that kind of detention. The washers and dryers were all housed one floor below us – in other words, the basement of the basement.

When I was clean and dressed and had reapplied all the cover up to my yellowing bruise, I stomped back upstairs and headed for my locker. I still hadn't decided the best payback but I knew I had to clean up the mess in front of my locker first. I would not allow Victoria to see the evidence of my humiliation. But the area around my locker was pristine, not a trace of dog food in sight.

"We'll thank Logan later," said Cambria, tugging on my arm. "Let's go." She turned and headed down the hall.

"Where are we going?"

Cambria's hold on my arm was vise-like, and I hurried to keep from stumbling as she dragged me along.

"You're pissed, right?"

My mouth hardened. "Yes."

"Like kill-her-when-she's-sleeping pissed, right?" We reached the lobby and Cambria turned, heading for the back doors.

"Yes."

"Right, so before you do something you'll regret, like punch her in the face and get expelled… again, I'm removing you." We reached the doors, and Cambria pushed them open and strode out into the morning air. It was still chilly enough that a sweatshirt or jacket would have been nice. I hadn't worn either. Goose bumps appeared on my bare arms and I looked at them, curiously. I couldn't remember the last time I'd gotten goose bumps when it didn't involve my body reacting to a Werewolf in close proximity.

"Removing me?" I echoed. Cambria was still leading and we were heading for the woods now.

"Normally I'm all for violence, especially in retribution, but I have to stop you. It would only get you into trouble and you're the most fun I've had in this place in a long while. I can't let you get expelled and leave me. I'll die of boredom."

I imagined Cambria being stuck listening to Logan as he told her all about his most recent experiment and her eyes glazing over and then rolling back in her head. Despite my anger, my lips curved up a little.

"Where are we going?" I asked.

"You'll see."

We took the path that led to the training area used for Defensive Maneuvers but cut away before we reached the spot. We were off the trail now, picking our way through thick trees. Cambria seemed to know where she was going, so I didn't stop her. We came to a new trail and Cambria veered onto it.

"I'm thinking what you need is some place to let out all that pent up anger and energy," she said. "Oh, look, we're here."

Ahead of us, I could see the opening of a small cave looming out of the ground. It looked out of place amongst the pines and oaks, half hidden under moss and brush. I couldn't see more than six inches inside it, and the fact that it was almost obscured from the path made me think no one had come this way for a long time.

Cambria walked towards it and carefully stepped around the vines that grew to one side of the entrance. She stopped inside and unzipped her bag, fishing around. She came away with a flash flight and clicked it on. She looked back at me. "You coming?"

I hesitated, not a huge fan of damp, dark places like this one, but in the end, I shrugged and made my way forward. "Sure."

Cambria led the way since she had the light, but I stayed close. No telling what sort of creepy-crawlies had made their home here. And while I had no problem taking down a full-sized, murderous Were, I'd definitely scream like an infant if I saw the slightest hint of a crawly bug right now.

After a while, I could make out the sound of rushing water. It grew steadily louder as we descended deeper into the cave. Up ahead, I could see the walls give way to open space. Cambria hurried towards it and into the space beyond, clicking off her flashlight. I followed and then stopped short when I reached the opening.

It was incredible; a large cavern with rock walls worn smooth by the trickling water that seeped in through the pores and cracks of the ceiling. Sunlight filtered in through the larger cracks, giving everything an orangey-red glow. In one corner, a rushing waterfall fell from some unseen opening above into a dark pool that lapped at the edge of its smooth, rock bank. Above me, giant, cone-shaped rock formations dangled from the ceiling. They looked like red icicles, ready to crash down around me at any moment. Their edges were pointy and sharp. I remembered the terms stalactites and stalagmites from Earth Science class, but I couldn't remember which was which. And I'd never seen any rock this huge. It was amazing. Several of them had grown together, making a giant blob of a rock formation. I stared at it until the blurry lines became a recognizable shape.

I felt Cambria come up beside me. "I see you've noticed our resident wolf. Cool rock formations, huh?"

"It's amazing," I said. "The whole cavern is."

Cambria grinned. "And the best part is the echo. Check it out." She spread her arms wide, tipping her head back so she was looking at the ceiling. "Hello!" she called. The echoing O-o-o could be heard for several seconds after she'd stopped. It seemed to bounce off every part of the room and back again, making the space feel even bigger and emptier.

I smiled. "Not bad."

"It's good for anger management." She shrugged. "At least that's what my last shrink said."

"You go to a shrink?"

"I did, before I came here."

"For anger problems?" I couldn't help but look a little skeptical. Cambria was the least angry person I'd met in a long time. She was always grinning or looking at me with the sparkle of laughter in her eyes.

"Let's just say it manifests differently in me," she said.

"What does that mean?"

"It means that I've been known to charm the ones who piss me off into doing things they wouldn't normally do."

I eyed her, thinking of the boys in the hallway. "Are those boys really going to check out gay porn at the library?" I asked, raising my eyebrows.

She shrugged. "Probably not since I doubt there's any there to begin with. But if they get up the nerve to ask the librarian where to find that kind of thing, they're going to have a tricky situation on their hands." She smiled but there wasn't any humor in it. "My mother says I'm evil."

"For using your gifts?"

Her expression clouded over with some memory. "A Hunter is only supposed to use their gifts negatively against Werewolves or their enemies. Never other Hunters. When I was younger, and I couldn't control it as easily, it would happen accidentally. I used it on my mom a few times without really meaning to, and she realized what was happening. She got pretty pissed off. I started boarding schools earlier than most. Third grade. I also had to see a shrink once a week, because I was so young to be away from home."

She trailed off, still caught up in seeing something that wasn't really there anymore, and I didn't say anything. I hadn't expected all of that and I wasn't sure whether to show sympathy or brush it off, like she seemed to do most of the time.

She cleared her throat. "So, give it a shot. Yell. Let it out," she added, when I stared at her blankly. She spread her arms wide, gesturing to the open space. "No one can hear you and it will make you feel better, trust me."

"I don't really feel that mad anymore."

"Really?" She eyed me with her hands on her hips. "You took a bag of dog food in the face for the entire junior class to witness and you're not mad anymore?"

"Okay, when you put it like that…"

"Exactly. Let it out. Rise above or whatever."

I nodded. Her words reminded me of something Grandma would say. And I had promised Grandma I would try to keep better control of my temper. It was worth a shot. If it didn't work, at least I could say I'd tried not to beat the crap out of Victoria. I'd at least attempted self-control. I let my hands fall loosely to my sides and tipped my head back, sucking in a deep breath. Then, I let it out.

"Aahhhh!" I yelled, with no specific words attached to the sound.

When the echoes stopped Cambria shook her head. "You can do better."

I tried again. By the third time, I was finally beginning to feel a release. Cambria was right; as stupid as it might sound, yelling into an echoing cavern was therapeutic. Before long, we were taking turns, seeing who could yell the loudest and whose echo could last longer. I only quit when my throat grew hoarse.

Cambria showed me the pool of water, and we drank from our hands and sat on the rocky bank, talking. Slowly, the story of how I discovered my Hunter side came out. Cambria couldn't believe it.

"So you just found out you were a Hunter a few weeks ago?" she asked, brows disappearing into her hair.

"Yeah. It feels like a lot longer, though, believe me."

"And you only found out because you were attacked by a Werewolf?" I nodded. "And that's when you met this Wes guy, right?" There was a glint in her eyes now. "Tell me more about him."

I laughed and shook my head, feeling not quite so alone and friendless after all. When I was done, I'd told her everything; from meeting Wes in the parking lot that night, freaking out on him, and getting my memory erased to inadvertently joining The Cause, in order to gain help in my fight against my murderous uncle. I left out the part about the weird almost-kiss moment with Miles because that was way too disgusting to say out loud, but I did end by telling her about the message I'd gotten from him on the way up here.

"So you think he's going to try and get to you here?" she asked.

"I think if he finds out this is where I am, then yes, he'll try."

"Hmm. Well, good thing you have a badass Hunter friend on your side."

"Who, Logan? Is he a good fighter?"

Cambria's fist shot out in a mock punch, but I swerved out of her reach and grinned. Talking about it all had definitely lifted a weight; I felt better than I had in days. The only thing missing was Wes.

It must've been obvious what I was thinking, because Cambria frowned and said, "So Wes is going to be the head honcho of the Cause now, huh? And that's why he isn't here with you."

I nodded.

"The same Cause that got his parents killed and destroyed your family."

"Yup."

"And now this Vera Gallagher believes you're next in line to run things, along with Wes, your soul mate."

"Basically."

She blew out a heavy breath, sending her bangs floating away from her face. "Wow. That's a lot."

"I know."

CHAPTER TEN

The rest of the weekend passed way too quietly compared to my first couple of days. Alex had cancelled our Saturday training. Something about his patrol schedule conflicting and he'd see me on Monday. I wasn't complaining.

Victoria was barely in the room when I was, which wasn't often. I was doing my best to avoid her because I'd caved and gone to Ms. Fincham about switching rooms. She'd wiped her flour covered hands on her housecoat – blue, with pink daisies – and shook her head, like she couldn't remember who I was in the first place.

"We don't got no vacancies anyhow. You need to work it out. Would you like a cookie?"

I'd edged away, remembering how Cambria had seemed a little scared of eating anything Ms. Fincham baked. "Um, no thanks. I'll go work on that."

When I'd realized I wouldn't be able to escape it, I'd even called Grandma to warn her.

"I know I promised to do better with my temper but this girl is going to push me too far, Grandma," I'd said into the landline I'd borrowed from one of the admin ladies in Griffin Hall. I was hunched over the desk while the secretary took a coffee break and whispering so no one else could hear me.

"You're better than her, Tara. That means you have to rise above and find a way to deal with her without violence. You can do it. I believe in you," she'd said. Then her voice changed to something sugary and forced and she'd said, "Oh, here's your mother, honey. Let me pass her the phone, and I'll talk to you later."

My mother's voice was just as fake. I could tell she was making an effort – they both were – not to let on that they were already sick of each other.

"How are you, sweetie?" she'd asked.

"Fine. Checking on you guys."

"Oh, we're all right. Grandma's been giving me ideas about how I can rearrange the furniture." Her voice lost some of the sweetness and let in more of the tension.

I smiled, able to guess how well that was going over. "Sounds great, Mom. I miss you guys."

"We miss you, too, sweetie."

The admin lady returned after that, and I'd hung up, knowing my only option left to deal with Victoria was to avoid and ignore. So that's what I'd been doing for the past two days. I didn't hold out much hope for my plan, long term.

My classes on Monday were a lot of the same information I'd heard on Friday, with the addition of English and Chemistry, which turned out to be a lab for the whole semester. I got partnered with the gangly kid Logan had sparred with in Defensive Maneuvers. His name was Justin, and today he was wearing black skinny jeans and a Megadeth shirt. He used the word vintage a lot.

My last class was history and I got out late, again. Professor Hugo seemed more determined than most of my other teachers that I make up any work I'd missed. Even though history was something that I was able to include on my old transcripts – unlike combat classes, which weren't exactly a part of my old schedule – he still wanted full-page essays on each chapter I'd missed since the semester began.

Between all the homework and trying to avoid Victoria and her posse, I'd skipped lunch, and by the time Professor Hugo had grunted that I could leave, I was starving and running late for Alex. Cambria was waiting for me when I rushed into the hall after last bell. Other than her, the hall was already empty of students.

"I better hurry," I said.

"Yeah, you don't want to be late for training." She winked, but I ignored it.

"I'm going to run back and change before I meet Alex," I said, as we power walked down the hall.

"You might want to inhale a granola bar or something, too. We both know Alex isn't going to go easy on you. You'll want the energy."

"Crap, I don't have anything in my room."

"No worries. I got this. Go change and meet me back here," she said.

I thanked her and then sprinted for the stairs. It wasn't so much that I cared if Alex had to wait, but I was determined to prove myself to him. And being late felt like letting him win.

In my room, I dug frantically for a pair of running shorts and a sports bra and then whipped them on in record time. I really needed to take the time to unpack at some point. Just not now. When I was done, I let the suitcase fall shut and slid it back under my rumpled bed. I pulled my hair into a ponytail while I jogged back down the hallway and up the stairs. Cambria waited for me in the lobby with a small paper bag in her hand.

"What's that?" I asked, eyeing it suspiciously. I didn't take it when she offered.

"Oh, for crap's sake." She reached into the bag and pulled out a bottled water and a gigantic muffin, prepackaged. "They're from the cafeteria. I didn't swipe it from Ms. Fincham or anything."

"Thanks," I said, already tearing into the muffin. "How'd you get these? Cafeteria's closed," I mumbled, around a mouthful of blueberry flavoring.

Her eyes sparkled. "I have my ways." I gave her an 'explain further' kind of look but she waved me off. "You're late."

"Right. I'll see you at dinner."

"Have fun," I heard from behind me in a very meaningful tone.

ALEX WAS ALREADY WAITING IN THE CLEARING WHEN I GOT THERE. I'D finished the muffin off before I'd even cleared the trees, and now I gulped down the last of the water. I dropped the bottle at the edge of the grass and walked over to meet him. He was already stretching so I did the same without offering a "hello."

He eased out of his stretch and clasped his elbow behind his head, pulling on it. I did the same. Still, neither of us spoke. A minute later, he pulled his foot up behind him, touching the sole of his shoe to his hip, and I followed.

The silence was starting to get to me. Not because I felt the need to talk but because I thought he, as the teacher, should've. Still, I waited him out. In the absence of words, all I had to occupy myself was the view, and it wasn't a bad one. Maybe having to listen to Cambria's innuendos was starting to get to me, but the way his muscles stretched against his shirt when he moved wasn't exactly a hardship to watch. I shook myself and turned away, continuing to copy his stretches by watching him in my peripheral.

When we were done he stood there, staring at me. I couldn't read his expression, and the silence was now officially driving me crazy. I wasn't one of those girls who had to talk all the time, but the way looked at me made me feel...weird.

"So? What are we doing today?" I asked.

"Does it hurt?"

"What?" I blinked at him, completely lost. Then I realized where exactly he was staring. I'd all but forgotten about the ugly yellow bruise on my cheek. Then something else hit me. Was he actually being concerned? It was so tempting to play right into it and say "yes", but my stubborn side wouldn't let me.

"Not really," I said, straightening a little and planting my feet. "I'm fine, don't you worry. I've had worse."

"I'll bet," he said, almost under his breath. "We're running. Come on."

"Running?" I repeated, shoulders sagging. I'd almost rather take another roll down the hill.

Alex glanced back with a look that said I should already be following and headed for the trees. I followed, practically dragging my feet, and found myself on a wide trail that led further away from school. I fell into step with him and he let me set the pace, which I made sure was slow. Like, tortoise slow. I might've been able to go faster but I wasn't taking the chance. I had no idea how far he was going to take us, and I didn't want him trying to challenge me by ramping up the pace to something that was going to make me throw up or pass out before we reached the end.

A mile in, we broke free of the trees, and everything opened up into gently rolling hills. There was green grass as far as the eye could see. Wrought iron fencing marked where the grounds ended and state property began. We ran parallel to the fence for a while. The terrain was easier to run on here, out of the woods, but the heat was worse. At first, I tried to be subtle about swiping at me forehead with my hand, but soon I didn't care. I used the sleeve of my shirt to swipe my face at regular three second intervals and prayed for a cold shower that would last until this time tomorrow.

At one point, I glanced over at Alex's expression. He was breathing in a slow, deliberate pattern; he didn't look uncomfortable at all. That pissed me off for some reason that I couldn't even name, and I vowed not to be the one who broke the silence.

We ended up making a circle and finished up in the clearing we'd started in. Alex retrieved a small cooler from the shade of a tree and threw me a dripping cold water bottle. I gulped halfway and had to stop to catch my breath. My lungs burned like a forest fire, and I wasn't completely sure if it was getting darker or my vision was going. I pressed my hands to my knees and let my head hang while I sucked in air.

"Not bad."

I looked up and found Alex watching me with a sort of amused expression. I noticed he wasn't wheezing or gasping for oxygen like I was, so I straightened and tried to pretend I could breathe normally without hyperventilating. The glint in his eye deepened, and his face did this thing where he looked like he was smiling without curving his lips. Something in my stomach flipped over; I told myself it was another symptom of running to the brink of death.

"Thanks," I said, between forced deep breaths.

"Same time tomorrow." He retrieved his cooler and slung it over his shoulder.

Then, believe it or not, he jogged out of sight. Jogged. Seriously? Was he a GI Joe in another life?

As soon as he was out of sight I let my knees buckle, and I slid to the ground, my limbs like liquid. I rolled onto my back and gulped in air like there might not be enough to go around. I looked up at the small piece of sky visible in the little clearing and let my mind wander. As usual, there was Wes.

The more I thought about him lately, the more I was sure something had been "off" during our phone conversation. He was always protective and usually extreme about it, but there had been something else. Desperation. Something he wasn't telling me. Maybe I was paranoid after all the secrets people had kept from me, but I felt like there was a missing piece. Had something happened back home? With the Cause? Had Miles come back for me?

I worried about my mom for a split second and then relaxed when I remembered that I'd talked to her a couple of days ago –and Grandma was there. It was probably kind of sad when a girl felt more confident about her grandma's fighting skills than she did her own mother, but there it was. And I knew the rest of the Cause could protect themselves. Derek and Cord would make sure Bailey was all right. And Jack and Fee had Wes with them. I felt better when I thought of it that way. No way could he get to any of them.

Finally, I was able to breathe like a normal human and not an asthmatic monkey. I got up and made my way back to Lexington Hall, opting again for the back door. I circled around and was surprised to see Cambria waiting for me.

"Finally," she said, practically jumping up and down with poorly contained energy.

"What's up?"

She opened her mouth to answer and then shut it again, eyeing me critically. "You look like crapola. Did you go for another tumble?"

I made a face. "Running."

"I see." She didn't seem to need further explanation. "You need to hurry up and shower. An announcement was made a while ago. Assembly in Griffin Hall in twenty minutes." She was bouncing again.

"Why?"

"Not sure, but it sounded serious and it's mandatory. Hurry up!"

"Why are we so excited about this?"

"Phillipe might be there. I want to introduce you. Go!"

"Okay, I'm going."

We booked it to my room. Cambria waited while I went in and got a change of clothes for the shower. Victoria looked up from her desk mirror as I came in and narrowed her eyes at me, pasting on the disgusting smile that had become her signature. I braced myself. This was the first time we'd come face to face with each other since Friday. My temper flared on sight, and I bit my lip and repeated the words rise above under my breath as I yanked open my suitcase.

"Tara, how did you like my present the other day?" Victoria asked in a tone filled with mock innocence. "I heard it was an explosion of success."

"Whatever," I muttered, doing my best to ignore her. I could feel the stirrings of temper rising but it didn't get far. I was too exhausted from the run. Victoria should count herself lucky on her timing.

"I didn't see you after that. Was everything okay? Or were you off enjoying your gift?"

I grabbed my clothes and shower bag and rounded on her. "Bite me, Victoria."

She made a tsk-tsk sound with her tongue and shook her head. "I should have known all you think about is biting. Such a mutt."

The last part was mumbled and low, but I heard it, and suddenly my temper was boiling, my exhaustion gone. I veered towards her, but

Cambria took a step towards us from the doorway and blocked my path.

"Tara, we've gotta go," said Cambria.

I ignored Cambria and stepped around her. I walked over to Victoria and leaned down until I was right in her face. I was shaking with the effort of controlling myself and my skin felt funny, sort of stretched too tight. I stared hard into Victoria's light blue eyes.

"Eat. Shit." I stayed where I was, waiting to see if she'd respond; hoping she would. She didn't. She sat rigid against the chair and her gaze never wavered from mine, but the snarl was gone from her face, and she kept silent. When I was sure I'd made my point, I straightened and followed Cambria out the door. In the hall I let out a loud exhale.

"Eat shit?" Cambria echoed. "That's the best you could do?"

"I don't curse at people on a regular basis. It's what came to mind."

Cambria laughed. "We'll work on that. Points for not punching her lights out, though."

I showered and changed, and we high tailed it to Griffin Hall. The assembly was being held in a large auditorium on the west end of the building. We were literally the last two through the door. A teacher I'd never seen before, with a crooked nose, shut the door behind us and gestured for us to hurry up and find a seat. I began scanning the rows when Logan caught my eye and waved us over.

"Thanks," I whispered, taking the seat next to him. "So, what's going on?"

"Don't know yet. I think it has something to do with the attacks last week," he said quietly.

"What attacks?"

"A couple of important families were attacked in their home. The parents went missing and everyone else was killed."

"Do they know who did it?"

He shrugged. "A rogue Werewolf pack is all they know. One of the families had a kid who goes to school here. He was flown out the day before you got here."

"You think the assembly has something to do with that?" I asked.

"Maybe. Headmaster made it sound serious and all the teachers are here. Not just our grade level."

He pointed to the stage where over two dozen teachers sat in rows behind a podium. Headmaster Whitfield was on the end, closest to the podium. Next to him sat Professor Kane. From here, his face looked almost normal. You couldn't even make out the scars. On his other side was a woman that could only be Professor Flaherty. Her red hair gleamed under the stage lights, looking like a ball of flames hovering over her face. She was leaning over and talking with a woman that looked vaguely familiar to me. I tried to place her but couldn't make out her features well enough.

"Who is that?" I asked Logan, pointing at the woman.

He shrugged. "Don't know."

I looked over at Cambria and caught her craning her neck and scanning the crowd.

"Is he here?" I asked.

"I don't see him."

Her lip stuck out in a pout and all the energy seemed to have finally contained itself. She slumped back in her seat, looking bored with the whole thing. Then Headmaster Whitfield stepped to the podium and tapped on the microphone.

"Good evening, Wood Point student body. I'm sure you are all wondering why you've been called here. It seems there has been a tragedy that involves two of our own. As some of you may have heard, a few days ago we received word that the Hilson family and the Romano family had been killed or taken from their homes by an unidentified Werewolf pack. Brendon Romano, a sophomore, was flown out to attend the funeral of his brother and sisters. Tonight we have learned that Brendan has also been reported missing, along with his escorts."

A rumbling of murmurs and not-so-hushed whispers went up around the room. I sat in silence. So did Cambria and Logan. Both of them looked as surprised as I was. Most of the kids did. I took that to mean this wasn't normal news for the Hunter world.

Headmaster Whitfield cleared his throat a few times and the room fell quiet. "The motive is not yet clear, though there will be a full investigation. In the meantime, the rules regarding student curfew remain in place and will be heavily enforced. Brendan was one of ours and even though he did not disappear from school grounds, every precaution will be taken. Security will be at a maximum and we have extra units on their way to help fill in until we're sure the danger has passed.

"I understand that many of you were friends with Brendan and this may be a shock or hard to handle, especially with so little information about the guilty party. The teachers seated behind me have agreed to stay after and speak to any students who feel emotionally affected by this tragedy. If you need someone to talk to, please see one of them. Otherwise you are free to go."

Headmaster Whitfield stepped back, signaling the end of the assembly, and everyone around us rose. I stayed where I was, still watching the woman seated next to Professor Flaherty. She was facing forward now, and I had a clear view of her face. It looked like… but, it couldn't be.

"You coming?" Cambria asked.

I kept my eyes on the woman on stage. "I need to talk to… someone," I said, moving against the stream of exiting bodies.

I made my way up to the stage and stopped. The woman had noticed me now, too, and watched me with equal interest. I waited until the crowd thinned, both on and off stage, and then stepped up to the edge of the dais.

"Vera."

She rose from her chair and descended the stairs. Her willowy frame and polished gray suit made her appear regal and cold. "Tara. It's good to see you." She smiled a tight smile that could have been a polite formality or evidence that it was, in fact, not good to see me. I wasn't sure which.

"What are you doing here?" I asked. I couldn't stand to beat around the bush and I knew enough about Vera to know she wouldn't tell me unless I came right out with it. Maybe not even then.

"Vernon asked me to come. I'm going to strengthen the wards around campus."

"Because of the attack on that student."

It wasn't a question, but she nodded anyway. An awkward silence fell and I regretted coming up here. When I'd recognized her from my seat in the crowd, I'd felt a connection and a need to speak to her. Now I realized it was only because she'd been a familiar face in unfamiliar territory. I wanted to ask her about Wes, but I couldn't.

"How is Jack doing?" I asked instead.

"He's recovering well. Fee is doing what she can to speed it up. We're waiting to see how far her healing ability can take him."

"And the rest of the group?"

"Everyone is fine. They say hello."

"They know you're here?"

For some reason it bothered me that they'd sent only Vera. She was in charge, basically, until Wes could finish training and take over for Jack, and she'd managed to get away for a day or two. Why couldn't Wes have come with her?

"Of course they know. My trip was voted on, like all decisions that affect the group. They send their regards. How are things here?"

"Um, fine I guess."

"You're training is going well?"

"Yes. Did something happen at home?" I blurted. "Is that why no one came with you?"

"Tara." Vera's expression softened slightly and I knew that she knew who I meant. "Everything at home is fine. You can't let yourself worry about that. Being here and learning how to fight properly is very important to your future. So is learning Hunter history and culture."

"Being with Wes is important to my future too, though, right?" We both knew I was baiting her.

"There are steps," was all she would say. "It's good to see you. I'll tell everyone you said hello." She turned to walk away and then stopped, a strange look on her face. It reminded me of the night she'd stopped me on the way out of Benny's house. "Tara?"

"Yes?"

"Your Lineage project. Have you started that yet?"

"No." I shook my head, completely confused as to why she would ask me about that.

"You should get started. It's an important assignment."

"Okaay." I walked away, still confused, and a little homesick.

Cambria and Logan were waiting for me at our seats. The rest of the auditorium was empty.

"Who was that?" asked Cambria as we walked out.

"Vera."

"Who's that?" Logan asked.

"She's a member of the Cause. She's more in charge of it, actually. And she sort of sees the future."

"Seriously?" Logan asked. He looked impressed.

"What's she doing here?" Cambria asked, looking back at where Vera now stood talking to Professor Kane.

"Strengthening the wards around the school. Headmaster Whitfield asked her to come."

"She creates wards?" Logan looked even more impressed. "Do you think she'd let me–"

"No," I said. "She wouldn't. She's sort of…" I tried to find a word that fit Vera but I couldn't find one. "Irritable," I finished, knowing that wasn't really accurate. Vera was stern and proper but under all that she seemed serious, to the point of unhappy, and I had no idea why. "Anyway, she was being her usual cryptic self and said something about my Lineage project and how important it was to get started."

"And you think she's fortune telling?" Logan asked. His eyebrows were raised, and I knew he thought I was being dramatic.

"Maybe. She said it in the same way she talks about her other vision of me; all 'mysterious, the-future's-coming' kind of thing.

"What other vision?" That was Logan again, and I realized I hadn't brought him up to speed.

"Vera had a vision of my future. I'm the next leader of the Cause, along with Wes, and we basically single-handedly bring peace to the two races." Logan stared at me. "Yeah, I know, right?"

"Do you think she's right?" he asked.

"Do you?" I shot back, only because I had no idea how to answer that.

He shrugged. "If anyone could do it, a hybrid could."

I didn't know what to say to that. We were back inside Lexington Hall now and climbing the stairs for dinner.

"I'll help you with your Lineage project," Logan offered as we got in line for food. "I can help you with the research. Did you bring your family's Draven?"

I nodded. "Grandma gave it to me right before I left."

"That'll make it easier. When is your project due?"

"Sometime before the end of the semester."

"Cool. We've got time. When do you want to meet?" Logan asked.

I grabbed a huge plate of Lo Mein and veggies and set it on my tray. "Good question. I have training 'til dinner basically every day."

"We can do after dinner. We can start on Friday. We get an extra two hours before curfew. That should give us enough time to get the research going."

"Sounds good," I agreed. "You want to tag along?" I asked, turning to Cambria.

"Eww. You guys are talking about the library aren't you?"

"Yeah." I smiled.

She wrinkled her nose. "No thanks. I'm allergic."

CHAPTER ELEVEN

Defensive Maneuvers was definitely my hardest class. I'd managed to get Professor Flaherty to let me hang back again on Monday, to watch. By Tuesday she wasn't having it.

"You come from such a strong line, and Alex says you're a fast learner. I think you'll do fine to jump right in," she said.

To argue would've basically been to call myself stupid, so I nodded, wondering how I was supposed to jump in and pick up the crazy dance-kung-fu moves that were a part of her drills. After stumbling through warm-ups, I got partnered with a girl named Iris, who wasn't nearly as fragile as her name implied. I spent more time on the ground than I did on my feet. I kept looking to Professor Flaherty for mercy, but she would either smile encouragingly like I wasn't getting my ass kicked or ignore me altogether. Iris didn't say much, either. She let her hands and feet do the talking, I guess. When it ended, she smiled down at me lying on my back in the grass and walked away.

Logan appeared and offered a hand, looking sympathetic.

"Don't say anything," I said, brushing myself off, and swiping my hair out of my eyes.

"Wouldn't dream of it." He settled his hat on his head and picked up both our bags. We headed for lunch.

“I really am a good fighter,” I insisted.

“I’m sure you are.”

I sighed. At least the week was progressing without incident from the Wicked Witch of the blonds. At lunch, she sat smug in her corner by the window and only sent me the evil eye like fifty or so times. I could handle that. Maybe what I’d said to her the day before had some effect and she’d decided to leave me alone. I could hope.

The school day finished and rolled right into training. It was basically a repeat of the day before. Running, running, and more running. Not much speaking in between. Me trying not to puke at the end. I wasn’t sure why we hadn’t done any more sparring. Maybe Alex was trying to avoid it turning into a kindergarten brawl again. I hoped it changed soon. Running could kill a person.

Alex had tossed me a water bottle, and I knew he was about to make his exit, so I decided to speak up and ask the question that had been on my mind all day.

“Hey, do you know anywhere around here that gets cell reception?” I hated, hated, hated having to ask him for anything, including this, but he knew the mountain better than anyone and he would know if there was a good spot.

Alex capped his water and looked into the trees, like he was thinking. “It doesn’t get clear until you get about halfway down the mountain, but you could try the roof.”

“The roof? Of Lexington Hall? It works up there?”

“Griffin’s roof is better, but students aren’t supposed to be up there.”

“Oh.”

“Cell phones aren’t allowed, you know.”

“Um…” I trailed off, sure I’d made a gigantic mistake.

He let me stew for several seconds and then shrugged. “Just keep it off when you’re not using it.”

“Right. Okay.” I stopped short of “thank you.” Instead I said, “See you tomorrow.”

He saluted me and then headed for the trail. I was pretty sure we’d just had our first non-antagonistic conversation.

I showered and changed and hurried through dinner. Logan had an essay to write on something called Rodgers Roundup, which I thought sounded like a bad western novel, but he said was something I'd learn in Hunter History next year; privileged information, courtesy of him being in honors classes. Cambria had something going with Phillipe that I purposely didn't ask for details on. We parted ways, and I headed for Griffin Hall.

Outside, the light was waning and throwing shadows on everything. Filtered sunlight trickled through here and there, throwing beams across the stone courtyard and glinting off the waterfall in the center. It was really pretty out here when I wasn't being stared at like it was the Salem witch trials. A couple of kids whispered and looked over. They looked a year or two younger, and I figured the rumor mill was making its way down the line. They had plenty to choose from, between my awkward tumble and the paper bag incident. Or my DNA.

I made it to the back entrance of Griffin Hall and slipped inside. The elevator dinged softly at regular intervals so I knew that was not the way to go. I slipped into the stairwell and prayed no one passed me on the way up.

At the very top was a heavy door marked 'Roof Access.' I slipped out and wandered forward. This part of the roof was flat and easy to navigate; lots of empty space broken up by large heating and cooling units and various chimneys. But that wasn't what got my attention.

I wandered closer to the edge, staring at the view. It was gorgeous. Every shade of green you could imagine covered the treetops for miles and miles. Beyond that, so distant they wore a ring of haze or clouds, were more tree-covered peaks. I stared until the line between land and sky blurred. Even then, I blinked and then watched some more.

The light faded, sending long shadows across the roof. I pulled my phone out of my pocket and powered it on. Three new voicemails and one text registered. I hit the button and pressed the phone to my ear, listening to the messages. The first was from Grandma, wishing me luck with my "social dilemma" and telling me to call when I could. The second was a hang up. I waited while the last message loaded, tapping my foot and hoping it was Wes.

The voice that came over the line was breathy and unrecognizable at first. "Tara. How are you?" Whoever it was seemed to be in the middle of a workout or struggling to lift something heavy. Or maybe they'd gone running with Alex. Then the voice leveled out and I realized who it was.

"Hope you're settling in alright at Wood Point Academy. I hear great things about that school. Very prestigious." I tried to swallow, but my throat was stuck. "Anyway, I've got a little project going now so my plans to reunite have been put on hold. As soon as I wrap this up, I'll come and show you what I mean. I only wanted to say Buongiorno. See you soon."

The message ended and I disconnected the call, not bothering to erase it. I finally managed to swallow, but it felt like there was a grapefruit in my windpipe. These messages from Miles were creepy. Miles himself was creepy, but his cryptic voicemails weren't helping. What project was he talking about? Whatever it was couldn't be good.

And how did he know where I was?

Had someone else in the group been turned? How else was he getting his information? If he knew where I was, wards or not, I knew he'd find a way to get to me. It was only a matter of time. Fear buzzed in the back of my mind. I clamped down on the feeling, refusing to let it get to me. I had to keep calm so I could figure out how to deal with this.

The phone rang, and I almost dropped it. I forced myself to breathe deep and checked the screen; not who I was expecting, but at least it wasn't Miles.

I answered it. "Hello?"

"Tara?"

"Hey, George."

"Oh, wow, you finally answered. How are you? Did you get to school okay?"

"Yes, I got to school okay. I'm fine," I said, and for some reason, my voice broke on the last word.

"Tay, talk to me," he said, quietly.

I wanted to. In that moment, I really, really wanted to. George had been my best friend until not so long ago, and part of me wanted that again; probably because life had been simpler then. But I couldn't tell him anything without putting him in danger. Or making him think I'd gone completely insane. "I miss home," I said, finally.

"Home misses you, Tay. Did you get my note from Ang and Sam?"

"Yes, thank you," I said, smiling and tearing up all at the same time as I remembered his Bon Jovi love letter. "It was sweet."

"I've been known to emit that quality." His voice was light, and I knew he was trying to cheer me up. "I've been bugging your mom about visiting you but she says they wouldn't let me in unless it's an official Friends and Family Day. Something about a list."

"That's okay, George. I'm fine."

"You don't sound fine. You can talk to me, you know."

"I know. I…." I trailed off, again searching for words that could be said out loud. "It takes a while to adjust, that's all."

"Are you sure that's all?"

"I'm sure." I swiped my eyes and forced my voice to be lighter. "I've gotta go, George, but I'm glad you called."

"Okay, well, call me if you need to talk. I'm here for you, Tay."

"Thanks. Bye."

"Bye."

I clicked the phone off and sat on a nearby vent, propping my chin in my hands. I blinked hard against the wetness in my eyes until I knew I wouldn't completely lose it. I picked up the phone again and wandered to the edge of the roof, looking down over the courtyard.

I could hear Wes' words now when I told him about the message from Miles. There would be lots of "don't worry, we'll find him, you'll be safe." And then some, "What?! I can't believe you didn't tell me he's called once before." Still, I missed him enough that hearing him rant about protecting me sounded pretty good right about now. I started to hit the button that would dial his number and then stopped.

Low voices drifted up from somewhere below me. I couldn't make out the words, but the tone sounded a lot like Vera. I crept forward, following the sound. I turned the corner and then stopped. There, below me, standing on a balcony, was Vera. Standing with her, and taking in every word, was Victoria. I dropped low and peered over the edge, close enough to make out the words now.

“I’m sure you understand the need for secrecy in this matter,” Vera was saying. “It is against school policy to use a student younger than a senior in a mission like this. It’s dangerous and there’s always a risk.”

“I understand.” Victoria sounded completely serious, almost to the point of reverent.

“We are trusting you to keep your involvement quiet. Arrangements are being made. We leave in two days. You’ll tell your friends you’re going home for a weekend visit.”

Victoria nodded. “No one will question it. I get special permission all the time.”

The way she said it, like that made her such a catch, made me want to gag.

“You understand, also, that we are relying heavily on your skills here. If at any time you are unsure of a direction, say so. It would be better than trying to bluff.”

“I understand. I won’t let you down.”

“Good girl. Get back to your room and we’ll talk in a couple days.”

“Yes, ma’am.”

Victoria disappeared back inside, and I jumped up, heading for the door. What could Vera possibly want with Victoria? And why was Victoria basically drooling over her? She didn’t strike me as the peace-loving type; I’d heard her make remarks about the Cause already. Only one way to find out. I slipped back inside and down one flight of stairs, guessing in the direction of the balcony where I’d seen them. Somewhere in the stairwell below me, I could hear the sounds of descending footsteps, and I knew it must be Victoria, trying to sneak away.

I stepped into the hallway and was glad that the lights were dimmed here. I stayed in the shadows and moved slowly towards the door I’d guessed as Vera’s. I was almost there when the stairwell door swung open behind me. I felt my heart jump into my throat and bolted. I made a left at the corner and ducked into a recessed doorway, praying whoever it was wouldn’t come this far.

A few seconds later, I heard someone rapping lightly on a door. The door opened. I leaned out of my hiding spot and peeked around the corner in time to see a scarred profile disappear into a dark room. Professor Kane. I glimpsed a crown of silvery hair as the door closed behind him. I couldn't take it. I had to know.

The term "peeping tom" crossed my mind as I ran back up the stairs and onto the roof to lean over and try to hear what Professor Kane would say to Vera. So did "nosy nellie," which is what Grandma would have called me. I still had to know.

I reached the spot and knelt down; peering over the edge and feeling my pulse pick up speed. They were both out on the balcony.

"You shouldn't have," Vera said. She was using a tone I'd never heard out of her.

I thought I caught a glimpse of red before she set whatever it was aside and came back to stand in front of Professor Kane. He stared at Vera, and I suddenly got a weird feeling in my gut.

"Jonah, I missed you," said Vera.

"I missed you, too."

And before I realized what I was about to witness, Professor Kane closed the distance and pressed his lips to Vera's. I snapped back like I'd been slapped and slumped over against the low wall of the rooftop, trying my best to blink the image away. I felt disgusting and dirty and like… a peeping tom. Eww. Okay, lesson learned.

"Nobody home tonight?"

Alex materialized from somewhere behind an air vent and walked towards me in the dark.

I tensed, hating how guilty I felt at getting caught. The fact that it was Alex who'd caught me was actually worse than if it had been a teacher. Especially when he was headed this way and directly below us was the grossest grown-up make out session ever. I absolutely could not let him catch me spying on that. I stood up and brushed myself off, walking towards him to head him off and praying he wouldn't come any closer to the edge.

"Home where?" I asked, trying to keep my mind on the conversation.

"You said you wanted to go somewhere that got a signal, so you could make a phone call. Here you are, but you're not on the phone, so I assume nobody's home."

"Oh, right. Yeah, that's what happened."

Alex stood directly in front of me now, looking down at me with an amused expression. He'd showered, and I caught the scent of soap and something musky.

"What are you doing up here anyway?" I asked, hoping to take the attention off of myself.

"I come up here most nights. It's a good place to sit and think without interruptions. Unless of course, you're hoping to be interrupted." His amusement turned to plain evilness and I already knew where this was going. "By, let's say, voices on a balcony."

He sidestepped me and went to the edge, where I'd been standing. He peeked over and then walked back over to me, wearing a mischievous grin. I'd never wanted to punch anyone more. Not even when I'd lost it with Cindy Adams and busted her nose.

"Quite a show, huh?"

"I wasn't spying. I heard something and–"

"Are you talking about now or the first time you were up here?"

I pulled my jaw shut and glared at him, debating whether to break his nose or kick him in his man-parts again. But I could feel the red heat of humiliation creeping into my face, and I knew it would be better if I made a break for it. I spun on my heel and headed for the door.

I'd gone two steps when I felt a hand on my wrist, pulling me back.

"Tara."

"Let go of me." I spoke without turning, hoping my tone was scary enough. Apparently it wasn't. The hand didn't budge. If anything, it got tighter.

"I was teasing, you. I'm sorry."

I was about to let him have it for grabbing me but those two words surprised me more than anything else he could have said. I turned to face him. "What did you say?"

"I was being an ass. I'm sorry." The evil smile was gone; I looked really hard for a trace of it, but his apology seemed genuine.

"Not the first time." I allowed my voice to soften by a few degrees. "But thanks for the apology."

"You can handle it. I knew that the first time I saw you in that warehouse. Whatever people throw at you, you can handle it."

I didn't really know what to say. The edge in his voice was gone. He was being friendly, and I wasn't sure how to deal with that. "Thanks."

He didn't respond, just continued to look at me with an openness that left me a little nervous. I felt his hand drop from my wrist, but I didn't move. He stepped toward me, close enough that I could feel his breath on my face, and I felt my knees tingle. Yeah, of all things, my knees tingled. It was weird enough to clear my head, though, and I stepped back.

"I should, uh, get back. Before curfew," I said.

The moment evaporated, and he stepped away, shoving his hands into his pockets and looking unsure. "Yeah, I'll see you tomorrow."

I nodded and power walked to the door that would take me back down and out of here. I didn't stop until I reached my room.

CHAPTER TWELVE

It didn't actually dawn on me until later the next day that I never called Wes. I thought about trying to get away and do it that night, but I was too scared to try in case Alex was there again. I'd seen him at training that afternoon but he'd pretended nothing had happened, and we'd run in silence. I went with it, since I had no idea what to say anyway. Like the day before, he tossed me a water bottle at the end and disappeared into the woods.

I spent the evening with Cambria and Logan, wandering the grounds and making up names for Cambria's relationship with Phillipe, like Cam-lippe or Phil-bria. I did my best not to think about Miles, or home, or where Victoria could be going for the weekend. I didn't see Vera again, or Professor Kane, which was good. I was still trying to get the picture of them out of my head.

Victoria left on Thursday, which was nice even if it was a mystery. I got a lot of my extra work done since I was able to spend time in my own room without fear of committing murder. I even managed to send an email to Sam and Angela, detailing my social standing and my class load for each of them, respectively.

I got re-partnered in Defensive Maneuvers, with some kid named Raj, who I could've easily beaten in a freestyle – or "street," as the kids here called it – fight, but since I couldn't remember the combinations we were supposed to be doing, I kept getting kicked in the shins when I didn't pivot like I should've.

The only good thing that came out of it was that Raj, along with a couple of other kids, came up at lunch and asked if we wanted to go to some bonfire on Saturday. Cambria and Logan seemed to know what he was referring to, and I let them do the talking about time and place and everything. I watched when he sat down again; one of the girls at his table was the one who'd made a nasty comment about "letting mutts into school" on my first day. When she saw me looking, she smiled and waved and then went back to her lunch. All I could do was stare at her suspiciously.

Training on Friday went exactly the same as the rest of the week. We ran until I hated my feet, and then Alex handed me water and went on his way. Like before, he acted as if our rooftop moment hadn't happened. I didn't press the issue. It was starting to feel like maybe it hadn't happened, or maybe I was imagining the fact that he might've been about to kiss me. Maybe he'd been about to say something or just hadn't realized he was standing so close. Whatever. I was determined not to think about it.

After training, I showered and hurried to get dressed. I was due in the library with Logan five minutes ago; we were supposed to start on my Lineage project. It sounded about as much fun as running with Alex. Okay, wait, running was worse. Barely. The Draven was still in my suitcase, buried underneath what was left of my clean pajamas.

I pushed clothing aside and pulled it out, brushing it off with careful fingers, even though it was already clean. Unlike the one Fee had given me, which had been covered in dust and smelled of mothballs, this one had a leather cover that shone with the evidence of regular polishing. It smelled of oil and crisp paper. I tucked it inside my bag and headed for the stairs.

Cambria was coming out of her room as I passed. She fell into step beside me, and I caught a whiff of some fruity smelling perfume. She wore a black lace top over a red tank and jeans with faux rips running over the knees and thighs. Her bangs fell over her eye, in their usual place on her forehead, and the rest of her hair bounced and shone from all the gel.

"Hot date?" I asked, bumping her with my hip.

"You think I get dressed up like this for just anyone?" I had to smile because, aside from the extra perfume, this was how Cambria always looked. "You're in a good mood. What's up?"

"Maybe because I am roommate free for the weekend." I'd already informed Cambria of Victoria's upcoming absence, but with all the homework and training with Alex, I hadn't had a chance to tell her about the real reason for Victoria's trip. Or what little I knew of it.

"Good point. I've been thinking about that, actually."

"What?"

"Well, this could be a good time to get some payback in, find out her weaknesses and all that."

I narrowed my eyes at her. "You mean go through her stuff. No way."

"I mean, you can find a way to get back at her."

I shook my head. "No way. I'm not going down that road."

"Oh, so you're just going to wait for her to piss you off so much that you haul off and break her face? That'll work out really well." She rolled her eyes.

I sighed. "Good point."

We were both quiet until we reached the top of the stairs.

"What do you want to do?"

"Yes!" Cambria clapped like she'd won something. "Okay, meeting in your room tomorrow. Before the bonfire. We'll strategize."

"Whatever." I was pretty sure I already regretted this idea. I shifted my bag higher up on my shoulder and caught sight of the time on the wall clock overhead. "Crap. I gotta meet Logan. You coming?"

"Eww. Allergic, remember? And I have plans." She winked and then headed for the lobby.

I turned and went up the stairs, bypassing the cafeteria and walking all the way to the end of the hallway. Large double doors sat propped open on my right, and I hurried in, scanning for Logan. There were a few empty tables near the front, a high counter to my right, and rows and rows of floor to ceiling shelving blocking my view of anything further.

I spotted an older lady behind the counter, so short you almost missed her. She threw me a polite smile and went back to stacking books. Other than that, the place was basically deserted. I scanned the reference signs and headed for the 'Lineage' section, passing markers that read 'Hunter History' and 'Weaponry'. Not your typical human library, although there were sections marked Fiction that displayed Harry Potter books on the end caps. Some things transcended race.

The lighting grew dimmer in the back of the stacks, and I found Logan at a table in the corner, between "Lineage" and the "Reference" section.

"Sorry I'm late," I said, sliding into a chair and setting my bag on the floor.

He looked up from a massive volume that lay on the table in front of him and waved his hand. "Don't worry about it. I got caught up."

It was sort of funny, seeing a tan-skinned, hat-worn-backwards, surfer looking guy with his nose in a book, all alone in a library on a Friday night. Talk about a contradiction. I looked down at his book and he spun it around so I could read the title. "Physics, As It Relates To Battle Technique," I read. "Wow. Light reading before we get to work?"

"It's interesting. You could probably use it to perfect your sparring defense. Not get kicked in the shins so much."

I stuck my tongue out at him. "Yeah, if it was in English. Two words in and I feel like I'm reading Russian or something."

Logan shook his head and closed the book, sliding it away. "Okay, where is it?" He held is hands out.

"Oh, right." I reached into my bag, pulled the Draven out, and handed it across the table.

Logan took it and stared, running his hand carefully over the cover. "Wow," he whispered.

"What?"

"It's really cool to be holding a book like this."

"Aren't all Dravens pretty much the same?" I was looking at Logan like he'd lost it, but he didn't notice. He was still staring down at my book like it was the Bible, original print, or something.

"Well, the first sections are. They all talk about our history and famous battles and basic fighting techniques. But after that it gets pretty personal to the family it belongs to. Not only family tree stuff but information about each generation and their role in our society. What they accomplished in their life, their legacies, special abilities, stuff like that. You feel how heavy this is?" I nodded, but he wasn't looking at me. "Your family line must be traced back pretty far. My Draven is only about half as thick as this one. Yours is definitely a lot older, too."

"Fascinating. Which means this family tree project is going to take twice as long, isn't it?"

"You're supposed to go back as far as you can."

"Right. Let's do this." I pulled out a notebook and a pen.

Logan opened to the page that listed my family line and read off the first few generations. "Elizabeth Godfrey, born 1971, daughter of Edith Godfrey, born 1948. Married to Lowell Godfrey, born 1945." Logan paused and scanned the page. "Huh. That's weird."

"What's weird?"

"Most Dravens list marriages and deaths, at least when the family remembers to update them. And yours is pretty well-kept because I see where they listed your grandfather's death in 1991, which was right around the time you were added. But it doesn't mention your father, or his parents, which is tradition since it lets you know where to go to trace his family's Draven…" Logan trailed off and looked up at me, his face reddening a little in the dim lighting. "Oh, yeah. Your dad wasn't a Hunter."

"Let me see," I said, ignoring his reaction. I refused to feel embarrassed about what I was, even with Logan.

I took the book and twisted it around so I could read the names. Sure enough, there was a line drawn from my mother's name, but it led to a blank spot. I shoved the book back across the table, confused. "I wonder why, though. I mean, Grandma has always seemed fine about it all. Neither of them talks about him much, but I get the impression he was accepted by my grandparents."

Logan cleared his throat, looking awkward again. "Typically, this project includes a section about your father. I guess you can talk to Professor Lopez about it if you want."

"Logan, I'm not going to be embarrassed about who I am. If I act ashamed, it will give people like Victoria more ammunition. I know my father's name was Jeremiah De'Luca. I'll have to dig up what I need to know on my own." I stopped. Logan's eyes had gone wide. "What?" I demanded.

"Your dad was Jeremiah De'Luca?"

"Yes. Why?"

"We learned about him in freshman history. He was a founding member of The Cause and a kick ass scientist. He did a lot of research on the differences in DNA between Hunters and Werewolves. It led to a breakthrough in the way we use metal against Werewolves."

I looked up sharply. "What do you know about metal?"

Logan blinked. "Um, just what every Hunter knows?"

It came out as a question, and he was staring at me with raised eyebrows, surprised by my ignorance, no doubt.

"Which is?" I prompted.

"It kills Werewolves faster and cleaner than a lethal blow landed in hand to hand combat. How do you not know this? It's basic."

I rolled my eyes, impatient. Ever since the moment I'd killed Leo and felt the weird vibration stemming from the metal, I'd wanted to know more about this. Unfortunately, it was one of those things my mother had shut down over. She'd insisted I wait until I'd reached that point in my studies to learn about it with my classmates – which, I'd learned, didn't officially happen until senior year. And in the whirlwind of almost dying I hadn't exactly had the extra time to ask someone like Grandma or Fee, who would've actually told me.

I sat back in my chair, completely forgetting about the family tree assignment.

"No details, remember?" I said, pointing to myself. "Start from the beginning."

"Oh, right," he said. He cleared his throat, and his voice took on this lecture-like quality that reminded me way too much of Professor Olbermeyer from Science. "Metal is a chemical element that conducts two things. Heat and electricity." He counted them out on his fingers as he talked. "It also attracts and forms bonds with non-metals. Which means, when it comes in contact with a Werewolf spirit, which are transient enough to begin with, the metal bonds with the second spirit, and is able to slice through it or pull it from the Were's body, making it a more effective kill."

"Uh-huh." I straightened in my chair. "I understood everything except second spirits being transient and forming bonds and pulling a spirit from the body."

He narrowed his eyes. "What did you understand?"

"And. Is. When. Kill."

Logan shook his head. "Look, I'll dumb it down. Werewolves have essentially two spirits – or souls – where we have one. You can kill a Werewolf by killing the human part of them, but it's not easy, which is why Hunters were created in the first place. We can actually compete with their physical strength and stamina. But their second spirit, the one that makes them a Werewolf, is susceptible to more than brute force. Its transient, which means it passes in and out of the body very quickly. That and the way it bonds to metal makes for a cleaner–and easier–kill, when done right."

"Huh." I chewed my lip, thinking back to those last few minutes with Leo. "So, why aren't we taught to fight with it until senior year?"

"Besides the side effects?" He shrugged. "They want to make sure you don't use it as a crutch in battle, obviously. I mean, metal's not always available to you. Fists and feet are."

"What are all the side effects?"

"Not many, if you do it right. You do feel it, though. You're essentially absorbing another living thing's life force into an object in your own hand–killing two living things at once–so you'll always feel something. If you do it right, it'll be a lot of vibrations, maybe some dizziness, elevated heart rate."

"And if you don't do it right?"

"Heart palpitations, seizures, vomiting, exhaustion, heart attack. Or worse."

I stared at him. "Worse?"

He shrugged. "It could kill you."

"But you're not sure?"

"It's been a long time since a death was recorded due to killing with metal. The research your dad is known for has the last recorded case."

"Right. My dad." I eased forward, finally remembering the assignment at hand, and what had started this conversation in the first place. "He discovered stuff about metal?"

"What we know about life force absorption largely came from his research. The way it affects the Hunter, and why. Before that, people thought it was magic."

"It isn't?"

"Magic is nothing but unexplained science. But if you want to believe in that sort of thing, the metal isn't magic. It's the spirit inside the Werewolf that is."

"I'm not sure what I believe," I mumbled. "What you're telling me is that my dad helped find ways to kill his own kind."

"It was all to help The Cause and deal with those who resisted peace, but yeah. I guess he did."

We sat in silence for a moment. Logan was watching me with an expression that looked a lot like pity. I didn't meet his eyes.

"You okay?" he asked, finally.

I shrugged. "Whatever. It's nice to be filled in, finally."

He opened his mouth to say something and then closed it again, his gaze locked on something behind me. I turned and found Cambria hurrying towards us through the stacks. Her black eyeliner was running vertical down her cheeks and it smudged sideways where she kept trying to wipe the tears away. She reached our table and fell into the chair beside me, looking somewhere between heartbroken and murderous.

"What happened to you?" Logan asked.

"Phillipe is what happened," she said, her voice cracking. "I went to meet him for our date, but he wasn't there, so I went looking for him." She sniffled, which made her look a tad more heartbroken than violent.

"Let me guess. You found him and he wasn't alone," I said.

She nodded, and her eyes narrowed, putting her right back in the murderous category. "He was with Demi. Of all the trampy, hooker-ific broads at this school, he had to pick Demi. He might as well have shacked up with Victoria."

"Oh." I looked to Logan for help, but he shrugged. I turned back to Cambria, who was sulking and chewing on a pen. I looked closer. My pen. I snatched it back. "This might be a bad time, but who is Demi again?"

"She's Victoria's second in command. Long brown hair, twisted smile. Possibly more evil than Victoria. She's been through pretty much the entire junior class and half the seniors."

"Oh, right." I remembered the girl I'd seen holding court instead of Victoria at lunch the other day.

I sighed. "I'm sorry, Cam. Are you sure? Maybe you misunderstood."

Cambria let out a harsh laugh. "I'm pretty sure there's no mistaking that pose. Not unless it's for medical reasons."

"Oh." I shoved the mental picture aside. "Want us to jump him?" I joked. "Or her?"

"That's really sweet of you, but I'll figure something out." Cambria was swiping at her makeup now that the tears had dried, and the way she said it let me know she hadn't been joking, like I had. I tried not to let that make me nervous, because Phillipe and Demi obviously deserved it. But then I remembered the boys who'd gotten busted for trying to check out gay porn from the library. It hadn't been pretty.

Logan and I exchanged a look while Cambria leaned forward and scanned the page I'd been taking notes on, already moving on from the horrific breakup – and then breakdown – she'd gone through.

"Jeremiah De'Luca, we studied him. Some scientist. Genius with metal. But wasn't he a Were…?" She looked at me with wide eyes, then back to the paper, tracing the lines of the tree I'd drawn, connecting all the names. "Crap. Is he your–"

"Dad? Yes."

"Geez. Sorry. I mean, not that he's your dad because I think it's totally cool to be half and half. I meant, sorry I didn't realize." Her brows knitted and she stared at me. "Wait. Dad was a science genius. Does this mean you're going to get all science-y on me and BFF it with Logan and do homework all the time?"

I laughed. "Uh, no. I must take after another part of my family. Trust me, no chance of that."

"Good. Does that mean you can take a break?" She glanced at Logan. "I'm already bored."

I laughed again. Logan rolled his eyes and looked genuinely irritated. "We just took a break. To hear about your–"

I cut him off, already anticipating the argument coming. "I've got something we should talk about. Victoria." That did the trick. Both of them shut up and looked at me.

"Why? I thought you said she was gone. Oh, do you want to brainstorm now?" Cambria asked.

"Brainstorm what? Where did she go?" Logan asked, looking suddenly very interested. He pushed the textbook aside.

"She left for the weekend," I explained to him. "Only, she didn't go visit her parents."

Cambria's brows furrowed. "But you said–"

"I know what I said. I was waiting until we were all together before I told you."

Cambria leaned forward. "Well? We're together. Spill."

I filled them in on what I'd seen and heard between Vera and Victoria that night on the balcony. I left out the part about running into Alex. That part was still confusing, and I didn't think I could handle Cambria's inevitable hot flash.

"She's on an official mission? That is so not fair," Cambria said when I was done. "We're not allowed to do that stuff until we're seniors."

"It makes sense, though," Logan said. Both of us looked at him with brows raised. "Because of her tracker thing."

"What tracker thing?" I asked.

"It's her gift. If you can take her back to the last known place of a Were, she can pick up on them. Sort of like an internal or mental scent. Then she can follow them, and if you follow them long enough, you'll find them. I bet they're using her to find the pack that kidnapped those Hunters."

"How do you know all of this?" I asked.

Cambria snorted. "Because it has to do with Victoria and Logan can't help himself."

"What?" I looked back at him in confusion because I couldn't bring myself to accept what it sounded like Cambria meant. Logan wouldn't answer or look at me, but I was pretty sure I'd never seen a guy get that red before. "No way," I said.

"Oh, yes way." Cambria laughed.

Logan glared at her. "Don't you have underclassmen to torture somewhere?"

Cambria chuckled and looked over at me, gesturing to Logan. "See?"

"Logan, but how? I mean, you know what she's like."

"She's not as bad as she pretends."

I gaped at him, positive I hadn't heard correctly.

"Whatever," he mumbled. "Can we get back to the project?"

I shot Cambria a look that said "what the hell?" She rolled her eyes. I looked back at Logan. He had his reddened face stuck deep into the Draven and was pretending to read some passage about my great-times-eight-grandfather. At least I assumed it was pretending, since the whole thing was in Latin.

"Let's get back to work," I said.

Cambria groaned.

"Ten more minutes," I promised.

We went back to the Draven, with Logan reading the names aloud and me taking notes. Cambria pulled out an iPod and began scrolling through playlists. We were up to my grandma's siblings and their children when a name caught my attention.

"Wait, go back. What was that last one?"

"Julia Crowne, married to Henry Gallagher." Logan re-read the 'born' and 'died' dates again, and I nodded, waving my hand to hurry him up. "One offspring. Vera Gallagher, born Nineteen-fifty-five. Still living."

Cambria looked up from her iPod. "What's going on now?"

I looked at Logan, trying to do the math. "Vera Gallagher. She's my..."

"Great aunt," he supplied.

"The Vera who has weird visions about you?" Cambria asked.

I didn't answer.

I stared back at Logan, without really seeing him. I couldn't focus. Part of me felt like this was par for the course. I mean, it's not like anyone had told me anything else important before now. At least not until I'd already figured it out for myself. Still... I'd sat in the same room with this woman. She'd been there when my mother had supposedly come clean about everything. I couldn't help but wonder what reason they'd had for keeping this from me. If it had been no big deal, then why hadn't they told me?

Lucky for me, Vera was here at school. And I was going to find out.

CHAPTER THIRTEEN

Training on Saturday sucked. Training any day sucked, but Saturday was bad because I had to wake up early to run. I thought that would mean my poor, tired body would reject itself by the end, and I'd finally throw up. When that happened, I was definitely putting my foot down that we end this and skip to the part where I actually learned something.

Alex still wasn't talking. Which had finally managed to crawl so far under my skin, I didn't care if we got into a knock-out, drag-down fight if it meant we were at least grunting at each other to break the silence. I waited until we were about a mile in, and I'd managed to level out my breathing, before I spoke.

We were out in the front field now, running parallel to the fence that separated the school from state property, about halfway through the course Alex had set for us. That left us roughly twenty minutes to converse without trying to kill each other.

"So. What exactly do you do when you're not running?" I asked.

He continued to watch the path in front of us. "Study," was his reply.

But I was determined not to be put off. "That can't be all. What do you do for fun?"

"Run."

I almost laughed, but then I realized he was serious.

"I haven't seen you on the roof lately," he said.

I looked up at him, surprised he was bringing it up. We'd spent the past week pretending it hadn't happened. "Um, yeah, I haven't had to make any calls…" I trailed off, knowing how lame that sounded.

"Don't worry, you haven't missed any good eavesdropping opportunities," he said.

I whipped my gaze up to his face, feeling myself reddening, and was surprised to find him looking back at me with a small smile. He was joking.

"Thanks," I muttered.

"All the good stuff goes down when Vera's around anyway."

I nodded like I agreed or had any idea what he meant.

"How's the hazing going?" he asked.

"What hazing?"

He glanced down, one eyebrow raised. "The paper bag?"

I groaned. "You heard about that?"

"Everyone heard about that. It gave the freshmen one more thing to be afraid of. Now, no one carries brown bags anywhere, and if they see one it's like a bomb threat. No one goes near it."

"I'm getting it worse than the freshman?"

"Victoria must really like you. She's pretty choosy about who she tortures on a regular basis like this."

"It probably doesn't help that we're roommates."

"Seriously?" He laughed and shook his head. "You never had a chance."

"You're trying to tell me you don't mess with the underclassmen like this?"

"No exploding presents. Although, I did steal a kid's underwear once."

My eyebrows shot up. "Was he wearing it?"

"How evil do you think I am?"

"You forget my experience is with the Victorias of this school. I assume the worst."

"Good point. No, he wasn't wearing it. Still, I don't think he was too happy when he kept waking up with no underwear. He started carrying it around in his backpack after that, so I let it go."

Logan. I bit my lip and tried not to laugh. "Maybe if that's all I had to deal with, I could handle it. Grandma keeps telling me to rise above, but one of these days I'm not going to be able to do that."

His expression turned serious. "You can't use physical violence against another Hunter. It's grounds for expulsion."

I sighed. "What's the down side? I'd get to go home."

Alex shook his head. "Probably not. There are plenty of other Hunter schools to choose from. And you're a Godfrey. They'd take you. You'd just be farther from home."

I tried to figure out what he meant when he said I was a Godfrey. Did that have some special meaning? But I was stuck on the part where he'd said I'd be further from home. That wouldn't be good. I was already a few hours away, and Wes and the rest of my friends felt millions of miles away. I couldn't imagine having to put any more distance between us.

We reached the place where we should've continued back up the hill to the clearing, but instead, Alex made a sharp right and took us back into the woods.

"Where are we going?" I asked.

"You'll see. Come on."

I followed him down and around a trail that eventually let us out onto a one-lane paved road. Thick trees lined both sides so we ran on the thin strip of asphalt which felt weird after so many days of running on grass and dead leaves. At the end of the road stood something I hadn't expected to see; an old garage, weathered and sagging in one corner, with a carport attached that looked like it had been pieced together from old scraps of siding and random plastic. A primer-gray pickup truck was parked underneath the carport. Various tools were scattered around near the hood.

Alex went to the front of the truck and felt around inside the seam of the hood. A second later he yanked and the hood came up. He propped it open and stood back.

“Is this yours?” I asked.

“You asked what I do in my spare time. This is it.” He gestured to the truck.

I came around and looked under the hood. I had less than no clue about cars, but I did notice several holes where I suspected parts were missing. “You work on this in your spare time?”

“It relaxes me.”

I felt my eyes narrowing and even though I didn’t want to ruin the friendly moment, I couldn’t keep from asking, “Why are you telling me this?”

He was slow in answering and there was an odd look in his eyes, like maybe he didn’t entirely know. “If we’re going to be spending so much time together, we should try to be friends.”

“You want to be friends with me?”

“Why do you look so surprised?”

“Because you haven’t spoken to me in days.”

“We had an entire conversation on the way here.” He eyed me. “Don’t you want to be friends?”

“Well, yeah, but… I’m a dirty blood.” He winced. Only a little, but I caught the reaction. “See? You have issues about that. It’s fine. I’ve accepted it.”

“You’ve accepted that I have issues?” An eyebrow arched as he said it. “That was nice of you.”

I could hear the sarcasm, and I would’ve backtracked since that had come out wrong, but the way he was looking at me was fanning my temper. I did not want to ruin the little bit of civility we were working on here. I looked away and breathed deeply to calm down.

“I’m saying that I’m dealing with the fact that you never have anything nice to say to me or always seem to be looking for a way to annoy me. I don’t expect anything more. So you being friendly and open enough to show me this hobby you have, it’s a little unexpected. That’s all.”

“You’re the one who started the conversation back there.” He jabbed a finger behind me. “Are you saying you were pretending? Would you rather I pretend to be friendly and not mean it?”

"No. It's called small talk. It's better than silence."

Alex took a step back and I braced myself, knowing what was coming; yelling or another wrestling match. Either way, I was sure he was about to let me have it. But he shook his head and paced back and forth along the truck. He stopped abruptly and walked up to me like he was going to say something and then shut his mouth again and stepped back.

"Training's over. I'll see you Monday," he said finally.

He turned on his heel and jogged back down the road. I stayed where I was, watching him go and feeling like whatever had just happened was all my fault.

CAMBRIA WAS WAITING AT MY DOOR WHEN I GOT BACK FROM THE showers. She had apparently already moved on from the Phillipe fiasco and was her usual energetic self. She followed me inside my room and flopped onto Victoria's bed.

"What's up?" I asked, throwing my laundry into the mesh bag the school used for washing.

"Plotting, remember? Now's our chance to get back at the Wicked Witch. Find her weakness."

I shook my head. "I changed my mind, okay? I'm not going through her stuff."

"We don't even need to. I've got the perfect solution. Photoshop."

"What?"

"Anne Price was talking about how Nevan Brown is gone for the weekend, too." She said the name like it held some special meaning.

"And who is that?"

"Nevan is the kid you don't even feel bad for not going out with. He's gross and dorky and crude, and I'm pretty sure the rumor about him dressing up in girl's clothes on weekends is true."

"Sounds like a winner."

"Right. And my friend Dave is a whiz with Photoshop. We just need to get a picture of Nevan and a picture of Victoria and voila! By

Monday, everyone thinks the two of them had a weekend getaway together."

"And why would anyone believe that?"

She raised her eyebrows, like the answer was obvious. "My natural charm will convince them."

"You mean you're supernatural charm."

"Whatever."

I stared at Cambria. "You scare me sometimes, you know that?" I wrung my hair out and sat down in front of the mirror, pulling it into pieces so I could braid it.

"Is that a no?"

"That's a 'hell no'. I'm not stooping to Victoria's level and playing her games. If she doesn't lay off with the comments, I'll–"

"Yeah, we all know your solution. It's not any better."

"I was going to say ignore her."

"That's completely lame. My idea's better."

"Your idea could get you expelled."

"So could yours."

Our eyes met through the reflection in my desk mirror and she held my gaze, eyes sparkling and pleading and willing me to say yes. For some reason, the fact that she was pressing me struck a nerve and something inside me sparked with temper. Even though I knew Cambria was trying to be a friend and have my back, I suddenly felt pressured and antagonized and my skin began to heat with temper. My eyes blazed with it.

"Look, I said no. Get it through your head," I snapped.

Cambria blinked at me, her smile disappearing as she realized how upset I was. "Geez, Tara. Fine. You don't have to snap."

"Apparently it's the only way to get you to stop nagging me," I shot back.

She gave me a strange look that was more confusion than anything. I wanted to take it back and calm down, but I couldn't. Something inside me was irrationally angry, and I couldn't put it aside. Cambria must've realized I wasn't going to back down because her expression hardened, and she got up.

"You're acting weird. And by weird, I mean bitchy. I'm leaving. Come find me when you get it together," she said. She slammed the door on her way out.

I finished braiding my hair, my fingers moving like a robot. I stared at my reflection, surprised at how much anger showed in my face, and sat there until I could finally feel my temper begin to fade. When it was gone, all I had was guilt. What had made me so angry in the first place? Why had I snapped like that? I knew I'd been a little short on sleep lately, but that wasn't me. I flopped onto my bed, trying to decide whether it was too soon to go find Cambria.

I MUST HAVE DOZED OFF BECAUSE THE NEXT THING I KNEW, I WAS waking up, on the floor, with a sore hip. I blinked, trying to clear the haze of sleep. I'd fallen off the bed. No, more than that, I'd thrown myself off the bed. I knew I'd been dreaming something terrible but it was one of those things that drifted farther and farther from memory the more you woke up. All I could picture were teeth. Lots of sharp teeth, aimed at me.

I got up, rubbing my hip. I checked myself in the mirror and made a face. My hair wasn't so much braided as it was knotted. I pulled the braid out and used my fingers to comb through it until it looked vaguely presentable. It fell in loose waves that looked like I'd been sitting in front of a fan for the last few hours, and I left it. I needed fresh air.

The shadows around Lexington Hall were long. I'd been asleep most of the afternoon. I zipped my jacket, glad I'd thought to grab it, and wiggled my toes inside my knee high boots. These boots so often held wooden stakes that they almost seemed roomy without a weapon tucked along my leg.

I didn't have a specific direction in mind, but I ended up on the trail that led to the bonfire Raj had invited me to. It was late enough. And maybe Cambria was there, and I could apologize. Not that I had any reason or explanation for why I'd gone off the deep end earlier. It was all sort of sudden and confusing. Hopefully a simple apology would be enough.

Inside the trees, I glanced down at my phone, which I'd turned on outside Lexington Hall in the hopes a signal would appear, but the readout was still blank. No signal. I kept walking.

The bonfire was happening as far away from school as we could get without being off school grounds. By now the announcement had been made that the wards were stronger and more complex and if any student stepped outside the perimeter, Headmaster Whitfield would know and there would be consequences. How he would know wasn't clear, and neither were the consequences, but it had done the trick. Sometimes the unknown was scarier, I guess.

From what Cambria had told me about the bonfire, it wasn't exactly condoned, but a lot of the teachers knew and chose to look the other way. As long as no one left the grounds or caused trouble, it stayed under the radar.

The further I walked, the more spread out the trees became, until finally everything opened up and I could see a gathering of people up ahead. It wasn't so much a clearing as a large space in between trees. And it wasn't so much a bonfire as a few pieces of kindling and a flame. I guess it was safer that way, considering we were still in the woods. At least the area around the fire had been carefully cleared of any stray leaves or brush. Someone had thrown a metal rack over some rocks and had hot dogs and burgers cooking. Logs had been pulled up and were filled with students talking and laughing around the small fire. A beat-up card table was set up nearby with plates and buns and a gigantic bottle of ketchup. Kids wandered around, munching on roasted meat.

At one edge of the clearing, a younger group of kids – probably freshman – were lined up along the ground and being yelled at by upperclassmen. They dropped to their hands and toes and began doing pushups at the barking command of the lead jock. I recognized Levi as one of the torturers. He walked along the row, at the feet of the freshman, kicking their feet out from under them as they tried to push up.

Smaller clusters of kids were scattered here and there, huddled against trees. Further out, couples were half hidden behind the bigger tree trunks and whispering close together – or whatever they were doing. I tried not to look too closely. Not because I was embarrassed. It made me miss Wes.

I turned back to the fire and searched the faces there. I recognized some of them from my classes and was surprised to see one or two wave at me instead of sneer or turn away. Only a couple, though. The rest didn't bother to acknowledge my arrival, sneer or otherwise. I hesitated, on the outskirts, wondering whether this had really been a good idea. If Cambria didn't talk to me, it wasn't like anyone else here would, either - except maybe Levi - And I didn't see Cambria anywhere.

I was halfway to retreating when Raj spotted me and broke away from the group nearest the fire. He was smiling, his expression friendly, and I relaxed a little.

"You came," he said. His dark skinned arm reached out and clapped me around the shoulder.

"It's pretty cool. How did you get all this back here?"

"I know a guy who helps out in the kitchen. And Cambria helped convince the lunch ladies to give us the food." He pointed and I spotted Cambria on the far side of the fire, talking to a girl with spiky hair that I recognized from my Chemistry class.

"Oh," I said, looking away before she saw me. "I didn't know you were cool with her doing her… thing."

Raj laughed. "Her thing comes in handy." He shrugged. "She knows better than to use it on another Hunter so we're cool. You hungry?"

"Sure." I let Raj lead me over to the table and make me a burger. The only topping available was ketchup so I made sure to douse it. "Thanks," I said, digging in. "This is great."

"It would taste better on a real grill but it's not bad. How's the shin?"

I made a face around a mouthful of smoky tasting hamburger. "Better. By the time they're done healing, it'll be Monday, and I'll have a whole new layer of bruising."

Raj grinned. "You want me to go easy on you?"

"No way."

"That's what I thought." Raj nodded like he'd expected that answer. "Besides, Hunter chicks don't really get breaks because they're female. We believe in equal opportunity mayhem."

"As it should be." I smiled and was pleased to know I meant it; I was having a good time, in the midst of a school full of haters. Maybe there was hope for me here, after all.

Raj got called back to the fire, and I finished the ketchup-drenched burger. More kids were arriving so even though the space was pretty open, it was filling up fast. I heard enough comments from passers-by to know most of the junior and senior class was here – along with whatever underclassmen they wanted to bring along for tortured entertainment.

Logs were dragged closer and sat on. Someone had brought a battery powered radio and found a station that played top twenty. The light was dimming to almost nothing and even though the sun was still setting somewhere, shadows covered most of the ground. I found an empty spot on a log a few rows back from the fire and sat.

"Hey."

I turned and saw Nina. Her hair was in its normal French braid but a few strands had come loose that she hadn't bothered to re-secure. It made her look more laid back. More approachable.

"Hey." I brightened. Probably because her face was both familiar and friendly. A rarity.

"Thanks again for showing me to the dorms last week," I said.

"No problem. Are you settling in okay?"

I nodded even though I wanted to say 'no, of course not, I'd rather be at home.' "I've learned a lot," I said instead.

She nodded, warming easily to the topic of education. "This school is one of the best in the country. You'll have to tell your grandma thanks for that."

"My grandma?"

"For giving so much," she said. Then her expression changed.

"Darn. I did it again, right? Put my foot in my mouth? Don't they tell you anything?"

"What does my grandma have to do with the school being the best?"

"She provides most of the funding for it. I mean, it was here before she was, but she's the real reason it's still open. She basically paid for the underground dorms to be dug out and the ventilation and plumbing and everything else that it took to create an underground dorm system. And she makes sure CHAS allows for proper training with new recruits and stuff."

"CHAS? Oh, the Committee, right?" I thought I'd heard Logan refer to it that way.

"Right." Nina looked a little relieved that I knew something. "Stands for Committee of Hunter Affairs and Security."

"My grandma is a member of CHAS?"

"She's all about making sure we don't get killed because of inexperience and stuff. She's pretty awesome, huh?"

"Mm-hmm." I nodded automatically, but my mind was already far away from Nina.

"And I'm sure the fact that you're going here will make it easier for you when you take over her spot."

The moment snapped back into focus. "Her spot on CHAS?"

"Um, yeah. You know, because it gets passed down to family members?" Nina seemed to realize she'd dropped a bomb of new information on me because at that moment, her attention turned to the kid sitting on her other side and she dove into a deep conversation with him about weaponry improvement in hand-to-hand combat.

I tuned it out and stared into the trees.

I was supposed to take over this CHAS position? Was it like a political office or something? Geez, I should be used to this by now. My family not telling me things. But I'd never really lumped Grandma in to the same secret-keeping category as my mother–until now. And if Nina knew about my supposed political future… that meant everyone knew.

I stood up and brushed myself off and marched over to where Cambria was still sitting with the spiky haired girl.

"I need to talk to you," I said, without waiting for a break in their conversation.

She eyed me from behind her bangs, and her expression was hard. "I'm busy."

"I don't care. It's important. Is Logan here?"

"Um, I think I saw him over–"

"Show me."

She shot her spiky friend a look and rose. "What is going on?" she hissed as we walked.

"There's Logan," I said, walking right up to him and stepping between him and a group that reminded me a lot of a chess club for some reason. Logan had a plastic cup in his hand and his hair tucked inside his hat. He looked like a frat boy lost in the wrong crowd.

"I need to talk to you," I said, interrupting another kid who was droning on about some War of Zombies game.

"Okay." He looked startled but he didn't argue. "I'll be back guys."

He stepped out of the circle and caught sight of Cambria. She shrugged and gave him a look that said she was as confused as he was and infinitely more irritated. I headed straight for the trees, in the opposite direction of any trail, and pushed my way through until we were far enough away from the party that we wouldn't be heard.

"So when exactly did each of you become aware of the fact that I'm an heir to a political office?" No answer. "I'll assume from your silence that each of you knew from the beginning. My grandma's position with CHAS? The funding she provides for Wood Point?" Still no answer. "Let me guess. You kept it from me for my own good."

I was vaguely aware that I was shaking and my voice was pitching from one octave to another. Both of them stared at me with wide eyes. I couldn't see much else of their expressions; it was a lot darker in here than it had been in the clearing. "So you have nothing to say about the fact that you lied to me all this time?"

"Tara, you really need to calm down," said Cambria.

"Are you feeling okay?" Logan sounded concerned.

I ignored that. It wasn't the response I was looking for. I ground my teeth together hard enough to make the noise audible. "Answer me."

"Seriously, Tara, what's wrong? You're shaking." Cambria put her hand out and touched my arm. I flung it back out of her grasp, and she backed away. "You're burning up. You need to calm down."

"Look, I don't know about Cambria but I didn't lie to you. I thought you knew about the CHAS thing already," Logan said.

I didn't answer. I looked at Cambria.

"I didn't bring it up because you don't like to talk about stuff like that," she said. "You're already freaked out enough by Vera's vision about you, and I didn't want to upset you. I didn't realize you had no idea." Her words came quickly, like she was trying to hurry to explain.

I didn't know what to say. And I hated how angry I was. Especially after how guilty I felt for getting this way earlier.

"Take a deep breath, Tara." Logan's voice was low and even. I did as he asked. "Good, now let it out slowly." I did. "Again."

All I could do was obey his instructions. I didn't speak, just concentrated on the sound of his voice and doing what he told me. After a few minutes, I could feel my heart rate begin to even out. The shaking had stopped. I still felt too hot, though, so I continued with the deep breaths even after Logan had stopped telling me to.

"Thanks," I said when I could speak again.

"Don't mention it," he said.

"Are you okay now?" asked Cambria quietly.

She was still standing further away than Logan was. It made me feel bad.

"Yeah, I think so. I don't know what happened. I just got so angry. I'm sorry. I would never have hurt you guys."

"Yeah, we know that." That was Logan. Cambria looked unsure.

"I'm sorry. For that and for earlier." I hoped she could see my face well enough that my sincerity came across.

"Yeah, okay. We're cool," she said finally.

"Does that mean we can go back to–" Logan fell abruptly silent and stared into the woods.

I didn't ask what was wrong. I didn't need to. I looked at Cambria and could make out the wide whites of her eyes. She, too, stared off into the trees, and I knew then that we all felt the same thing.

Goose bumps.

They ran up my spine first, past my neck and over my scalp.

Snap. Dead leaves and brush crunched somewhere nearby.

I whirled. It was coming from the opposite direction of the bonfire, but I couldn't let it get closer. We must have all had that same thought because we all took off running at the same time. I squinted into the darkness, willing my night vision into focus. Even with it, though, I knew whatever was making all that noise could see far better than I could.

The branches and heavy bushes weren't helping. We'd been standing in the middle of what could only be described as a thicket. Trying to get out was like fighting with a rosebush; the rosebush always won. By the time I broke free, I knew I'd torn my shirt and my skin in several places.

I kept going.

Behind me, I could hear Cambria and Logan crunching over the same leaves I was. We were making enough noise that I couldn't hear anything else, but I still felt the goose bumps, and I knew something was close. I put my hand on each of their arms and signaled them to stop.

Up ahead, I heard the faint crunching of leaves. I took off. The way was clearer now. The trees were further apart and easier to get around. Logan inched next to me and then past me, running full speed. Cambria and I were shoulder to shoulder, parting only to sidestep a tree or fallen log. I knew the moment we passed through the wards. A sort of jolt ran through me and I felt my stomach rise into my throat for a split second, like when you go over an unexpected hill in the car. Cambria and I glanced at each other, but we kept going. Logan hadn't even slowed, and we sprinted ahead to catch up.

We ran for what felt like longer than it should've taken. After a while, Logan stopped and froze in place, listening. Cambria and I did the same. I strained my ears against the silence of our muted breathing.

Nothing.

We stood, unmoving, for a few more minutes, but I never heard anything else. The goose bumps began to recede. When they were gone, Logan turned and walked back to Cambria and me.

"What the hell?" Cambria hissed.

I understood her reason for whispering. Our bodies told us we were alone, but I still felt exposed.

"How did that happen?" I whispered.

Logan didn't answer. He took his hat off and wiped his forehead with his hand and then shoved his hat back on, brim facing backwards. "We need to get back inside the wards," he said. "Now."

"Right, like that'll help. A Werewolf got inside the wards. We need to tell everyone to get the hell back to the school," Cambria said.

"We can't," said Logan. "If we tell people what happened, they'll panic. Some will go running back to school but think of who you're dealing with, Cambria. The first thing most of them will do is run straight into the woods to find the Werewolf and be the one to kill it. We can't put them in danger like that."

"We'll explain to them that we chased it off. It's gone," I said. "We can't just leave them out in the open like that."

Cambria sighed, eyes still darting around in the dark, looking for any sign of danger. "Logan is right, Tara. These kids are Hunters. A.k.a. glory seekers. They aren't afraid, and they don't run from a fight. If anything, they'll run straight into it."

Logan nodded. "And we don't know how many Werewolves were here. It could've been a whole pack."

"So what are we supposed to do? Let them party out here all night until the pack comes back for them?"

"I don't think they're coming back," said Logan. "I mean, there are only three of us so why did they run in the first place? Unless there was only one and it couldn't take us. But either way, what was it doing here?"

No one had an answer.

"Until we know, we have to assume it's not safe," Logan went on. "We'll go back and stay at the party until the last person leaves and make sure they all get back okay."

Cambria and I nodded. It was the best plan we had. We made our way back to the bonfire and slipped into the clearing. In the added light from the fire I got a good look at Cambria and Logan, and my eyes widened. Then I glanced down at myself.

"You guys. We're a mess," I hissed at them.

They each looked down at their ripped shirts, caked in dirt. All three of us had drying, bloody scratches up and down our arms. I inched back towards the edge of the thicket we'd come out of. Cambria and Logan followed. I was about to disappear, figuring it might be better to watch from a distance, when a familiar face appeared from the trail that led to school.

I froze long enough for Alex to meet my eyes and then, like a five year old, I dove into the bushes anyway. Cambria and Logan stayed where they were, and I cursed under my breath. I closed my eyes and waited. I don't know why; I guess I was hoping it was a 'if I can't see you then you can't see me' situation. It wasn't.

"Tara." Alex's tone let me know he wasn't amused.

I stepped out of my hiding place with as much nonchalance as I could muster. Thorns pulled at me, and I had to pick them free before turning to face him. "What's up?"

He took in my appearance which he'd, no doubt, already noticed about Logan and Cambria, and his eyes narrowed. He looked pissed. "Headmaster Whitfield wants to see you. Now."

I sighed in relief. "That's good. I guess that means the wards did their job after all." I looked over at Cambria and Logan, but they didn't look nearly as relieved as I felt. I looked back at Alex. He still looked pissed, which confused me. "He wants to see me about the breach, right?"

Alex's lips tightened into a thin line. "Good guess. But not only you. All three of you went off grounds. You all need to come."

Cambria looked startled. "All three of us? Can we go one at a time?"

"No."

I stepped forward, seeing the problem this presented. "But one of us needs to be here. Is anyone else with you?"

Alex looked at me blankly. "I'm pretty sure I can handle bringing the three of you in by myself."

"Not for us. For the Werewolf," said Cambria.

"What are you talking about?" Alex's gaze swiveled to Cambria, full of frustration and impatience.

Cambria crossed her arms. "The whole reason we crossed the wards," she said, just as impatiently. "We were chasing the Werewolf that breached our side first."

"Nobody said anything about a Werewolf to me," said Alex.

"Oh, so then it must be a lie." You could almost hear Cambria rolling her eyes. "Look, you're cute, but you're not cute enough to keep me from going off on you for being an idiot. Why would we cross the wards unless we had a reason?"

Alex stepped up so he stood toe to toe with her. "I have no clue why you crossed the wards. Not my business. My job is to take you to Headmaster Whitfield. Now move before I have to carry you."

He and Cambria locked eyes. Neither one moved.

"Uh-oh," Logan whispered under his breath.

I wasn't quite sure whose temper would snap first, but I really didn't want to find out. I put a hand on each of their arms. After what felt like forever, Cambria backed up and headed for the trail. Logan and I exchanged a look and followed.

CHAPTER FOURTEEN

No one said another word on the way back to school. A part of me wanted to negotiate, beg, whatever, with Alex to let one of us stay and keep an eye on the kids at the bonfire, but I knew it was useless. He'd made up his mind. Any possibility of convincing him had gone out the window when Cambria had called him an idiot. Not to mention the fact that he was probably still mad at me for earlier. So I stayed silent and hoped Headmaster Whitfield would be easier to convince.

Griffin Hall was deserted and quiet. Our footsteps were annoyingly loud on the marble floors, and we didn't pass anyone else on the way. All of the admin offices were dark, the doors closed. Alex stopped outside Headmaster Whitfield's office and knocked twice. There was a mumbled response, and we waited while Alex disappeared inside. A second later, he reappeared and motioned for us to enter.

We stepped inside, shoulder to shoulder, and found ourselves facing Headmaster Whitfield, Professor Kane, and Vera. They watched the three of us with matching expressions of disappointment that couldn't have been more identical if they'd planned it.

Vera glanced behind me and said, "Thank you Alex. You can get back to your patrols."

The door clicked shut without a word.

"Come sit down," said Vera, looking at me and gesturing to the chairs. She remained where she was, standing next to Headmaster Whitfield behind the desk. Professor Kane stood off near the corner, watching us intently.

We shuffled forward and sat.

"So," said Headmaster Whitfield, folding his hands on his desk and looking back and forth between us. "Who wants to tell me what happened tonight."

I spoke up, looking at Vera instead of Headmaster. "You should already know. If you sensed us crossing the wards, you sensed the Werewolf."

"Yes, Alex said you mentioned something about a Werewolf, but I'm afraid you're mistaken. No Werewolves passed through the wards." When I opened my mouth to interrupt, she raised her hand to stop me. "I would've felt it if they had. Just like I felt the three of you when you crossed outside of school grounds and when you re-entered. Maybe you heard a small animal or a deer and mistook it for a Werewolf."

"But I felt it. We all did," said Cambria.

"I'm sure you thought so," said Headmaster Whitfield. "And if you thought you felt one then I commend you for going after it and trying to keep our school safe. Although, the right thing would've been to send for help and let us take care of it." He nodded towards Vera and Professor Kane and then went on. "Your intentions were good. So, I'm simply going to issue each of you a warning. Keep in mind that if it happens again there will be serious consequences."

We all mumbled a simultaneous, "Yes, sir."

But Headmaster Whitfield wasn't finished. "Safety is our number one priority, and I can assure you that the wards are checked daily. If a breach was made from the outside, we would know. You needn't worry."

We all nodded, and I guess that was enough for him because he finally let us go with instructions that we all go directly back to our rooms. Apparently, they were still okay with turning a blind eye to the bonfire activities, as long as the three of us didn't attend.

We all filed out and made sure to click the door closed. We slowed our pace once we were away from the office.

"Something's wrong," said Logan quietly.

"Definitely," agreed Cambria. "They should've sensed the breach."

"We need to do something," I said.

We reached the door, and I followed them out into the darkness. Up ahead, twinkling white lights lit the way across the courtyard to Lexington Hall. I'd gone exactly three steps when a figure stepped away from the side of the building and blocked our path.

"Can I talk to Tara alone?" Alex asked.

His hands were stuffed into his pockets, and his expression was neutral. Still, I was pretty sure he didn't want to tell jokes and hang out. He hadn't seemed happy about the way we'd kept insisting that we'd felt a Werewolf tonight, and I was not in the mood to hear anyone else tell me I'd imagined it. Before I could formulate a reason why I shouldn't stay and talk, Cambria and Logan had nodded and given me a look. They were gone before I could muster a hateful glare at their backs. Some friends.

"We need to talk," Alex said, walking over so that he blocked my path of escape.

I was trapped between him and the building. I sighed.

"If you're going to lecture me about imagining things save it. I heard enough of that inside. I'll be keeping this sort of thing to myself from now on."

His eyes flashed and his neutral expression vanished. "You need to realize that I'm responsible for you. Everything you do comes back on me. Remember that."

"Oh, so you're here to make sure I keep my nose clean? Make sure you don't get any marks on your permanent record because of me? Message received. Can I go now?"

"What is your problem?"

"My problem? Maybe that you're more concerned with being teacher's pet than you are about the fact that a Werewolf breached the wards. A Werewolf. The only security system the school has against being invaded just became compromised. Which wouldn't be a problem except that apparently someone out there wants to invade. And all you can think about is yourself and how you look on paper."

I shoved my hand into his shoulder to move him aside. I had every intention of having the last word and marching off to my room to invent new curse words to use on him, but my shove must've been pretty weak because he didn't budge, and I almost ran into him.

"I'm not done," he said.

"Believe me, I am," I snapped. But I backed up because it was either that or stand nose to nose.

"Are you sure there was a Werewolf out there tonight?"

I blinked, too surprised by the question to answer right away. "Um, yeah," I finally said.

"You don't sound sure."

"I didn't expect… ." I glared at him. "Why? Do you believe me?"

He shrugged. "Maybe."

"Whatever, Alex. Why would I lie?"

"That's what I've been asking myself the whole time you were in there."

"And?"

"I guess you wouldn't," he said slowly. "You're the most Werewolf-friendly Hunter I've ever met. I can't see you crying 'wolf' for nothing."

I didn't answer.

"What do you think it wanted?" he asked.

"I don't know, but since no one's going to take it seriously, I'm sure we'll find out soon." I thought of Miles but pushed it aside. There was no proof he was behind the intrusion, and until I knew more, I wasn't going to freak anyone else out.

"And that's why one of you wanted to stay behind, at the bonfire."

I nodded. "Logan and Cambria said we shouldn't tell anyone else. That they'd race off into the woods to try and take it out on their own. We were going to watch and make sure it didn't come back, until the party died off."

Alex rubbed his jaw. "They've got a point. Too many glory seekers."

"That's what Cambria said."

"She called me an idiot."

"You were being one," I said. "She also thinks you're hot."

"Really? Huh. A hot idiot. Not sure how I feel about that."

I rolled my eyes for effect, but I had to fight a smile.

"You realize we're conversing calmly–almost pleasantly–again." He sounded on the verge of a smile. "If a stranger heard this and didn't know any better, he'd think we were friends."

"Huh. Imagine that."

Alex's eyes stayed on mine for a long moment, and just like that, I knew we'd become friends. I wasn't sure how–or why–it had happened; I was pretty certain he still despised the Werewolf side of me, but right now, it didn't matter. We were no longer enemies. It felt nice.

Behind me, the door to Griffin Hall creaked open, and I jumped. A senior emerged and headed off down the trail, whispering into an earpiece hooked onto one side of his face.

"I need to get back," Alex said, staring after the other boy for a moment.

I nodded. "I guess I do, too. I was ordered back to my room for the night." I sighed. "I hate that I can't go back and keep an eye on things."

"I'll do it. You go."

"You will?"

"My patrols take me right by there, and I'm on duty most of the night."

"I don't understand, why are you guys patrolling if the wards are in place?"

Something passed over Alex's face and was gone. "Protocol. Training. And there's more of us tonight because of the bonfire."

"So they do care about the party?"

He nodded. "They let it happen because they know it's good for morale. And Headmaster tries to be cool. Anyway, I'll get some extra guys to help, and I'll keep an eye out."

"Thanks, Alex. I appreciate it."

"You can owe me. I'll collect at training on Monday. We'll add a mile to our run or something."

I groaned. "Maybe saving lives isn't worth it."

He laughed and jogged away. "Later," he called. Then he disappeared into the moonlit trees.

I WAS HALFWAY ACROSS THE COURTYARD WHEN A SHADOW MOVED, blocking the twinkling lights, and I realized I wasn't alone. I assumed it was Alex, wanting to add one more torture to the list for Monday's training. I slowed and changed direction, heading towards it. I rounded the corner of a low-lying wall that surrounded the center fountain and a hand clamped down on my wrist. I stifled a scream.

"Sshh!" Cambria hissed. She pulled me down beside her in a jerky movement, and my butt hit the concrete.

"What the heck?" I demanded.

"We're going to Logan's room. I need you to be quiet, and do what I say."

She grabbed my hand and jumped up, keeping her back bent and her head low, and headed for the far side of Lexington Hall. I followed, trying to keep low with her. She stopped at a side door that I'd seen before but always avoided. It said, 'Staff Only'. Cambria pulled it open, and we slipped inside.

The doorway led directly down to the landing above the boys' dorm. Cambria darted through and headed down the stairs. She still had my hand in hers and I struggled to keep up without tripping. At the bottom was a fork of hallways like in the girls' dorm. Cambria took a right and we ran. Somewhere behind us, on the main hall, a door opened. We darted around the corner and leaned against the wall, trying to breathe without making a sound. Cambria pulled on my hand and urged us on. We ran halfway down and stopped in front of a door with the number eighty on it. Cambria opened it without knocking and yanked me inside.

Logan was seated at a desk identical to mine. The only real difference between my room and his was that at some point, someone had painted the walls ocean blue. And the bed opposite his was bare. He didn't have to worry about a roommate.

I looked at Cambria, but she held a finger to her lips. We all waited, and even though I never heard anything in the hall, she must've decided the coast was clear because she exhaled and sank onto Logan's bed, pulling her ankles up and tucking her feet underneath her.

"We can't stay long," she said. "Kids will be back from the bonfire soon and we won't be able to get out."

"Why are we here?" I asked.

"We need to figure out what we're going to do about tonight," she said.

"There's nothing we can do. No one believes us," said Logan.

"Alex does," I said.

Both of them looked at me, eyes wide with surprise, so I relayed my conversation with Alex. Minus the part where'd I'd told him Cambria thought he was hot.

"Well, that makes him slightly less of an idiot," Cambria said.

"That covers tonight, but what about tomorrow and the next day?" Logan asked. "There's a Werewolf out there who knows a way to get through our wards. He'll come back, probably with his pack. It's only a matter of when."

"I know," I said. "But there's not much we can do if Headmaster doesn't believe us."

Logan didn't say anything.

"So we're going to pretend like it never happened? Wait to be attacked by a pack of Werewolves and know we didn't do anything to stop it?" Cambria jumped up and began to pace.

I sat on the edge of the bare mattress to stay out of her way. "I think we need proof of what happened before anyone will believe us."

"The only way we could get proof is if it happens again," Logan said.

"That'll be too late," Cambria said.

I agreed but didn't say anything. Something was nagging at me. If not for the goose bumps, my money would've been on Miles. But Miles wasn't a Werewolf. A dirty blood, yes, but his DNA had turned out like mine and made him a Hunter instead of a wolf. His presence had never caused a reaction for me. Whatever it was in those woods tonight had definitely been a Werewolf.

Had Miles sent someone after me?

"We need to know what it wanted in the first place," Logan said.

"And we need to know how the hell it got through," Cambria added.

The problem was that none of us had any clue about either.

"What's really weird is Vera not sensing it," said Logan. "Any Hunter with the ability to work wards should be able to feel that. It's the whole point of wards. She should've felt that before she felt you." He looked at me.

"You think something's wrong with her ability to work the wards?" I asked.

"Or she's lying," Cambria said. Logan and I looked at her, letting that possibility hang in the air.

"So, wait. Vera's a traitor?" Logan asked.

"No way," I said. "She's a leader of The Cause. She wants peace. Letting a Werewolf through her wards to terrorize a high school is the opposite of what she stands for."

"I don't know," said Cambria. "It would explain a lot about her denying that she felt it and how the Werewolf got through in the first place. I mean, what is she doing back? I thought she was gone on a mission with Victoria."

"Victoria." I groaned. "This means she's back, doesn't it?"

"And just in time to have a Werewolf come though her wards," Cambria went on, ignoring me.

I squeezed my eyes shut. I was getting a headache, and I didn't want to think about Vera being evil. "There's got to be another explanation."

"So, we're back to needing proof," Cambria said. "Any ideas?"

"None that don't involve those consequences Headmaster was talking about," Logan said. "And I really don't want to get expelled. My parents would kill me."

"All we can do is wait for an opportunity. Keep our eyes open," I said.

"We need to get out of here." Cambria stood. "But we all agree that we need to find a way to prove this, right? And none of this information leaves this room."

We all agreed, and Cambria and I slipped out.

CHAPTER FIFTEEN

Victoria was back.

And she wasn't ignoring me, or giving me space, or skipping out of our room early to avoid me in the mornings. She was there. All the time. With her acidic smile, and nasty comments, and at least two minions beside her at all times. She seemed to be extra full of herself after being away on whatever secret mission Vera had taken her on and more determined than ever to make my life miserable.

I'd come to realize being a junior had saved me from the outright hazing the freshman got because I'd overhead enough stories to know what I was missing. Midnight walks into the woods wearing thin pajamas with nothing but a broken compass to guide you back; being woken at three a.m. so you could perform your best karaoke version of 'Twinkle ,Twinkle' using your bed as a stage–and getting yelled at by half the dorm floor when you woke them up because of it.

Those were just the girls. The guys had it even worse. Something called liquid sit-ups sounded particularly horrific. A group of freshman lined up on the ground, single file, and began doing sit ups, while the upper classmen slowly poured water on their face. I was really glad I wasn't a freshman.

So, I understood it could've been worse. And since I'd managed to miss all that simply by being in the eleventh grade, Victoria was forced to think of new and creative ways to torture me. Dirt in my suitcase led me to finally unpack on Monday. Tuesday was worms in my bed. Wednesday morning, I woke up to Demi and another girl, Merona, leaning over me with a razor in their hands and evil smiles on their faces.

They were staring at my eyebrows.

My reaction wasn't pretty.

I'd jumped up so fast I'd knocked Merona over in her haste to get away. Demi was faster than her friend and made it out of reach, but Merona wasn't so lucky. My temper flared in a way that was so automatic it was primal. I was still half asleep when I reached down and plucked Merona up by her hair.

"What the hell do you think you're doing?" I demanded.

"Victoria said–" Merona broke off and bit her lip. She was trying not to cry.

Behind her, near the door, Demi leaned against the wall and watched, cool as ice. Merona definitely wasn't cut out for evil.

"Stay the hell out of my room," I yelled into Merona's face. She squeezed her eyes shut and nodded vigorously. I jerked my eyes to Demi's and stared her down.

"Message received," she said. She sounded bored.

It was all I could do not to bruise her flawless face with my knuckles. I let go of Merona's hair, and she sank to the floor like a ragdoll. That's when the water works started. I rolled my eyes. No way was I going to feel bad. They were going to shave my eyebrows! But Merona wasn't moving and Demi made no move to help her. She was eyeing her with annoyance and looked ready to leave her there. Victoria was, of course, nowhere to be found.

I sighed and grabbed my shower bag. I stomped to the door, pausing to glare at Demi.

"Be gone when I get back," I said. I jerked a thumb at Merona. "And take her with you."

"Whatever."

I marched out, seething.

THE REST OF WEDNESDAY, AND INTO THURSDAY, REMAINED INCIDENT free but I was on edge even without Victoria's torturing. Knowing a Werewolf stalked the woods nearby and being able to do nothing about it was making me crazy. Cambria and I had talked about patrolling on our own, but there wasn't time, between classes and my training with Alex. Three of us wouldn't have been sufficient to cover the entire perimeter anyway.

By Friday, classes were getting easier, and I could feel myself adjusting–if that were possible–to life at Wood Point. I learned the names of more of my classmates and people were saying hi to me in the hallway. The paper bag incident was already forgotten. Based on the gossip I got from Cambria, everyone was talking about a fight that had gone down between Levi and Jeremy – a kid from my Defensive Maneuvers class. Both were sporting serious bruises so I didn't doubt it. I was glad the gossip train had moved on from me.

Even Defensive Maneuvers was getting easier, which was still the hardest of all my classes. Raj had assured me he wasn't going easy on me, but I noticed he was landing fewer hits during our sparring exercises, and I could feel a rhythm in my movements that hadn't been there before. It felt good. Now if only Algebra was that easy. Then again, that was universal and had nothing to do with being at a school designed to ready you for combat. If all I was going to do was fight Werewolves for the rest of my life, why did I need to know what x equaled?

In the back of my mind, I knew the comfortable feeling was an illusion. It wouldn't last. For one, I still hadn't heard from Wes. Not that I had time. Most of my free time was still taken with training. Alex had added an extra half hour to our time this week for toning. I never knew until then, but I hated lifting weights almost as much as I hate running.

Alex thought it was hilarious–he'd never met a Hunter who hated exercise as much as I did. I let him give me a hard time because even though he snickered whenever I complained, it was friendly between us and that was progress.

He'd been keeping me updated on anything he heard in patrols about any breach or Werewolf sightings, which was zilch, and even though I knew he believed me about the night at the bonfire, he'd made it very clear I should be letting the senior patrols handle it from here. I wasn't sure I could do that, but I kept my mouth shut.

WHEN TRAINING ENDED THAT AFTERNOON, I LEFT ALEX IN THE GYM. He'd decided to stay and do some extra reps of his own on some machine he called the Bodycraft. The name alone sounded sweaty and painful, so I got out of there as quick as he'd let me go–partly to escape the exercise and partly to escape the view. At first I'd chalked it up to being stressed about Wes and our lack of communication since I'd arrived at Wood Point, but I knew it wasn't that. And I caught myself staring more and more lately, especially when he got going on the free weights. The sight of all those muscles bunching and moving along his back and shoulders was mesmerizing. I told myself it was more of a general appreciation for toned anatomy and not physical attraction, but even I knew I was full of crap.

On the way back to the dorm, I was so caught up in lying to myself about Alex's toned abs that I turned the corner and ran smack into Vera.

"Oh, sorry," I said, stepping back and wiping the stray hair out of my face.

Her lips tipped up in a polite smile. "Tara, it's good to see you again. Settling in okay?"

I nodded, suddenly nervous. Cambria's biggest theory still pegged Vera for a traitor. I couldn't see it, but standing in front of her, speaking to her now, I couldn't help but wonder.

"I wanted to touch base with you again about our conversation last weekend," said Vera.

"What about it?"

"You said you thought there'd been a breach in my wards."

"I didn't think there was a breach, I know there was," I said, frustrated at her choice of words.

She went on without acknowledging the difference. "I want you to know I looked into it. I've been checking on the wards daily, and I can tell you that everything is intact. There's been no break, authorized or not. We are completely sealed here."

"You keep saying that, but I know what I felt." I was determined to make her believe me. "Is there some other way that someone could come through, without you feeling it? Any possibility at all?"

Vera frowned, and I knew I'd hit a nerve. Then her expression cleared and became neutral again, unreadable. "The only way to come though without my body reacting is with the bypass phrase."

"What's that?"

"It's a backdoor of sorts, through the fault lines."

"Like a password?"

"Precisely. But no one, save a few trusted friends, know it."

"Is it possible someone who knows it gave it out?"

Vera's frown deepened and she straightened, peering down at me. "Tara, you can't go around making accusations simply because you think you felt something. I know what it's like to be your age with all of those hormones. You can't tell one feeling or emotion from another. I assure you there's nothing to worry about with the wards."

"And I assure you there is." My hands knotted into fists at my sides, and I was literally biting my tongue to keep from snapping back. She was blaming this on teenage hormones? "Either someone close to you is a traitor or there's another way in. I'm not imagining things."

Vera sighed and the polite, distant look she always wore dropped away, revealing an expression of frustration and an exhaustion I hadn't noticed before. "I don't want to believe you're imagining things, Tara, but you've given me limited information to go on. I've been out to that spot every day since. There's no sign of a breach. Except for you. I felt you and your friends the second you stepped over the line. Which is as it should be. The bypass phrase is a possibility I honestly hadn't let myself consider, but I will. Will that suffice?"

I nodded; surprised at the small glimpse of honesty she was giving. "Thanks."

She blinked, and the mask was back in place. No emotion shown in her eyes, and the tired lines had been smoothed over. "Now, how is that Lineage project going?" she asked.

"It's fine," I said, instantly nervous again. "Why do you keep asking me about that, anyway?" She didn't answer; I thought I knew why. "Is it because we're related?" I blurted.

"What?" Her only reaction was a slight widening of her eyes. I had to give it to her, she was always composed. Even when I'd seen her gunning for Benny, come to think of it, she'd remained cool and calm. "No, I'm not asking about the project because we're related."

"But you didn't want me to know," I pointed

"I didn't think it mattered."

"Why not?"

"Because you barely know me. How is knowing that I'm your great aunt going to help you trust your destiny?" I didn't answer. "I wasn't trying to lie to you, but your mother made it clear a long time ago that she wanted nothing to do with her family. She thought it would protect you. I had to respect her wishes."

"But that's over now. I'm here, aren't I?" I waved an arm around, gesturing to Wood Point–and my life in general.

"You are." She nodded. "But for the rest of these kids, being here is the end of their education as a Hunter. For you, it's just a beginning. I'm also trying to respect that."

"Then why do you keep asking me about the project?"

Her eyes glazed over, and I finally realized the real reason for her questions. "You had a vision."

She stayed quiet for several seconds, her eyes glassy and faraway as she relived whatever images she'd seen before, and then her eyes came into focus again. "Yes," she said simply.

"Well? Are you going to tell me what it is?"

She shook her head. "It was a mistake to tell you the first one. Destiny is something better left unknown. It needs to be discovered in layers, not run at like a finish line. This one is much better left unknown, but it will be a piece to your puzzle. Without it, you will not become the leader you need to be."

"What does that even mean?"

She smiled a tight smile, and I knew that was all I was going to get. "You should get going. Dinner is already being served."

She turned to leave and then stopped, looking over her shoulder at me. "And Tara? You should try getting a better handle on that temper. It will get you into trouble if you're not careful."

I opened my mouth and closed it again. It was no use even asking. When she was gone, I turned and headed for the dorms, and a shower.

"I MISSED YOU TOO, HONEY."

The sound of Victoria's baby talk wafted into the hallway, and I halted before I reached the door to my room. I had a pretty good idea what I would be walking in on and there was no way. Not again. I stood there and debated while my wet hair dripped onto my shoulders. Deciding to chance it, I leaned over, so I wouldn't have to actually see into the half open doorway, and knocked.

"I'm giving you a warning. I'll be back in ten. Be done," I called out.

"I can be done in five," Levi called back. "Want to come back early and test me?"

I made a show of gagging, and Levi laughed.

"Get a life, mutt. Come back tomorrow," Victoria called.

I sighed, knowing full well she'd still be in there two hours from now, just to spite me. I shuffled down to Cambria's room and had to force myself not to stop at Mrs. Fincham's office and report her for being physically unsanitary.

Cambria let me in and shook her head when I told her why I was here.

"My roommate is out. God knows where. She has a better social life than you and I put together so you can hang here 'til later," she said.

"Thanks." I used her desk mirror to pull my hair back and then we sat on her bed. "You'll be interested to know I talked to Vera."

"Did you call her auntie and everything?"

"I told her I know we're related."

"What did she say?"

"She said she wasn't allowed to tell me before, because of my mom, and now she's trying to keep her distance out of consideration since I've had so much to settle into lately. She asked me about the lineage project again."

Cambria wrinkled her nose. "Just like a great aunt to keep bringing up homework."

"It's more than that. She had a vision about it. She won't tell me what it is, though."

"Why not?"

"She talked about destiny and how its better left discovered slowly instead of something to chase after. Whatever the heck that means. She talks in riddles."

Cambria nodded. "All old ladies do that. It makes them sound wiser or something. Did she say anything about the wards?"

"She said she believes me. At least I think she does. But she says there's no sign of it in the wards. She's been checking on them more often, though, so that's something."

"Now she admits to believing you?" Cambria's eyebrow–the one visible underneath her bangs–shot up. "Sounds fishy."

"I found out something else. She says there's something called a bypass phrase. Sort of a password to get around the wards, and if someone uses it, she wouldn't feel them pass through."

"Do you think that's how the Werewolf got in?"

"I don't know. She insists she only tells people she trusts what it is."

"Well, maybe she's wrong about who she can trust. Maybe that person is the traitor."

I nodded. "She says she'll look into it, but I don't know. That would mean investigating the people she trusts, and I don't know if she'll take it seriously."

"Hmm. We'll have to keep an eye out. I wish Logan would quit staring after Victoria and actually help us figure this out."

"What the heck does he see in her? I don't get it."

Cambria snorted. "Good guys and bad girls... Hmm. Speaking of impossible relationships, what's up with you and long-distance-lover-boy?"

I sighed. "Absolutely nothing. I haven't talked to him in forever."

"Yeah, the no phone policy sucks. You could email."

"Actually, I have a phone."

Cambria's eyes popped. "You do? And you didn't tell me? What kind of new best friend are you?"

"It doesn't matter. The only place it gets reception is the roof of Griffin Hall, and I'm not going back there again."

"What's the problem? And how do you know it gets reception there?"

"Alex told me. But he hangs out up there. I can't call Wes in front of him."

"Why not?" Cambria's eyebrows disappeared underneath her hair. "He's just your trainer… right?"

I could hear it in her voice. She was dying for me to admit Alex was yummy. Which meant there was no way I could tell her how jittery I got every time he spotted me on the weights. I wasn't even admitting that to myself yet.

"Whatever," I said. "I don't want to see Alex unless I have to. The point is, I can't call, and when I do, Wes doesn't even pick up. I miss him but I don't even know if he feels the same way anymore." A sharp pain shot through my chest as I said the words. Until now I hadn't realized that was the real problem.

"Duh. Of course he misses you. But he has a job to do now. Besides, you're destined to be with him, remember?"

"I don't know if I believe that. The future changes all the time based on our actions. What about the destiny of me being a part of

CHAS like my grandma? That's like working for the other side, so which one is my true future?"

Cambria reached out and squeezed my hand. "Visions aside, you still have a choice," she said.

I looked at her, thinking of Wes and the pull I felt even when he was gone. "Do I?"

CHAPTER SIXTEEN

Alex was in the clearing, already stretching, when I got there for Saturday's training session. I hung back near the tree line and watched as he extended his arms high over his head, my attention taken first by the utter concentration that showed on his face. His eyes were free of the harsh business-like expression he wore when we were together. Instead, he looked calm and completely absorbed by the movement of his own body. His biceps flexed as he bent his elbows and pulled slowly from side to side. He wore a thin gray shirt, and he was facing slightly away from me, but I couldn't help but wonder what the muscles would look like, flexing across his bare chest when he pulled himself that way. I shook the thought away, as I'd done every other time I'd caught myself thinking along these lines. Alex was my trainer. I needed to learn from him, and this line of thinking would only distract me.

"Hey," I said, stepping clear of the trees and walking towards Alex.

He turned and let his arms drop. "Hey."

"So, what are we doing today?" I stopped a few yards away and turned sideways before I started stretching. I needed the action as an excuse to look away. I kept my eyes on my toes while I mimicked the arm stretches I'd seen Alex doing.

"Tracking."

I looked up in mid-stretch, surprised he'd said anything other than running. I would've liked to hear sparring, or combat, or weapons training, or something interesting, but tracking was still better than running any day. I'd take what I could get.

"What do I do?" I asked.

"Watch and listen, for now." I scowled but he ignored me and kept talking. "Learning how to properly track is just as important as learning how to fight. If you can't track your enemy, you'll never get close enough to do battle, so even the best fighting skills are worthless."

"Unless they find and attack you first," I pointed out.

Alex gave me a look and I shut my mouth.

"We're going to stay together today, so I'll start by showing you how to track smaller animals, like rabbits and squirrels. Let's go."

I followed Alex into the woods and within seconds, we were off the path, wandering through close-knit trees and fallen limbs. There seemed to be no real direction or destination to our movements; or so I thought until I looked at Alex's face. He wore an expression of such deep concentration that I wondered if he even remembered I was beside him. It was clear he was totally into this.

"There," he said in a hushed tone. He pointed ahead, but I couldn't figure out what he meant.

"What?"

"That broken twig there. That's a rabbit."

"How do you know?"

"See how the leaves are parted like this?" He bent over the twig and pointed gingerly, careful not to disturb anything.

I still couldn't see what he meant, but I nodded so he'd go on.

"Now, we look for the next marker." His eyes scanned the ground in every direction. "There." He shuffled a few feet away to another spot that looked exactly like the first one. "See how this one is broken and turned? And these leaves are parted from the body dragging as it hopped."

"Okay," I said slowly.

Alex looked up, finally realizing I had no idea what he was talking about. He sighed and stood up. "We're going to have to start small. C'mon."

I didn't want to mention that I wasn't sure you could get any smaller than a rabbit so I stayed silent and walked with him.

"Tracking is basically a matter of being able to see the forest for how it is, untouched, and recognizing the signs of an intruder. Whether the intruder means harm or not, whether it's a bird or a human or a strong wind, it will leave a mark. The trick is learning to recognize the difference. Watch." He bent down and picked up a fallen branch and cracked it over his knee, snapping it in two. He held it out to me, broken sides up. "Do you see how the ends are jagged from being snapped?"

"I guess so," I said.

"Now look over there, at that fallen branch." He pointed. "No one pulled it loose. It fell on its own. Do you see the end that broke off the trunk? See the difference between that one and this one?"

I stared for a minute and then slowly nodded. "That one is a cleaner break than yours."

"Exactly. So you can tell where nature left its mark versus a human or an intruder. Those are the things you look for when you're tracking. The larger the animal, the bigger the mark. Understand?"

"So far. How do you know so much about this?"

His jaw tightened but his expression stayed neutral. "My father was a tracker."

"And he showed you," I finished for him.

"He used to take me with him on his days off. We would hunt small game for dinner and he'd show me what to look for, how to track." His voice had an edge to it that hadn't been there a moment ago.

I remembered what Cambria had said, about Alex's dad drinking after what happened when Alex was a kid.

"Do you still talk to him?" I asked.

Alex shook his head, his gaze far away. "He died last year. Liver failure."

"Oh. I'm sorry."

"Don't be. It was his own damn fault for letting the bottle win. Well, his, and the pack that started it all."

"What do you mean?"

Alex took a deep breath, like the weight of the world rested in whatever memory he was about to divulge. I waited, unsure if I'd overstepped but unwilling to take it back.

"When I was a kid, a pack of rogue Werewolves attacked my family. My dad had been tracking and killing their pack members for weeks, one by one. On orders from CHAS. The pack leader followed him home one night and waited until he left for work the next day. Then they attacked. I was getting ready to leave for school. I opened the door and there they were. But they were men. I didn't understand what was happening until they'd shoved into the house and began to shift.

"When I realized what they were, I yelled for my mom to get out, but a couple of them had already pushed their way into the kitchen. She screamed, and I tried to get to her, but the pack leader had stayed human. He grabbed me and locked me in the basement."

"How did you get out?"

"I didn't, at first. They–" He stopped and turned away.

"I'm sorry. You don't have to tell me," I said.

He looked back at me. "I haven't told many people this story, and maybe I'm crazy for saying it, but I trust you, Tara." He inched closer, his chest rising and falling with heavy breaths. "Can I trust you?"

"Yes," I whispered. I was completely caught up in the story – and this moment.

He nodded, like that was all the reassurance he needed. "That day, they tortured me. They used their claws and other weapons so I wouldn't be too wounded to walk. When evening came, they brought me upstairs to wait for my dad. They had me on the porch when he came home. He saw me from the road and called for backup. Then he charged the house."

"How did you guys get out, though? I mean, your dad against a whole pack?"

He shook his head. "You didn't know my dad. He was insanely focused in battle. He'd have made a great general for the human army. Strong. Strategic. Lethal. He took down a few on the porch before they could even shift. He threw me into the car and then went back inside the house, looking for my mom. When he found her – the way she looked – I think it broke his concentration. A couple of them managed to get their teeth in him. But then backup came and drove the rest of them off."

"Your dad recovered from the bites?" I asked.

"They weren't that bad. Mine were worse. They'd waited until right before my dad came home so I would be alive when he saw me, but…" A shudder rippled through his body, and the ghost of whatever replayed through his mind flitted over his face.

And in that moment, I understood his hatred for Werewolves.

"But you're okay. They saved you," I said.

"Yeah." His voice was heavy. "But my mother wasn't. And neither was my dad, after that day. Drank himself to death, in the end."

The haunted look in his eyes dimmed, but I could still see the pain and loss he felt, and I wished there was something I could say. But there was nothing. All around me, birds chirped and sunlight streamed down, warming the chilly forest floor. It seemed out of place in its cheerfulness after the conversation we'd had. I wrapped my arms around myself to chase away the melancholy.

"Alex, I'm sorry," I began.

"Let's keep walking." His tone was brusque and devoid of any emotion.

It was a tone I'd heard him use before, and I suspected it was his way of dealing with it all. It changed the way I reacted when he spoke that way. I nodded and fell into step beside him.

And for the rest of the afternoon, Alex talked about tracking.

He went on about the difference in how a trail would look if left by a rabbit versus a cat or even a Werewolf. He showed me what to look for if a trail seemed to end out of nowhere, and how to find it again. Under any other circumstances, I would've been bored out of my mind with a subject like this, but it was fascinating to watch Alex's excitement. The way his whole mind seemed to submerse itself in the process; trying to guess what his prey was thinking. I couldn't look away. Something about his expression in those moments was more open than I'd ever seen him. It was easy to picture Alex as a boy, in the woods with his dad, being taught these very same things.

"Okay, same time tomorrow."

"On a Sunday?" I wrinkled my nose. Sundays were my only day off.

"We're going out again, separately, and you're going to track me. I want to show you how to avoid leaving a trail."

"Okay." I turned to head back to the dorms.

"Tara?"

"Yeah?" When he didn't say anything, I looked up and met his eyes. He watched me with an unreadable expression. "What?"

He shook his head like he was clearing it of whatever had held his attention and seemed to remember I was waiting for him to say something.

"Vera said she talked to you," he said. "She believes you about the breach, I think."

I nodded slowly. I wasn't sure what I'd been expecting him to say, but it hadn't been this. There was still pain in his expression, though he'd pushed it to the back. "She told me. She didn't seem very bothered by the possibility that someone she trusts helped get that Werewolf through."

"But you understand now, right? About her, I mean?"

"Um, sure," I said, tilting my head in confusion.

He rubbed his head and paced, obviously frustrated by whatever I was supposed to understand. "With the disease, it's hard for her. I think she won't admit how weak she is," he said. "I'm glad she told…" He trailed off as he met my eyes – and realized I had no idea what he was talking about. "Shit."

I stepped closer. "What disease? What's wrong with Vera?"

Alex tipped his head back and stared up, mumbling to himself. He ran a hand over his face. "All right, look. I wasn't supposed to say anything, least of all, to you. I don't know why she cares if you know."

I tapped my foot. "What are you talking about?"

"Vera's sick, Tara."

"Sick?" There was some small part in the back of my mind that understood the depth of the meaning behind the single word—that this wasn't some flu virus or head cold–but I couldn't go there yet. It was too unexpected and confusing. "No, I saw her yesterday. She was fine."

"You're right. She does look fine, mostly. But it's not good." His lips pressed together in a grim line. "I'm sorry, Tara."

I waved a hand, ignoring the last part. I didn't need sympathy, and I was pretty sure Vera wouldn't want it, either. "What is it? Cancer?"

"No one knows. She's had all the tests. They all come back inconclusive. But she's exhausted and weak. It's getting worse. That's all I know."

"So this virus does what? Makes her numb enough to miss the feeling of a Werewolf passing though her wards?"

He shrugged. "She won't admit to it, because she refuses to say how bad off she is. Kane's got a nurse checking on her but she's fighting him on it. She doesn't want anyone to know she's sick. I thought when she said she'd talked to you… I thought you knew."

We sat down on the grass and fell into an awkward silence. I fumbled with the cap to my water bottle until I couldn't take it anymore. This was too much. First, Vera was having visions again–of something other than me leading The Cause, something that would directly shape my future, then she's my great aunt, and now she was dying? And I was supposed to what? It wasn't like I didn't care. I felt sympathy – just not the kind I would've felt if it were someone I actually felt a connection to. She didn't feel like family.

Alex watched me, waiting. I wasn't sure for what. It was obvious he knew Vera and I were related. I didn't really want to get into that, though, so I left it alone. His expression was sympathetic, bordering on pity. The thing was I had no idea how I felt – or how I was supposed to feel, so it irritated me.

I stood up. "I've gotta get ready for dinner."

"Don't say anything, okay?"

"The wards aren't secure. You know what this means, right?"

"What happened Saturday will happen again."

"Exactly –"

I was about to say that we needed to do something about the problem. Vera's illness was too dangerous to keep it a secret. Alex cut me off, his tone biting and rough.

"They'll keep coming until they get what they came for. It's in their nature. They're animals."

My jaw hardened, and he seemed to realize what he'd said. He opened his mouth like he was about to say something, but I didn't want to hear any of it. After what he'd told me about his past I might be able to understand why he despised Werewolves; but he had a bad habit of lumping me into a category of killers, and I couldn't overlook that.

"Save it." I turned and ran for the trail.

I RACED DOWN THE HALL, MY SHOES SQUEAKING ON THE LINOLEUM floor, my wet hair flung out behind me. I was twenty minutes late to meet Logan. I'd raced through a shower and back upstairs for dinner. By then, the dining hall was basically empty. I'd had just enough time to grab a pop tart and a soda before the lunch ladies chased me off and closed the door behind me with a thud.

I slowed my pace to a walk a few steps outside the library doorway. Even so, my heavy breathing and mussed hair had the librarian glaring at me and shushing me, even though I hadn't said anything. I hurried past her and disappeared into the row labeled 'Combat', cutting through to what had already become our 'usual spot' in the back of the stacks.

Logan was there with his nose in some thick volume with numbers in weird formulas written all over the front. I didn't bother reading the title. I was surprised to find Cambria there, though. She hadn't joined us since her tragic ending with Phillipe.

"What's up?" I slumped into the chair beside Cambria. "What are you doing here?" I asked, breaking off a bite of pastry. I froze with it halfway to my open mouth.

She ignored me, or didn't see my reaction, because her face was stuffed inside a book.

"Are you reading?" I gaped at her.

"Hang on," she mumbled, still scanning the page.

I looked from her to Logan, who smirked. "Has hell frozen over? Because I missed that memo," I said.

Logan grunted and went back to his book.

Cambria looked up at me, stuck out her tongue, and went back to reading. A minute passed. I munched the pop tart, waiting.

"Okay, got it," she said, looking up and pushing the book away. Her eyes were bright and her fingers tapped the open pages to a beat only she could hear.

"Got what?" I asked.

She held the book up and read a passage. "A bypass phrase can be used to breach a protective ward only if spoken exactly as it was programmed into the wards by the original maker. If the words are spoken precisely, the maker will not feel the presence of whoever crosses the threshold."

"You're doing research?" I asked.

"It's a one-time deal, trust me. Logan said he'd do my math homework if I helped find out more about this bypass phrase thing."

"No, you said I could do your math homework since you were doing research on our pest problem. I never agreed," said Logan.

"Same difference," Cambria mumbled.

"That's great, but I'm afraid it's a waste of time," I said, leaning back against my chair and staring down at my soda can.

"Don't say that. We'll figure this out."

"Guys. I don't think the bypass phrase is the answer." They looked at me, waiting for me to go on. "Vera's sick," I said, finally.

"What do you mean 'sick'?" Cambria asked.

"It's serious. I don't know exactly what but it's bad. Her senses aren't working properly which is why she didn't feel the Werewolf come through last weekend."

"How do you know?" Logan asked.

"Alex told me."

"He's sharing information now?" Cambria's brow went up. "Huh. Well, that doesn't get him off the hook for being an idiot," she said. Then she looked at me with something resembling pity. "Are you okay? I mean, is she going to be okay?"

"I don't know what she is. And I'm fine. I barely know her." My tone sounded more defensive than I'd intended but what did she expect? I felt bad, but just because we were related on paper didn't make me connected to her any more than a stranger off the street. I looked at Logan. He hadn't said much. "What are you thinking?" I asked.

He cleared his throat. "Does anyone else know Vera's sick?"

"I don't know. Alex made it sound like a pretty big secret. Why?"

"Even if the Werewolf that came through last weekend doesn't know about the reason for her weakness, it won't take them long to figure out that they have a free pass inside, either. It's only a matter of time."

We all exchanged a look. Logan was right.

"What should we do? We can't exactly go to Vera," Cambria said.

"No, we can't," I agreed.

"We need to patrol," said Cambria. "The seniors only go out so far. They don't go all the way to the wards, and they stick mostly to the front entrance perimeter."

"How do you know?" I asked.

She smiled. "It's probably best if I don't tell you his name. Protect the innocent, and all that."

"Cambria," I said. "Please tell me you haven't been out compelling senior patrols to give you secret information."

"It's not secret. I asked. He told me."

"Willingly?" I narrowed my eyes. "Or under duress?"

She shrugged and looked at me with wide eyes.

I sighed, long and loud. "I don't want to know."

"You're probably right," she agreed. "The point is, the eastern and western boundaries are wide open. No patrols there unless there's a student event–like the bonfire–to supervise. Anyone could come through."

"We need to be ready," said Logan. "I'm going to see if I can find us some stakes to carry. We need to be armed."

"They have weapons here?" I asked.

"They keep them locked up. Only seniors can check them out for training and stuff," he said.

"So how are you going to get a hold of any of it?" I asked. "Do you want me to ask Alex?" They both gave me a look. "Yeah, okay, good point." Alex might believe me when I said there'd been a breach, but he was still way too much of a rule follower to condone something like this.

"I'll do it," said Cambria.

Logan and I exchanged a look and finally, against my better judgment, I nodded. "Okay. But be careful."

"Of course," she agreed, in a voice that I knew meant she wasn't concerned nearly enough.

"We'll start tomorrow," Logan said.

"It'll have to be in the afternoon. I have training in the morning," I said.

"Fine. We'll meet at the back doors after lunch. Cambria can you have the weapons by then?" She nodded. "It's set, then."

We worked on my lineage paper after that. Cambria got bored and left, saying something about rather being poked in the eye with a stick. I knew how she felt. Family tree stuff wasn't the most exciting, even for someone who was seeing the names for the first time.

"So, this lady was my great-great-grandmother? And she was on something called the high council?" I stared down at a black and white photo of a woman in a high-necked dress. Her expression was solemn and her eyes were sad. She had my mother's cheekbones.

"Looks like it. Back then, they called it the High Council. It disbanded after a bunch of the members were killed in an attack, and when it reformed it became what we know as CHAS."

"So, my family, at least my mother's side, has always been on the council?"

He shrugged. "You come from a political background."

"Yippee."

Logan looked at me. "You know, it could be a good thing. The chance to make a difference and all that."

"I've thought of that, but how many of them do you think will listen to me? Especially knowing I'm a–"

"Hybrid?"

"What?"

"It's easier to say hybrid than dirty blood."

"Isn't that a car with good gas mileage?"

Logan rolled his eyes. "Or it's a mix of two completely different elements. Like you. Anyway, you were saying?"

"Huh?" I tried to remember what we'd been talking about. "Oh yeah, the council thing. I don't know. I don't think people will want me to be a part of something like that if they know I'm a hybrid," I said, putting emphasis on the new term. "It wouldn't win me any votes, that's for sure."

"It's not about votes with them. It's a lineage thing. Your family has a spot and since your mom doesn't want it, your grandma will probably hand it off to you."

"So, I don't have a choice?"

"It's not a democracy if that's what you mean."

"Well, it should be. That's part of the problem with this culture. Probably one of the reasons everyone's so cold. Nobody gets a say in anything."

Logan leaned back in his chair and folded his arms behind his head. "So, change it."

I tilted my head and looked at him. "You'd make a great council member."

"Nah. I'm going to close myself off in a lab somewhere and not come out until I'm rich enough to date supermodels."

I rolled my eyes. "Seriously. You're diplomatic and patient and good with people. Cambria wouldn't be bad either."

Logan laughed. “Good one.”

“Well, she can be convincing anyway.”

“But will she use her powers for good or evil?” He made a face as he said it and changed his voice to a creepy tone.

I laughed. “When she picks a side, we’ll decide whether to add her to our council list.”

“Deal.”

CHAPTER SEVENTEEN

"Hook this around your ear." Alex handed me what looked like a blue-tooth device. I took it and hooked it on while he adjusted his.

It was Sunday. Time to test my tracker skills; I'd already hunted Alex, with zero success, earlier that morning. Now, Alex was going to hunt me. I watched while he pressed a button on the earpiece.

"Testing." His words echoed in my headphone.

I nodded and tested back.

"I'm going to give you thirty minutes and then I'm coming in full speed. You know where the wards are, right?" I nodded. "Make sure you stay inside them."

I narrowed my eyes at him. "You think I like breaking rules, just for fun, don't you?"

"That's not what I–" He broke off, ending the argument before it could begin. Then his expression changed. He looked concerned. "Did you have a chance to think about… what I said the other night?"

My jaw hardened. I'd done everything I could not to think about what he'd said about Vera. At least not directly. Mainly, I'd focused on how to compensate for the weak wards without actually letting her–or anyone else–know that I knew about her condition. I didn't know why, but the whole thing made me feel weird and self-conscious about my reaction.

"I'm good," I said.

His concern only deepened. "Look, I'm really sorry. I guess I shouldn't have said anything. I just thought you should know."

"We aren't close. Her and I." I watched him, waiting for the look of sympathy to go away. Needing it to. I really didn't want his pity.

"I know that. I mean, well, I've heard her make comments about your future with The Cause. I'm sure that complicates things for your role in CHAS. It's a lot of pressure, that's all."

He shrugged, and finally, the look of concern eased into a sort of 'whatever, I tried to help' look. Unfortunately, I wasn't relieved. Not after that.

"How do you know about that? Vera told you about her vision?"

"I may have heard her talking about it." His eyes shifted. "In passing."

I stared at him. It took a minute to pinpoint what was going on. "You eavesdropped?" My jaw slid open. I pictured Alex peeking down from the roof of Griffin Hall, like I had. The image was almost funny.

"You of all people should know how something like that can accidentally happen," he said.

His cheeks were pink, and he looked defensive. I'd never seen him embarrassed and the vulnerable look he was trying to cover up made it impossible not to laugh. I snickered and he glared at me. For some reason, the whole thing was adorable; the way he wouldn't quite meet my eyes and seemed so unsure of himself when normally he had such control. Geez, since when was blushing hot? I shook my head. Alex was mean. Alex was not hot. I repeated it until my head felt clearer.

I cleared my throat. "What exactly did you hear?"

"She was telling Kane about a vision she'd had. Something to do with abilities manifesting inside you. I didn't hear exactly what it was."

"What else?"

He shrugged. "That's basically it. After that they weren't so much talking anymore as… never mind."

"Oh. Eww." I squeezed my eyes shut against the mental picture left over from the night I'd seen them for myself. "Are they a couple?"

"It's not a shock if you've been around. They were engaged once. A long time ago."

"Seriously? What happened?"

"Werewolves happened. At least to Kane."

"So, his scar is really from–"

"Werewolves? Yeah. He and Vera were in The Cause together."

"I thought The Cause was formed by my parents and their friends."

"It was. The one we know today. Back then it was a different version. A true peace-keeping group."

"Different how?"

"A lot less fighting, for one. It was more about protests and peace marches and lobbying to CHAS for changes. Paperwork and speeches, mostly. The Werewolves took advantage of that and became violent. They launched night attacks, stalked the group and picked them off one by one when they were alone. It wasn't pretty."

Even though there was no way he'd been there–or even born yet, for that matter–there was disgust in his voice. I tried to ignore it for once and focus on the story.

"They were on a peace mission together, the two of them," he went on. "Vera was attacked and knocked from behind before she saw it coming. I think she passed out. Kane stepped in to save her. He took on four by himself. That's how he got the scars. After that, all he wanted was vengeance against the Werewolves. For her and for him. Vera didn't want any part of it. She said she was more convinced than ever that peace was the way to go, to end things like that from happening. They couldn't agree so they split. Kane went back to CHAS and offered his services as a team leader for special ops and Vera left."

"Wow, so they walked away from each other over that?"

"Politics are a major part of our lives, like it or not. Even without a leading role on either side, you'll end up caught in it somewhere."

Alex moved away, checking his earpiece again, but I stayed where I was, lost in thought. I didn't know why, but there was something completely ominous about those words. I couldn't escape the feeling that someday I'd have to choose, and that choice would draw a line between friends that couldn't, or wouldn't, be crossed. It made me sad to think about.

I wondered if Vera and Kane had truly worked things out and found a middle ground or if her sickness had been enough to push everything else to the side. Would being sick be enough for me to be with someone who thought so little of my morals and values?

"You ready?" Alex asked.

I adjusted my mouth piece and nodded. "Where should we meet after?"

"After what?"

"After the exercise is over," I said, with a look that said 'duh'.

He smiled, nice and wide. "That's cute. You think you'll evade me." He shook his head and went back to the magazine he'd already pulled out to pass the time.

I crossed my arms. "It could happen."

Alex's response was nothing more than a grunt and I could feel my defenses go up automatically; even though I knew he was right, evading him was a long shot. He was made for this kind of thing. He was probably an Indian in another life or something.

I slugged off into the woods and tried to pick a direction. I should've thought this out ahead of time, made a plan. Maybe it would've given me a better shot at beating him. I headed for the only place I thought Alex might not know about. The cave Cambria had taken me to. I could at least hide there for a while until enough time had passed that I could lose with dignity.

It was still early enough to be cool in the woods, so I had my jacket zipped up. I tried remembering some of the things Alex had told me about not leaving a trail and went slowly so I could watch my steps. At the thirty minute mark, I shed my jacket and sped up. I was still a few minutes away from the cave, and I decided hiding would be better at this point, with my sad skills of invisibility.

Out of curiosity, I pulled my phone out of my bag and checked the signal strength. Zero. I sighed and put it away, unsurprised but still disappointed. I hadn't talked to Wes in days and I was quickly passing anxious and heading towards paranoid. What if he wasn't answering his phone because he didn't want to talk to me anymore? Or something was happening back home. Something dangerous. What if Miles had shown up? His messages had been ominously vague when it came to clearing the way for us to be together.

I was distracted. I knew the moment something moved out of the corner of my eye that I had no one to blame but myself for Alex finding me so quickly. So when a hand closed over my mouth and yanked me backwards against a chest, my first reaction was confusion. Alex hadn't been specific about the terms of being found, but I was pretty sure assault hadn't been the plan. I inhaled sharply through my nose, struggling for air with a hand pressed so tightly against my lips – and caught a whiff of a familiar scent. Hair products and crazy.

My eyes went wide, but any noise I would've made was silenced by the hand that gripped my jaw.

"Hello, darling. Nice to see you again. I missed you." Miles' tone was completely relaxed, as if we'd run into each other at a dinner party and were both equally charmed by the other.

"Mrrmph," was all I could manage.

I struggled against him, but his arm had mine twisted up behind me at an odd angle, and every time I moved, it sent a sharp pain up my elbow and shoulder. There was nothing else to do but wait this out. I stopped struggling. He wasn't here to kill me. No, his plan would be so much more twisted than that.

"Good," he said, his breath blowing hot against my ear as he spoke. "Now, I'm going to take my hand away and you're going to behave. We need to have a quick chat and then I'll let you get back."

I nodded to show my agreement. Whatever got his flesh off my face was fine with me. I felt dirty.

Slowly, he eased his hand away from my mouth. He didn't loosen his grip on my arm until he was convinced I wasn't going to scream. When I felt the pressure fall away, I took a step to get clear and turned to face him.

"What are you doing here?" I demanded. Now that I was out of his grasp I could afford to have attitude.

"Checking on you," he said, his eyes glittering in a way that made me feel like Lysoling my entire body. He was wearing a fake leather jacket, and as usual, his hair was slicked back and shiny. He looked like he was auditioning for Grease. "How are you? How's school? Is it everything they say it is, being in a school strictly for Hunters?"

I narrowed my eyes. "I guess so."

"And you're keeping your grades up?"

"Sure." I was frantically trying to figure out how to handle this. I didn't even have a weapon. But I'd bet Miles did. Could I disarm him? He was a lot stronger than he looked, judging by the way he'd hung on to my twisted arm.

"Why are you looking at me like that?" he asked, cocking his head to one side.

My mind was whirring in overdrive and my words came out breathless. "I'm trying to understand. Your messages said you were working on something."

"Right, the project." He frowned. "It has its kinks but we're working them out." Then he smiled. "I'll be ready for you soon, don't worry."

His expression had changed so fast it was creepy. He was reminding me a lot of Leo–as in, completely off his rocker. He'd seemed so much more 'together' back in Frederick Falls. I was torn between wanting to take him out, end this here and now, and trying to pry information out of him. Whatever this project was, it couldn't be good. I was willing to bet people would get hurt.

"What sort of project are we talking?"

"It's a surprise." He grinned like a small child would over a colorfully wrapped birthday present.

A voice buzzed in my ear and I jumped. "Getting close now, Godfrey. You suck at this, you know that?"

Alex. Crap. He was going to walk in on this. And Miles would bolt. I really didn't want to lose this opportunity. I eyed Miles, who was taking it all in, and slowly brought my hand up, pressing the talk button.

"How close?" I asked into the microphone.

"Two minutes," he replied.

He sounded confident of it, and I didn't doubt him. I had two minutes.

Miles' eyes narrowed. "This was supposed to be a private reunion." He took a step towards me.

I lowered my hands away from the earpiece but kept my muscles tensed and ready. "I'm in the middle of a training thing."

He took another step, and I realized he wasn't coming towards me so much as moving away, in the direction of the wards. Time was up.

"How did you get in here anyway?" I asked. I crouched and got ready to make my move.

He shrugged. "Apparently, I can come and go. Must be a Hunter thing." He winked.

The way he'd emphasized the Hunter part had a little bell going off in my head. I stared at him. "You sent that Werewolf in here last weekend."

"I wasn't sure what sort of setup they had here. Seriously lacking, if you ask me. Especially when they have a hot commodity like you nearby."

I didn't answer. I couldn't. What was I going to do, defend Vera? He was right. The wards sucked, especially if he could simply walk right through. Which he obviously could, or Vera and the cavalry would've been here by now.

Miles was only half-looking at me now. Every few seconds, his eyes would dart into the trees. He was searching for Alex. I waited until his eyes swung away again and then I charged.

I swung my leg out in a move I'd been practicing with Raj and knocked his feet out from under him. Miles went down on his back but managed to roll with it, coming up in a kneeling crouch. His eyes blazed. Somehow, he managed to look threatening and excited all at once.

I charged him again, not wanting to hear whatever creepy comment he was about to make.

Miles straightened and met me head on, blocking my fists with his forearms, and driving me back.

“This is no way to greet your future mate,” he said between blocks. He still hadn’t tried to hit me back.

“I am not your mate, now or in the future,” I said between heavy breaths. I swung out again, and followed it up with a kick. It landed, though barely, and Miles stepped back.

“We’re going to rule the races, you and I. You know that, right? It’s what should have been…what would’ve been if my father hadn’t let revenge take over his thoughts. Over a stupid Hunter woman.”

I stopped to catch my breath. “You knew about him and my mother?”

“Of course. He never made it a secret.”

“So, you see why this whole vendetta is so wrong.”

He nodded. “Completely. Obviously it’s you and I who belong together. You and I who are destined to lead together. It makes perfect sense, you and I being the half-breeds. And when my project comes together, we’ll have even more on our side. No one will be able to stop us.”

I opened my mouth to argue, but he cut me off and waved his hand. “Wes, but he’ll be dealt with and then it will be just you and me.”

My blood boiled. “I’m not going to rule with you,” I said, gritting my teeth to keep my voice even, and the bile down. My hands balled into fists at my sides. I took a step forward and swung out, catching nothing but air as Miles stepped out of reach once again.

He didn’t look upset at being turned down. If anything he only looked more determined. “I’m confident you’ll change your mind.”

My earpiece buzzed, distracting me.

“I’m closing in,” said Alex.

I looked up, but those few seconds had been enough; Miles was already slipping away into the thickest part of the trees. I stood and watched him go, knowing I should do something to stop him but unable to make myself move. I was frustrated at my pathetic fighting skills. They worked so well on wolves; not so much on humans.

I was still standing there, staring at empty forest, when Alex caught up with me.

“Um, you could’ve made it a little more difficult,” he said, coming towards me. "Maybe tried hiding or something instead of standing here in the…" He trailed off when he saw my face. "What happened?" Just like that, his voice went from friendly-training-exercise to all-business.

I wrenched my eyes away from the direction Miles had gone and forced myself to focus on Alex. "It's nothing."

"Nope. Not working on me. Let's try it again. What happened?"

I bit my lip. Cambria and Logan had said not to trust him, but I'd seen Alex in action and he was definitely someone you wanted on your side. And the way he was looking at me now… there was a fierceness in his eyes that reminded me of the protectiveness I'd seen in–

"It was Miles. He – he came to see me."

"Who is Miles?"

"He's–" I stopped. How did I answer that question? "He's a Hunter. Or… well, he's like me. A hybrid."

"A hybrid?" His eyebrows went up. The fierceness was turning to amusement.

"Yeah, like the car, whatever. Anyway he's the son of the guy I killed at the warehouse that night."

Amusement faded, and he eyed me intently. "Did he hurt you?"

"No. He wanted to talk." I sighed, knowing it had to be said. "He's convinced himself he's in love with me and that we're going to rule the races or some crap." I shivered because the creep out factor was back, big time.

"And he's evidently going to pretend you're on board with this plan," he said, piecing it together. I nodded and stayed quiet, both of us digesting the possibilities of that, should Miles actually get his hands on me. Finally, Alex looked up, towards the empty woods. "Which way did he go?"

"Alex, he's gone. He's good at escaping, believe me. Besides, he's harmless, for now. Until he finishes whatever project he's got going, he's going to leave me alone."

Anger flashed across his face. "Oh, so no problem then. We'll just wait for him to come back, when we're not expecting it, and drag you off like a caveman to be his new bride. No wonder you're always in the middle of drama with a plan like that."

My temper flared. I raised my voice to match his. "I don't intend to wait for him to come and get me. I'm doing what I can do protect myself. What do you care anyway? Besides the mark on your record."

"I'm in charge of you, and you're not getting abducted or killed on my watch."

We were toe-to-toe and I could feel my blood beginning to heat. I tried taking deep breaths but this stupid temper wouldn't quit. I was going to have to let it out; tell him exactly what I thought of him, his prejudice, and his teaching methods in general.

"You are an ass–" My words were cut off.

I must've blinked and missed seeing it about to happen because there was no time to push him away or react at all before his lips were pressed against mine. At the same time, his hand came around the back of my neck, holding me still. He didn't come any closer or move in any way; just held his mouth to mine for what could've been three hundred years or three seconds, and then jerked away so he was looking down at me again. There was still fire and temper in his eyes. Mine, on the other hand, had evaporated.

Neither of us spoke.

I had no idea what to say. I wondered if that was his problem, too, because the longer he looked at me, the more his anger faded into something else. I couldn't read what that something was, or maybe I could've if we'd stood there long enough, but eventually he dropped his hands to his sides and turned away, making a show of staring out over the woods where Miles had gone.

"It's more than a job," he said, completely surprising me again. "Come on, let's get back," he added, when I didn't respond.

He sounded resigned, and I realized I felt something similar, though I had no idea why.

CHAPTER EIGHTEEN

Somehow, I made it back to Lexington Hall. I couldn't remember walking there, but I found myself looking at Cambria and Logan, who were blinking at me and moving their lips. I struggled to tune in. Everything felt foggy and sort of removed.

"...Can't believe we got this lucky," Cambria was saying.

She was smiling and excited and holding something out to me. I looked down and registered that it was a wooden stake, smooth and pointy. I took it.

Cambria frowned at me. "Tara? You okay?"

"Hmm?" I looked at her and blinked to clear the fog. "Yeah, I'm good."

I could see she wasn't convinced, but she let it pass.

She handed another stake to Logan. "Seriously, we got so lucky," she said, returning to her original comment. "I got there as the deliveries came in and those dudes will never even know I swiped an entire box."

"You were careful, though, right?" Logan asked.

"That's the beauty of it. I got to the delivery guy before he made it to the front door. I never had to compel any staff or students. And one little human is not going to matter. Easy peasy."

"Good girl." Logan took the stake, stuffed it into his cargo jeans, and adjusted his hat. "Let's do this," he said.

I slipped my stake into my boot and we headed into the woods. We'd gone a short distance into the trees when Cambria stopped and turned to me. This time, her eyebrows were raised and she even pushed her bangs out of the way so she could stare at me with both eyes.

"Okay, what's wrong?"

"Nothing is wrong, exactly." I looked from her to Logan, who was looking more curious than anything else. "Alex kissed me and I saw Miles," I blurted.

"What?!" They spoke in unison.

"You saw Miles?" Logan asked.

"You kissed Alex?" Cambria asked, her voice raised at least two octaves.

"Yes, I saw Miles. He was in the woods, waiting for me, I guess. He grabbed me when I was alone and said some weird crap about his project and that he would be back for me when it was ready." I turned and looked at Cambria. "And no. I did not kiss Alex. He kissed me. Big difference."

"Okay, fine, he kissed you but–"

I cut her off with a look and made sure my tone left no room for argument. "And I do not want to talk about that. End of discussion."

She huffed at me but let it go. I could see it in her eyes, though. She'd corner me later.

"Fine, but let's keep moving. We only have a few hours before dinner and we've got a lot of ground to cover." Logan led the way without really waiting for an answer. "Let's start in the spot you saw Miles earlier."

I gave them the location, and at their prompting, I went over the full conversation I'd had with Miles. Both of them already knew the history so at least I didn't have to go back and explain all of that, but neither one knew about the creepy almost-kiss in the warehouse so I came clean about that, and tried not to gag as I said it.

"He's crossing a line," said Logan. His eyes were hard and shiny, and he looked more capable of actually damaging someone than I'd ever seen. "You realize he's threatening to basically kidnap and rape you, right?"

"I guess so," I said.

"You guess so?" Cambria asked. "Tara, please tell me you're taking this threat seriously. This is bad."

"I know that, guys. I'm not going to leave with him. Alex was right behind me and scared him off. If he hadn't left, Alex and I could've taken him."

Logan's expression cooled. "Let's keep moving," he said.

We started walking again. For a few minutes, none of us spoke. We made it back to the spot I'd seen Miles but there was nothing there. Not that I'd really expected there to be. It made me think of Alex again, though, and I felt antsy.

"Now what?" I asked.

"We should head out closer to the wards and walk the perimeter," said Logan.

"You realize that's going to take hours," I said. "We don't have that kind of daylight left. Not in here, anyway." I glanced up at the thick canopy. Most of the branches were still bare but there were enough pine trees mixed in that only a limited amount of sunlight came through.

"We could split up," said Logan.

"Uh, no way," Cambria said. "Too dangerous. Even with our weapons, I don't trust it. Miles is out there, and so are his little friends. And they all know they can get right through the wards. We stick together."

"Cambria's right," I said. "Too bad we don't have earpieces, like the ones Alex and I used earlier. Then we could stay in contact."

"I can help with that."

We all froze. No one even went for their stakes because we all knew that voice and we all knew how busted we were. I turned, slowly, and felt my face flame red as Alex got closer. He pretended not to notice, which didn't make it any less embarrassing.

"What do you mean you can help?" Cambria asked. Her eyes narrowed and she'd let her bangs fall completely over one side of her face. She looked suspicious and pissed. Apparently, Alex was officially out of the "too cute to be mad at" category for her.

"I mean, I have ear pieces," he said. He held them up, one in each hand. The same ones we'd used earlier.

We all waited for him to go on.

"Okaay," Cambria drawled, when he didn't continue. "Why are you telling us? Is Headmaster Whitfield on the other end? So he can lecture us while we're on the way to his office to get lectured some more?"

"No lectures. No Headmaster. I'm offering them to you for patrolling." There was no mistaking it; Cambria and Logan's eyes lit up. "On one condition," he added.

Logan still looked excited, like he was ready to agree to whatever came next. Cambria didn't look so convinced. I continued to stand there, mute, and wishing I'd evaporate or combust or anything to get me out of here.

"What is it?" Cambria asked.

"I get to patrol with you."

Cambria exchanged a look with Logan. He shrugged. They looked at me. I didn't move.

"If we let you patrol with us, we can use the earpieces and you promise not to rat us out?" Cambria asked.

"Absolutely," Alex said, meeting her eyes dead on.

"Huh. Well."

"Cambria, no!" I hissed at her. "He cannot help."

Cambria looked at me, her brows drawn in an apology, and then turned back to Alex. He handed her an earpiece and proceeded to show her how to use it. I threw up my arms and stomped away to pace. I caught Logan's eye a minute later.

"Sorry," he said, putting his hands up in defense. "If we don't take the deal, he'll talk. And besides, we can cover more ground this way."

I glared at him.

"There are only two earpieces," said Cambria, turning back to us and adjusting the one in her ear. Alex had the other one in his ear already. I knew where this was going. "We're going to split up into doubles. We'll cover more ground but still have each other's backs."

I opened my mouth, ready to claim Cambria as my partner, but Alex cut me off.

"Oh, one more condition," said Alex. He looked at Cambria. "I'm with Tara. It'll be part of her training for me to see her in action."

Whatever argument Cambria might've had, Alex's reasoning shot her down. She nodded. "All right. Check in every fifteen minutes. We'll head east, you head west. We'll meet at the back line."

"See you then," he said with a nod.

Cambria didn't answer. Her eyes found mine, and I glared at her with what I hoped were death ray eyes.

"Sorry," she whispered. "He is sort of your teacher. I couldn't say no."

"Traitor," I hissed.

She fell into step beside Logan who started walking without a backwards glance.

I turned to Alex. His face was expressionless. Pretending, then. Okay. I could do that. I started walking, staying a half step ahead of him, and tried to think of something to say that wouldn't sound completely awkward.

"How did you know we were out here?" I asked.

"Lucky guess." He sounded amused, like he might be smiling, but I didn't turn to look. If he was, I might've punched him.

"Why are you helping us? If you get into trouble, it could go on your permanent record."

"I'm not worried. We're trying to protect the school. Besides, Vera would have to admit the wards are weak to let us publicly get into trouble for this, and I don't think she's willing to do that."

Damn. I hadn't thought about that; which meant, we were sort of blackmailed into taking his deal in the first place. I hoped Cambria was really mad at him when she found that out later. I heard a distant voice come through the speaker of his earpiece. I didn't turn. A minute later, I heard Alex say, "All good here. Check back in fifteen."

He fell silent and we walked on. The wards were somewhere on our left, but I didn't bother looking over. If there was a Werewolf nearby, I'd feel it before I saw it, anyway.

"You feel different," Alex said, jolting me out of my carefully blank thoughts.

"What?" I turned to look at him before I remembered not to.

He looked at me with something close to curiosity. "You feel different," he repeated.

Oh crap, I could feel myself blushing again. Feel different? From one kiss? What did that even mean?

"I didn't say anything before now, because I was sure you'd think I was trying to insult you somehow, but I thought you should know."

I realized he wasn't referring to earlier and curiosity got the better of me. "What do you mean different?"

"You know how we can feel a Werewolf nearby, with the tingling? Kind of like that but.... different. You don't feel like a Werewolf but you don't feel like a Hunter either."

"You can sense me?" I asked, so surprised that I forgot about my earlier embarrassment. "How is that possible? I thought Hunters couldn't feel each other."

"They can't. Well, some can, but it's rare. It's more of a subconscious recognition. We can look at each other and know that we're more than human. But with you, I don't know. There's something else."

"Like what?" I was intrigued. No one had ever told me this before. "What does it feel like?"

"I don't know. It's faint. Like a pulse or vibration." His eyes sharpened. "It got stronger when I kissed you, though."

I almost tripped over a fallen log. Alex's hand reached out and steadied my arm.

"Ow," I yelped, yanking free of his grip.

"What's wrong?" Alex was beside me, frowning down at my arm while I cradled it against my body and rubbed at my shoulder.

"I don't know. I think I strained something when Miles–"

I broke off, but it was too late. Alex's eyes were on me, a lot like Cambria's had been when she'd forced me to talk earlier. "Miles what?" he prompted. I didn't answer. "The guy you saw in the woods earlier? The dirty bl–, I mean hybrid?"

I nodded.

"You said he didn't hurt you."

"He didn't. Not really. He may have grabbed my arm and held it behind me for a minute. That's it."

"That's it," he repeated, looking totally unconvinced.

I nodded again. Alex stared at me and for a second, I thought maybe he was going to kiss me again. Panic shot through me, and I wondered for a second if I would even stop him if he tried. At the last second, he stepped back and his jaw hardened.

"From now on, I go with you every time you step foot in the woods. If you guys do any more patrols like this, I'm coming. If I find out you've been out here alone, I'll turn you in and get you put on house arrest." Every single bone of his body vibrated with the sincerity of his words.

"You can't do that," I protested. "I can take care of myself and I will not be babysat."

"Tara." Alex closed his eyes and opened them again, taking care to keep his voice even. "Don't argue. I have the authority to make sure the house arrest sticks. Possibly for the rest of the year. Don't push me."

I glared at him and bit my tongue. "This is blackmail."

"Call it whatever you want."

I was angry enough to want to put him in his place now, whatever it took. "I didn't kiss you back," I said. That shut him up. "In case you're acting this way because you think I feel something for you. I thought I should point out that I didn't kiss you back." No need to mention it was due more to shock than attraction or emotion.

Alex stepped closer and leaned down until his lips were only a breath away from mine. "If I'd wanted you to kiss me back, you would've."

He stayed there, his lips so close they were almost brushing mine. I could feel his breath on my face. His eyes were angry and glinting, in a silent dare. He wanted me to close the distance. The worst part was, I kind of wanted to. I could feel myself leaning closer, itching to give in.

At the last second, I stepped back. Alex straightened and his lids drooped, heavy with silent satisfaction. I glared up at him. "You're a jerk. I think I liked it better when you hated me."

He didn't say anything, and I spun, walking faster and staying ahead of him. He let me go without further comment. A few minutes later I could hear him speaking into his earpiece, checking in with Cambria. Then he fell silent again but I could hear his footsteps. No matter how fast I walked, he stayed behind me. Never any closer but never out of sight.

We finished our patrols without sighting–or sensing–a single Werewolf. When we reached Cambria and Logan, I was still walking ahead of Alex with a set jaw. I could see their expressions change the second they saw me. They looked nervous.

"I'm going to shower," I snapped, cutting straight across the lawn and heading for the school. I didn't wait for them or look back to see who followed, but after a few seconds, I could hear someone padding up behind me on the grass. Cambria appeared, power walking along side me.

"That bad?" she asked.

"Worse. He offered himself as a body guard to me. And by offered, I mean blackmailed me into agreeing."

"Oh."

"Oh?" I glanced over at her. "He's a jerk. I wish he still hated me."

"I think it's a little late for that."

"What does that mean?"

"Nothing. You go on up and shower. I'm right behind you."

She slowed and I sped up, heading for Lexington Hall and trying not to scream.

CHAPTER NINETEEN

I kissed Alex. No, wait, Alex kissed me. For some reason, it was important to remember that. I didn't know why; it's not like remembering it that way made it any less confusing.

It was dawn on Monday morning, and I'd barely slept the night before. I couldn't. Alex had kissed me! What was I supposed to do with that?

Was I supposed to pretend it hadn't happened? Go back to being the student? I mean, I had Wes. What was I going to tell Wes? I groaned and earned a muffled curse from Victoria, still trying to sleep across the room.

I sighed. Might as well get up. It wasn't like I was going to sleep anytime soon. I threw the covers back and sucked in another groan. My arm, the one Miles had twisted and held behind me, burned with sharp pain. I lowered it and cradled it to my side. I'd have to be careful about that today.

I gathered what I needed for the shower and headed down the hall. The bathroom was empty this time of morning, and I took my time, using probably all of the hot water, and then spending an extra few minutes on drying and combing through my hair. The humidity of the bathroom counteracted the blow dryer, though, and I shut it off when I started getting sweaty. My hair would have to be its usual style; somewhere halfway between straight and wavy.

I dropped my stuff off back in my room, thankful that Victoria was still sleeping, and headed upstairs in search of an early breakfast. I was relieved to find the dining room open already and decided to go all out. Bacon. Eggs. French toast. Coffee and cream. The works. I was halfway through stuffing my face when Logan came in. He went through the line and came over with eggs and toast.

"What are you doing here so early?" he asked, plopping his tray down across from me.

"Couldn't sleep. You?" I inhaled another forkful of syrup-drenched French toast.

"I want to get over to the library at Rockford Hall for this essay I've got next month."

"Next month?" I shook my head, letting it go. "Why Rockford Hall's library?"

"They aren't all the same. Rockford's specialty is the sciences. Biology, chemistry, physics."

"What's Lexington's?"

"Philosophy, poetry, the classics. Ashton's is math." I made a face. "Taylor's is World History. And Griffin is Lineage. All of the libraries carry books in all categories, but each building specializes and has more books in that genre. I need something on quantum chemistry."

"Quantum huh? Okay, whatever. I'll come."

"You will?" He blinked, like maybe I was messing with him.

I rolled my eyes. "Not for the physics books. I want to send some emails. They have internet there right?"

"Oh, yeah. Only in the senior libraries."

We dumped our trays and headed over to Rockford Hall. It was set up exactly like our building. The artwork was different, along with the flyers announcing clubs and events, but otherwise, it was the same; a grand staircase leading up from the front doors, with the monstrous cafeteria at the top, and the library at the far end of the second floor.

Once inside, Logan wandered off to find his book, and I found an empty computer station. One benefit to being up early was internet access. It wasn't available during school hours since we were all supposed to be in class, and since the library only had two stations with internet capability, getting to use one usually involved standing in a line five people deep for a chance at ten minutes in your email box. But since the roof at Griffin Hall was out of the question, emailing was my only option.

I logged in with my student ID and booted up my email. I scanned through one from Sam; it was a single paragraph all about her weekend trip to DC with her older sister and the crazy clubs she'd stood outside of. It ended with a question about when visiting day was, and exactly how many 'hotties' to plan on seeing when she came. It made me smile.

The next was from Angela. Hers was a lot more laid back. She was busy with piano and school and trying to keep Sam from going completely insane on some girl who was dumb enough to try and flirt with Sam's flavor of the week.

There was one from my mother. A couple of sentences:

How are you? How are your grades? Grandma says hello.

And one from Fee, which surprised me in a way that made my chest pang with homesickness. I didn't even know she had my email address. I read slowly, trying to soak in every word:

Dear Tara,

Hope all is well at your new school. We miss you here, but we know you are safe and learning a lot more than Jack and I could teach you. I hear Wood Point is the best on the east coast and the weapons training is top notch. Keep those grades up. Jack says he's going to test your combat skills next time he sees you, so be ready. Which is to say, he's worried about you and misses you but won't come out and say it. Just like he won't come out and say when he's overdone it for the day. I swear, nurses have infinite patience. I could never do this for a living. Wes being here is helping. I know he misses you, too, but summer will be here before you know it. Your Grandma has been coming around.

She's an amazing woman. Completely unprejudiced even though she refuses to join us outright. Did you know she's a member of CHAS? Could be useful someday. There I go, being all political again. Either way, she's a good friend to me. Oh, Jack is calling for me, and Wes sounds a little frazzled. Talk soon.

Love,

Fee.

I read it four times. By the end, tears had gathered in the corners of my eyes, and I blinked them back. I hit reply and fired off a quick email, answering the basic questions about school and assuring her that Grandma was definitely someone good to have on our side. Then I stopped. I wanted to ask more about Wes or have her give him a message, but I couldn't. He'd been there. When she'd typed the email, he'd been in the next room. So he wasn't hurt or too busy or whatever. And still I hadn't heard anything from him. No emails. No voice mails. What did that mean?

I left the email as it was and sent it off, depressed and homesick. I clicked on the next one. It was from George. He missed me, he wanted to be friends, and I could call and talk to him anytime. I sat back and sighed, long and loud, and ignored the look it earned me from the librarian. I was homesick enough to miss George, but I wasn't going to write and tell him that.

Instead, I opened a blank email and addressed it to Wes. My fingers hovered above the keyboard, frozen and unsure. I had no idea what to say. I'd already sent him three other emails, none of which had been answered. And email was definitely not how I wanted to do this.

I logged off and went in search of Logan.

He was all the way in the back with his nose in a book that looked like it might've helped put me to sleep last night. I waved to let him know I was leaving and kept walking. He barely looked up.

I hadn't meant to do it, but I ended up on the roof of Griffin Hall searching like a spy for Alex. When I finally convinced myself I was truly alone I relaxed and slid down to the ground, leaning back on a massive air handler that was silent and still in the chilled mountain morning. I pulled out my phone and dialed Wes.

"Hello?"

My heart flipped over and jumped up and down. "Wes?" My voice shook, and I bit my lip to steady it.

"Tara? What's wrong?" Any trace of sleepiness vanished.

"Nothing's wrong. Just calling to say hi."

I could hear him letting out a breath and relaxing. "It's really good to hear your voice."

"You, too."

His tone matched the way I felt. It was comforting and heart wrenching and for a second, I closed my eyes and pictured how he would look saying these words. It was beautiful and way too painful, so I forced my eyes open again and tried to remember what I wanted to say.

"Where have you been?" I asked.

The connection crackled and then cleared again. I froze, unwilling to move away from whatever sweet spot was allowing the signal to remain. "What?" I asked.

"… Phone was broken," he was saying. "I couldn't get a new one until yesterday. Been trying to call you ever since."

I'd missed the first part about whatever had caused his phone to break. His tone was changing from longing to fierce. "I can't believe you went outside the wards. After you promised."

"What? How do you even know about that?"

"Vera called."

"Oh. So you know about the Werewolf?" For a second I forgot all about the protective tone he'd taken and was relieved there was someone else I could talk to about it all.

"The what?"

Vera must've left that part out. I sighed. "I only went out of the wards because I was chasing a Werewolf that had come through."

"No one said anything about a breach in the wards," he said. He muttered a stream of curses that was a little harsh, even for him.

"Wes?"

The sound of tires screeching against asphalt.

"Wes?"

"I'm sick of being kept outside the loop. I'm supposed to be in charge. This is ridiculous," he said.

His voice was just short of a growl, and I felt a stab of temper. I'd barely spoken to him the past few weeks. No wonder he felt out of the loop.

"If you wanted to be in the loop, you could've called me," I said.

"I didn't mean you."

"What did you mean?" The static was back, full force. I had to pull the phone away from my ear because of the noise. I spoke into it like a walkie-talkie. "Wes?"

Nothing.

The connection ended.

I dialed him again, but it went straight to voice mail. That meant my signal was fine. His was the one screwing up. Great. I ended the call and set the phone down, resting my knees on my chin and staring at nothing.

I'm not sure how long I stayed that way, but when I finally pulled myself out of whatever blank daydream I'd been having, the first thing I noticed was that it was hot. Like sticky, sun beating down with no branches to shield me hot. As if in response, the air handler I was leaning on groaned and jerked and came to life, sending cool air into the building below me. It sounded like a helicopter was landing behind my head.

I stood up and brushed my pants off, not wanting to stay near the noise but not sure whether I was ready to go yet, either. If it was this warm out, I'd no doubt missed a class or two, and I wasn't sure if that would go unnoticed.

Another one of the giant air handlers kicked on a few feet away and was irritating enough to send me on my way. I was still distracted, thinking about Wes and the way he'd peeled out, and trying to imagine where he might be going, that I wasn't even focused on what was in front of me anymore. I barreled out of the door at the bottom of the stairwell and ran smack into a brick wall of a body. Large hands reached out to steady me. I stepped back and the hands fell away.

"Ms. Godfrey."

I looked up into the scarred face of Professor Kane. "Professor."

I stopped there, unsure what else to say. I was so busted. And he looked mean enough to make it very unpleasant. But instead of lecturing me or sentencing me to the dungeons (it seemed like a possibility for someone like him), he stood there, watching me with a mild expression –it might've been amusement, but he couldn't really pull it off with the scars and all–and a raised eyebrow. "In a hurry?" he asked.

I glanced at the exit behind him and met his gaze. "I guess so. I didn't see you there. I'll be more careful."

Now there was definitely amusement. "Somehow, I doubt that." He looked around. "Your trainer doesn't know you're here?"

"I, uh, no." Crap. So was I allowed to come and go from the rooftop as long as Alex was with me? For a rule follower, he seemed to have a lot less boundaries than the rest of us.

"He's probably working on that truck of his, if you're looking for him," he said.

"He's not in class?" I asked, and then clamped my mouth shut.

"His schedule is a little different than yours," he said, pointedly.

I nodded and waited for the lecture.

His gaze sharpened. "You know, I've wanted to speak to you for some time. You're a very skilled fighter, especially for someone with no training or background."

"Thank you," I said, and even though it was sort of scary, the way he looked at me like a tool instead of a person, I couldn't help but feel a little proud that he'd noticed.

"Do you have any plans after graduating next year?"

"Not yet."

"You'd be a real asset to any of our search terms."

"Search teams?" I repeated. I tried not to show my horror. I knew exactly what search teams he meant. "Search and Destroy" would be the proper term, and I knew I could never be a part of something like that, even if I wasn't half Werewolf.

Kane nodded. He didn't seem aware of my revulsion. "Something to think about. I'd mentor you myself, if you were serious about it. You've got potential."

"Uh, thanks. I'll think about it."

"You do that." He winked, which made me almost take a step back. It was supposed to look friendly, I'm sure, but all it did was scrunch up his scars and make him menacing. "Get going now, and we'll both pretend you weren't skipping class."

I hurried out without looking back.

CHAPTER TWENTY

Training was strained. It felt like Alex was waiting for me to do or say something, and I didn't know what it was. He didn't bring up Miles again, or anything that had happened that day, and neither did I. We worked on tracking some more, and then evading. Alex was really good at that part.

When I failed to find him for the third time, he dropped silently from a tree branch above my head, straightened, and smirked.

I crossed my arms over my chest. "Evading females is a trait all men are born with."

"I thought it was evading questions?"

"Same thing."

"True."

His smirk turned into a genuine smile, flashing white teeth at me, and my stomach jumped into my ribs. I found it hard to look away from his mouth, and an awkward moment passed where all I could do was stare. He looked back at me without a word, and again he seemed to be waiting for something. I swallowed hard, surprised and irritated at my body's reaction. It was reflex; I hadn't meant to do that, so it didn't count… right?

We ran after that, which I was grateful for. I still hated running, but at least it left me out of breath enough that I had an excuse not to talk.

"You feel stronger today," he said, when we finished. He popped the top on a bottle of water and drank deeply.

"What do you mean?" I guzzled my water in shorter bursts, so I wouldn't hyperventilate in between sips.

"I don't know. You feel different today. Stronger, more alert."

"Hmm." I frowned, trying to figure out what he meant. I felt the same to me. Still ragged after running three miles.

"Maybe you're getting better with the running," he said.

"Maybe," I agreed, letting it go.

We parted ways after that – Alex jogging back into the trees to finish his run and me heading for civilization.

I met up with Cambria and Logan in the cafeteria and we headed out for more patrolling. I hoped and prayed that Alex wouldn't realize this was going to be a regular thing. But I could tell Cambria and Logan were kind of hoping the opposite, since Alex had the earpieces. In the end, it didn't matter; he showed.

When he held out the earpiece, Logan actually slapped him five, and I glared so hard that my eyes almost closed. Logan purposely didn't look at me, but Alex noticed.

He cleared his throat. "I was thinking we could mix it up today. You girls want to go together?" He was looking at Cambria, whom he'd clearly decided was in charge.

"Sure," she said, reaching over and taking Logan's earpiece out of his hands. "Let's go," she said, jerking her thumb to the trail and looking at me. I didn't waste any time following.

"Check in every fifteen, like yesterday," Logan called out to our backs.

Cambria held up a hand with a thumbs-up as we disappeared into the trees.

"So…?" she asked, when we were out of earshot.

"Not talking about it," I said.

I didn't have to look at her to know she was pouting. "You're no fun sometimes, you know that."

"I talked to Wes today," I said, instead.

She perked up at that. I guess any boy gossip was good gossip right now. "About time. What did he have to say for himself?"

I sighed. "Nothing, actually. The connection went bad and cut out." I quickly told her the conversation we did manage to have.

"Where was he off to in such a hurry?"

"I don't know. I guess things must be stressful for him there, learning to lead. He said there's been resistance because he's a… you know, hybrid."

"That's stupid."

I gave her a sideways glance. "Not everyone's as willing to live outside the rules as you are," I said.

Cambria smiled, flashing her teeth and making it look half menacing and half winning. "I am one-of-a-kind, aren't I?"

I felt a smile forming in response. "Definitely."

Daylight was beginning to fade around the edges of the blue sky that poked through the branches overhead. I could feel the temperature dropping as the sun dipped lower. Air tickled the back of my neck, drafting down my spine. I drew my jacket more snugly around myself and stopped. Yes, it was getting cooler out, but not enough to be cold. And I didn't have goose bumps. So, what was I feeling then?

I stopped walking and concentrated.

Cambria stopped too and looked at me with an eyebrow raised. I waved a hand to keep her quiet and concentrated on my body. I took a step forward without realizing it. Then another. I stopped and stared down at my feet like they were strangers. I was pretty sure my brain hadn't told me to do that. Cambria was watching me like I was a new brand of crazy. I tried to ignore that and looked in the direction my feet were pointed.

Cambria's earpiece crackled signaling it was time to check in with the guys, but I didn't pay any attention. I was staring into a darker part of the trees, straight towards the wards.

Something was there.

I wasn't exactly sure how I knew it, especially without goose bumps, but I did. Just like I knew I had to get to it.

"Everything's fine," Cambria said into her earpiece.

She didn't sound convinced of her own words, though, so I turned to her and nodded in reassurance. I didn't know how to explain this to the guys until I knew what this was. Even then, I wasn't so sure I wanted them to come running. Whatever I was walking towards – it didn't feel like a threat.

Logan seemed to be satisfied with Cambria's answer, and the line went quiet.

"What's up?" Cambria hissed at me as soon as the boys signed off.

"There." I pointed at a dark stand of trees where I could feel the pull originating. "Something's there."

"Werewolf?" she hissed back, even sharper.

"No," I said slowly. "I don't think so. No goose bumps. But it's something." I bit my lip trying to figure it out. I didn't put it past Miles to have some sort of trap laid out, but I couldn't ignore it. Not even if I wanted to. My feet twitched again and my whole body felt itchy with the need to move.

Cambria squinted into the trees. She stayed like that for what felt like forever to my twitchy limbs and then bent down and took out her stake. "Right then. Let's do this."

I took my stake out, too, and we set out. I let my body lead me, or pull me, towards the shadows and concentrated on keeping my pace even and slow. Part of me wanted to run, but I managed to tell that part to shut it.

We walked in silence; our footsteps sounded too loud as we crashed through the fallen branches and pine needles. Whoever – or whatever – was waiting definitely knew we were coming.

I gripped the stake tight enough that my knuckles turned white and I had to ease up to let some of the blood flow back in. Cambria fell in behind me when the way became too thick, and I knew she was wound as tight as I was. The way was blocked by thorn bushes more than trees. We were getting seriously close to the wards line. Cambria must've felt it, too, because I could feel her hesitating behind me.

I knew what she was thinking. We could not let ourselves cross that line unless we wanted to bring the cavalry running. I slowed my pace, feeling my way forward with instinct so I didn't wander too far towards the line. I couldn't see anything except a face-full of thorn branches. I pulled them apart with careful fingers, but even so, I stuck myself and drew blood. I sucked on the injured fingers absently and kept moving.

All at once, the thorn bushes gave way and the space in front of me was open woods again. The vibrating feel of the wards was stronger here, and I knew we'd come as far as we could. I stopped and Cambria came up next to me, both of us scanning the trees for any sign of movement.

"We can't go any farther without alerting Vera," she whispered.

"I know." My feet still felt twitchy, and I was frustrated. "There's something here, though. I know it."

"Tara–"

"There." I pointed to a large oak twenty yards away. Something behind it had moved – I was sure of it.

Cambria didn't answer. She squinted at the tree. We waited.

A face appeared from behind the tree and then the body that went with it. I sucked in a big gulp of air.

"Wes," I said, letting all my breath out on the one word. I lurched forward, ready to run to him, but Cambria's hand came down on my arm. Hard.

"Whoa. What do you think you're doing?" she demanded.

"It's okay. It's Wes," I said, frustrated at having to explain it – and that she would stop me from going to him in the first place.

He walked towards us with a small smile on his lips and his eyes on mine, locked in some private, silent reunion.

"You can't cross the wards, remember?" Cambria hissed at me.

"She's right," Wes said. He was still coming closer, and I wondered why he didn't just break into a run already. Didn't he miss me as much as I'd missed him? He was still looking at me with an intensity that I figured would be impossible to achieve if he didn't feel happy to see me.

"You can come to us," I said.

He had almost reached me now but came to an abrupt halt about eight feet away, eyes still shining but sad. "No, I can't," he said, shaking his head. "I tried. Before you got here. I even changed into wolf form and tried that way but it didn't let me through either way. Vera's got pretty good security going on here."

Cambria and I exchanged a look. For a second no one spoke.

"Well, that sucks," Cambria said. "Of course it would work on him and not the rest."

Wes' eyes, which had been glued to mine, flickered to her. "And you are?"

"This is Cambria. She's a friend," I said.

"It's nice to meet you. I'm glad Tara found someone she can trust." He smiled at her, big and dazzling, and I had to force myself not to stumble forward and go to him.

Cambria smiled back. It took me a minute to realize she was too busy staring at him to really respond. That might've made me laugh, seeing Cambria speechless, but I was too frustrated with the situation. Wes stood right in front of me, a few feet away, after weeks of being separated, and I couldn't touch him. I couldn't hug him or hold his hand or anything. That is what he'd come for… right?

"What are you doing here?" I blurted.

He broke off in mid-conversation with Cambria and turned to look at me. I waited, but he didn't say anything.

"Right, so, I'm going to wait for you over there," said Cambria, waving her hand indistinctly behind her. "See ya." I listened to her retreating steps until they faded behind me.

"Why did you come?" I asked when we were alone.

"I missed you and–" He broke off and looked away, like the answer wasn't easy.

"And?" I braced myself. If there was an 'and' then it wasn't good, obviously. If he'd missed me, which is all the reason I would've needed, he wouldn't have stopped himself. What else was there? "Wes? Did something happen? Oh gosh, is my mom–?"

"You're mom's fine. Everyone is fine." He ran a hand through his hair. "You said on the phone that there was a breach here, in the wards." I nodded. "I wasn't told about that."

"Probably because they don't believe me," I muttered.

"No excuse." He shook his head, waving away the entire explanation with a frustrated hand. "This is the last straw. It's been like this for weeks now." He took a step and for a second, I thought he was going to come to me, but then he turned to the side, pacing. "They say I'm in charge, or going to be, but they still only tell me what they think I need to know in the moment. I've been dealing with it and biting my tongue until now, but this… this is the last straw. Keeping things from me about you." His voice dropped to a growl and he stopped pacing to stare at me over the empty space that separated us. His gaze was so intensely personal that for a second, it was like I was across the wards and in the circle of his arms. He blinked. "They shouldn't have done that. You shouldn't have done that."

"Me?"

"You have to keep me informed. I need to know you're safe. I've been going crazy…." He trailed off and ran a hand through his hair. He was looking past me now, into empty space. "I need you to tell me everything, okay? No secrets."

"I am telling you everything. That's the whole point. I told Vera and Headmaster Whitfield everything, too, for all the good it did." I took a deep breath. Here goes… "Okay, there is one other thing." That got his attention. I let the breath out that I'd been holding and blurted, "I saw Miles."

"Miles was here?" He didn't sound happy but he didn't seem too surprised, either. I nodded. His body had gone rigidly still, with his hands held in fists at his sides. The only thing that moved was a small muscle in his jaw that always twitched when he was angry and trying to keep control. "When?"

"Um, yesterday. I was going to tell you, but I can never get a hold of you with the stupid signal up here."

His eyes narrowed and he looked at me, but I couldn't read the expression he wore. Like deep concentration.

"Wes?" I prompted. "Why did you come this way instead of going through the front gate?"

He blinked, and something like guilt flashed across his features before he forced it back. I knew there was something he wasn't telling me, but he changed the subject, and I let it slip away.

"How did you get away from him?" he asked

"Huh? Who?"

"Miles. How did you get away from him?"

"I, uh, well, we talked." Crap. I really didn't want to bring Alex into this. "And someone scared him off."

"Who?"

"My trainer. Alex Channing."

I so did not want to be having this conversation right now. I still hadn't decided exactly how to handle the whole kiss thing. I mean, I wasn't that girl who hid it from her boyfriend and then ran around and did whatever. But I knew telling him would almost certainly provoke some sort of violence towards Alex, or at the very least, we'd fight. I didn't want to fight. I'd missed him too much to fight with him.

"How?"

"He was showing me how to track and we got separated. Miles found me alone and said some things and then Alex showed up and Miles ran off."

"I see. Lucky for you he was there." His voice was hard around the edges. I prayed I was imagining the guilty blush I could feel creeping into my cheeks.

"Yeah," I managed.

His eyes flashed. "Yeah? That's it? That's all you're going to say to me? Wow." He stepped away and went back to pacing.

I stood there, surprised at his sudden reaction and unsure what it meant or how to respond.

"Are you mad?" I asked, finally catching on.

He whirled. "Am I mad? I don't know. Would you be mad if you found out I'd kissed someone else while you were locked away here at matchmaking boarding school?"

My jaw dropped. "How did you–?"

"Um, Tara." Cambria's voice broke through our brewing argument. She sounded a lot closer than I'd last seen her.

I turned and saw her coming straight toward us, her eyes urgent.

"We have company. Sorry." She gave me an apologetic look and then with a crunch of branches, Alex and Logan appeared behind her. They saw me – and Wes – at the same moment, and I saw both of their eyes widen.

"This is why you were acting weird?" Logan demanded, glaring at Cambria. "Who is that?"

Alex didn't say anything. He looked at me with a stony stare. He didn't try to break up our little party, either, which let me know he probably understood what was going on. Something inside me, a tiny little part, felt bad for him, and I refused to feel that. I turned away from him and back to Wes.

Wes eyed the guys with open hostility. I could feel the tension coming off him. "Who are they?"

"Wes, this is Logan. He's a friend," I said, pointing him out where he stood locked in hushed conversation with Cambria. "And that's Alex, my trainer." I made sure to keep my voice even but Wes' eyes narrowed, and I cringed.

Silence followed, lasting long enough to become awkward. Logan was the one to break it.

"You must be Wes." He stepped forward until he was shoulder to shoulder with me. "I'd shake your hand but…" He made a gesture to the invisible line that separated us. "I don't want to get expelled over a handshake."

Wes, who'd wrenched his glare from Alex, relaxed and looked at Logan. "I understand. It's nice to meet you, too. I was telling Tara that I'm glad she's made trustworthy friends here."

"How do you know we're trustworthy?" Cambria stepped forward with eyebrow raised. It seemed she'd recovered from her earlier shyness and was back to her old self.

"She told you about me, didn't she?" he asked. They didn't answer. "And Miles?" This time they nodded. "Then she trusts you. And I trust her judgment." Cambria and Logan smiled and I knew they'd officially been won over. "What I can't figure out is what you all are doing out here. Isn't that sort of dangerous if there's been a breach in the wards?"

"We're patrolling," Logan explained.

"Patrolling?" Wes frowned. "Why would you need to? That's what the wards are for."

Logan opened his mouth to answer, but Alex was suddenly at his side, laying a hand on his arm and shaking his head. Logan turned back to Wes and gave him a helpless shrug. Wes glared at Alex again, only this time, Alex was much closer.

"What's your problem?" Wes all but growled at him. "We were talking. Private conversation."

"The subject matter is not his to tell." Alex let go of Logan's arm and stood with his hands loose at his sides. He glared back at Wes without flinching. At a glance he might look relaxed and unconcerned, but I could see the tension in the muscles along his shoulders and arms.

"If it concerns the wards it concerns Vera, so it's my business as well."

"Not this time it isn't. Vera works for Wood Point right now. Not your Cause."

"And Tara out here patrolling unsecured woods is also my concern," Wes went on.

Alex snorted. "Tara can take care of herself pretty well from what I've seen."

Something about his tone made me think back to that first day when I'd kicked him in his…

Wes barked out a laugh, and I froze. He was looking at me and seemed genuinely amused by something.

Then it dawned on me. I rejected it at first. There was no way; he wouldn't do that to me twice. But the way he'd laughed right at the exact moment I'd thought of it…

"Logan, what's today?" I asked.

Wes quieted; the smile disappeared.

"Sunday, why?" Logan answered, sounding confused.

"What moon phase is it?"

"Um, full, I think. Why does that matter?"

I couldn't answer him. All I could do was stare at Wes. I couldn't even think, which was a good thing, since whatever thoughts I did have would've been plucked right out of my head, anyway.

"That's how you knew about Alex. That's why you're here now," I said.

"No, it's not why I'm here," he said, shaking his head, looking incredibly guilty.

I could feel my temper beginning to rise. Seeing him look at me like that only confirmed my suspicions.

"What the hell does this have to do with me?" Alex demanded.

I ignored him and stared at Wes. I was angry, yes, but I also couldn't help but feel hurt and betrayed and used. He'd come here to find out what sort of things Vera–or I–was keeping from him. Only, he didn't trust me enough to tell him the truth out loud. He picked the one day he could get it from me whether I was willing or not.

"No, Tara. It's not like that." Wes took a step forward, and Alex moved closer to me.

Wes' gaze swiveled and locked onto Alex, full of fire and venom.

"I can't believe you," I whispered, still trying to process all of the reasons he'd come, and all of the thoughts he'd heard from me so far.

"Tara, it's not because of the full moon. I missed you." He put extra emphasis on the last part, but it was too late.

"You should go now," I said, not meeting his eyes.

"I'm not leaving like this."

"She said go," Alex said.

Wes glared at him and took another step forward, this one towards Alex. I could feel a vague vibration in the ward's line. He was getting dangerously close to crossing.

"I'll go when I'm ready. This has nothing to do with you," Wes growled at him.

"She's on my side of the line right now, pup. Which means she's my responsibility, and I will protect her, even from you." Alex hadn't stepped forward but he hadn't backed up either.

Through the veil of tears covering my eyes, I finally realized how serious this was getting. Wes was shaking, struggling to stay in control of his human form. I needed to do something before someone crossed the line.

"We'll go, then," I said. I turned to walk away, but Alex stayed where he was. I sighed and grabbed hold of his arm, pulling on him. "Let's go."

"You think because it's a full moon I can't take him?" Alex spoke through clenched teeth, his eyes on Wes.

I dropped my hand from his arm. "Are you serious right now? You actually think any of this has anything to do with you? Let's go!" I was shouting now, with fisted hands, and I could feel myself shaking. In three seconds, I already felt closer to the edge than that night in the woods with Cambria and Logan.

"No, I don't think it's about me. Are you okay?" Alex's expression had gone from pissed to concerned, and he held me lightly by the shoulders. His arms shook along with me.

"Tara?" Wes' voice was urgent and close. "Tara, what's wrong?"

I turned to look at him, and all I could see was how mad I was for what he'd done. I couldn't think in coherent sentences, much less talk in them. All I could do was glare. Some sound erupted from deep in my throat. I couldn't hold it in. I opened my mouth and uttered a growl.

Everyone stopped and stared.

It surprised me enough that the shaking ceased, and I felt a little calmer.

"Um, okay. Feel better?" Cambria asked.

I nodded. Wes and Alex were still watching me, but with totally different expressions. Alex looked concerned, and a little confused. Wes looked… almost animal. His head was cocked to the side in a gesture I knew wasn't even conscious, and he looked curious more than anything else.

"We should go," I said. I was glad my voice sounded somewhere close to normal. "We're losing light anyway and we're not done with patrols."

As I'd hoped, reminding Alex of the job at hand got his attention. "Right. Let's get going," he said.

No one else looked back at Wes but me. He stayed right where he was, watching with a painted expression until I reached the briars and waded inside.

CHAPTER TWENTY-ONE

Monday and Tuesday passed. That was the only way to describe it. I didn't know whether the days had been quiet, or loud, or easy, or hard. They simply… passed. I was in too much of a haze to notice the details. I went to class, did my homework, ate with Cambria and Logan, and trained with Alex. None of them brought it up. I guess they all knew I wasn't going to talk about it until I was ready.

Alex seemed the most out of sorts, which surprised me. He was usually so good at putting up a front, but there was serious tension on his part. So much that we'd gone back to running for the entire session, in silence. Victoria had even given up on torturing me since nothing she said seemed to get a reaction. I guess I wasn't even a fun victim at this point.

All I could think about was Wes and how he'd ruined it. I should've been happy to see him that day in the woods, even if it sucked that I couldn't touch him, but he'd had to ruin it by coming on the full moon. Did he really distrust me that much? And then there was all the extra information I'd handed to him, through the power of my wandering thoughts. The one that bothered me most was, of course, Alex. I'd convinced myself that I would've told him had I been given the opportunity. I wasn't a two-timer. But now, Wes had only my disjointed and guilty thoughts as explanation. Did he even know I hadn't been the one to initiate the kiss? Had that come through in what he'd heard?

Not that I cared what he thought. I mean, I was mad at him. And for good reason. So, why did I care so much how he felt?

And then there was the pull. That was all I knew to call it at this point. That strange magnetic feeling I'd gotten that, in the end, had led me right to Wes. It scared me enough that I couldn't bring it up to anyone, not even Cambria. I'd felt a similar–though not nearly as strong– pull to him when we'd been together back in Frederick Falls. So was this pull somehow responsible for my attraction to him? Would I even be drawn to him without it? And where did it come from?

By Wednesday morning, I was deep in my own pity party. I was so distracted by it that I didn't notice anything wrong right away. I was halfway across my room, my eyes still heavy with sleep, when I caught a whiff of something foreign and wrinkled my nose. I looked back at my half of the room and froze.

All of the laundry that had scattered the floor had been shredded. It looked like giant claw marks had cut my clothing into little pieces and let it lay where it fell. Scraps were scattered on every surface, including my desk and bed. I ran back over and yanked on my dresser. Everything had been pulled out of the drawers, down to my underwear. No piece of clothing remained intact.

I sniffed the air again and frowned. What was that scent? It smelled like something burning.

I followed it all the way to the floor underneath my bed. The only thing there was my empty suitcase. I yanked on it and pulled it out, flipping it open with caution. I stared down at it in horror. I'd forgotten. It hadn't been empty. I'd been keeping the stakes and weapons Cambria had gotten for us in here when we weren't on patrol. Now, they were a pile of ash and burnt wood. The smell of smoke burned in my nose and I knew whoever had destroyed them had done it recently. I had a sinking feeling I knew who that someone was.

I marched down the hall and banged on Cambria's door. She

opened with a protest about beauty sleep but quickly shut her mouth when she saw the look on my face. I stepped inside and told her what had happened.

"Crap. You think she's going to rat us out for the weapons?" she asked.

"No. I mean, if she did, she'd be telling on herself for burning the evidence. She's got something else up her sleeve."

"You want to borrow something?" Cambria asked, looking sympathetically at my pajamas.

"Oh, um." I hesitated. Cambria's style wasn't something just anyone could pull off. I mean, her pajamas consisted of a black lace cami with black leggings that had skulls going up the side of each leg. She topped it off with kitten slippers.

Cambria must've noticed my scrutiny. She rolled her eyes. "Not me, my roommate. Her style is a little more…you."

I ignored any underlying meaning to her words. "Won't she be mad?"

"Always absent, remember?" She gestured to the closet that was opposite her own, and I tried not to show my relief. It was filled with plain jeans and tee shirts.

"Thanks," I said, walking over and rifling through until I found a size that would work.

"Don't mention it." She waited until I pulled out a shirt and then said, "But seriously, don't mention it. My roommate will be pissed if she finds out."

"My lips are sealed," I promised.

We showered and dressed and headed up for breakfast, and I was glad, for Victoria's sake, that I'd had time to cool off before facing her for destroying my property. But as soon as we walked into the dining hall and I caught sight of her perched at her usual window table with all her loyal subjects fanned out around her the fury was back.

"Come on. Let's get this over with," Cambria said, marching straight for Victoria's table.

That surprised me. Cambria was usually the one who tried calming me down or talking me out of a scene, since we both knew I was unpredictable in a face to face.

"Well, well, look who it is. Love your outfit, Tara, is it new?" Victoria's smile lit up and shined a new level of evil over the rest of her features.

I opened my mouth to respond, but Cambria beat me to it. "All of you." She was looking at the rest of the kids gathered at the table and her gaze meant business. "Scatter," she said, once she'd made eye contact with them all.

One by one, they all got up and walked away, taking full trays of food with them. Most of them relocated but some actually left the dining hall completely. I stared at Cambria until I began to recognize the intense way she was watching the last of the retreating kids.

"What the hell do you think you're doing?" Victoria demanded, rising.

"Sit down," Cambria said. She seated herself across from Victoria, looking calm and controlled.

"I don't take orders from you," Victoria snapped "How did you do that? You better not be using compulsion."

"I'm charming, what can I say? Now, sit down, and don't make me have to use my powers of persuasion to get you to do it," Cambria said.

I watched Victoria from across the table with my arms crossed and had to hold back a smug smile as she lowered herself into her chair.

"What do you want?" she snapped. She sounded impatient, but I thought I saw a small glimmer of fear pass over her before she replaced it with her usual bitchiness.

"A truce," said Cambria.

"And why would I do that?"

"Well." Cambria leaned back in her chair and eyed Victoria like you would a prisoner; all confidence and a little bit like you had a secret. "So far this war has been pretty much one sided. We've let you have all the victory."

"Let me? Please." Victoria snorted and tossed her hair, refusing to be intimidated.

I could feel my temper threatening to break. Logan walked up beside me, eyebrows raised, and I gave him a look that said "not now."

"Yes, let you," Cambria went on. "But if you insist on amping up the battles, we'll be forced to retaliate." Cambria leaned forward, elbows on the table, and stared straight at Victoria with wide eyes. "Our patience is running thin. Do you understand?"

Victoria stared straight at Cambria for a long moment, without blinking. Then she nodded her head methodically – like a puppet on a string. Her pupils were unfocused and I heard her say, "I understand. A truce," although it sounded whispery and nothing like the Victoria I knew; full of venom and loathing.

Cambria leaned back and looked away, breaking whatever spell she'd weaved, and Victoria shook her head, obviously trying to clear away whatever had held her. Her eyes narrowed and she glared at Cambria like a snake ready to strike. The fear was back in her eyes, though, and this time she couldn't gloss over it with her attitude.

"You think you can compel me?" she hissed, looking at all of us. Logan shifted uncomfortably, but I met her eyes unflinchingly. "Think again. Wait until I tell Headmaster–"

"I wouldn't if I were you," Cambria said, cutting her off mid-threat. "That'll only snap our patience and then the war becomes two-sided. Consider this an example, a whetting of the appetite. So you know what we're capable of. And consider yourself lucky we allowed the pranks to go on this long. Your roommate has a bit of a temper, you know. You're lucky she hasn't taken a bite out of you in your sleep by now."

Victoria's eyes widened like that possibility had just dawned on her for the first time. I almost laughed.

"Which brings me back to my original offer. A truce," said Cambria.

Victoria glared for another minute and then she finally seemed to realize her acid-stare tactics were no longer effective, at least with us. She sighed almost imperceptibly, and I felt some of the tension go out of me. It was the closest to an admission of defeat I'd probably ever see out of her.

"Fine, whatever. A truce," she said. "For now."

"It'll last until I say it doesn't," said Cambria. She pushed back from her chair and stood.

Victoria remained sitting, looking sullen, and I knew that no matter how much Cambria threatened her, our truce really would last only as long as Victoria could reign herself in.

I followed Cambria out with Logan trailing behind me. We didn't stop until we were out of the dining room and halfway to the staircase. My adrenaline waned, and I stopped to catch my breath and grin at Cambria. She grinned right back. We stayed that way until Logan interrupted.

"You both look like lunatics right now, you know that?"

I shrugged and kept grinning. "That was awesome," I said, looking at Cambria. "You can be pretty scary when you want to."

"You're both lucky Victoria's not the type to rat you out," said Logan, shaking his head. He looked at Cambria. "You're pushing it and one of these days you're going to push too far."

My smile faded. "What does that mean?"

Cambria sighed. "He means if any of the staff found out I used my uh, skills, for something other than killing Werewolves, I'd be expelled." She glared at Logan. "Buzz kill."

"So?" I countered. "Why is that even so bad? This place sucks anyway. You could skip it and find a job or something."

"You think anyone in the Hunter world would hire her or even trust her if she's known for using her power against her own people?" Logan said. "She'd be a scarlet letter. She'd have to join the human world and be shut out from Hunters forever."

"Oh," I said, finally understanding the severity of the situation. "Maybe you shouldn't have done that."

"Please." Cambria rolled her eyes. "It was as much for me as it was for you. The ice queen's reign has come to an end. I'm happy to be the one to let her know. Quit worrying about me. I'll be careful."

I didn't know what else to say, so I nodded.

"Now, let's go to class and enjoy this truce while it lasts," she said, smiling again.

We parted ways, and I headed for English, feeling a little lighter than I had before.

It wasn't until Defensive Maneuvers that I started feeling anxious again. I'd managed to push away all thoughts of Wes, Alex, and the problem that was always in the back of my mind–Miles–for most of the morning. I walked into the classroom and found Professor Flaherty waiting at the doorway. I mumbled "Hello" and kept walking, but she stopped me and motioned for me to follow her to the corner of the room.

"Tara, I want to check and see how things are going for you here," she said.

"Um, fine, I guess," I said.

She nodded and then lowered her voice. "Listen, I've been made aware of a proposal offered to you by Professor Kane about training with him next year, and I'd like to offer one of my own."

"Okay." It came out sounding more like a question. I hadn't really given much thought to Professor Kane's offer. Or any thought at all, really. But I wasn't going to tell her that.

"You have a lot of potential, Tara, and from what little I've seen of your combat skills, you're going to make a great fighter, a real asset to the Hunter community. I'd like to offer myself as a mentor for next year and work with you personally on further developing your combat and weaponry skills." She looked like she was going to say more, but another group of students walked in behind me and she broke off, watching me expectantly.

"Uh, thanks." She blinked at me, waiting for more. "Can I think about it?"

"Of course, it's not a light decision by any means. Your mentor will play a significant role in what sort of Hunter you will become. Take all the time you need."

I nodded, and she ushered me to my seat. We were doing in-class lectures today about new techniques. We wouldn't start drilling on them until tomorrow, so I had a day to do nothing but think. I would rather be outside, kicking and punching at someone, but I didn't have a choice, and my thoughts immediately wandered back over my conversation with Professor Flaherty. She was right about one thing. A mentor did play a significant role in my life. At least mine did. Whether I wanted to admit it or not.

BY THE END OF THE DAY, AND ANOTHER INFINITELY LONG AND EERILY quiet training session with Alex, I couldn't take it anymore. I waited until I thought Alex would be heading in for a shower and I slipped up to the roof of Griffin Hall. I powered my phone up and crouched down behind one of the AC units. Two new voice mails. I clicked the button to retrieve the messages, held my breath, and listened.

"Tara, it's me." Wes' voice was low and thick, and something squeezed itself around my heart listening to it. "I know you don't want to talk to me right now. I get it. I want you to know I'll be here when you're ready. I just – I miss you. A lot." The last word was nothing but a whisper and then the line went dead.

I pressed the button to save the message and listened to it over again, enjoying the sound of his voice. There was longing in it, along with every other emotion that should've been there when we'd seen each other face to face. After the third listen, I sighed and skipped to the next message. This voice brought on exactly the opposite reaction.

"Hello, darling." Miles' voice dripped with psychotic sweetness. I tensed and swallowed against a horrible taste in my throat. "Time is running a little short, and we've had to bump up our schedule a bit. I know I said I'd come for you when I was ready but I think it best if we rearrange that a bit and have you come to me. We need to be moving on from here. It's getting a little crowded with all of your boyfriends, and what-not. I'm in Luray. Not too far from you as the wolf runs. Keep your phone close, and I'll call you tomorrow morning with further instructions. Won't be long now, darling. Ciao."

The line went dead, and I closed the phone and let it fall into my lap. I stared ahead, seeing nothing, my mind racing.

Miles wanted to meet me and was giving up a location to do so. It would be crazy to go. Walking right into a trap. Then again, he didn't want me dead this time. He just… wanted me. Eww.

I knew I should probably tell someone–or everyone. That would've been the smart move. Take a team with me; try to close in on his location and take him out once and for all. But if I brought anyone with me, I had no doubt that Miles' gentle streak would come to an end. If I betrayed him, he could very well change his mind about wanting me alive. But if I went alone, willingly, I'd have a shot. I could get close enough to take him out myself. And in the meantime, I could find out what his little project was all about.

I stood up and brushed myself off, tucking the phone back into my waistband and heading for the door. I was sick of sitting around, waiting for the danger to come to me. I was being handed the chance to end this and I was going to take it. Even better that I wouldn't have to involve or risk anyone I cared about.

My hand faltered at the knob. Wes would be severely pissed off when he found out. So would Alex.

It didn't matter; let them be mad. They'd get over it once they realized I'd taken care of it, and Miles was no longer a problem. It bothered me a little that I would have to kill again, but it bothered me more to have psycho-perv Miles after me for the rest of my life. I shook it off and took the stairs at a run. I had to hurry if I wanted to slip away without being noticed.

That's when it hit me. There was no way I'd make it off school grounds – and through the wards – undetected. Unless…

I checked my watch and made a beeline for the dining hall.

Cambria and Logan were at our usual table, plates loaded with rice and beef. Chinese night.

"I need your help," I said, sliding in across from them.

"What's up?" Cambria lowered her fork and looked instantly suspicious. "Don't tell me Ice Queen ended the truce already because I'll–"

"Not about that," I said, cutting her off. "I need your help getting through the wards."

Cambria cocked her head at me and seemed to consider. Then she exchanged a glance with Logan who gave her a knowing look. "Let me guess," she said. "Time to make up with hottie boyfriend."

"Um." I blinked.

Cambria nodded, like that was all the answer she needed, and I felt guilty enough that I had to look away, but I kept my mouth firmly shut. It was better than having to explain Miles and then somehow convince her she couldn't come.

"Can you do it?" I asked.

Cambria shrugged. "Easy peasy. When?"

CHAPTER TWENTY-TWO

"I can't believe we're doing this," Logan muttered.

"Ssh!" I hissed at him through the earpiece and heard Cambria do the same thing from right next to him.

"You aren't doing anything," I heard her say.

Cambria had swiped the earpieces from a gullible senior – it would've been too risky to ask Alex – and although I hadn't asked and she hadn't said, I was pretty sure she'd had to use her powers of persuasion to get him to hand over the goods. I would've felt bad for making her use her powers because of me, but that was nothing compared to what she was about to do. I wasn't allowing myself to think about what would happen if she got caught.

Logan had the earpiece so he could signal me when the coast was clear but he'd kept it set to "two way," so he wouldn't have to press the button to talk to me; which meant I could hear all of the bickering going on between them as I made my way towards the invisible border in the woods.

It wasn't quite dark yet but it was close enough that there were shadows everywhere. It was eerily quiet, save for the sharp call of a bird at regular intervals, and I had to concentrate to block out the feeling of being so completely alone out here. Alone was a good thing. Having company would be a problem.

I was on alert for it, too, but there was no sign of movement, or goose bumps, or a pull of any kind. That last part was sort of disappointing, although I didn't know why. It's not like I could expect Wes to still be waiting for me three days later. Besides, a part of me was still angry. I was clinging to that part because it made missing him a little easier.

I trudged on, slowly, careful not to leave a trail, like Alex had taught me. Until I was clear of the wards, I needed to make sure there was no evidence of having been here. If I didn't return soon–that thought left a lump in my chest too big to swallow–Alex would come looking and I didn't want him following.

Through the earpiece, I could hear Cambria whispering to Logan and him shushing her. A door banged closed, and I knew they were inside Griffin Hall. I picked up the pace. I was supposed to be in position when they found Headmaster, and I still had a fair distance to go.

A few minutes later the silence on Logan's end was broken by a faint, echoing knock. It was followed up by a pause and then Headmaster Whitfield's surprised voice coming through the line.

"Mr. Sandefur. Miss Hebert. What brings you here at this time?"

"A quick question about our schedules, actually," said Cambria. She was talking slow, and I could hear the hypnotic quality already seeping into her tone.

"Sure, sure. Come in. Sit down. I was heading out for the night, so let's make this quick," he said.

He must've led them to the chairs in his office because there was a pause and then fabric rustling.

"What exactly do you want to know, Ms. Hebert?" Headmaster asked.

"Well, it's not so much about my schedule as the wards," said Cambria, in a sing-song tone.

I stilled without even realizing it and held my breath. I could picture the way she'd stare at Headmaster Whitfield, intense and unblinking, a gentle expression on her face.

"Wards? What about them?" Judging from the tone of his voice, the charm was already working. He didn't sound the least bit alarmed about her comments.

"I need to know the bypass phrase, sir. It's a small favor, just this once."

Cambria's voice was soothing and even without the power of her eyes on me I could feel myself wanting to give her what she was asking. I shivered and my head cleared. Wow. That girl had some serious talent. She hadn't even laid it on this thick with Victoria. A stab of guilt shot through my gut. Please don't let her get caught because of me.

"Bypass phrase. Of course," I heard Headmaster say. It was a mumbled response. He was fully under Cambria's influence now.

"Yes, sir, what is it?" Cambria prompted.

"Semper Tutus."

"Semper what?" Cambria's voice sharpened, and I cringed. We didn't need Headmaster coming out of it before she was done.

"Semper Tutus," Logan whispered. "It's Latin. Finish up."

"Thank you for your help, sir. We're going to head back now. Can you do me one more favor?" Cambria asked, back to her smooth tone. "Forget we were here, sir."

"Of course, Miss Hebert. Already forgotten," said Headmaster Whitfield.

Chairs scraped; I could hear Cambria and Logan shuffling for the door.

"Oh, one more question, sir," said Cambria. "How long is this bypass phrase good for?"

"It will be changed tomorrow," he said. He didn't sound nearly as out of it as before, at least not on my end.

My pulse sped. "Get out of there," I hissed into my mouthpiece.

"Thanks," Cambria called. A door clicked shut.

I resumed up my pace. Silence followed, and I knew they were booking it back to the dorm, or at least somewhere far away from Griffin Hall.

"Tara, you there?" Logan finally came back on.

"I'm here," I said.

"How far away are you?"

"Almost there."

"You heard the bypass phrase?"

"Yeah. Latin."

"Doesn't seem like Vera's style, does it?"

I shook my head. "No," I murmured. "Let's hope it works."

I reached the thorns and got through them as best I could without getting bloodied up. It was completely dark when I came out the other side, and I stood still for a moment, using the thorns as cover and waiting for my eyes to adjust. Slowly, the dark shapes of trees and bushes came into blurred focus. When I realized that was as good as it got, I walked forward.

"I'm starting to feel the pulse. I'm almost there," I whispered.

"You know what to do," said Logan.

Static crackled over the line, like fabric rustling. Hissed whispers. Then, "Tara, its Cambria. How are we doing?"

"Okay, so far."

"Did the bypass phrase work?"

"We're about to find out."

"Be careful," she said.

"I will. And Cambria, thanks for doing this."

"Are you kidding? School hasn't been this much fun since Logan got his underwear stolen. Off his body."

"Shut-up," I heard Logan hiss.

"I don't want you to get in trouble because of me," I said. I was almost there and feeling guilty now that the deed was done.

"Don't worry about me. It's been a long time since I had a friend worth doing it for," she said. Her voice was thicker and lower than usual, and I could tell she meant it.

"I don't know how I would've survived this place if I hadn't met you," I said. I really was grateful to have found Cambria–and Logan, too.

Logan's hissing voice came through my earpiece, pulling me out of my thoughts. "We do not have time for this."

"He's right. We'll bond later," said Cambria. Her tone was all business. "Listen, when you're through we're going to have to sign off so I can get this earpiece back before anyone notices."

"What about mine?"

"Bury it for now and then bring it to me when you come back through."

"No one will notice it's gone?"

"You'll be back before they do," she said, sounding overly sure. She paused, like she wasn't sure whether to say the next part. "I don't know if you heard, but Headmaster Whitfield says the bypass phrase is only good until tomorrow."

"I know." I tried to sound unconcerned. "Here goes," I added, wanting to cut off any further conversation. There was nothing left to say, anyway, that wouldn't lead to more questions.

I took a deep breath and stepped as close to the pulse as I dared without stepping into its direct line. Then I exhaled and whispered, "Semper Tutus".

The pulse in the air waned and disappeared. I wasn't sure how long it would last, but I didn't want to find out. I shot forward, running several yards and taking cover behind a tree, before stopping and looking back. There was nothing to see, of course. I wondered if the wards were down around the whole school or only in that spot. No time to find out.

"I'm through," I said into my mouthpiece.

"Good girl," said Cambria. In the background I heard Logan sigh. "Now get going and find your man."

"Um, right. I'll see you guys… soon."

"Don't forget you have a curfew."

"I won't." We said goodbye, and I powered off the earpiece and removed it. I found a soft spot in the dirt at the base of the tree and buried the earpiece like Cambria had suggested. I covered the spot with leaves and stared at the tree until I was sure I would remember where I'd left it.

When I was finished, I turned and ran.

CHAPTER TWENTY-THREE

The sound of my phone ringing woke me up. I groaned and grabbed for it, yanking it free of where it was wedged between my pocket and the hard, wet ground. I rolled to a sitting position, pulling leaves and debris from my hair and answered it, still half-asleep.

"Hello?" My voice was a croak. I desperately needed water…and a toothbrush. Yuck.

"Tara, darling." Miles sounded wide awake and ecstatic.

I came awake at the reminder of why I was here, alone in the woods, sleeping on the ground.

"You came," he said.

"Yes, I came," I answered, scanning the trees warily. "How did you know?"

"I have my sources. I've sent someone to bring you to me. He should be there shortly. Stay put and we'll see each other soon."

The line went dead before I could argue.

Great, so I was supposed to sit in the woods like a painted target until someone–or something–came for me? I pulled a bottle of water out of my backpack, slugged half of it down, and stood up to brush myself off. My jeans were damp and stale but I didn't have anything else, thanks to Victoria. I looked around, trying to find someplace to wait it out where I would see what was coming. There wasn't much to choose from.

On one side were widely spaced trees that got thicker the further you went. On my other side was a shallow river that separated the forest from a trail that led into town. The faint trickle of water could be heard as it was pulled over rocks in the riverbed. Part of me wanted to get in and wash off, but I didn't dare with company on the way.

I went back to scanning my surroundings, and in the end, I climbed into the low branch of the tree I'd slept under. I hung my backpack on a curved branch next to me and checked on the wooden stake I'd packed into my boot–a replacement for the burnt one, thanks to Cambria–before settling in to wait.

I felt the newcomer before I saw him. The goose bumps ran up my arm and onto my neck and I clamped down against the creepy crawly feeling. A second later, a husky brown wolf emerged from the thick of the trees, heading in my direction. He stopped and looked around, his brown wolf eyes confused, as he scanned the forest floor for me. He sniffed the air and grew agitated; probably because he could smell me, but it hadn't dawned on him to look up. It might've been a funny prank under other circumstances.

Suddenly, the wolf's eyes sharpened into slits and his hair stood up. He fell into a crouch at the same moment the wave of goose bumps swept over me, intensifying exponentially. The brown wolf had just enough time to pull his lips over his teeth and growl before an entire pack of Werewolves shot into the clearing and pounced on him. There had to be at least seven of them, maybe more. It was too hard to count with all of them moving so fast. Half of them piled onto the brown wolf, taking him down in a flurry of fur. The other half spread out and began sniffing; the air, the ground, the leaves, the river's edge.

Their eyes gleamed with the hunt.

Below me, a sandy wolf circled the tree, sniffing excitedly. It did a full lap of the tree trunk and stopped in the spot where I'd slept. Then it raised its head and looked up – right at me.

I froze.

The wolf tore its eyes from mine long enough to glance back over its shoulder and growl, long and loud, followed by, "She's here."

The rest of the wolves, who weren't already occupied with killing, raised their heads and met my eyes, one by one. I felt the goose bumps rise and the creepy crawly feeling intensify. I was pretty sure this wasn't good. Even if they couldn't get up here in wolf form, all it would take was one of them changing back to human form and pulling me down to the others to end it. I had no choice but to fight.

Without taking my eyes off the wolves, I reached into my boot and pulled out my stake. I let it fall into a comfortable position in my palm and narrowed my eyes. I shoved aside every thought that didn't involve ending the Werewolves below me. Then, with a deep breath, I pushed off my branch and dropped to the ground.

The sandy wolf was waiting.

He leapt toward me the moment my feet hit the ground. I knocked him aside with my free hand and sent him sprawling. Another one was there to take its place, and I used a combination kick-hit move that I'd learned in Professor Flaherty's class. I was so pleased with myself when it worked to knock the wolf aside that I almost missed the one coming at me from the other direction. At the last second, I kicked my foot out and nailed the wolf in the shoulder. I spun, using my body's momentum, and pushed the stake into its chest as I came around. It slid in and out in a clean motion and the wolf dropped to the ground, breathing heavily. It made no move to get up.

One down.

Six to go.

Two more were already on me and even though I managed to deflect their teeth away from my flesh, I knew this wouldn't last long. Out of the corner of my eye, I could make out the still form of the brown wolf I'd seen first, the one Miles had sent to get me. It wasn't moving, and I didn't need to check for a pulse to know it wasn't breathing, either.

I was on my own.

The knowledge of that threatened to paralyze me, but I kept on. If I was going to die here, I was going to take as many of them with me as I could.

I pressed my lips together and swung my stake towards the nearest wolf. It lodged in the Were's rib cage, and I yanked it sideways before pulling it free. The wolf let out a high pitched howl before falling at my feet. I stepped over it to meet my next attacker, using another move I'd learned in Flaherty's class to block it and keep its teeth from breaking my skin.

All around me the sounds of the forest were dimmed by the incessant growling and snarling of my attackers. I used that to see them coming, even from behind me. I twisted and turned in every direction, trusting my body and my instincts to block whatever came at me.

The Werewolves teamed up, coming at me in groups of two. It wasn't quite as easy to block two at a time. I could feel myself getting tired. It felt like I'd been fighting for hours when in reality it had been what, two minutes? Three?

I spun again, maneuvering away, this time losing my balance and sidestepping so I wouldn't fall. Unfortunately, I sidestepped right into the path of an oncoming Were, and before I could get clear, I felt the stinging swipe of claws rake down my back, ripping my shirt and flesh all at once. Tears formed in my eyes, and I blinked them back, shutting out the stinging pain.

I whirled and leaned away from the teeth already headed straight for my face. I brought my stake down in an arc and smashed it into the wolf's eye. It yelped and jerked away and I barely managed to pull the wood free before the wolf took off, yelping in pain in a haphazard circle around the clearing.

I didn't have time to fall back again before another wolf was on me. With claws extended, it leapt at me, pushing me to the ground and pressing its claws into my shoulders. I flinched from the pain and was surprised enough to be going down that I didn't even have a chance to roll away. The wolf landed on top of me, pinning me underneath it. Its jaw was only inches from my face. It panted and stared down at me with glassy, yellow eyes. Saliva pooled at the corners of its mouth. I cringed away, more grossed out about a face-full of drool than I was about getting hacked up by those teeth.

"You're a fighter, Tara Godfrey," it growled, bearing down on me so that its claws dug into the wounds it had opened on my shoulder. I grimaced. "But we are stronger. You made a mistake. One that needs to be rectified. The only way to make it right is with death. And now it is your turn."

His paws bore down on my throat, making it harder to breathe. "What mistake?" I managed.

"You half-breeds think you're God but you're not. You're monsters, same as us, and monsters should be destroyed, not created," it snarled.

Hot drool leaked from its jowls onto my shoulder, and I tried to shrink away, but its claws held fast to my punctured skin. The rank odor of its breath wafted into my face and there was suddenly nowhere left to go, to get fresh air.

My lungs felt like they were closing up on me. I was vaguely aware of the other pack members advancing towards us, waiting for the signal to close the gap and tear into me with their razor canines. I tried to focus, to find a way to break free of the one holding me still, but it was like my brain had overloaded or short circuited.

For the first time in a long time, I felt scared. Not just a little afraid, but well and truly terrified. I didn't want to die like this at the hands of a rabid Werewolf pack. I squirmed and struggled, but my attackers only crept closer. I could see the feral glee in their glowing eyes; the murder they craved.

This pack was different from other Werewolves. Different from Leo or even Miles. They were clearly all about the hunt and even more about the kill. There was no perverted craziness here, only cold blooded hunger for death. Maybe that's what made me so afraid. A part of me knew–could feel–how much they were going to enjoy this. They wouldn't make it quick.

My heart pounded. They were close now. A hush had fallen over them; the only noise was a soft growl emanating from somewhere deep in their throats. It blurred together until it became one sound, instead of several.

The one pinning me leaned towards me again, its sweaty muzzle only inches from my face.

"You should've kept yourself far away from the likes of him. You've brought this on yourself." He paused and then leaned even closer and lowered his growly voice so that I was the only one who heard the next part. "I will enjoy killing a half-breed like you. You smell too much like me but fight too much like them."

Then he raised his head and opened his mouth, to give the signal to attack, no doubt.

A noise came from somewhere at the edge of the clearing and all of the Werewolves' necks snapped that way, alert and attentive to the distraction.

I tried craning my neck around, but I was pinned. Any movement I made only dug the claws further into my flesh. I stayed still and prayed for a miracle.

More rustling and then a figure broke free of the branches. All I caught was a blur of motion out of the corner of my eye and two wolves went down. A sharp cry went up among the remaining four, including the one who still held me pinned. He nodded his head at the three still standing somewhere behind me and they rushed off. Their growls were menacing and still held a hunger for a kill. Whether it was me or someone else didn't seem to matter.

I crossed my fingers for whoever was out there fighting for me and tried to summon the strength to push the Were off me and take him down while the coast was clear. I shoved as hard as I could, still aware of the claws digging into my shoulders, and managed to shove him a few inches sideways before he bore down with his full weight, paralyzing me against the dirt. I squeezed my eyes shut against the stinging pain and bit my lip until I tasted blood.

"No you don't," the Were growled. "I am going to finish this while I can." He reared his head back and revealed the sharpest, grimiest canines I'd ever seen. I could see the intent in his eyes. He was going to strike.

Something inside me snapped, and I felt a guttural sound rise up in my throat. I let it loose without thinking and was shocked when a vicious snarl escaped my lips. I think the Werewolf was a little surprised, too, because he paused to blink at me. Then he must've regained his concentration because his eyes narrowed to slits and he snarled back, sounding a lot more intimidating than I had.

Then an arm–a human arm–grabbed him from behind and yanked.

The Werewolf went sprawling backwards and the arm let go. A shadow fell over me. I blinked into the glare, waiting for my eyes to adjust so I could see exactly who it was rescuing me. If it was Miles, would I have to say thank you? Would I be forced to be grateful?

That question was never answered. When I blinked again and the face came into focus, I almost choked. It wasn't Miles who stood over me, watching me with the worst combination of concern and outrage I'd ever seen.

"Are you okay? Did they hurt you?"

"Alex? How did you find me?" I pushed myself onto my elbows and Alex extended his hand to help me up. I started to reach for him, but a glimpse of fur behind him distracted me.

"Look out!"

He swiveled and brought his hands up, sidestepping and delivering a blow all in one motion. The Werewolf that had pinned me was thrown to the ground. It was up again, and circling, in a blink. Alex fell into a fighting stance, letting it circle but leading it away from where I still lay in the dirt.

I pushed myself up and crawled to the base of a tree to keep out of the way. I glanced over, wondering what had happened to the rest of the Weres who'd been about to take a bite out of me, and found the ground littered with furry bodies. Some of them had gaping wounds that seeped red. Wooden stakes protruded.

None of them moved.

I turned back to Alex and the remaining Werewolf and took a deep breath. I needed to get a hold of myself so I could jump in if Alex needed me. The Werewolf he faced was huge, determined, and completely focused on the kill. I could feel it when I looked at him. I could see it in his eyes and the set of his jaw.

Alex didn't look any less determined, though. He never took his eyes off the Were and was still circling, though I knew he was waiting for the Were to make the first move. That was Alex's style.

Alex repositioned the stake in his hand, and I caught a gleam of metal on the tip as it began to arc through the air and cut a path towards the wolf.

The Were came, teeth first, but Alex spun and deflected it easily. The stake grazed fur but didn't penetrate. Alex completed the turn and rammed his fist into the Were as it went by, sending it flying forward, legs sprawled. It was completely off balance and Alex took full advantage. He ran and leapt at the Were, stake extended, and caught the Were in the stomach. There was a definite hiss in the air as the stake pushed through fur and into flesh.

Alex pulled his stake free and stood, looking down at the Were. It was trying to get up and move away as Alex stalked towards its head, but it faltered. It couldn't seem to put weight on its front left paw and blood was already seeping heavily from the stomach wound.

Alex showed no reaction to the Were's injury, at least not outwardly. He walked right up to the Were and stood over it, and even though I couldn't see his eyes, I had the distinct impression that if I could, I would see the same killing intent there that I had in the pack.

He didn't hesitate or give the Werewolf any chance at last words. He simply reached down and plunged his stake into the Were's shoulder, yanking on it to move it through the heart.

The Were jerked once and opened its mouth in a silent growl and then went slack. Its eyes were open but unfocused and pointing towards me.

Something rippled in the air and then it was still. I could only watch–and wonder if this was what it had been like when I'd killed Leo. I couldn't remember anything except the ice cold, excruciating pain of it.

I felt the air ripple again as the stake was pulled free.

CHAPTER TWENTY-FOUR

"You want to tell me what the hell made you come out here alone?"

I didn't answer.

"Or why you decided to try and fight an entire pack of Werewolves who don't enjoy killing unless it's slow and painful?"

I kept my eyes averted. If I looked up, I knew I'd be drawn back to the empty stare of the Werewolf pack leader where he lay bleeding in the dirt. All I could think was that it was almost me, glassy eyed and lifeless in the middle of the woods. It was almost me…

"Tara, dammit!" Alex stepped in front of me, blocking my view of the river, and crouched down until we were eye to eye. "Answer me!"

I brought my eyes to his and saw the coldness in his stare give way to something else. I wasn't sure what, but something hot and dangerous looked back at me.

I swallowed, and focused on his eyes instead of his mouth. I suddenly felt stupid for what I'd done, which only made me angry. "It was dumb. I was dumb," I said. "Is that what you want to hear? Or thank you for saving me, how about that one?"

His eyes flashed, and his chest rose and fell with heavy breaths. I wasn't sure if it was from the fight or from being so angry with me. He leaned closer. I blanched, sure he was going to kiss me, and not sure if I'd be able to stop him right now with my heart pounding so hard in my chest and the panic of near-death still in my veins. But he stopped an inch away and did something completely unexpected.

He sniffed.

Then he sat back. "Huh."

"What?"

"You smell like…"

He didn't finish, and I was sure I didn't want to know, but I couldn't let it go. "Like what?"

"Well, like them, a little," he admitted.

"Probably because the alpha over there rubbed himself all over me and drooled a little for good measure," I said.

Alex nodded, really slow, and I knew neither of us was convinced with that answer; but now wasn't the time.

"Did they hurt you?" he asked. His voice was quieter now and whatever had been in his eyes was cooling.

I allowed myself a deep breath. "No. I mean, yeah, some scratches. No teeth, though, so I'll be fine."

"Good. Can you walk?"

"I think so."

"Let's get going then. I really don't want to wait around to see if there are more on standby."

"You think?" I asked, stricken with the idea.

I was sort of ashamed I hadn't thought of it, but Alex was right. Even if the rabid pack was taken care of, Miles would surely be sending someone else to check on me any minute; I was running late for our little reunion. And after what had just happened, I was in no shape to carry out my plan.

"Let's get out of here," Alex said.

I nodded and let him help me to my feet. When I was sure I was steady enough, we headed through the trees. On the other side was a path I hadn't seen on my way in. Probably because it had been pitch black. Alex led me onto the path and we veered around and splashed across a shallow portion of the river, downstream from my rendezvous point. The path was leading us straight towards town.

"Are you sure this is a good idea?" I asked, slowing my steps and hesitating.

"We don't have a choice. If we stay in the woods we risk another attack–and you're not up for that."

"Yeah but..." I wanted to say that Miles was that direction but I wasn't ready to admit to my real reason for being out here yet.

"You need to get cleaned up. We'll get a room and then rent a car to drive back to school."

My shoulders sagged in relief at the mention of a hot shower. Alex must've taken my reaction for disappointment, though, because he glanced at me with something close to sympathy.

"I know it's a lot to handle right now, but it'll get better. You should really stand up to Victoria. Let her know not to mess with you," he said. "I'm sure she'd back off."

I gaped at him. "You think this is about bullying? You think I ran away?"

"Didn't you?"

I bit back a laugh because for now, until I worked up the nerve to tell him why I was really here, it was as good excuse as any. "Okay," was all I said. "Let's get to that shower."

Alex nodded, and we started walking again.

Less than an hour later, we were unlocking the door to a motel room that wasn't exactly five stars but smelled clean, as long as you didn't mind the scent of mildew mixed with bleach. Alex still hadn't asked me more about what I was doing here so I hadn't asked him how he'd found me. I figured it was sort of a mutual understanding and tried not to think about what I'd tell him when he ended the truce and demanded answers.

I walked inside and clicked the door shut. I eyed the single bed, did my best to ignore the weird ping I got in my chest, and headed for the bathroom.

"Wait," Alex called to my back. "Your shirt is pretty shredded. Here, let me."

He came up behind me and began picking and peeling at the fabric on my back. I watched through the mirror as he grimaced with each poke and pull, and bit my lip against the pain. The blood must've dried on the scratches, making the shirt stick in places, because peeling it off wasn't easy. When all the small pieces had been removed, Alex met my gaze through the mirror.

"Lift up your arms."

I felt his fingers go around the fabric and gently pull up. The shirt caught a couple of times, and I made a face, but Alex managed to pull it free and work it up over my head and arms. He dropped it into the trash can and met my gaze again, still hovering close behind me.

I stood in full view of him, in only a bra and beat up jeans, and I knew I should've moved away, but I didn't. I stared back at him, caught in his expression. He'd made it a point not to let his eyes wander from mine, which I found frustrating and sweet at the same time. A part of me wanted him to let his eyes roam over my body, but the other part of me knew where that could lead – and knew better.

"Thanks." My voice came out in a hoarse whisper, but it was enough to shatter the tension.

Alex nodded and turned away, his face carefully blank.

"I'll find you some clothes," he said, scooping up the room key and heading for the door.

I walked into the bathroom and closed the door, leaning against it and just breathing. What had happened out there? We hadn't even touched but it felt no less powerful than if we had.

I peeled off my jeans and dropped them in a heap on the floor, hoping Alex was true to his word about finding me clothes. Cambria wasn't going to be happy when she realized I'd ruined her roommates outfit. She might not let me borrow anymore. I'd have to get Alex to take me to a clothing store in town before he took us back to school – and I'd have to use my emergency cash so my mother wouldn't find out.

The water finally waned from hot to warm and I shut it off, my skin flushed pink from the heat and the steam. It was the best shower I'd had in weeks. It didn't get this hot in the drafty dorm bathrooms at Wood Point.

From the other side of the door I heard, "I'm back."

I hurried to dry off.

I debated whether I could walk out in nothing but a towel without my face bursting into red hot flames when there was a sharp rap on the door. I yanked the towel around me as the knob turned and the door slid open a crack.

"Here," Alex grunted. He shoved some fabric through the opening, careful to keep his face turned away.

It was a motel-issue robe; once made of soft, fresh terry cloth, it now looked like a worn, faded washcloth. I looked up to mutter a "thanks," but the door had already closed.

I pulled the robe on, used the towel for my hair, and eased out into the room. There was a full length mirror outside the bathroom door, and I caught sight of my reflection. I went closer and pulled the neckline of the robe aside, inspecting the puncture wounds on my shoulders left by the Werewolf's claws. They were small and had already stopped bleeding, but they stung and ached like I'd been punched. Repeatedly.

The pain radiated out onto my arms and chest, so I pulled the robe a little further down and gasped. I was a collage of bumps, bruises, and scrapes. Some were newly forming, so they were blue and swollen, but some – thanks to my speedy healing – were yellow, gross, and looked three days old. I looked like a painter's palette.

"Feeling better?"

I turned and found Alex watching me, frowning at the sight of the bruises and cuts.

"Yeah, thanks," I said, trying to decide whether I could sit on the bed without revealing too much. The robe suddenly felt very small.

"Let me see," he said, walking closer, eyes on my shoulders.

I braced myself against a shiver when I caught sight of his expression. It wasn't passionate or suggestive or any of the emotions you might see in a guy who had a semi-naked girl in front of him. It was soft and gentle and made me wonder how in the world I'd ever overlooked this Alex. Or how different things might be if this were the version of himself he always carried.

He stood in front of me and waited, almost like he was asking for permission. Without a word, I pulled the fabric aside, revealing my wounds. My skin felt overly exposed under his sharp gaze, but I didn't feel embarrassed or self-conscious.

Alex examined the wounds with the intensity of a scientist with his microscope. At one point, he pressed against a bruise and I winced. He pulled back and continued the rest of his exam without further contact.

A minute later, he walked away, and I felt some sort of loss I couldn't explain.

He came back and produced a tube of antibiotic cream. He rubbed a small amount into the open cuts on my shoulders and bandaged them with gauze. I waited for the tension, like before, but his expression remained blank and his demeanor was precise and brisk–like a doctor.

When he was finished, he stepped back and his gaze swept over the rest of me. He frowned, and I wondered if he'd felt any of the sweeping heat and emotion that I had while he'd examined me. If he did, there was no trace of it now.

"Looks like you had quite a workout before I got there. Care to tell me about it yet?"

"If I say no, will you leave me alone or keep asking until I give in?"

"What do you think?"

I cocked my head to the side, not ready to answer. "How did you find me?"

He shook his head. "You snuck off school grounds. By yourself. Got attacked. Almost died." He crossed his arms. "That means you go first."

I stared back at him, pretending to think it over. My mind raced as I tried to figure out what story to give him. The ghost of a smirk appeared on his lips.

"And don't give me that bull shit about meeting Wes like you told Cambria," he said.

"She ratted me out. That's how you knew?"

He shook his head again, refusing to answer. "You first."

"All right, fine." I decided to come out with it. If there was anyone I knew who'd be on my side about my fighting alone, it was Alex. "I'm here for Miles."

"Miles?" Alex's eyebrows shot up and his arms fell away. He apparently hadn't seen that coming. "What about him?" His eyes narrowed, and I knew I'd better talk fast.

"He called me yesterday and left me a message. He said I should meet him instead of waiting for him to come get me." I started to pace back and forth in the small space between the bed and the door. "He didn't say why but I think something must've happened to spook him. Anyway, he said to come here, to the edge of town, and he'd call me with further instructions on where to meet up."

"So, you decided to rush right into it. Head first." Alex sat on the bed, stiff and impatient. He'd gone back to glaring at me. "You never even thought to ask for help, did you? Just had to be the hero."

"Of course, I thought about it," I said. "I thought about how unfair it would be to ask any of you to come. Cambria, Logan… they don't deserve this kind of danger. And you…"

"What about me? I don't deserve it, either?"

"My best chance was going alone. Miles won't hurt me. He wants me alive. I can get close enough to him to end this. Any other way would've meant more violence. This was easiest."

"Uh-huh. And how'd that work out for you?"

I sighed, putting all my frustration into it. "Obviously, not well. But those Werewolves weren't sent by Miles. They ambushed that clearing and killed Miles' guy before I had a chance to stop them. I took out as many as I could before…Well, you know the rest. So, thanks for that."

"If they weren't sent by Miles, then who were they?"

He'd completely ignored my thank you, which grated on me, but I bit my tongue. I wouldn't say it again. "I don't know. The one who had me pinned said something about a mistake and death being the only way to right it. I think I did something to piss them off."

Now it was his turn to get up and pace. "Great. Just great. You're a magnet, you know that? Damn."

He ran a hand over his face and the gesture, combined with those words, reminded me of Wes. For a moment, the emptiness I felt was more painful than the aching and stinging of my wounds, and I couldn't even see Alex's face in front of me. Only a mental image of Wes. Of the way he'd looked on our last day together before I'd come to school.

He'd told me not to forget him.

It made me feel guilty for standing in a motel room, with Alex, wearing nothing but a robe. But then the memory of the full moon came crashing back in, and I hardened myself against the guilt and pushed it away.

"You never said how you found me," I said, moving to a new topic to clear my head.

"Cambria."

"She told you I left but not where I was going."

"Oh, that was easy." His lips crept into a smirk. "I tracked you."

"But I made sure not to leave a trail," I said.

"You really need to work on that."

He was still smirking. And looking at me. And standing way too close. I stepped back and his smile faded, like he understood my reason for putting distance between us.

"I found you some clothes," he said, pointing at a pile of fabric he'd dumped on the bed. "I'm going to go find us a car and then we're heading back. I trust you not to leave while I'm gone."

I blinked, totally giving away my intention with my lack of response. He doubled back and grabbed the clothes off the bed and tucked them under his arm.

"Unless you want to go see Miles wearing nothing but a bathrobe. Bet that would make his day."

He sailed out the door like he couldn't care less whether I stayed or went.

I paced for a while before finally admitting the aches and pains of my body were getting to me and stretched out across the bed. I didn't think I could sleep, after all the adrenaline that had pumped through me that morning but I guess the aftermath of panic tended to make one drowsy. I drifted off to the mental replay of me growling.

A HAND ON MY ARM WOKE ME. NOT THE PRESSURE OF THE TOUCH BUT the pain it caused.

"Ow," I muttered, rolling away from whatever had pressed on my bruises. I eased onto my other side and came face to face with Alex.

His eyes were closed and his breathing was even. He was curled on his side, still in the same clothes he'd worn earlier. There was a small smudge of dirt under his right eye that I hadn't noticed earlier. Actually, there was a lot I hadn't noticed earlier. Like the exact texture of his skin, or the smooth olive color of it. I'd never been close enough to take in the details.

I held my breath as he shifted and brought his arm up to tuck under him. The arm that had fallen over me and woken me. I knew I should get up, move away, anything to put distance between us, but I couldn't. Alex asleep was mesmerizing. The intensity he always wore when he was awake was gone. It made him more approachable. I wanted to enjoy being this close to him and not wanting to kill him.

"You're staring at me," he said, his lips barely moving, his eyes still closed.

I tensed. "You're awake." He didn't answer and I felt awkward. I tried to think of something else to say. "Did you get a car?"

"I did." His eyes opened slowly, almost lazily, and met mine. Something in my stomach leaped into my throat. I couldn't speak. "Your clothes are over there," he said, nodding his head towards the bathroom counter. His voice was low and gruff from sleep.

"Right. I'll get dressed," I said, scooting away and turning my head before he could see the redness creeping into my cheeks.

I felt his hand close over my wrist and pull me back to the pillow.

"I wasn't telling you to get up," he said.

"What are you telling me?" I asked, hating that I'd even voiced the question at all; afraid of the answer.

He didn't respond with words, though. He leaned in and closed the gap, quick enough that neither of us had a chance to change our minds. Our lips met and held for a long moment and then his mouth moved against mine. This was bigger than the first time we'd kissed. That had been almost chaste, the way his lips had planted themselves on mine, unmoving and hard. This was different. Like a dance, starting slow and building into something heavier, something I wasn't sure I could stop.

Alex pulled away first. He stared back at me with a fierce expression, and for a second, I thought it wasn't over. But then he sat back and blinked and the moment faded. I pushed myself up onto my elbows and tried to breathe normally. Alex seemed like he was trying to do the same.

He cleared his throat and did a complete subject change. "You handled yourself pretty well on your own. I almost forgot to tell you that," he said. "As for Miles, your plan wasn't a bad one. But you need a team to help coordinate all of the possible what-ifs. We'll go back to school and regroup and then try again, okay?"

I was too shocked to argue. Partly about the kiss and partly that he was so willing to, not only help me, but do it my way. "Okay," I said, knowing my skepticism was showing.

"You don't believe me?"

"I don't think you're lying," I said carefully.

He laughed. "I'm serious. We can try again once you have time to heal."

"You would let me walk in there alone?" I asked, eyebrows raised, fully expecting him to correct me.

"As long as I was nearby in case you needed me, yes. It's a good plan." I stared at him. "What?"

"Nothing. I…I'm not used to being treated like an equal," I admitted.

"Why? Because you're a Dirt- a hybrid? Or because you're a girl?"

"Both, I guess."

He nodded. "Hunters are pretty good with gender equality, as a rule. I've seen enough women in action to know you girls are just as good in combat, if not better. And I've seen enough of you personally to know you can handle yourself."

"Thanks," I said, understanding the level of compliment I was getting from him and that it didn't come often.

"And if all else fails, you could always kick him between the hips."

I stuck out my tongue.

He smiled. "Now, you can get dressed."

ALEX WAS WAITING FOR ME WHEN I EMERGED FROM THE BATHROOM IN tight sweats – he said he'd swiped them from the lost and found at the front desk–and a white tee shirt. He'd opened the curtains a few inches and sunlight slanted in from an angle.

"What time is it?" I asked, pulling my shoes on.

"Three. If we leave now we can make it back by curfew."

He looked out the window, scanning the parking lot. All traces of humor and closeness were gone, replaced by the rigid, almost military-like attitude he carried when it involved anything to do with Werewolves; it was as if the kiss had never happened.

I hadn't missed the slip he'd made a few minutes ago, when he'd almost called me a Dirty Blood. Did he still think of me as nothing but a half-Werewolf? Did he still despise that part of me? He must be a little more accepting of it, if he wanted to kiss me. I didn't know how to ask without making things awkward or way more complicated than I was ready for.

"Ready?" he asked, glancing at me and then back out the window.

"Let's go."

"Keep your head down," he said as we headed for the car.

"You really think they're looking for us?"

"I think you left a pretty obvious trail on the way in," he said, wrenching open the door of a beat-up pickup and climbing into the driver's seat.

I got in and pulled my seat belt on while he fired up the engine, which sounded less like a truck and more like a lawn mower with a cold.

"What does that mean?" I asked.

"It means you had a certain odor coming off you when we got here. You smelled… animal."

I shifted in my seat. "You said that already. I'm sure it was those Werewolves."

"I don't think so. It was different. It was mixed with your scent, part of you." He shook his head, steering us out of the lot and onto the main road. I wasn't sure why, but I wished he'd let it go. I didn't like knowing I'd smelled like one of them since I wasn't sure exactly what that meant.

The subject fell away as he concentrated on getting us out of town. The way he watched the road and the mirrors, you would've thought we were being followed by Secret Service. I sat back and let him obsess; trying to figure out what the heck I was going to say to Headmaster Whitfield to explain my absence over the last twenty-four hours. Or worse, what I was going to say to Cambria.

My phone rang, jolting me out of my panic. I grabbed it from my pocket and looked at the readout. I glanced at Alex.

"Miles," I said, my heart pounding.

"Answer it. Maybe he knows who attacked you."

I nodded and pressed the button. "Hello?"

"Tara, you're being a tease. What exactly happened out there earlier? I thought you were coming to meet me." Miles sounded irritated underneath the smooth cockiness he exuded.

"I got held up. A pack of pissed off Werewolves with bad breath and rabid eyes tried to kill me. You wouldn't know anything about that would you?"

"Kill you? Of course not. I don't want to harm you." Miles sounded genuinely surprised. "I want you by my side, an ally in the war. The future first lady of our kind."

I gagged a little, and glanced at Alex who was watching me with a questioning expression. "So you have no idea who sent the pack of killer Werewolves after me?"

"No, but rest assured, I will find out. In the meantime, you will be safer with me than on your own. Why don't we try this again?"

"No, Miles. Not today. Soon."

Miles paused. I could feel his annoyance through the silent speakers. Something crashed in the background, and I thought I heard a muffled whimper.

"Soon," he repeated in a tight voice. "I won't accept any more delays. The next time I call you, be ready, my dear."

The line went dead before I could answer. I dropped the phone into my lap.

"What did he say?" Alex asked.

I leaned my head back against the seat and tried to shake off the threat that had come across in Miles' tone. "He's pissed. No idea who wants me dead, but says he'll try to find out. He wanted me to meet him. I think I pushed him too far when I told him no."

"Do you think he'll call again?"

"Eventually. He says to be ready this time. It sounded kind of ominous."

"Good. It'll be easier if he thinks he has to work for it. He'd be suspicious if you gave in too easily."

"Typical guy then," I muttered.

Alex smiled wryly. "You do have the whole 'play hard to get' thing down."

"Whatever." I was definitely not responding to that one.

My phone beeped. Seven missed calls. I cringed and looked at the list of numbers. It wasn't as bad as I thought. Only two were from Cambria. Four from Wes. One from George.

I called into my voice mail and listened to only the first half of the messages until I got to George. It wasn't that I didn't care; they were just full of lectures. First Cambria, hissing at me to get back to school before the bypass phrase changed. Then Wes going on about how sorry he was for reading my mind. By the last message from him, he sounded distraught and irritated, and I felt bad for him so I skipped the rest of the message to save myself from having to deal with that yet.

George's message was, surprisingly, the most pleasant.

"Tay, oh wow, you're never going to believe it. I secured the scholarship to Brown. Ivy League, baby! I can't believe it! The recruiter said I have more potential than any rookie he's seen in years. I'm on cloud nine. I...." His excitement faltered and I could hear him struggling to maintain the happy attitude. "I wanted to share it with you. I – I miss you. Talk to you soon."

He hung up quickly, and I could tell he wanted to say more but held back. I knew that feeling all too well. I was genuinely happy for him about the scholarship, though. It was everything he'd ever wanted, and I was glad that at least one of us had a promising, normal future ahead of them.

CHAPTER TWENTY-FIVE

"How bad is this going to be for me, exactly?" I looked over at Alex, but there wasn't enough light left to make out his expression. We'd been driving for over an hour, and I knew we were getting close to Wood Point.

"That depends," he answered.

"On what?"

"On our method of entry. Do you want to announce your return?"

"Um, do I have a choice?"

"Yes." He pulled the truck to the side of the road, throwing up a spray of gravel in our wake, and shifted into park. The truck idled like a weed whacker.

"Where did you say you got this truck again?" I asked.

"I didn't say."

"It's not a rental, is it?"

"No."

I waited but he didn't say more.

"Okay. Why are we stopping?" I asked.

"We go on foot from here." He killed the engine and wrenched the door open. The road was free of any traffic, and the air smelled like pine and darkness.

I got out and followed him as he cut a path straight into the trees. "But what about the truck?"

"Someone will be by to pick it up," he said cryptically.

"Okaay. And the wards?"

"Not a problem."

His tone was clipped, and he walked fast enough that he stayed ahead of me. Not that I would've been able to see him, even if he had been walking next to me. It was pitch black in the trees and even with my heightened sight, I could only make out the outline of his body. Still, I could tell the difference between 'all business' Alex and 'don't talk to me' Alex. This was definitely the latter.

"Alex, wait." He didn't slow, and I grabbed his arm, halting him until I could come around and face him. "What's your problem?"

"Nothing." He shifted like he wanted to sidestep me, but I held onto his arm and waited. "We're almost back to school. I assume you'll want to forget about anything that happened between us once we're there. I'm simply switching gears to accommodate."

"Switching gears to accommodate? What are you, a robot?" He didn't answer. "Look, I didn't say anything because… well, it's complicated. You know that." I squeezed my eyes shut and then opened them again. "You haven't said anything, either," I said quietly.

"You're right. I guess I figured I'd made my feelings clear."

I laughed before I could catch myself. "Have you ever actually had a girlfriend? Because you really suck at this." I held up a hand to silence him. "Don't answer that. Seriously, though, you can't kiss a girl and expect her to automatically know your feelings through osmosis or something. Besides, when I met you, you hated me. And now you're kissing me. So, pardon me if that leaves me a little confused."

"I didn't hate you."

"Pot-ay-toes, pot-ah-toes," I said. "You were disgusted, at least."

"You don't disgust me, Tara. You amaze me, impress me, surprise me, and entertain me. You definitely don't disgust me."

He fell silent, and like before, he seemed to be waiting for something. I didn't answer. I didn't know what to say.

"Do I do any of those things for you?" he asked, quietly. There was something very serious in the question, and I knew he meant something much deeper than the words implied.

"Yes," I whispered.

"And does Wes do any of those things for you?" he asked, his voice strained.

"Yes," I repeated, feeling miserable.

I saw him nod in the darkness and was glad I couldn't see his face, and he couldn't see mine.

"I think its best that we leave it here then. For now."

I swallowed a lump in my throat and stayed silent. A minute passed.

"Let's get you back to school and focus on getting Miles," he said.

"Okay."

I moved aside, and we began walking again, this time shoulder to shoulder. The silence was different, more relaxed, and I knew that while it bothered him to pretend nothing had happened, he had accepted that things were this way, for now, and was letting me off the hook about it. I wondered how long that would last.

Within minutes, I began to feel the vibrations of the wards line. We were coming in at a different angle than when I'd left but the feeling was there just the same, and I halted.

"Cambria said the bypass phrase was being changed today. How are we going to get in?"

Alex answered by turning back towards the wards line and whispering, "E Pluribus Unum."

All around me the vibrations fell away, and I knew the lines had been removed. I whirled on Alex.

"How did you know?" I asked.

"You aren't the only ones with tools of manipulation," he said.

He was walking again, and I hurried behind him.

"What does that mean?" I asked.

"Well, how did you get the phrase yesterday?"

"Cambria um…"

"Right. Details are sketchy."

"She might've convinced Headmaster Whitfield to give it to us," I said.

"There you go." He reached into his pocket and pulled out a small cell phone. He pressed a button and the screen lit up, revealing a text with the same phrase he'd whispered.

"Cambria strikes again," I muttered. "I can't believe she sold me out so quickly and then jumped up to help you drag me back."

"Not quite accurate," he pointed out. "The dragging part, I mean. You're not exactly kicking and screaming. Yet."

"What do you mean?"

He halted and let out a sigh, like he was finally accepting some hard reality. "I think him showing up had something to do with it." He gestured to a grove of trees up ahead and a figure standing in front of them.

I froze, unsure who it was at first. But then the figure stepped forward, and I heard the rustle of leather, and I knew.

"Wes!" I ran to him, not even thinking about whether reaching him would mean crossing the wards, and not caring, either.

He caught me and held me to him like a life raft. I buried my face in his neck and inhaled the scent of him, holding on just as tight. We stayed that way for a long moment, and then I could hear him whispering my name against my hair and I remembered where we were, and how I'd gotten here. Reluctantly, I pulled away.

"What are you doing here?" I asked. "How'd you get inside?"

"That would be your friend Cambria's doing."

"Huh. Seems she's been handing out that password like its candy." My smile faltered when I remembered Alex. I turned, feeling embarrassed and guilty, but he was nowhere in sight.

"He left," said Wes. "I can't even smell him anymore."

"Oh." I turned back, determined to focus on the moment before me and not the one I'd left behind.

"Is everything okay?" He was still smoothing my hair, running his hand over it and wrapping it around his fingers.

"Yes, I...It's been a long day."

He nodded, looking unsure. "I'd like to hear about it, if you want to tell me."

"I think we should talk about the other night first."

"We should." He hurried on before I could interrupt. "I'll start. Tara, I'm sorry. There's no excuse for what I did. I could lie and say it was a bad coincidence, me coming here on the night I did, but it wasn't. I wanted to see you, to know everything that had happened to you since we'd been apart. I knew I could get the information quicker if I picked it out of your mind than waiting for you to explain it all. Selfish, completely, I know. But I never meant to use it as a weapon. I just didn't expect to see everything I saw. And then the stuff with Miles." He stopped and ran his fingers over my hair, onto my shoulders, down my arms, and folded my hands into his. "I'm sorry," he repeated.

"For what it's worth, he kissed me," I said. It sounded weak, even to me.

"I know. I saw that. But you didn't push him away, either. And I know you're confused by it. Should I be worried?"

He sounded entirely too calm and rational, and it broke my heart. "No," I insisted. "You shouldn't be worried. It was–" I stopped. I couldn't say it was a fluke, or a one-time thing, because it had happened again at the hotel. And that one had been mutual. I sighed. "It happened again."

"Twice?" It was too dark to see his face but I could picture his brows raised.

"Yes," I whispered. I stood very still. My arms were wound lightly around his shoulders, and I waited for him to take a step back or pull away, but he didn't.

"All right," he said.

"All right? That's it?" I stared up at him, wishing I could see his face better.

"I don't know. Is that it?" he asked, carefully.

"Yes. No. Not at first. But it is now." I stopped, knowing I was probably screwing this up beyond repair. I took a deep breath and started again. "At first, I thought maybe I had feelings for him. Then I thought maybe it was because I missed you and we weren't getting along. Either way, it doesn't matter because I love you. I don't want us to have any secrets." I held my breath and waited for him to answer.

"So, you might have feelings for him, but it doesn't matter because you love me," he said, slowly.

"Um, right." It didn't sound nearly as noble and romantic when he broke it down like that.

"Okay."

My eyebrows shot up. "Okay?"

"Well, not okay, but you're being honest, and I can appreciate that. Besides, it's partly my fault for not being around more. If I want to keep you, I guess I'm going to have to fight for you."

I couldn't believe how good it felt to come clean. "So you're not mad?"

"I'm furious," he said and the low tone of his voice proved it. But that was the only reaction that gave any indication he meant it. He was holding back, I knew. "But again, I can't fully blame you for this. Or him," he added, though his voice became more brittle when he said the last part. "Although, if I see him, I may have to make sure he feels the weight of his responsibility in all this." There was extra emphasis on the word feel, and I decided to make sure they didn't meet again, if at all possible.

"You should be mad at me, then, too," I said. "I'm as much to blame."

"It doesn't matter," he said.

"Yes, it does."

"No, it doesn't."

"Why not?"

"Because I love you."

"I love you, too." I was on the verge of tears, and I didn't know why.

"I know. So, it's okay to be confused, as long as you choose me in the end."

"Why are you being so nice to me?"

"Because I snuck into your head, and I shouldn't have."

"So, it would be different if you couldn't read my mind?"

"Exactly."

I shook my head. That logic made no sense to me, but if it kept us from fighting, I'd take it. "I would've told you about Miles, even if you hadn't seen it," I said. "I'd been trying to get a hold of you for days. You never answer your phone."

"About that… I don't want to fight so I'm going to be up front with you, too. No more secrets. There've been some attacks. I've been away a lot trying to find the group responsible. A lot of prominent Hunter families have been targeted. A couple of kids from your school, even."

"You were a part of that?" I asked, remembering the hunting party Vera had mentioned.

"Vera brought me in, along with Cord and Derek. We kept to ourselves, sort of a side team, but we fed off the information from the Hunters. There was a girl with them, a tracker. She led us to their base, but they were already gone. We lost them after that."

"Victoria. She's my roommate."

He nodded. "I wanted you to know. No more secrets. Things have been rough." He ran a hand through his hair, sending it sprawling in new directions. "Training to lead hasn't been smooth. There's been a lot of opposition. Then these attacks happened and some of them weren't only against Hunters. Some humans have disappeared up and down the coastline, under suspicious circumstances. Some have turned up dead, blood drained from their bodies. Everyone needs a scapegoat, and The Cause seems to be shouldering the brunt of it. No one wants peace when there's a war brewing."

He broke off, preoccupied with thoughts of the battles he spoke of. I took a closer look and realized he did look pretty disheveled, even for Wes. His shirt was only half tucked in and his leather jacket had new creases that didn't really add to the stylishly unkept look he always wore.

"I'm sorry. I wish you'd told me things were this bad. Do you think Miles has anything to do with it?" I asked.

"I hadn't really considered it until I heard he'd made an appearance here. I mean, I assumed all he wanted was you, but then I didn't take into account his need for revenge against me, and possibly the rest of The Cause. Maybe."

"He says he's got some sort of project that will make us invincible or something. He wants to rule both the races and thinks he's figured out a way to do it. With Miles, it's a given that would involve killing innocent people," I said.

"Maybe. Like I said, it wasn't his style, but it's possible. I've put Derek on it until I get back. He's digging up what he can, using what's left of our contacts, which aren't many." He pulled me closer. "We'll figure it out, don't worry. I'm glad you're safe."

"About that," I said, hating that my entire explanation of the past day was going to completely ruin the reunion.

"Not yet," he said, holding me tighter, as if he knew what was coming. "I want to enjoy holding you."

I didn't argue and when he leaned down and pressed his lips to mine, I forgot all about Miles and angry packs of Werewolves. All I could think about was how much I'd missed this and how completely perfect and right it felt to be kissed by Wes. All of the tension and guilt fell away and I kissed him back with an intensity that left us both breathless by the time we managed to come up for air.

"I missed you," I said, by way of explanation.

I could see Wes grinning. "Good. I missed you."

Then he was pulling me down so we were sitting on the ground, in each other's arms, and kissing me again.

We didn't come up for air for a long time after that.

When we did, it was Wes who pulled away first. His breath was labored and his fingers slowly uncurled from where he'd grabbed fistfuls of my hair.

"I can't believe I'm saying this, but I think I need a break," he said. His voice was gravelly and low. I shivered. "I'm not – I mean, not in the woods, like this."

"Right," I said, sitting up and attempting to clear my thoughts.

"So, let's have it. Where were you really for the past twenty four hours?"

"Promise not to say anything until I'm finished," I said. "Promise?" I prompted, when he didn't answer.

"Yeah, okay. Promise," he muttered. "This ought to be good."

In a very condensed version, I told him what had happened from the time Miles had called, until the time Alex had brought me back.

"So, you have no idea who the pack of Werewolves was? Who they worked for?" he asked, as soon as I was done.

"No. They never said." I braced myself for the torrent of lecturing sure to follow, but Wes was curiously silent.

"Alex saved your life," he said finally.

"Yeah."

"I guess I owe him a thanks for that. Damn. I really want to hate him."

"You can still hate him and be grateful," I said.

He cocked his head to the side with an unreadable expression. "I'll take you up on that."

"You will?"

"Yup. And I won't even lecture you about how utterly stupid it was to go off alone."

"You won't?" This was starting to feel way too easy. I could feel a punch line coming.

"Nope. I'm going to give you a taste of your own medicine."

"What are you talking about?" Definitely a punch line coming.

"I'm sending in reinforcements. I've spoken to Vera and it's already arranged, too, so don't even try to argue or go around me to change things."

"What things?" I demanded, my voice rising. This couldn't be good if he wouldn't tell me who the reinforcements were.

"Cord. She's on her way. We've enrolled her in your classes, and she'll be rooming with you as well."

"What? You can't be serious." I shoved him away and sat back, hoping it wasn't too dark for him to see my venomous glare. It would've done Victoria proud. "I already have a roommate."

He was shaking his head before I'd even finished my sentence.

"Cord's staying with you and that's final. You only make this harder if you argue, and I really don't want to fight."

"Then stop trying to run my life," I snapped. "What are you, my dad?"

Wes flinched at that but otherwise didn't back down. "Look, we both know you're not done trying to deal with Miles, am I right? And chances are you're already cooking up some sort of plan to go after him again, on your own, or at the very least, without me. Cord is not a babysitter. She's the best Hunter we have and she'll be useful to have on your side."

"She hates me," I pointed out.

"She hates Miles more."

I glared at him, wondering what I was going to say to Vera, to get out of this one. I really didn't know who was worse as a roommate, Victoria or Cord.

Wes sighed. "It's the only way I can protect you. And it's better than having me hovering like a worried grandmother, right?"

"My grandmother gives me more credit than you do, so I wouldn't know."

"Tara…"

"Whatever."

"You can still hate her and be grateful for her help," he said, somehow keeping a straight face as he threw my own words back in my face.

I glared at him, wanting to say something to shut him up. "You're right. I am going after Miles again. Alex and I already talked about it, and he's agreed it's a solid plan. Unlike you, he believes I can handle myself."

Wes didn't respond.

It was a low blow. Even lower than the 'dad' remark, and I knew it, but I was pissed and tired of being treated as incompetent or "less than" by all sides. School, my mother… that was bad enough but Wes, too, was a little much.

I shuffled to my feet. "Cord can stay, not that I have a choice." I felt tired, like I hadn't slept in a week. "I better get back. Hopefully, I can get away with playing hooky, but I need to be in my room for curfew."

Wes rose, too, but he didn't try to touch me. "You're right. Cambria's waiting."

"She is?" I turned and scanned the trees. "Cambria?" I called. At the sound of her name, she stepped out of the trees several yards away and waved.

I turned back to Wes.

"I know you're angry but it's the best way to protect you," he said.

I closed the space between us and, despite my anger, wrapped my arms around his neck in a fierce hug. I pushed away the irritation and resentment, for one moment, and felt his arms come around me, too.

"Be safe, Tara. Even if you're angry, just be safe."

"I will." I stepped back and let my arms fall back to my sides. I gave him one last look and then turned and went to join Cambria. When I was halfway there I looked back, but he was already gone.

CHAPTER TWENTY-SIX

The sound of muffled sobs took me off guard. I'd finally reached my room after apologizing to Cambria enough times that she might actually speak to me again someday. She'd let me off the hook only when she saw how exhausted I was, with the threat that I "owed her big time," and she'd be thinking of a way to have me pay her back. With anyone else, the thought wouldn't have worried me, but with Cambria, there was no telling what she'd come up with.

So, I was preoccupied with thoughts of indentured servitude, and it took me a moment to realize the sound of someone crying was originating from my room. That confused me even more. Victoria didn't cry. She wasn't human enough or something. And Cord wasn't here yet. She was stuck in the office, filling out paperwork. I threw the door open and stepped inside, expecting to find some poor freshman kid huddled in the corner; a hazing ritual Victoria had taken too far.

I stopped short just inside the door and stared at a red-faced, swollen-eyed Victoria through the reflection in her desk mirror. Tears ran in tracks down her cheeks, cutting through her makeup. I hated that she was still pretty, even with mascara running down her face.

"Look who decided to show up," she snapped. She angled away so

I couldn't see her face and concentrated on moving her jewelry around inside a silver jewelry box.

"What happened to you?" I muttered, closing the door and crossing to my side of the room. I fell into bed and let my body settle against the softness of the mattress. I didn't even care that all my clothes were gone, as long as I had my sheets. "Did you break a nail or something?"

Victoria glared at me through wet eyes, but it withered before it could really gain any venom and her face crumpled into another mess of sobs. I watched her, feeling uncomfortable and awkward. Victoria always had a comeback. She should've at least threatened me with bodily harm or something by now. I could handle that Victoria, because I knew what to expect. This was something else, something foreign, and I had no idea what to say.

"Um, are you okay?" I asked, a minute later, when she showed no signs of letting up.

"What do you care, anyway?"

"Fine, I tried." I rolled over and closed my eyes.

"My parents. I just found out. They've been taken." Her words were broken and halting, and I knew from the amount of pain in her voice that she wasn't lying.

I sat up. "Victoria, I'm sorry. Do they know what happened?"

She regarded me suspiciously, like she wasn't sure whether to believe my sincerity, but then she seemed to give in. "They said it was that pack of Werewolves. The same ones that killed or kidnapped the other parents and students."

Victoria's expression was far away. Her eyes were filling with tears that threatened to spill over at any moment. For the life of me, I couldn't think of a single thing to say. I finally let out a heavy breath that seemed to break the spell over Victoria and pull her out of her private thoughts. "Wow, I'm s–"

"Sorry. Yeah, you said that already," she snapped. She blinked, and the tears cleared away as someone knocked on the door.

Victoria got up and swung the door open. Quiet words were exchanged between her and the visitor and then Victoria moved away to grab her bag. I caught a glimpse of Demi standing in the doorway.

She flipped her hair back and glared at me. I glared back, because I couldn't allow myself not to. It was like reflex with these girls; show no signs of weakness.

"Heard you had a wardrobe malfunction, mutt." Demi's lip curled back.

"Heard you sold your sole for a latte and rip-off Jimmy Choos," I shot back.

Demi sniffed the air. "Is something burning?"

I narrowed my eyes. "You."

She just smiled and turned to Victoria. "Ready?"

Victoria nodded. The two of them left, plunging the room into silence. I stared at the closed door, feeling something I never thought I would feel: sympathy for the ice queen.

A SHARP KNOCK BROUGHT ME OUT OF SLEEP, AND I ROLLED OVER AND stared at the clock uncomprehendingly. The readout said 1:13; the only proof in the windowless room that it meant AM was the little red dot that glowed next to the time stamp. That and how groggy I was. The knock came again, and I fought back a groan. I pushed to my feet and went to the door, pulling it open and blinking against the light that streamed in from the hallway. I blinked faster when I saw who it was.

"Hey." Cord stood in front of me, blond and glowering and looking all around pissed to be at my door in the middle of the night. That made two of us.

"Hey," I grunted back. We stared at each other.

"Well? Are you going to let me in?"

Her tone was demanding and not at all like she expected a "No," which is why I was seriously tempted to give her one. Back in Frederick Falls there'd been a time when I'd cared that she hated me. A big part of me had craved her acceptance because she was a part of Wes' circle. But now, after being in a place where I was so overwhelmingly despised at all times, having her approval didn't seem so important anymore. Then again, telling her to get lost and slamming the door in her face wasn't an option, either.

I sighed, and stepped back to let her enter.

She flipped on the light switch and looked around the room. I went back to my bed, mainly so she wouldn't get any ideas about claiming it for her own, and pretended she wasn't there. Where was she supposed to sleep anyway? I didn't think Victoria would be too pleased to come back and find a strange new roommate in her bed. Then again, that could be interesting.

Someone rapped on the still open door. I turned over to see who it was. One of the admin ladies from Griffin Hall stood there, along with a sleepy-eyed Ms. Fincham.

"Cordelia, we brought you a fold out with fresh sheets on it," said the admin lady. She gestured behind her, where Ms. Fincham was holding the strap to a wheeled cot.

Cord grimaced. "It's Cord. Thanks."

"And Ms. Fincham will be up the hall at all times, in case you need anything else." She glanced at me and then quickly back to Cord. "Well. You have your schedule and classes start early, so I'll let you get some sleep."

Cord didn't respond and Ms. Fincham gave the rolling bed a shove into the room.

"Here you are," said Ms. Fincham. She reached into her pocket and came out with a napkin covered bundle. "And I've just pulled a batch of these out. Help yourselves."

She handed the napkin to Cord and smiled crookedly. Then both of them nodded and left, pulling the door closed behind them. Cord dropped the napkin onto Victoria's desk, where three burnt cookies rolled free.

I made a face. "I wouldn't eat those," I said.

"Wasn't planning on it."

Cord moved the bed further into the room, laying it flat. She kicked her shoes off and climbed onto the cot with her back to me. I stared at her.

"What?" she snapped after another minute, and even though she hadn't rolled over to make eye contact, I still felt 'caught' somehow.

"I didn't ask you to come here," I said. For some reason, her knowing that seemed important.

"I know," she said.

"Wes made you, didn't he?"

"No one makes me do anything."

My eyebrows shot up. "So you're here voluntarily?"

She rolled over, and we locked eyes. Hers weren't friendly. "Look, I'm here to watch your back and to take Miles down. That's all that matters. In the meantime, we're not going to become BFF's, so let's try to make the best of a crappy situation, okay?"

"You read my mind," I said.

We stared at each other a minute longer–I was not willing to be the first to look away–and then she finally got up and switched the light off before crawling back onto her cot. Five minutes later, I could hear Cord's steady breaths that let me know she was already asleep.

It took me way too long to fall asleep after that.

CHAPTER TWENTY-SEVEN

The sound of Victoria's shrill voice woke me.

"What the crap?! Who the hell are you?"

I sat up and held back a smile. Victoria stood at the edge of the roll-away bed with hands on hips, glaring down at Cord. This was going to be good.

"I'm your new roommie," she said, sitting up and shaking her mess of blond hair back. It hung thick over her shoulders and, even with bed-head, managed to look model-mussed and ready to go.

Victoria straightened. "Oh, really? Since when?" she snapped. "Because, as you can see, we're all full up here at Club V. So, you must have taken a wrong turn."

Cord stood up, managing to look half-awake and half-violent all at once. Victoria looked completely violent. I braced myself for fireworks.

As soon as their eyes met, they both broke into a grin and all traces of anger evaporated. To my horror, they took it one step further and actually hugged. My jaw fell open in shock and awe. The awe part was mostly due to seeing the two of them willingly being affectionate to another human being. I felt somehow cheated. They let each other go and stepped back. A smirk that was definitely friendlier than the one she reserved for anyone else crossed Victoria's lips.

"Decided to admit you don't know everything and slum it at our Were-hating school?" Victoria said.

"More like, you're sorry asses can't survive without me," Cord shot back.

I stared, trying to figure out what was going on. They were trading insults and smiling at each other. "You two know each other?"

Victoria's smile withered as she switched her gaze to me, and her expression became closed. "We've met," was all she said.

Neither of them elaborated on that explanation. There went the chance to witness the best girl fight ever. I needed coffee.

"I'm going to shower," I said.

"Probably a good idea," Victoria said, wrinkling her nose.

I froze, remembering my clothing situation. I whirled and stalked past Victoria to her closet. I grabbed jeans and a shirt before she could protest.

"I'm borrowing these," I said.

"And why would I let you do that?"

"Because you'd rather let me wear your clothes than explain to Headmaster why all of mine are ripped to shreds."

"Whatever. I never liked that shirt anyway," she muttered.

Cord raised an eyebrow but didn't comment.

I eyed Victoria, a nasty retort on the tip of my tongue. Her eyes were red and puffy, and even though she was pretending to be fine, I could still see the lines of grief in her face. I bit back my reply and stalked out.

Cord must've caught up with me at some point because when I pulled the door that led to the shower area open, she caught it before it could swing shut and walked in behind me. I ignored her and found an empty stall to shower in.

Under a steady stream of hot water my thoughts wandered away from ice queen and warrior princess and back to Wes, and from there, Alex. It seemed that lately, thoughts of one inevitably led to the other, and I didn't know how to react to that. I was pretty sure thoughts of my boyfriend were supposed to make my heart race, and they did, but not for all the reasons they should. There was way too much to be angry about and I had a feeling that was part of the reason my heart pounded when I thought of him.

Then there was the pull.

I knew now that it wasn't imagined; that it had become a real, physical reaction. I also knew the longer we were apart, the stronger the pull would feel when he was close by again. What I didn't know was if it made my feelings for him stronger, or if it was made stronger by my feelings. How much of it was I actually in control of?

The problem of my heart racing when I thought about Alex was that there was no anger or temper left to blame it on. He could still make me angry, with his quirks and prejudices, but overall, I understood why. It was hard not to be prejudiced in a culture like this one. And he was willing to let me be myself; a fighter. He was willing to risk me. Wes wasn't.

I wasn't sure what that said about either of them, and I was pretty sure that I wasn't being completely fair in my reactions over it, but being in this situation at all was unfair.

I left the quiet solitude of the shower only when the water ran cold. Even then it was tempting to stay inside the safety of the stall, compared to what kind of day it would be with my new shadow tagging along. I promised myself I'd find a way to repay Wes for this, and it wouldn't be pretty.

Cambria and Logan were already there when we got to the cafeteria. They, along with every other student we passed, eyed Cord with a mixture of friendly curiosity and outright awe. She did have the sort of hair that could air-dry into runway perfection, damn her. The stares turned decidedly more hostile when they turned to me. Even being seen with Cord wasn't enough to cure my popularity leprosy.

I slumped down across from Logan with a bowl of cereal and flavored coffee in a paper cup.

"Rough morning?" Logan asked, between bites of pancakes. He was glancing from me to Cord with raised eyebrows.

"Guys, this is Cord. Cord, this is Cambria and Logan."

Cord gave them the once-over and then said, "The other misfits, I take it."

Logan looked a little offended, but Cambria smirked. "Takes one to know one."

"I won't argue that," Cord said.

They were eyeing each other in a way that suggested they hadn't yet made up their minds about the other.

"You're from Frederick Falls? With Tara?" Logan asked.

"I'm from there. Not with Tara," Cord said.

I rolled my eyes and glanced over at the sound of metal scraping. A crowd was gathered around the elite table near the window, with Victoria the center of attention – as usual. I almost went back to my cereal, but the expression on the faces gathered was so different from the usual plastic smiles and flirty eye-batting that I did a double take.

The other girls seated at the table were huddled together in a tight group and leaning across the table with Demi at the head, each one looking concerned and murmuring in low voices. All of their sympathetic expressions were aimed at Victoria.

She, on the other hand, looked like a caged animal. Her eyes were wide and even from this distance I could see her muscles coiling, like a snake. She was riveted on whatever Demi was saying, like she was concentrating very hard on the message being delivered. There were a couple of guys standing behind them; they looked shifty and uncomfortable.

The conversation came to an abrupt halt when Victoria pushed back from her chair and stood, glowering at the girls across the table from her. Her spine was rigid and her lips were moving in some retort. The girls shrank back, and the guys were edging away from the table, but Victoria beat them to it.

She did a perfect pivot on her booted heel and strode away, her fists clenched and shaking at her sides. Her hair had fallen across her cheek so I couldn't actually see her face until she passed right in front of me, and even then, it was only a glimpse. But it was enough to witness the red face. And the tears.

And then she was gone.

It took me a full five seconds after the door banged shut–and echoed after–to realize how completely silent the rest of the cafeteria had gone. Apparently, I wasn't the only one to notice whatever had gone down at the head table, or the Ice Queen melting down long enough to shed a liquid tear.

Slowly, the noise returned and the volume built back to normal. Over at the table by the window, Demi sat straighter than before, and all the boys huddled closer to her than the others.

Had we just witnessed a power shift?

"What the hell do you think that was?" Cambria asked, still staring at the door Victoria had exited through.

I looked back at her and Logan. "Her parents were taken. She found out last night," I said.

"Seriously?" Cambria's eyes went wide. "How?"

"That pack of Werewolves that's been targeting alumni," I said.

Logan stared hard at the door, as if he could will Victoria to reappear. "That's horrible," he said.

Cord pushed back from her chair and headed for the door without so much as a backwards glance.

"Where's she going?" Cambria asked.

"To find Victoria, I think. They know each other."

"How?"

"They didn't say. The kicker is that they actually like each other. Still trying to figure that one out," I said.

Logan stood and grabbed his tray as the bell rang. "I've gotta…" He was gone before he could finish.

Cambria and I shared a look and headed for class.

Cord didn't show up for my first two classes. Neither did Victoria. Demi was there, and from the glaring look she gave me she seemed to be up to the challenge of 'head bitch' just fine. On my way out of Chemistry she blocked my path up the aisle. I stopped and waited for her to finish whatever point she thought she could make by standing in my way. I was not in the mood for this.

She ended our silent standoff by hissing one word. “Dog.”

A couple of jocky guys that were lined up behind her laughed and began barking.

I rolled my eyes. “What’s your name again? I keep calling you minion number one,” I said.

Her eyes narrowed. “It’s Demi Johanssen, mutt. Don’t forget. I’m in charge now.”

“Whatever,” I said.

“And tell you’re freak friend she shouldn’t feel bad. Most girls wouldn’t be able to handle someone like Phillipe. Then again, I’m not most girls.”

“You’re with Phillipe?” My brow went up. Cambria had said she’d seen them together, but how any guy could pick Demi over Cambria was too unbelievable.

“I would’ve thought that was obvious, judging from the intricate position she found us in.” Demi flipped her hair, her lips twisting at the corners.

I didn’t give her the satisfaction of a response. Besides, what do you say to that kind of sexual reference anyway? Um, gross.

When it was clear to her that I wasn’t going to respond, she spun on her heel and left.

I watched her leave and realized my assumption had been correct. Whatever had happened at breakfast had been big. Power shifting big. And Victoria was out.

I slid through the door to Defensive Maneuvers as Professor Flaherty reached over to close it. The rest of the room was empty.

“Cutting it close,” she said.

“Sorry, Professor.”

Someone knocked on the door behind me, and I stepped aside so Professor Flaherty could open it.

“Can I help you?” Professor Flaherty asked.

“Hi, I’m Cord, your new student.”

“Nice to meet you, Cord. Come in.” Professor Flaherty stepped back and let Cord enter. "I was told you'd be arriving today. You're from Frederick Falls, with Tara, right?"

"I'm from there. Not with Tara, though," Cord corrected.

Professor Flaherty glanced between us, looking a little confused at Cord's answer, but she let it pass. "Well, we're glad you're here. Is this your first time at a Hunter school?"

"Yes."

"You'll do great. Tara's adjusting just fine so I'm sure you'll have no problem. The rest of the students are assembling down the path for drills. Tara can show you where it is. I'll be along in a moment."

Cord nodded, and I led her out the back door and onto the path.

"How's Victoria?" I asked. I wasn't sure exactly why I was asking, but basic compassion seemed to require it, and there was a part of me that did feel bad for her, in spite of everything.

"She's a wreck, of course," Cord said with a shrug.

"Demi must've really known what button to push to break her like that," I said.

"Demi." Cord spat the word like it made her mouth hurt to say it. "Not a fan."

"So, is Victoria going to kick her ass and take her spot at the top again?"

Cord gave me a look that reminded me of the way my mother looked at me when I did or said something wrong. "Her parents were kidnapped, genius. I don't think she cares about being Miss Popular right now."

I bit back my retort because maybe Cord didn't know Victoria as well as she thought. Maybe she knew some other version of Victoria that I didn't know existed.

"Then what's she up to?" I asked.

"She's talking to Headmaster Whitfield about what comes next."

"What do you mean?"

"It's all up in the air since her parents were a big political deal. They can't decide whether to keep it quiet until the pack can be tracked down and held accountable or hype it up so more Hunters will want to join the search for the guilty party. If they decide to hype it they want Victoria to be a spokesman of sorts."

"How do you know all of this?" I asked.

"Vera told me."

"Vera told you?"

She shrugged. "I'm in the loop. I guess you're not."

I gritted my teeth because she was right. For some stupid reason. She'd been here less than a day, and already she knew more than I'd been told my entire time here. I wanted to know more, but I couldn't bring myself to ask and further reveal how little everyone told me compared to her.

We joined the rest of class, and I drifted away from Cord and huddled up with Logan until we broke up into pairs for sparring. Cord stayed next to Professor Flaherty for most of class, watching like I had done the first week. I concentrated on my partner for the day, Justin. I hated to say it, but he wasn't exactly skilled at combat, and it was almost too easy to move and block his thrusts and kicks. I went through the motions of the moves I'd finally gotten the hang of, and concentrated on perfecting the rhythm of my body as I executed each one. I had to bite back a grimace each time I twisted wrong and upset the scratches that ran the length of my back.

Halfway through class, I glanced up to see Cord fall into a fighting stance in front of another student. Professor Flaherty said something to the student and he stepped up to meet Cord's advance, crouching in a way that spoke of over-confidence and grinning recklessly. Levi.

I blocked Justin and danced away, making sure to keep him at an angle so I could watch the fight beginning across the clearing.

Cord advanced toward Levi, who was still crouched but a little too relaxed. He was obviously going to let her make the first move and go way easy on her. A couple of his friends had given up their own sparring and were drifting closer to watch. Cord didn't seem to notice. Her eyes were fixed on Levi, her lips pressed together in a tight line. Levi held up a hand and beckoned to her with his fingers. She charged.

Her expression never even changed as she whirled a leg through the air and brought it up sideways against his cheek.

Levi was thrown to the left and his face went with him, like he'd been slapped. He stumbled and turned back to Cord with wide eyes.

Professor Flaherty said something and motioned for them to continue. She was smiling.

I held up a hand to Justin as Cord and Levi faced off again. This was getting good. The rest of the class must've been thinking the same thing. Everyone else had stopped their session and drifted closer to the main event. Justin shrugged and fell into step beside me as we crossed the clearing to get a better look.

A round of cheers went up, and I broke through the wall of bodies in time to see Cord drop down into a crouch and throw her foot out, clothes-lining Levi at the ankles. He went down on his back with a thud, and I heard the breath whoosh out of him. He stared up at Cord, stunned.

She, on the other hand, looked down at him completely satisfied.

"Nice!" Logan appeared beside me and offered his hand to Cord for a high five. Cord smiled and slapped his palm, stepping over Levi to do it.

"Well done," said Professor Flaherty, stepping into the circle. "All right class, that's all we have time for today."

She offered Levi a hand. He ignored it and rolled over, pulling himself up knees first and looking dazed. The crowd broke apart and everyone drifted back into the woods, headed for school. I followed behind Logan and Cord, sulking over how easily Cord had gained the acceptance of an entire class, while I was still treated like a scarlet letter.

"YOU REALLY DON'T HAVE TO TAG ALONG WITH ME EVERYWHERE I go."

"Yes, I do," Cord said, from beside me.

I was on my way to meet Alex and was already running late thanks to Cord's newfound popularity. The entire junior class had heard about Cord beating the crap out of Levi, and she couldn't walk down the hall without someone stopping to talk to her. A few had even attempted to include me in the conversation, like being seen with Cord cancelled out my otherwise nonexistent social status.

"Woot Woot!" Cambria came up behind us, smiling at Cord. "I heard about the take down. Looks like new girl can hack it."

"More like jock-boy can't," Cord replied.

Cambria nodded appreciatively and simple as that, the connection was made. Cambria was officially off the fence and had huddled up on Team Cord's side.

I glared at her.

"What?" she asked.

"Traitor," I muttered.

She shrugged, feigning innocence.

"I've got training," I said. I shoved out the door into the courtyard, leaving Cambria behind.

I was making sure to walk fast enough that Cord and I were single file instead of side by side.

"Wes invited you here to help me with Miles, not be the big sister I never wished I had," I said over my shoulder. A hand closed over my arm, yanking me to a stop. I whirled so I was face to face with a glaring Cord. "What is your problem?" I demanded.

"If we're being technical, Wes invited me here to babysit you," she said. "Which we both agree isn't one of his best decisions. But I'm here. And we can either make the best of it and find a way to take Miles out, or kill each other in the process. I don't really care which way it goes, but I would prefer the first. Personal reasons."

"Personal reasons? What does that even mean?"

Cord didn't answer. I could feel my temper rising. Not the slow building kind of way that would be normal, but the fast-moving, body shaking kind that left me feeling a little less than human. A big part of me wanted a fight and didn't care what I had to say to get one.

"You don't even like me," I said. "Are you sure you don't want to skip to the kill each other part and see where that takes us? If you win, you're free to hunt Miles down on your own."

I struggled to stay in control. I knew that one word from her would send me over the edge. I wasn't exactly sure what waited for me there.

"Tempting," she said, and for a second I thought she was going to take me up on it and tackle me. I felt my muscles coiling. But then her shoulders dropped a few tiny inches and her expression relaxed enough for me to see she wasn't going to do it. "You're right. I don't like you. But only because you're getting it all handed to you. I had to work for mine. Just remember what a sweet deal you're getting."

Her unexpected answer was enough to lower my body temperature. I felt my temper fading. "What does that mean?"

Cord sighed. "It means you're lucky. Everyone's already put you on a pedestal, with respect to go with it. I had to earn mine, fight for it. And it wasn't pretty, or character building, or any of the things that might have made it okay.

"What pedestal?" I asked. "You do realize everybody here hates me."

"I'm not talking about them," she said, looking disgusted. "Vera's vision. Automatic pedestal."

I tried to think of something to say to that but came up empty. I didn't feel like Vera's vision gave me any sort of extra respect or handouts. If anything, it made things more complicated. Apparently, Cord didn't see it that way. "Are you saying you could be my friend if it weren't for Vera's vision of me?"

Cord shrugged. "I'm saying that if you don't abuse your position, maybe I won't always want to trip you when you walk by."

"Is that supposed to make me feel better?"

She shrugged again.

I shook my head and continued up the path, trying to figure out what had happened. Was that Cord's version of a truce?

Alex was waiting in the clearing and looking extremely pissed. He held a water bottle in one hand, and when he saw me he threw it down and stalked over.

"Where have you been?" He didn't even look at Cord.

"Uh, I got caught up," I said.

"Caught up," he repeated. "I've been here for almost a half hour already. I thought –" He stopped and pressed his lips together. "I thought you –"

"You thought she, what?" Cord asked.

"You thought Miles got to me," I finished.

Alex eyed Cord. "Who is this?"

"Alex, Cord. Cord, Alex. She's the newest addition to the babysitter's club. You two should coordinate schedules." I walked away to see if there were any water bottles left in the cooler. Alex followed.

"So, we're back to this? I'm your babysitter again?" His voice was quiet but there was an edge. I'd offended him.

I turned to face him. "Look, I'm just stressed."

"And I was worried." He brought his hand up and brushed hair back from my face. Something I probably wouldn't even have noticed if Cord hadn't wandered over at that exact moment.

I froze – and so did she.

Alex noticed but not until he'd completed the gesture and the damage was done. "What is it?" He looked at Cord and then back to me again. "What?" he repeated.

"Alex, Cord is here at Wes' request. She's a part of The Cause, and she's here to help us deal with Miles."

Alex tensed as soon as I mentioned Wes. No one said anything for what felt like a year.

"Wow. Awkward moment." Cord dropped her bag and crossed her arms. "I can get the details later since no one's in the mood to share right now. I'm pretty sure you two supposedly train together around this time, so whenever you're ready to start..."

"Your orders are to watch over Tara, correct?" Alex asked.

"Sure," said Cord.

"Good. The best view is from twenty yards back. Let's get going." He turned and gave me a pointed look before jogging towards the trail. I hurried to catch up and fell into step next to him.

Alex waited until we were well onto the path to speak again. When he did, his voice was hushed. "He can't be here himself so he sent you a stalker?"

"Alex..." I glanced back at Cord, following us at a distance. Her expression was hostile.

He shook his head. "Don't answer that. Are you really going along with this, though?"

"I don't have a choice. She's here."

"Give me a break, Tara. There's always a choice."

I couldn't respond to that because something in his tone told me he was talking about more than Cord, and I wasn't ready for that conversation. Besides, it was easier to keep up with Alex if I didn't waste my breath on talking.

"She knows about Miles?" he asked, a few minutes later.

"Yes, Wes told her."

He snorted. "And this is his solution."

"What is that supposed to mean?"

"It means he doesn't trust you to handle yourself, obviously."

"You think he loves me less because he sent her?"

"You think he loves you more?"

Was there a safe answer to that question, especially when I was having this conversation with Alex? Not to mention the fact that I might agree with him. "We should talk about something else."

"Fine. Miles. What are we doing about him?"

Alex's tone was all business; no hint of emotion or a clue about the conversation we'd been having remained. I wasn't sure whether it was a point for or against him that he was able to switch gears like that.

"I don't know. It's not like we can leave school to hunt for him. I think all we can do is wait for him to come for me."

"You really trust Cord to have your back for that?"

"In a fight? Yes, I trust Cord for that no matter how much she doesn't like me."

"Why doesn't she like you?"

"She thinks I'm spoiled."

Alex looked at me and then threw his head back and laughed.

"What?" I demanded. His answer was to laugh harder. "Shut up," I muttered.

He managed to get himself under control, and by then, we were back to the clearing. Cord brought up the rear. Alex threw her a water bottle from the cooler when she emerged from the trees. She caught it and tipped it in our direction as thanks before uncapping it and drinking deeply.

"So, what's on the schedule for tomorrow?" I asked. "Please don't say more running. I'm willing to tolerate Cord as long as we don't run."

Alex chuckled. "Fine, no running tomorrow. I'll think of something equally torturous, though. Especially if you bring her." He nodded at Cord, and I made a face. "I almost forgot, we'll have to meet in the morning. I have a security meeting in the afternoon."

"Do they know we were gone?" I asked.

"No. Kane wants everyone there to redo the patrol schedule. A few seniors are being sent with Victoria to CHAS headquarters, to help deal with the Lexington's disappearance."

"She's leaving?"

"CHAS wants to hype it up, help get support for tracking these Werewolves down." He shrugged. "They want Victoria to cry on camera and make people feel bad."

"She's okay with that?" I couldn't imagine being thrown into the spotlight when my mother had gone missing.

"I guess so." Alex leaned down to grab his cooler. "See you in the morning," he said, and then he disappeared into the trees.

"You ready?" Cord asked.

I chugged the rest of my water, and we grabbed our bags. We weren't even out of the clearing yet when Cord started in.

"So… you two are what? Friends with benefits?"

"What? No!" I glared at her and took a deep breath, trying to unclench my jaw enough to speak. "Alex and I are just friends."

"Whatever. You don't want me to tell Wes. Fine. But at least call it what it is."

"I am. And you don't need to tell Wes because there's nothing to tell."

"Okay, either you're lying to me or you're lying to yourself. And you suck at both."

Cord sped up, and I hurried to catch up with her. I could not leave this conversation to end this way.

"Fine, Alex has… feelings for me. I haven't done anything to reciprocate those feelings."

"But you haven't done anything to stop it, have you?" Cord eyed me. "Take it from me, this sort of thing will knock you right off that pedestal you're enjoying. I hope he's worth it."

I let out a harsh laugh. I could feel the temper inside me building. It didn't help that I felt guilty that she might be right. It only made the anger worse.

"And what would you know about relationships?" I snapped. "I don't exactly see the guys lining up for you. Don't expect me to take advice from someone who can't put away her bitch card long enough to snag a man."

"You don't know me." Cord spoke through clenched teeth. "You don't know a single thing about me. So don't pretend like you do. You think because you have two of them falling all over you, you can stand there and judge me? There you go, misusing that pedestal again." She stepped closer to me, and I could feel the hot anger rolling off her, onto me. "I'd be happy to knock you off it, though. If you need to be reminded where you came from – and where you'll return to, in the end."

"How many rejections does it take to make someone a bitter, old hag who can't stand to see someone else in the spotlight? One? Five? Everyone she's ever met?"

Cord blinked and backed off, like someone had thrown a switch in a dark room. "You're a bitch," she said, with less anger and more of a "matter-of-fact" tone.

I bristled, the desire for a fight still making my blood boil. "And you're nobody. So, stop sticking your nose in where you're not wanted."

"Stop giving me a reason." Her expression remained clear. I wondered how she could let go of the overwhelming anger that had been there moments ago. "And you might want to get that insane temper checked out. You look like you're about to either explode or rip my head off. Neither one would leave you in one piece."

"Try me," I said.

"Not my type." She grinned, like she knew her lack of angry response would only make me angrier.

It did.

"I'm bored of this so I'm going now. Try not to explode."

She walked away and I let her go, not entirely sure she was wrong about my two choices had she stayed. I took deep breaths but it was a long time until I felt my control return.

CHAPTER TWENTY-EIGHT

Logan walked out the front door of Lexington Hall as I came in the back.

"Logan, wait up," I called, but he was out the door before he heard me. I picked up the pace. Through the glass doorway, I could see him carrying a suitcase in each hand. I slowed when I realized who was walking next to him.

Victoria had her own, smaller version of the bags Logan carried slung over her shoulder. Logan was walking faster than her and must've realized it because he stopped and waited for her to catch up before resuming his trek. He said something I couldn't hear and she responded. He slowed his pace to match hers and they continued on, either oblivious of the looks they were getting from the kids scattered throughout the courtyard, or ignoring them.

Most of the stares were filled with curiosity at seeing the unlikely pair together, but I caught a few glares aimed their way as well; mostly from minion-looking wannabes.

"That's new," I muttered to myself.

Cord appeared next to me. "What is?"

I sucked in a breath, determined to be civil. If nothing else, I had to prove to myself that I was in control of my temper. "Logan and Victoria. I mean, I didn't think Victoria even knew his name."

"I thought she was with that Levi guy," Cord said.

As if on cue, Levi appeared from around the hedged corner that led to the courtyard's atrium. He halted in front of Victoria and it looked like he was saying something, but I couldn't hear. Then a girl appeared beside him and his arm snaked possessively around her shoulders. Victoria's back stiffened, and Logan pulled Victoria away, towards Griffin Hall. Levi and his partner continued this way, and I saw who his new flavor was.

Merona. Victoria's former minion number two.

Demi came up beside them and said something to Merona and Levi, and they all turned their backs on Victoria and disappeared around the hedge.

A low whistle sounded beside me. I looked over and found Cambria staring out the window. "That was an official dethronement right there," she said.

"But how? Or why? I mean, even with Victoria's parents missing, she would never step down, or let someone else do that to her," I said.

"She'll be alright. She's strong," Cord said.

"I wonder what Logan is doing with her," I said.

"Um, I would think it's obvious." Cambria grinned. "He's making his move."

My eyes widened. "No way. You think?"

"Only one way to find out." Cambria planted her feet. "I'll be waiting right here when he gets back."

"Hmm. Tempting, but a shower's calling my name. Fill me in," I said, heading for the stairs.

"Yes, please, don't leave out a single detail," said Cord, rolling her eyes.

I threw her a look.

There were moments that Cord's sarcasm reminded me a lot of Sam, but there was a different edge with Cord, something darker and altogether nastier underneath the light bickering that made it hard to laugh at anything she said.

Cambria leaned against the front doors, waiting, when Cord and I got back upstairs.

"Where's Logan?" I asked.

"Being secretive, as usual. He didn't even stop or say hi when he saw me. Just took off for his room."

"Were you already interrogating him at that point?"

Cambria stuck her lip out. "Maybe."

I laughed. "I'll catch up with him later. See if I can get anything out of him."

We went up to dinner side by side, talking about anything I could think of that would leave Cord out of the conversation. She seemed content to trail behind us, anyway. I looked back once and saw she had her phone out and was texting.

My eyes narrowed. "You get service here?"

Cord looked up and slid the phone into her pocket. "Looks like."

"Who were you texting?"

"What are you, my mother?"

I rolled my eyes and let it go.

Victoria's table was as loud and annoying as ever with the jocks vying for the attention of the new queen bee–Demi–and the girls laughing and crowing over something the guys had said. The horsing around was reminiscent of junior high, and even though I didn't like her I had to admit, the whole thing had held a much classier element when Victoria had been in the spotlight. At least they hadn't been loud enough to interrupt my meal before. Well, not much.

"Um, hi. Cordelia?" said a voice behind me.

I turned and found Nina standing there, twisting the corner of her shirt in her hands, and looking completely terrified of the blond sitting across from me.

"It's Cord." The tone of her voice made it clear what she thought of being addressed by her full name.

"Oh, uh, Cord. Okay, well, Vera said to come get you. There's a meeting with her, Professor Kane, and Headmaster in ten minutes. She wants you there."

Cord rose. "Thanks."

Nina nodded and looked relieved to be done with her message delivery. She drifted off, towards the line for food. Cord dumped her tray and headed for the door without a word to me.

I slumped in my chair and watched her go. "They could call her in for a top secret meeting, and not me?"

"Stop pouting, it doesn't look good on you," said Cambria.

"She –"

"Gets under your skin, doesn't deserve the attention, you don't need a babysitter, blah blah blah. Yeah, I know. But has it even dawned on you that you actually have some alone time, without her shadow weighing you down, for as long as that little meeting lasts?"

I blinked.

"That's what I thought. Why are you still sitting here? Go." Cambria shooed me away.

I hurried out and raced down the steps and out the front doors, into the darkening evening. I stopped there and caught my breath as a few people passed by, into the building behind me. The courtyard wasn't empty yet, but it would be soon. We weren't allowed out here after dark without a senior escort.

I hesitated.

If I wanted to talk to Wes, I had to get on that roof before the meeting ended and get back to Lexington Hall before curfew. But when Cambria had pointed out my few precious minutes of freedom, I knew I didn't want to spend it fighting on the phone with Wes. And I didn't want to be alone with all my thoughts. Too many of them were scary and involved danger I couldn't do anything about right now. There was only one person I thought of.

I stopped, not sure where I'd find him. The only place I knew to try besides his room was the garage, but if I was wrong it would be dark before I could get back and getting caught would mean trouble. I hesitated only a second more and then plunged into the woods, cutting through brush to get to the trail that would take me to the garage.

I was almost there when I heard it. Grunts and growls that were unmistakably Werewolf – and unmistakably violent. No sooner had the sound reached my ears than I felt the goose bumps spread over me. I broke into a run and tore through branches and leaves. I knew better than to call out and alert them to my presence, but I was terrified Alex needed me, and I wouldn't get there in time. I had to bite my lip to keep silent.

I broke through the trees into the gravel that led to the garage and Alex's truck. I scanned the yard. Nothing moved. From the other side of the garage came a growl, before it turned into a yelp and was cut short. Then, nothing.

I slid up against the wall of the garage and peered around the corner. The fractured moonlight was made brighter from the break in the trees but not by much. All I could make out was the form of two bodies, lying motionless, not far from me. My heart constricted as I tried to see who it was on the ground. I blinked and everything adjusted.

A man lay less than five feet from where I stood. He was bloody and naked and unmoving. I saw the steady seep of red liquid from small, rounded wounds; one in his arm and the other in his neck.

What struck me weren't the gashes in his flesh but the fact that he was flesh. The only other Werewolf I'd ever seen become human again in death was Liliana. I'd always assumed it was some sort of personal choice on her part and had basically forgotten it. Seeing this guy made me wonder again. I moved beyond him without bothering to check for a pulse; I knew there wouldn't be one. The goose bumps had already faded to nothing along my skin. The threat was gone.

I hurried to the next body.

Alex lay in the dirt several feet away, unmoving except for an almost imperceptible rise and fall of his chest. I ran to him and dropped down beside him, searching for some sign of consciousness.

"Alex." I shook him by the shoulders, gently at first and then harder when he didn't respond. "Alex!"

Even though he was breathing, panic crept in. Alex couldn't be this hurt. He was invincible. He was… Alex. Unless that Werewolf had gotten his teeth into him. I yanked on his shirt and scanned his chest and abdomen for wounds. I didn't see anything except a vicious line of scratches trailing down one arm. I eyed his pants, unsure. I had to know, because what if he'd been bitten. Was I going to let him die because it would be inappropriate to check for wounds? I reached for the snap on his pants and hesitated. I had a better idea and reached for the hemline and yanked the pant leg up as far as it would go. The fabric bunched at the knees. Alex's calves and ankles were wound-free. I reached for the zipper again, already blushing in spite of the panic and worry.

"Are we at second base yet?"

The sound of his voice was so unexpected I forgot to be happy that he was awake and talking. I froze like a deer in headlights. A really guilty, really blushing deer.

"I was checking for wounds."

"Good excuse, I guess. Here, want me to help?" He reached for his own zipper, and I smacked his hand, mortified.

"Geez, no! I thought you were –" I couldn't say it but even the thought of it must've sobered him. His smile disappeared and he looked military-serious. "Are you okay?"

He sat up and shook his head, looking dazed. "I went down on that last round and must've knocked my head." He was rubbing a spot on the back of his scalp and wincing. He caught sight of the dead Werewolf and his eyes narrowed.

"Here, let me see," I said, moving behind him to look at the bump. It was raised and tender, like a golf ball, which meant a killer headache was on its way, but there was no blood.

"Is he dead?" Alex asked, walking toward the body.

"Yeah. He's dead. What happened?" I followed for a little ways and then stopped. I didn't really need a second close up.

"I don't know. One minute, I was working on my truck, and the next, I was up to my ears in goose bumps and this guy comes barreling out of the trees. I didn't even have a weapon on me."

"But you staked him."

"Yeah, with this." Alex held something in the air.

I stepped closer, squinting. Whatever the object was, it was too dark to see. "What is that?"

"Screw driver." Alex shrugged. "It's what I had."

For some reason, I thought of my plunger handle, and I had the irrational urge to laugh and high five him all at once. I held back on both counts and bit my lip. "Nice," I said instead.

"We need to get back to Griffin Hall and alert everyone. There could be more." Alex was already scanning the trees as he said it and I felt my whole body stiffen, on instant alert. But there was no trace of a physical warning so, for now, we were okay.

"Wait," I said. Alex stopped and turned back. "Before we do, there's something I want to say. The reason I stopped by tonight. I'm sorry about the way things turned out last night –"

"Let it go, Tara."

"What do you mean?"

"I mean, let it go. I have. Well, maybe not completely, but I'm working on it. It's the best thing. You're involved with someone else, and it's already way too complicated without me. I'm backing off. I'm going to let it go."

"Oh." I tried to think of something else to say, but I couldn't. I wasn't even sure how I felt about it. He was giving up? Of course, that was the right thing to do. I was with Wes and this was complicated.

"It's the right thing," he said quietly.

The sound of his voice pulled me out of my thoughts and I forced a smile. "You're right. I'll let it go." And as I said the words, I forced myself to accept them and put it behind me.

He nodded and just like that, it was over. I wondered how he could do that so easily.

"We need to get going now. Alert the others," he said.

"Right." I struggled to focus on the task at hand. I could think about what this meant later. "Vera, Kane, and Whitfield are all in a meeting. If we hurry we can catch them all together."

"Let's get going then. I think it's time Vera admitted her weakness and helped plug the holes it's causing."

He was still patting at the knot on his head, and I knew he was right. Vera's illness had made it way too dangerous to be kept secret any longer.

"Did he say anything?" I asked. "The Werewolf that attacked you."

"No. Just charged at me like he wanted to have me for dinner."

"But he changed back to human form after he… you know."

He shrugged. "Some do. It's involuntary, subconscious. Some of them are more in touch with their human side than their animal side." Alex shook his head. "Which is odd for that one, since he seemed all animal when he was coming at me. Definitely the most vicious I've fought in a while." He rubbed his head again.

We made it back to Griffin Hall and right inside the lobby came face to face with Vera, Professor Kane, and Cord. They were coming from the hallway that led to Headmaster Whitfield's office and speaking in hushed voices. Vera looked more tired than I'd ever seen her, with lines under her eyes and creasing her forehead. She walked very close beside Kane and for a second, I thought she was leaning on him, but when I looked closer, they weren't touching.

"Tara? Alex? What are you two doing out so late?" Vera asked.

Cord narrowed her eyes at us like she could only assume. Great.

"I was attacked out at the garage. Single Werewolf," said Alex.

Vera's eyes widened and Kane took a step towards us.

"That's not possible," Vera said.

"How long ago?" Kane asked, ignoring Vera's denial.

"About thirty, forty minutes ago. The body needs to be disposed of. And a perimeter check done," said Alex.

Kane nodded. "I'll go start with the body. You take Cord and round up some others to help with a perimeter sweep. Radios on silent. Check in with me in twenty."

Alex nodded and Kane turned to Vera.

"I really didn't see this. How could I not?" Vera said.

"I know. We'll sort it out after the perimeter's been secured. Wait for me in the conference room," Kane said. His voice was lower now, almost soothing.

It was the most vulnerable I'd ever heard her, and it made me uncomfortable. Vera was like Alex; invincible. Add to that the aura of 'untouchable' she exuded and it felt wrong somehow to hear her sound so lost and unsure.

"Tara, you stay with Vera. We'll be back when we're done," Kane said, pulling my attention back to the conversation.

"What? No, I want to help check the perimeter," I argued.

"Only seniors can be assigned patrol duty," he said.

"Cord's not a senior," I pointed out.

The look Cord gave me could've melted steel.

Kane looked momentarily at a loss, like he didn't know how to respond to an argument. Maybe he wasn't used to being questioned. The scar on his face twitched, either in frustration or deep thought. "Cord's not technically bound by school rules, either," was all he said. Then he headed for the door, with Cord and Alex in tow.

I crossed my arms.

"Come, Tara," Vera said "Let's go upstairs to wait. I need some tea."

Vera moved slowly, but she was still halfway to the stairs before I caught up with her. I really didn't want to sit in a room with her for the next hour, waiting for everyone else to decide if we were safe or not. And I didn't need any tea, but it was either that or risk getting sent back to my room.

Dim sconces with glassy red covers lit the stairwell and the second floor hallway, casting a burgundy glow on everything. It made Vera's face look even more shadowed and gaunt, and I couldn't believe I hadn't seen it before. She definitely didn't look well.

"Alex told you, didn't he?" she asked.

I looked away, startled and guilty. "Yes."

"I suspected he might've." She turned into a room with giant double doors and crossed to a sitting area near a set of French doors. On my right the room went on forever, with a polished, wooden table running the length of it. The tapestries and carpet were all neutral tones and matched the sofa and armchairs that made up the sitting area Vera had settled in. It was like any other board room in the world, with nothing in particular to set it apart as a place where Hunters discussed the killing of Werewolves.

I sank into an oversized chair that overlooked the view of twinkling lights from the courtyard below, and beyond that, Lexington Hall.

"You two have grown close in your time together," Vera said.

It took me a minute to realize she was talking about Alex and me. "Oh. I guess so," I said after a lengthy beat.

"You are friends then?"

"Um." What the heck kind of conversation was this? She wasn't my mother. And she might've been blood related, but we were so not having the 'boy talk.'

"Yeah, we're friends."

"Good."

She seemed satisfied with that answer. I held my breath, praying that would be the end of that line of questioning.

"You know, Tara, I thought we'd have more time, but tonight is a glaring reminder that things are progressing much more quickly than I'd hoped. I am glad for the chance to speak with you alone, despite the circumstances being what they are."

"More time for what?"

"To talk about your future." She leaned back and shifted, like she was settling into the deep cushions of the couch. "You will have many options available to you in the next couple of years. More than most young women your age."

"So I've heard," I said.

"What exactly have you heard?"

"Well, your vision for one," I said slowly. "Apparently, I'm seen as the next leader of The Cause. Along with Wes." Saying that last part gave me a pang in my gut. I ignored it and went on. "But being a Godfrey means I'm also next in line to serve on the council for the school, and for this CHAS thing, right?"

"Those are both choices, correct," she said. "All of which are affected by your DNA. The biggest part of it is obviously that you are a mixed race. It complicates your choices, in the eyes of some." I felt my spine stiffen and Vera noticed. "I'm not one of those people, but there will be those who oppose you, no matter what choice you make."

"And what if I don't want either choice?" I couldn't help a little bit of attitude creeping into my tone.

Vera looked surprised, like she couldn't imagine someone turning down one, much less both, of those options. "It's your decision, so you have the right to refuse." Her expression changed then, her eyes faraway and unfocused, like she was looking at something not in this room anymore. "But you're not the type to walk away, Tara. You want to make a difference. In the end, it will be a matter of where you can do that best."

"You sound sure."

"As sure as you are of your own identity."

"And you think I'll do the most good being with The Cause." It wasn't a question. It was clear which world she'd chosen to live in.

"It was the right choice for me." Her gaze sharpened. "I faced the same crossroads that you do, Tara. There were reasons and regrets for both choices. Don't forget that. You have to be willing to live with both, whichever road you choose."

"I'm not a politician," I said, needing to argue because her words were heavy and scary, and I believed her.

"Good. The only way you will make a difference anywhere is to be yourself."

I sighed. I couldn't argue with that answer.

"I'll admit, there is another reason I wanted to speak to you alone," she said after a moment. She tilted her head and her expression turned curious, watchful. "Have you been feeling any differently the past few weeks? Anything out of the ordinary?"

"What do you mean, like sick?"

Vera shook her head. "Not necessarily, though that is one way of putting it. I mean, has anything happened that made you feel not like yourself."

"No," I said, drawing the word out slowly to prove I had no idea what she was talking about, even though, for some reason, the memory of my bad-ass temper was rolling around in my mind. "Why?"

"Your grandmother and I have spoken about you and we want to alert you to the possibility that you may have special gifts that have lain dormant inside you. We want you to be prepared, should any of them surface."

"What sort of gifts?" I gripped the armrest extra hard.

"I don't know, exactly. It could be anything, since you have the blood of both races inside you."

"But you must suspect something if you're bringing this up to me," I said. "Did you see something?"

"No, nothing all that specific," she said, waving her hand.

And in that moment, I knew she was lying. It surprised me, and I wondered if I was imagining it, because Vera wouldn't do that. She had no reason to, right? But I knew with every piece of me that she was holding something back.

"You're lying," I said.

Her brows shot up. "And how do you know that?"

"I just do. What are you not telling me?"

Vera's shoulders sagged in a sigh. She seemed to let go of all her poise and rigidity in that one exhale. It left her looking entirely too human and frail, and for a second, I caught a glimpse of the heavy fatigue she must be feeling. The lines that etched her face were deep and the haunted look in her eyes evidenced pain. Then she straightened, and the façade was back in place. There was still a hint of what lay underneath but you wouldn't see it unless you were looking.

"I'm not well, Tara." She smiled, but her expression was hard and humorless. "Dying, if you want to be technical. Maybe sooner rather than later, no one really knows. I've never been good at 'seeing' anything about myself. I had hoped to work with you more, help you develop your knowledge about this world, yourself, and anything else you need to assume the role given to you at birth. You're a leader, Tara. You come from leadership on both sides of your blood line and those of us who know your DNA is not a curse believe that you hold the key of bringing the races together, more than anyone else in our recent history – maybe ever."

She paused to take a breath, and I waited, needing to hear her out. I felt like she was being honest with me for the first time since I'd met her. I felt like this was the most honest any of my family had been up until this point, and I desperately wanted to hear it.

"I've seen you in my visions. An older you. A different you. You're amazing, breathtaking. But there are two paths. You may or may not find your way. If you do, it'll be the best thing that ever happened to either society. If you don't, it will kill you."

She said the words gently, as if to soften the blow, but I felt it like a brick wall. Kill me. So, if I didn't choose right, I would die?

"I have seen that you have gifts, as well," she went on. "And I know you would rather me tell you what they are, but I will not. If I do, it will make it harder, not easier. You will have to come into them in your own time. It's the best way, trust me. I will be here as long as I can to help you."

We sat in silence. I knew she was giving me time to process everything she'd said, but there wasn't nearly enough time in the world for that. And I couldn't really stay focused on the whole "it could kill you" aspect, anyway. It was like my brain had decided that was too much to carry and skirted it in favor of the other things she'd said.

"Why will you be here for me?" I finally asked, and there was more than a little accusation in my voice. "Why now? You haven't been here for me at all before, so why all of a sudden? Because you're dying? Because you need to feel better about your successor?"

Vera's only reaction at my outburst was to blink. "I stayed away out of respect to your mother, and your grandmother. I told you in the beginning, I never knew you lived so close by, and even after, your mother wanted nothing to do with my vision. Or your grandmother's politics, for that matter. I've respected her wishes. But you're old enough to make your own decisions now, or close to it, anyway. If I'd waited until you're legally an adult, it might be too late. I might not be around that long."

I felt the sting of guilt when she said that. She was right. And she didn't owe me anything. "I'm sorry. I didn't mean it like that," I said. "Is there anything I can do? For you, I mean?"

"Let me help you," she said.

The intercom next to her buzzed with static. I jumped and the tin sound of Kane's voice came through the speaker; I hadn't even noticed the radio sitting there until now.

"Vera, you there?" he asked.

Vera pressed a button and said, "Go ahead."

"All clear out here. Guess he was a loner. We're heading back. Get Whitfield, and we'll see you in ten."

"Understood," she replied. She let off the button and pressed another, next to it. "Nina?"

"Yes, Vera." The reply took several seconds and sounded half asleep, but it was there.

"I need you to summon Headmaster Whitfield to the second floor conference room. Can you do that?"

"He went to bed, ma'am."

"I know. Do it anyway," she said.

"Yes ma'am."

The static ended, and we went back to sitting in silence. I think both of us felt like we'd said everything we could for now.

"Tara, would you mind fixing me some tea?"

"Sure," I said, getting up and heading for the mini kitchen counter. There were mugs sitting out, upside down, on the faux granite countertop and packets of tea and instant coffee in bins along the wall.

It dawned on me that if Vera had asked this of me when we'd first arrived at the room, I would've refused. Now, I felt like it was the least I could do. I knew my view of her had changed, and it had nothing to do with sympathy. I saw her as real, approachable, and possibly, someone I could trust.

CHAPTER TWENTY-NINE

Kane and Cord came in first. Kane's hands were dirty, and he went straight to the sink and began scrubbing, so I was pretty sure there was more than dirt on them. Cord took a seat in one of the rolling chairs at the conference table and drummed her fingers on the wooden tabletop. She looked impatient to be moving again.

"Any evidence of where the breach occurred?" Vera asked.

"Hard to say for sure until it's light out. Looks like the southwest corner, though, off the main road. No vehicle in sight, so we're wondering if he had help, after all. Jackson and Hekler are going to ride out a ways and see if they find anything." Kane finished scrubbing and dried his hands with a paper towel. When he was done, he came over and sat next to Vera, looking her over like he expected an injury in his absence. "How are you feeling?"

"Responsible," she said. "But otherwise, fine."

"Did you call Whitfield?" he asked.

"Here." Headmaster Whitfield stood in the doorway, taking up every inch of open space between the frames. He wore a rumpled suit and his hair had some serious bed head going on, but he looked wide awake and ready for the crisis. "Someone please tell me why I'm up," he said, walking to the counter and pulling out a mug and the makings for tea.

Kane filled him in on what had happened, and I saw him glance my way a few times, like he didn't get why I was here, but he let it go.

Alex came in while Kane discussed the patrol efforts. Alex had a water bottle in one hand and a packet of a single serving Aspirin in the other. He set his water on the table, tore into the packet, and knocked the pills back in a single motion. He didn't even seem to need the water chaser. I got up and went to him.

"So, nothing?" I whispered.

"Possible trail to the main road. Couple of the guys went to check it out, but it looks like he was alone."

"What do you think he was doing?" I asked.

Alex eyed me, his expression grim, and it wasn't hard to see what he was thinking; probably because I'd been thinking it, too.

"You think it was Miles?" I asked.

"I think it's time we clued everyone in on the details," he said.

"They already know," said Cord.

We both looked over to where she was twirling absently in her chair.

"You told them?" I asked.

"Well, how else was I supposed to get them to let me shack up with you?" she shot back.

"It makes it easier, to not have to explain it," Alex said. He sounded as irritated as I was, though, and he was glaring at Cord like he wanted to knock her out of her chair.

I wasn't ready to let it go. "But that means… They know I wasn't lying about the first breach, then."

"Correct," said Kane, coming up behind me.

"And I still got in trouble," I finished, making sure to avert my eyes from his face. It was a little difficult to stand up to him when he stood this close. His size was intimidating enough without the scar.

"Did you?" His eyebrow shot up; just one and it made the scar elongate.

I turned towards the door as a couple more kids entered the room.

They took seats at the conference table and sipped from bottled water. One was a tall, lanky guy with freckles. I'd seen him patrolling out by the gate near the main road on my runs with Alex; one of the few areas that got patrolled in daylight. The other was a girl that was butch enough to pass for a boy – or a high school gym teacher. She was grinding her teeth and staring at me.

I looked away, and caught sight of a familiar figure entering the room. Professor Flaherty was dressed in all black and even though it was casual, it contrasted starkly with her bright red hair, and made her look like she'd just come from a Cat woman try-out. Even her movements were fluid and almost feline. She smiled at me and then went to the kitchen counter and took a mug.

"All right, everybody take a seat," Kane said.

He stood right behind me and I scurried forward, sliding into an empty rolling chair, across from Cord and the future-gym teacher girl. Everyone else fell quiet. Professor Flaherty was last to sit, with a steaming mug of tea. She slid in next to the freckled boy and sipped at her drink, while watching Kane over the brim.

"Everybody knows why we're here," Kane began. "There was a breach tonight. Single Were went after Alex and got taken down." There was a definite note of pride in his voice at the mention of how Alex had handled things.

"By a screwdriver, no less," said the freckled boy with a grin aimed at Alex.

"Carver, congratulations are being saved for the end," said Kane, but his lips curved at the edges, too.

The boy –Carver – nodded, but he was still grinning at Alex.

"We did a perimeter sweep and came up empty. There's a possible trail to the main road that we'll confirm when it's light out. No vehicle. Looks like the guy came on foot," Kane said.

"Any ID on him?" Whitfield asked.

"No. We'll contact the local pack leaders tomorrow, via Vera's people, and see if anyone's missing," Kane said. "In the meantime, we need to talk about the wards." Kane hesitated like he didn't want to bring it up, but we all knew he didn't have a choice.

I glanced at Vera. She sat expressionless, all business; the usual Vera. She nodded at Kane and rose to address the group.

"Some of you have heard, and some of you have been kept unaware. I am not well and my illness has begun to affect my ability to feel a breach. It doesn't mean the wards aren't effective. It means my body's alert system isn't working like it should. In light of the recent attacks on our fellow students and alumni, I feel it's in the best interest of the school that I step down as head of security and let someone else take over." Vera finished and took her seat again.

Everyone looked back at Kane, but he was watching Vera and didn't say anything right away. Finally, he cleared his throat and nodded.

"We'll start searching for someone tomorrow. In the meantime, Betty, you can fill in." Kane nodded at the butch girl across from me.

Her eyes widened in surprise. "But sir, I'm not capable of the level of security that Vera is."

"You'll do fine," he said, cutting her off. "I've seen what you can do and it's perfectly acceptable for our needs. Go ahead and get started. It'll take you awhile to link the entire grounds. Carver, go with her. Assemble the others and have them patrol double time until we're secure again."

"Yes, sir," they said, in unison.

They pushed back from their chairs and left the room, single file.

"All right," said Kane when they were gone. "The usual suspects will need to be hunted down."

"What does he mean by 'usual'?" I whispered to Alex.

Alex shook his head and Kane went on, watching me now.

"There are a couple of new possibilities to consider," he said. "One, we've got a nasty pack of Weres with a taste for alumni tearing things up. School grounds could be next for them." He paused, letting the possibility hang, and his gaze returned to me and sharpened. "The second is Miles De'Luca. Son of Leonard De'Luca. Twice as crazy and twice as capable of destruction due to his ah, DNA structure. Add to that an unhealthy infatuation with our girl Tara here and we've got a serious problem."

Everyone in the room looked at me. I could feel myself going red at the mention of Miles' "unhealthy infatuation." Was that worse than "stalker?" Because I was pretty sure "unhealthy" didn't even begin to cover it. No one looked all that surprised by the information Kane provided, though, which was pretty good evidence that everyone had been informed like Cord claimed. Even Professor Flaherty nodded calmly, like she'd heard it all before.

"Do we think this is the De'Luca boy then?" Professor Flaherty asked.

Alex opened his mouth, probably to tell her "yes," but Kane cut him off.

"We think there are multiple possibilities," Kane said. "We can't discount the Were pack as we've yet to identify them."

Alex stayed quiet. He shifted in his chair and it squeaked.

"Um, have you considered the Were pack and Miles are working together?" I asked.

No one said anything right away. They all looked at each other.

"It's a possibility," Kane said finally. "Either way, we'll get people out into the field to see what we can learn. Our contacts in the area are reliable enough, and we should be able to find out more about both groups within the next twenty four hours. In the meantime, Tara, you and Cord stick together."

Cord and I wore mirrored grimaces.

"Vera, you can assist Betty with the new wards, yes?"

Vera nodded. "Of course."

"Alex, how's the bump?" Kane asked.

"I've had worse," he said.

"Your eyes are glassy. Get a good night's sleep, and check in with me tomorrow. I can use you for extra patrols."

"I've got training with Tara," Alex said.

"Cancelled," Kane shot back, shaking his head. "I need you in the field." Kane turned back to Cord. "Cord, here's an earpiece. We're on frequency six unless there's an emergency. Then it's frequency one."

He tossed her an ear band that looked identical to the ones Cambria and I had used the night I'd left for town. Seemed like forever ago, when really, it had been only a day. Cord took the earpiece and strapped it on looking less than thrilled.

"Anna, you and I can make a patrol schedule that doubles things up. We'll split shifts. That work for you?" Kane asked.

Professor Flaherty nodded, her red hair bouncing where it had come loose from its bun. "Sounds good," she said.

"Anything else?" Kane asked. No one spoke. "Dismissed."

Cord stalked out first and disappeared into the hall. Alex followed behind me. Vera was still talking to Kane and Professor Flaherty had taken a seat closer to the front, to work on the patrol schedule, no doubt. Headmaster Whitfield looked around, like he was uncertain whether he was still needed here or not. I heard Vera telling him to get some sleep and they'd call him if they needed anything.

"I can't believe this." Cord pushed off from the wall when she saw me and put a hand on her hip, blocking my path. "I leave you for five minutes and not only do you run off, but you manage to stumble upon the only dead body within miles. How am I supposed to keep an eye on you?"

"I'm confused," I said. "Are you mad because I ran off without you or that I found a dead body and you didn't?"

She glared at me and then huffed out a breath. A high pitched beeping sound cut off whatever nasty response she'd been trying to come up with, and I looked around, panicking, for the source of the sound.

"I think that's your phone," Alex said.

I grabbed it out of my pocket and stared at it like it was a foreign object. I wasn't used to it ringing anymore. The number that came up wasn't one I recognized but I needed to get it to shut up. I flipped it open.

"Hello?"

"Tara, did you get my message?"

"Miles?" A shot of adrenaline instantly pumped itself into my blood stream, and I couldn't catch my breath. Cord and Alex fell silent and stared at me like they were straining to hear Miles through the phone. "What do you want?"

"I sent a messenger to tell you the answer to that. Did he not reach you?" Miles' voice held the usual calm and crazy, but I put his meaning together.

"That Werewolf that attacked Alex. That was your guy." It wasn't a question but Miles answered anyway.

"Yes. A special message for your new boyfriend and then a message for you. It's time we were together. The project is complete."

I stared at Alex in horror. "You tried to kill him? But he's not – what project?" I couldn't keep up with everything Miles said. And the fact that he only alluded to the violencc he caused didn't help in knowing where to start a conversation with him.

"You'll see. Now where is my messenger? I need him." Miles was growing impatient; I could hear it in his voice. It irritated my temper.

"Your messenger boy's dead," I snapped. "I'd take it as an omen and surrender now. Where are you?"

"Dead? You can't seriously tell me that little Hunter-in-training managed to take down my newest pet?"

Miles was a combination of disbelief and anger, and my temper wanted to push him. "Believe it. With a screwdriver, of all things. I hear Werewolves are seriously susceptible to metal. You should look into it."

"Watch your tone with me, girl," Miles snapped. I could hear the anger in his voice now, and I was glad to have finally caused him to lose his control, no matter the consequences. "I'm tired of waiting. You will join me."

"Not if the human race depended on it, or any race for that matter."

Miles' voice went quieter but there was more violence in it. He reminded me of a coiled snake. "I've been far too patient with you. I will have you, though, one way or another. Mark my words. You will come to me, in the end."

The line went dead, and I lowered the phone.

"Well? What did the ass have to say?" Cord demanded.

"The usual. Threatened me with affection, then with death, I think," I said. "He's determined to get me to come to him."

"He sent that Werewolf tonight, didn't he?" Alex asked. His hands were balled into fists at his sides.

"Yes." I nodded. "He said the guy was supposed to kill you and then come get me and tell me where to meet Miles."

"He still thinks you'll go willingly?" Alex asked.

"He says I will one way or another, whatever that means." I shuddered without meaning to because there had been a real threat in the way he'd spoken the words. I couldn't shake the fact that Miles was way too determined to give up or utter empty threats.

"You think he'll try again," Cord said, watching Alex.

"Without a doubt," he said.

"Good." She raised her chin and her eyes glittered. "He doesn't know I'm here and I, for one, can't wait to see him again."

There was something underneath Cord's threat, but I had no idea what it was. There was no way she was acting like this out of protection for me. Or duty to Wes. There was more. But I knew better than to ask, or expect an honest answer if I did, so I let it go.

Cord blinked and the hungry look in her eyes faded as she focused on Alex and me again. "Say good night and let's go already. I'm tired."

I looked at Alex, feeling suddenly very self-conscious with Cord so close. I wanted to ask how his head was feeling, and if he was okay, but I was pretty sure that wouldn't be appropriate as far as Cord was concerned. "Um, I guess I'll see you later," I said.

He nodded. "Be careful."

I followed Cord down the stairs and out into the courtyard towards the dorm. The last thought I had as I drifted off was of Miles and how he'd described that Werewolf as his pet.

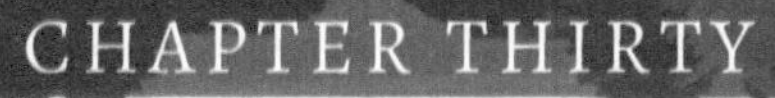

CHAPTER THIRTY

Cambria woke me up on Saturday. It took me a minute to realize it wasn't an emergency. I wasn't used to her being so wide awake before me. Even on school days she was dragging and gulping coffee until the end of second bell before she resembled a person. But today, she was wide awake, shower bag in hand as she stood over me and shook me awake.

"What the hell?" Cord mumbled, from her cot across the room. "Shut the noise off. It's the middle of the night." She wore a padded eye covering, like something you'd wear in a spa, and didn't bother removing it to yell at us. Then she rolled over and went back to sleep.

"I'm going to shower," Cambria said. "You coming?"

"Sure." I grabbed my stuff and followed her out. Cord didn't move except to burrow further underneath her blankets. At least I'd get the morning away from her.

"She's a dream in the morning," Cambria said.

"Late night, remember?"

Cambria stuck out her tongue.

I'd made a stop at her room last night on the way in from Griffin Hall and filled her in on what had gone down at the garage, and then at the meeting after.

"And again, I miss the action. I'm getting real tired of that, you know," she'd said when I was done.

And that was it. No "Wow, you've got a big, political choice to make," or "What are you doing about Miles-the-crazy-stalker?" or "How pissed do you think Wes will be when Cord calls him behind your back about Alex?"

Those were all the things going through my mind, but all Cambria could think about was how often she was left out of the action. I'd give almost anything to be left out of the action, for once. I didn't tell her that, though.

We reached the showers and Cambria slipped into the stall beside mine. "So, what are we doing today, Mission Impossible?" she called over the steady stream of hot water.

"Mission Impossible?"

"That's your new nickname. You're always on something new and dangerous and against the rules," she explained. "A girl after my own heart."

I shut off the water and stepped into the stall to change. "I hate to disappoint, but I was going to find Logan and make him help me with my lineage project."

"Eww. You're talking about the library, aren't you?"

"That's the place."

Cambria sighed, long and loud. I rubbed a towel over my hair and stepped into flip flops before yanking the curtain aside and heading for the mirror.

"You don't have to come," I said.

Cambria's curtain slid open, and she followed me to the mirror, adjusting her lacy black sleeves. "I'll manage. Nothing else to do. I can't even sleep in these days. Too wired with everything going on. Besides, I want to hear from Logan anyway. He needs to spill the details about how he came to be walking Victoria to her getaway car. I need to hear this."

We found hot coffee and prepackaged donuts in the cafeteria and that was fine by me. I swiped a helping of each and went in search of Logan. I figured we could head to the library first since, even on a Saturday, that was the most likely place to find him.

I wasn't wrong.

Logan sat at our usual table, surrounded by stacks of books – all of which could rival Webster's in thickness and word count – and was hovered over an open one on the table in front of him. His hat was pulled down low, facing front, so it was hard to see his expression except that he seemed to be concentrating extra hard.

"Hey," I said.

Logan's head snapped up, and he quickly pulled his hands underneath the table and into his lap. I caught sight of a black cell phone at the same time shades of red began creeping up his neck.

"Hey," he said, trying – and failing – to sound casual.

"What are you doing?" Cambria asked. She stared down at Logan with a sharp gaze.

Logan shifted, and I was pretty sure he was sliding the cell phone into his pocket. "Nothing, um, I mean reading," he said, gesturing to the open book in front of him. "What are you doing? In the library? On a Saturday?" His brows went up, turning the attention back to Cambria.

It worked, a little. "I'm at an all-time low for boredom. And I needed a good story to go along with my liquid breakfast." She raised her coffee cup in salute and sank into a chair. "So? Are you going to tell us?"

"Tell you what?"

"We want to know how you came to be the one walking Miss Ice Queen herself to her getaway vehicle yesterday. It's a mystery no one can seem to unravel," Cambria said.

Logan looked from Cambria to me. I sipped my coffee and waited. I wanted to hear this as much as Cambria did. The redness was creeping in again; up Logan's neck and into his cheeks. He pulled his hat down lower over his eyes and glared at us.

"None of your business, that's how," he said.

Cambria and I exchanged a look, eyebrows raised.

"Wow, that sounds sort of serious," I said.

Cambria nodded. "Kind of covert. And pre-meditated. Maybe I should call him Mission Impossible."

Logan's brows wrinkled. I laughed and that must've finally pushed him over the edge. Logan glared at Cambria, then at me, then at Cambria again.

"Look." His voice had lowered to a sort of hissed whisper. It got our attention. "I don't have to explain myself to you two. Just because I hang with you doesn't automatically make me one of the girls. I'm not going to sit here and gossip with you about my love life, okay? You have each other for that. I'm a guy. Guys don't feel the need to share about that crap. And I'm not dumb enough to tell you, anyway, since all you're going to do is give me a hard time seeing as how you hate her."

He stopped and let that sink in. I stared at him and neither Cambria nor I said anything. "And for your information," he went on, "She's not as mean as she pretends, you know. She's got layers."

With that, he slammed his book shut and stuffed it into his backpack and stalked out. Silently, of course, but still… it was Logan. I'd never seen him mad before, so it was kind of shocking.

"Did he say the Ice Queen has layers?" Cambria asked.

I looked at her. "I think he did."

We stared at each other for a beat and then burst out laughing.

"Like an onion?" Cambria hissed, between giggles.

That made us both laugh harder, and I had to put a hand on the table to keep from falling onto the faded carpet. I couldn't breathe. Cambria was wiping tears from her one exposed eye.

That's how Cord found us.

"What the hell, you two? Are you off your meds or what?" Cord took Logan's empty seat and gave us a dirty look and the stacks of books an even dirtier look. She had her hands wrapped firmly around a coffee cup and still looked half asleep.

I wheezed, trying to catch my breath, but I didn't bother to answer her. Cambria was pulling it together, too.

"Oh, man. I feel kind of bad for making him so angry. I've never seen him like that before," I said.

"He'll be fine," Cambria assured me. "For all his talk about being one of the guys, he's really kind of sensitive, but he'll get over it. Always does."

"He really likes her," I said.

"Are you talking about studious surfer boy?" Cord asked.

"Uh, Logan? Yeah, I guess you could call him that," I said.

"He's not bad looking. If you're into that type," she said.

"And what type is that?" I asked.

She shrugged. "Smart. The kind of smart that's also sensitive. Not my thing."

"What, smart? I agree," I said. Cambria snorted.

She sneered. "Funny. I was thinking the same about you, two-timer."

That hit a nerve. I could feel my temper kicking in. I set my coffee cup down a little harder than I'd anticipated, sloshing warm liquid onto the table. "I'm not two-timing anyone."

"Okay, now that we've got that settled," Cambria cut in, "What's today's plan? Besides sit around and wait for Miles to attempt a snatch and grab?"

Neither of us answered. I was too busy biting my tongue, still trying to prove I could control my temper, instead of the other way around.

"Okaay," Cambria said, drawing out the word.

"I'm going to call Wes," I said.

I stood and grabbed my coffee and what was left of my donuts. Cord stood, too, but I avoided her eyes. I wasn't calling Wes because I felt guilty, despite what she probably thought.

"So… roof then?" Cambria asked.

I nodded and we headed for the exit, earning a nasty look from the librarian on our way out.

Halfway across the courtyard, Cord's earpiece went off. It was set to vibrate, but I could still hear the pulsing it gave off. Cord switched it on and said, "Go ahead." A voice on the other end was speaking but I couldn't make out any words.

I watched her as she listened and realized I was holding my breath. I let it out and forced myself to calm down. Cord's comment had me all wound up. The Hunter in me wanted a good fight, some way to let out some of the energy that was building.

"Nope, nothing new to report here… Yeah, okay." Cord signed off and gave me a sideways glance. "Problem?"

"What did they want?"

"Just checking in."

"Oh." I forced myself to relax.

I expected Griffin Hall to be busy in light of the attack, but it was as deserted and low key as usual. There were a few staff people coming and going in the lobby, all disappearing down one of the hallways. A few students, probably working as aides or needing extra credit, wandered by, heading for the administrative offices, but no one I recognized enough to speak to, and no one interested in stopping us, thankfully. I guess if they had, I could use Cord's presence to smooth it over, but I didn't really want to resort to that. It would feel too much like owing her one. And I did not want that.

I led the way to the access stairs and then up and out into the open air. The sky was bluer today than it had been, with an added hint of warmth that made the breeze feel good against my arms and face. It was amazing how different the weather felt up here, compared to down in the coolness of the trees. Down there, it seemed like all one season. Cool and damp. Up here, it was spring already.

I wandered off to the side, away from Cambria and Cord, and took out my phone, waiting for a signal. It came up, and I dialed Wes.

He picked up on the second ring. "Hello?"

His voice did things in my stomach and I stopped walking and dropped down to lean against an air handler.

"Hey," I said.

"Tara. It's good to hear your voice."

And it was obvious he meant it. I could hear the relief and happiness that came through in his words; it fueled the guilt that I'd been pretending I wasn't feeling. I squeezed my eyes shut and focused on how the sound of his voice made me forget all of the confusion and stress I'd been carrying. It dropped away; none of it mattered. All that mattered was Wes.

"Yours, too," I said, and my voice cracked.

"Is everything okay?"

"Everything's fine. I assume someone called you about last night?"

"Yeah, Cord called while they were disposing of the body. Alex took care of him?"

"Yes." I held my breath, waiting for whatever he was going to say next. I was terrified Cord had told him whatever she thought she'd seen.

"I still want you to keep Cord close. And maybe that Cambria girl, too. Don't go anywhere alone, okay?" There was the usual concern in his voice, but otherwise, he sounded like business as usual.

I let out the breath I'd been holding. "Okay," I said.

Wes paused, and I wondered if I'd agreed too easily, if I should've argued more.

"Are you still mad at me?" he asked.

"No, I'm not mad. I just –" I stopped and took a breath. "I just miss you. Things are really… different here."

"It doesn't feel the same without you here, either."

I supposed what he'd said was close enough to what I'd meant, though it was so much more than that. But I let it go. "How are things going for you? With The Cause, I mean. Is it getting any easier?" I asked.

"It's a process," he answered. "What about you and Cord? She is still alive right?"

"Ha ha. Funny," I said, but I let a smile creep into my voice. "We're managing. She gets a daily quota of nastiness she's allowed to exude, and then I cut her off."

"Seems fair," he said, and I could tell he was smiling back. It was the first light moment we'd had since I'd come here, and it felt so good it literally warmed me. Then, just like that, it was over, and we were back to serious. "I know you're not happy with her being there so I appreciate your effort."

"I don't get why she has to hate me so much," I said. I left the usual anger out of it because deep down I still really didn't know what the problem was. She'd said she didn't like how everything was so much easier for me, but now that she was spending time with me, she could see it wasn't as simple as it appeared. I felt like I was missing something.

"She's had it rough. Her past isn't as cut and dried as she likes to make out. I'm not defending her," he added quickly. "All I'm saying is she's got reasons to hate the world. It hasn't been very friendly to her."

"Well, the world is a large target. She can only aim at one person at a time, and so far, it's me."

"Then remind her to focus on Miles. He deserves it."

"What's the big deal with her and Miles?"

"They dated, sort of."

"Seriously? As in, a couple? When?"

"Before I met you. Miles was really new to the group. I'm not sure how exclusive it was. It's not like either one of them shared the details with me. We just knew. It's a small group."

"Wow. So, she's got extra reasons to be pissy about him. Good to know."

"Don't use it against her, Tara," he warned.

"I wasn't planning on it." But if it came out by accident, like if she pushed and pushed and made me mad enough, well… I couldn't help that. I didn't say that part out loud.

"Any day, Tara," Cord called.

I looked over my shoulder and saw her standing near the door, tapping her foot and looking all-around impatient. I sighed. "My babysitter said my time is up," I said into the phone.

"Fine, I'll let you go. But, Tara?"

"Yeah?"

"We're good, right?"

I wanted to say yes. I ached to say yes and end the weird, back and forth, fighting-or-not thing we'd had since I'd gotten here, but the truth was, I didn't know. Not until I could see him face to face, talk to him in person, and know what I felt and whether it was real.

"We're good enough until we can talk this out in person," I said instead. "And we're good enough for me to tell you I miss you. A lot."

"I miss you, too. Be careful."

"I will," I promised.

I hung up, and immediately the phone rang again. I could hear Cord's exasperated sigh from here. The screen said George. I wouldn't have answered it except I knew it would piss Cord off, and I was in the mood to get to her.

"Hello?"

"Tara, hey!" George sounded excited and a little breathless.

"Hi, George. What's up?"

"I'm so glad you answered. I'm coming to see you." I could hear his grin through the phone, and I froze.

"What are you talking about? Visitation day isn't for another two weeks," I said. And more importantly, George didn't know where I was.

"Yeah, I know. But I didn't want to wait that long. Did you get my message about the scholarship?"

"I did. That's pretty awesome," I said. His enthusiasm was contagious. I couldn't help but smile. "Congratulations."

"Yeah, my mother is beside herself. I had to share it with the person who did the most to help get me here, and that's you, so I decided to surprise you. We need to celebrate. Are you free tonight?"

"Tonight?" My brain went completely numb. I couldn't think. George was coming here tonight. "I don't know. How do you know where to find me?"

"You're cousin… Miles? He stopped by and gave me directions. He said you get free time on the weekends, and I could probably sneak in for a couple hours."

"You talked to Miles?" I worked hard at keeping the shrieking panic out of my voice, but plenty of stress had come through. George caught it easily.

"Yeah, why? He seems like a great guy." His answer wasn't so much concerned as defensive, guarded.

I narrowed my eyes. "George, you sound weird."

"I thought you'd be happy to see me, that's all. You can meet me, right? We'll be there in about an hour."

"We?"

"I drove up with Miles, to save on gas. Like I said, cool guy."

My throat dried up, and I couldn't breathe. I turned around and locked eyes with Cord. She stiffened at whatever she saw in my face. I gripped the phone too tight and my cheek hit a button. It beeped loudly in my ear and brought me back enough to make me coherent. I walked towards Cord and Cambria. They watched me with matching expressions of concern and tension.

"Tara? You still there?" George asked. There was some background noise and then he said, "Miles wants to say hi, hang on."

There was silence and then, "Hello, Tara."

"This is war," I spat. I could feel my temper rising, and I knew I was shaking because the phone kept pulling away from my ear.

"It always was. It was simply a matter of whose side you're on, lovely."

"Not. Yours." My muscles literally ached to do damage to him and my jaw felt tight, like it was too big for my mouth.

"The choice is no longer yours. I've decided to take out an insurance policy." His voice was light, like all crazy people seem capable of when innocent lives hang in the balance. He reminded me of Leo. No more affection, no more creepy crush, just plain psycho. George probably had no idea what he was in the middle of, or that Miles was threatening his life at this very moment.

"I will kill you if you hurt him," I said, trying to keep my own voice as calm and nonchalant as his. I didn't want him to know he was getting to me. It would only endanger George further.

"You may try. We're going to pull off and come in the back way. Since the wards are sketchy at best, what with the new girl taking over, I think we can sneak in fairly easily through the woods. I'll call you when we find a quiet spot, and we can meet up."

"How do you know about Betty?"

"I'm everywhere, darling." His voice was smug and silky.

Somehow, Miles knew about the wards being down, and that Vera was no longer in charge of them. Someone was giving him inside information. My mind raced. "Fine, I'll come. But you will let George go when I get there," I said.

"Of course, whatever you want."

His tone was entirely too accommodating, and I didn't believe him for a second. I grit my teeth and stared at Cord. She was figuring it out, I think, because her eyes were blazing and she looked just as ready as I was to rip into someone.

"Call you soon," Miles said, and then he disconnected.

I lowered the phone.

"What the hell's going on? Who was that?" Cambria demanded.

"Miles," I said, glancing at her. She looked worried but not nearly as violent as Cord. I took a deep breath and kept focused on her. The shaking wasn't letting up and my thoughts were getting jumbled behind the rage. I needed to think clearly.

"Tara, are you okay?" Cambria asked. She reached towards me and then seemed to think better of it. "You don't look so good. You're sweating. And your cheeks are really flushed."

"I'm fine," I said. I took another deep breath. I wasn't fine, though. I wasn't calming down. I was shaking worse, and I couldn't keep still much longer. Something in me had to move.

"What did he say?" Cord asked in a low voice.

"He has George."

"Your ex?" Cambria's eyes were wide.

I nodded, jerking and shaking. "They're driving here. Miles is using him as blackmail so I'll leave with him. He's going to call back when they find a place to meet."

"What about the wards?" Cambria asked.

Cord shook her head. "They aren't up and running yet." Cambria looked at her with wide eyes. "I know they told everyone they're up, but they're not. Not completely anyway. Butch Betty or whatever her name is, she's new and slow. It's taking time. He'll get through."

"He knows about the wards being down," I said.

"How?"

"I don't know."

"How long?" Cord asked.

I blinked, trying to clear my head and remember the answer to her question. "Um, an hour?"

"Geez, Tara, you're shaking worse," said Cambria.

I couldn't take it anymore. I stepped back, my legs feeling stiff and unused, and paced towards the edge of the roof. Cambria and Cord stayed where they were, watching. I ignored them. I couldn't concentrate. My thoughts felt jumbled and shifty; I couldn't focus on anything except my desire to hurt Miles. A vision of taking him down was on replay in my brain and I couldn't shake it. I didn't want to. It was the only thing keeping me sane, imagining myself killing him, over and over again.

CHAPTER THIRTY-ONE

I don't know how long I paced, but eventually a pair of hands appeared in front of me, bracing tightly on my shoulders and bringing me to a stop. Their appearance was so unexpected that my head came up and I let out a snarl at the face they belonged to.

As soon as the sound reached my ears, I stopped and blinked.

It felt as if I was waking from a dream, coming back to myself. I had no idea how much time had passed, only that my muscles felt loose – and better – and the shaking had stopped.

And I was looking at Alex.

"What are you doing here?" I asked. I looked around, confused by his presence. I was still on the roof. Behind him, Cord and Cambria were huddled up, watching our exchange. Logan was with them. He watched me with worry etched into his expression.

"Tara? Can you hear me?" Alex's tone was low and soft, like the way you'd talk to a child or a wild animal.

"Yes." I stepped out of his hold and he tensed. "What are you doing here?" I repeated.

"Cord asked me to come. You were…not yourself. She and Cambria couldn't get you to respond when they called you."

"What? When? I didn't hear them."

"Yeah, that's what we're trying to tell you," Cord said, coming up behind Alex. She kept her distance. "You were standing right here, or well, pacing right here, and you wouldn't answer me. Even when I screamed at you. It's like you were hypnotized or something. I got Alex because if you attacked me or something, I wasn't going to be responsible for throwing you off a roof, even if it was self-defense. Better to let Wes kill him." She finished by jerking her thumb at Alex.

He rolled his eyes.

I looked back and forth between them. It was clear they were serious. I glanced farther back, at Cambria. She was watching me, too, and she wasn't scared, but she looked seriously concerned, and sort of lost.

"You're okay now?" Alex asked.

"I guess so," I said. "I'm not shaking anymore. And I don't feel ready to punch anything that looks at me funny."

No one was amused by that. They all nodded with serious expressions.

"Good, can we figure out what to do about Miles now?" Cord asked. "Thanks to Tara's one-woman drama act, we're down to forty minutes before show time."

The words were meant to be a barb but her usual bite wasn't there. I could tell she was still bothered by the whole thing and unsure how to respond. That made two of us.

Cambria and Logan walked up. "You told them?" I motioned to Alex and Logan.

"No choice. We're going to need backup," said Cord.

I stared at her with a sinking feeling. "Who else did you tell?"

"Relax. Just these two," said Cord.

"Why can't we tell Kane?" Logan asked. "We could use the help. Especially if Miles brings any backup of his own."

Cord shook her head. "If we tell Kane, they'll give plenty of backup, but they have their own way of doing things. They may not let Tara play 'bait' and then who knows where that'll leave her friend George."

"But he's a hostage," Logan argued.

"He's a human," said Cord. "Are you really arguing this? You know how Hunters operate. He won't be a priority."

Logan didn't answer.

"So, we're letting Tara walk right up to him?" Alex asked. "Not my favorite plan."

"It's the only way Miles will let his guard down long enough for you guys to get George out," I said. "No matter what, you have to get him out."

"We will," Cambria assured me.

"And then we go after Miles," Cord finished. The gleam in her eye made it easy to see which part she was looking forward to.

"Then we call for backup," Alex said.

Cord eyed him, like she didn't agree.

"I thought you'd be the first to run to Kane," I said to her.

"I don't think we'll need anyone else," she said, and her eyes gleamed with malice. "Not like I – we – can't handle him ourselves."

"Okay," I said. Even if I didn't understand her reasons, I agreed. If bringing Kane would endanger George, we'd have to do this ourselves. "You guys get George and then call Kane."

"Hey, what about me?" Cambria asked. Everyone turned to look at her and I'm pretty sure their stares were as blank as mine. "I can help with Miles. I can be convincing, remember?"

Her meaning dawned on me, and I felt like an idiot for not remembering before. "That's a good idea, Cambria. You can make sure Miles decides to live up to his end and let George go. But how close do you need to be?"

She shrugged. "I only need a visual on him."

"What's she talking about?" Cord interrupted.

Cambria and I exchanged a look. "Cambria has a special gift," I said.

Cambria smiled; sweet and evil all at once. "I can compel him to let George go."

Cord raised an eyebrow, either doubting or impressed, I couldn't tell which. "Will he know what you're doing?" she asked.

"Not if I do it right."

"And can you compel him to, say, not fight back?" Cord asked. Her eyes were alight with the full possibilities of Cambria's ability. "To sit there and take it?"

"Um, probably not." Cambria's smile fell away. "I mean, that's a basic Hunter instinct, especially when you're under direct assault. He'd probably fight out of reflex."

"Too bad. We'll make it work regardless," Cord said.

Once the plan was made, everyone wandered off to do whatever they could to pass the time. We couldn't leave the roof until Miles called; we needed the cell service to find out the location. Besides, it was the best place to hide out from Kane and the other patrollers until it was time to make our move. I wandered to an empty corner of roof, the one that overlooked the western corner of the woods. Nothing but green treetops were visible as far as I could see but I barely noticed them. I was too preoccupied with mental images of Miles to see anything in front of me.

A hand on my shoulder made me jump. I whirled and Alex stepped back, apologetic.

"Sorry, I didn't mean to scare you," he said. He looked wary, like before, when I'd been out of it – like I was a little too unpredictable. It made me defensive.

"No, I'm fine," I said. "Thinking about Miles. And George." Alex stepped up so we were shoulder to shoulder and gazed out over the trees.

"You and George, you were a couple?"

"We broke up a while ago but we're still friends. I've known him for a long time."

Alex didn't say anything, and we stood there for the next few minutes, wrapped up in our own thoughts and plans. It felt nice, not having to talk but knowing he was there and had my back. We stayed that way until my phone rang.

I pulled it out, and George's number came up. I braced myself. I still had to act like everything was fine to him.

"Hello?"

"Hey Tay," George said. The line was crackly, and I knew he didn't have long before he lost signal. He must be close. "We're about there. Miles said there's some cave on the grounds, off one of the smaller trails. He says we can hang there. Do you know it?"

"I think so," I said. I remembered Miles had found me near the cave that day in the woods.

"Cool. We'll be there in twenty, so I'll see you then."

"I'll be there."

"I can't wait," he said, his smile evident in his voice.

We disconnected, and I turned to find everyone had crowded back together again, waiting for me to fill them in.

I looked at Cambria. "They're going to that cave you took me to."

She nodded. "I can get us there. It's going to be tricky for me to get a good visual without being seen, though. Not many places to hide, especially if they get there first."

"Then we need to get there first," Cord said. "Let's move."

No one argued with that. I think we were all sick of standing around, waiting. We moved for the door that led downstairs, but Alex stepped in front of us and put up his hand.

"I'm going down first, alone. If you hear me being stopped, I'll distract them and you guys slip out another way," said Alex. "No one can know where we're going. Cord, turn your earpiece on. Give me three minutes and then head down."

She flipped a switch and Alex told her what frequency to tune into, so he could let her know when the coast was clear. Then Alex disappeared through the door.

After a few minutes the rest of us headed down the stairs, single file and silent. The hallway and lobby were pretty empty; it was mostly student aides and kids cutting through to the courtyard. The staff didn't come downstairs much on a Saturday. Except Kane, who always seemed to be on duty, but there was no sign of him. From the doorway, Alex waved us over.

"Here, take these," he said. He held out a handful of stakes. We all grabbed one and shoved it someplace concealing.

"Where'd you get these?" I whispered, eyes darting around.

"I stopped by my room. They're mine, not school issued, so no one will miss them."

I looked closer at the rough stake in my hand. Near the point, the initials A.C. had been carved into the wood. I looked up at Alex.

"I like to claim my kills," he said. Intensity blazed in his eyes. This was a different Alex; a battle-hungry version with little or no emotion, except the satisfaction of making a kill. It unnerved me, but I told myself it was worth it, if it meant saving George. And stopping Miles.

"Let's go," Cord said, breaking the silence and pushing on the door.

We filed out into the courtyard and followed Alex when he took a sharp left, away from the buildings and open spaces in between. It was all I could do not to break into a run. Even though I couldn't see anyone out who would stop us, I knew that didn't mean we weren't being spotted. Plenty of kids were wandering the courtyard; I could hear talking and laughing coming from around the hedge, near the fountain.

As soon as we were well into the cover of the trees, Alex broke into a run. The rest of us were right behind him. I was, for the first time, actually grateful for all the running Alex had made me do. Right now, it was the only chance we had of arriving at the cave first and getting Cambria in a position to save George. I kept up easily with the rest of the group, which said a lot for my progress, considering all of them had been training like this for years.

Alex went first. I crouched behind a tree and watched as he approached the cave cautiously, sticking to the tree cover until he was directly across from the opening. He stepped through and was swallowed up by darkness. I felt a moment's panic as I imagined him being ambushed inside, but then he reappeared and motioned for us to join him. We moved across the trail, single file, into the darkened mouth of the cave. I blinked until my eyes adjusted enough to make out the damp walls on either side.

Alex motioned for Cambria to take the lead with him. No one spoke as we moved down the pathway. I forced myself to breathe evenly and put one foot in front of the other at a normal pace. My anxiety was working overtime; between the darkness and the danger George was in, the walls felt like they were closing in.

We made it through the tunnel and into the cavern below without incident. My heart pounded as we neared the open area. I could see the trail lightening, and I stepped forward into open, airy space. It was exactly as I remembered. From across the cavern, the sound of rushing water could be heard from the waterfall. High above us, a natural skylight allowed enough sunlight through the cracks to make it bright but not hot. There was too much dampness and shadowed edges to heat the room.

We fanned out, without anyone having to give a single order. We all searched for two things: a concealed enemy and a decent hiding place. Cambria found a spot where the rock split to form a small alcove. She slipped inside and ducked down, watching me from around the corner with a question in her eyes. I angled around to check for visibility, and when I saw that it hid her from sight, I gave her the thumbs-up. She nodded back and sent me a strained smile.

Across the room, Cord handed Logan her earpiece and slipped around a vertical rock formation, to wait. Logan slid the earpiece on and hurried forward, still looking for a spot to hide. I scanned but didn't see Alex. He must've already hidden himself. I kept going, looking for a place to wait, and watched Logan disappear behind the edge of the waterfall. I was alone – or at least appeared to be.

I didn't bother to hide. I wanted to be visible when Miles showed. I wanted him to know he hadn't gotten the drop on me; I'd still gotten here first. But I didn't want my back exposed, either. I ended up leaning against the rock wall as far from the entrance as I could get, arms folded across my chest in a stance that I hoped looked confident and sure.

I didn't have time to wonder, because there was the sound of shuffling feet on the darkened trail and then George, with Miles behind him, appeared inside the cavern. I forced myself to relax – and smile. Even if it was fake.

"Tara, hey!" George broke into a jog and held his arms out for me, a big smile on his face.

"Hi George." I stepped forward and allowed him to pull me into his embrace, keeping my eyes fastened on Miles. He hung back, near the entrance, like he didn't expect to stay long. Or he didn't trust that I was really alone.

George's arms tightened around my waist, and I let him hold me for a second longer than friends normally would. It was George. And his life was in danger. I didn't care if he was a little affectionate right now. In fact, the closer he stayed to me, the safer he was. So I squeezed him back, and when he pulled away, I kept a grip on his arm.

"How are you? You look great. Have you been working out?" George asked.

My eyes flickered to him but stayed mostly on Miles. "Uh, yeah, some," I said. "They make you do a lot of physical training here."

George laughed. "I'd love to meet the person who got you to agree to more P.E."

I almost smiled at that because he'd probably enjoy meeting Alex about as much as he'd enjoyed meeting Wes.

Miles stepped forward, and George noticed my expression change.

"Oh, come say hi, Miles," he said.

Miles walked very slowly, very deliberately towards me. I couldn't hold my tension back any longer with him this close. I reached out and took George's hand firmly in mine and faced Miles squarely. I couldn't pretend anymore. God, I hoped George didn't make this too difficult. I didn't even have time to wonder what he would think of me now.

"Let him go, Miles. That was the deal," I said.

Miles stopped several yards away, watching me with bright eyes. He looked excited, like a child presented with a new toy that had been kept from him for too long. I resisted the urge to glance towards where Cambria was hidden. I hoped her compulsion would work because the look in Miles' eyes made me wonder if he'd even heard me, much less had any intention of letting George go.

"Let me go?" George echoed, looking back and forth between us. Out of the corner of my eye, I could see confusion twisting his brows. "Go where? What are you talking about, Tay?"

"I'll explain, I promise," I told him, still staring at Miles and holding tightly to George's hand. "But right now, I need you to trust me. Miles isn't your friend, or mine. He brought you here as a threat to me."

George turned to Miles. "Is that true?"

"You make a wonderful insurance policy," Miles said, his eyes flickering to George. He smiled a little, a polite brush off, and then looked back at me. "Letting George go was your deal, not mine. But I won't stop him. George, would you like to leave?"

"Uh, no, considering I just got here. What I would like is for someone to explain what's going on." George's voice had risen. Anxiety tinged with confusion. He moved closer to me, angling himself protectively.

"Probably a good choice," said Miles. "While I wouldn't stop you, my new friends probably would. They don't like humans."

There was movement at the entrance and then, one by one, a group of people streamed into the cavern. They stayed near the wall, their eyes wary and shifting as they took in the three of us. Goose bumps flowed over me, and I realized what they were. A few of them didn't look any older than I was. I wondered where Miles had recruited such young Werewolves to fight for him.

Somewhere inside the cavern, someone gasped.

"Ah, yes, your friends are here after all," said Miles. "Good, it means mine will be entertained." Miles raised his hand and snapped his fingers.

One by one, the people against the wall shimmered and shifted at the edges, and then... they were wolves. Scraps of clothing rained down around them as they changed forms. They sniffed the air and growled. A couple of them broke off from the group and moved along the wall, nose to the rock, searching. A heavy ball formed in my stomach, and I knew this was way worse than any of us had anticipated.

"Tara?" George's voice was shaky and the confusion I'd heard in it moments ago was replaced by a building panic and sheer disbelief as he stared at the animals. "What the hell is going on?"

"Exactly what it looks like," I muttered.

"But –"

"I'll explain later, I promise. Stay with me, okay?" I squeezed his hand in mine, trying to pass enough comfort along that he would accept my answer and not freak out yet.

He nodded slowly, his eyes locked on the wolves. I couldn't look away from them, either. My breath was caught in my throat. Any second now, my friends would be found, and taking care of Miles would be left up to me. My hand itched to go to my stake but I held still, my mind racing. Miles stood there, calm and collected, and completely himself. Was Cambria's compulsion even working?

"Miles, I'm taking George and leaving now," I said.

"Well, that was fast. I have a car waiting not far. I'll show you. Come." Miles waved his hand for me to follow him.

"No, not with you. Alone," I said.

"Oh, I don't..." He trailed off, and his expression turned blank. "Well, if that's what you want. Go ahead." His voice had changed. It sounded far away and child-like.

I took a step forward, watching Miles suspiciously for any sign of sudden movement, but he remained where he was. His eyes were unfocused.

I took another step. And another. George was right next to me, his hand still firmly in mine. We were standing almost in front of Miles now. Maybe this could work. I took another step.

Across the room, a wolf yelped. The faraway look in Miles' expression dissolved and he blinked, confused. The wolf yelped again, and I saw Cambria slide out of her hiding place before the Werewolf could corner her. The wolf darted forward, teeth bared, but she was already in motion, bringing her fist around hard against its jaw.

"Sorry," Cambria muttered, and then she sprang into motion again, ready with a second hit as the wolf came at her.

I looked back at Miles. He was frowning.

"That was strange..." He was talking to himself. A growl echoed off the walls from somewhere behind us. It must've broken his concentration, and he blinked and focused on George and me. "That was rude. And a mistake."

I backed up a few paces and watched behind him as a Werewolf found Logan. He jumped free of his hiding place behind the waterfall, getting soaked as he leaped straight through the rushing water, and lunged at the wolf, stake held high. The wolf dodged him, and Logan chased after it. A second Werewolf noticed and went after Logan.

Alex appeared a few feet from where I stood clutching George's hand and flew past me towards the snarling wolves. He wore a look of intense concentration and didn't even look at me as he passed.

"Cord!" he yelled.

I followed his gaze. Cord had come out of her hiding place and was already locked in battle with a large, brown Werewolf. She wielded a stake in each hand and was alternating between swinging the pointed end and turning so her first connected with fur-covered flesh.

She whirled at the sound of her name and brought her stake up as another wolf, a burly black one, went for her neck. She managed to leap aside but lost her balance and rolled a few times before getting to her feet again. The black and brown Werewolves were already coming again.

These Werewolves were insanely fast. They reminded me of the pack that had attacked me in the woods near Luray.

I watched the fights raging across the cavern, and I itched to help. My feet shifted, impatient to get moving, to be a part of the violence, but I couldn't leave George. I knew if I did, Miles would hurt him to get my attention. But I couldn't watch and remain still any longer. I turned to glare at Miles.

"This wasn't part of the deal," I snarled.

"If you'd come alone, it wouldn't have needed to happen."

With my free hand, I clenched and unclenched my fist.

"You want to fight, don't you?" Miles' lips twisted up at the corners like he was sharing some secret with me. "You're such a little warrior. It's one of the things I love about you."

I felt George tense even further. "Okay, this has gone too far," George said. He stepped forward and pointed a finger at Miles. "You're crazy, man. And what I'm seeing over there, that's crazy, too. I don't know what's going on, but I'm leaving, and Tara's coming with me."

He might've been convincing if he'd had a chance of making it happen. But he was the weakest one here, whether he knew it or not.

Miles shook his head. "I don't think so. I'm in charge of when this meeting's over."

Somewhere behind him, a Werewolf yelped and Cambria cried out. I moved, out of instinct, but stopped when George yanked on my hand. I craned my neck but couldn't make anything out beyond the blur of fur and weapons. Everything was happening too fast, and I wasn't sure if we were winning.

I took a step towards Miles.

"This ends now," I said. "George, let go of me and stay against the wall."

"Tara –"

"George, do it. If not, I'll have to knock you out. I really don't want to do that."

Something in my voice must've convinced him. Either that or he knew he was out of his league, because after a final squeeze he let go of my hand and stepped back against the wall. I advanced towards Miles. The mental images of me destroying him were back, replaying in my mind. I used them to stay focused and gave in to the desire to make them come true. The sounds of the fights around me fell away. All I could see was Miles – and all the ways I was going to kill him.

"I thought you would've been more impressed with my project," he said. He hadn't moved back a single step. He didn't seem concerned at all as I advanced.

"You're finally offering to tell me about that?" I shot back. "Why? Because you know I'm about to kill you?" I was only a few steps away now.

"I wanted to wait until I was sure it could be done. Really surprise you," he said. "They are my best work and proof of my success." He waved a hand towards the group of Werewolves behind him.

"What are you talking about?"

"The Werewolves you see before you are my own creation, darling. I made them."

CHAPTER THIRTY-TWO

I faltered, all of my concentration on the words he'd spoken. Images of violence against Miles vanished. I struggled to understand what he was saying. "What do you mean 'made them'?"

"It wasn't easy, believe me. There were a lot of mistakes before we got it right. It took a lot of blood, sweat, and tears, as the saying goes."

"But that's not possible," I said

"Just because something has never been done does not mean it's impossible."

"But how?"

"Ironically, Hunter blood was the missing ingredient." He winked, conspiratorially. "It's what makes them unstoppable."

As if in response, someone cried out.

I couldn't look.

I was too close to Miles, and I knew if I took my eyes off him for one second, he'd have me.

"We will create our own army," said Miles. "And then no one will be able to stop us. The fact that they will all be dirty bloods, it only makes it more satisfying. They won't be able to shun us any longer, when we make them all like us."

His voice had dropped to almost a whisper and his eyes were shining. This was his project; this was what he wanted complete before he came for me. He'd found a way to make more of us – more hybrids. Except these hybrids were destructive and craved violence even more than any other Werewolf I'd seen.

"You want to turn the entire Hunter population into hybrids?" I said.

"Greatness takes vision. Then, I will be in control, with you by my side. You can still choose it, you know. I will still show you mercy."

I barely heard him. My mind was reeling. He'd changed them. Somehow, he'd found a way and infected them with something. And he'd changed a Hunter into a Werewolf.

I stared at him, shock giving way to anger. "You're the one who's been kidnapping all those Hunters. You changed them into this."

He smiled wide. "Brilliant, isn't it?"

My answer was to rush him.

He didn't see it coming and I actually managed to take him down and pin him, my stake poised over his heart.

"You're faster than I remember," he said.

He actually looked like he was enjoying it, which made me feel gross, but I didn't move away. No way was I going to let him up because he was disgusting enough to be getting some weird sexual fulfillment out of this.

I gripped the stake, ready to plunge it into his chest.

A hand closed over my hair and yanked me back, and I was lifted off Miles and dragged backwards. I landed in a heap, with hair in my eyes and stinging pain running the length of my scalp. I was pretty sure my hair was thinner than it had been a moment ago, by whole chunks.

I brushed my hair out of my face and looked up at my attacker. It was definitely a human hand that had grabbed me, so I half expected to see one of the Hunter-Werewolf hybrids back in human form looming over me. Instead, I saw–

"Demi?"

I was too shocked to move out of the way, and her kick landed extra hard in my gut. I hunched over and blinked against the black spots in front of my eyes.

"The one and only, loser," she said. "And I don't like you putting your hands on my man."

"Your man?" That was almost funny but still too disgusting to laugh at. I rolled away from her and managed to get to my feet. "You two are together?"

"Didn't your friend Cambria tell you?" she snapped.

"Cambria?" I was completely confused.

I glanced over at where Cambria was fighting one of the Werewolves. She shoved it back, and her eyes met mine. Her expression contorted to something unreadable when she saw Demi. Then the wolf was coming at her again, and she looked away.

"I only want to get close enough to kill him, trust me," I said. "What are even you doing with him? He's insane."

Demi rolled her eyes, so they disappeared under her perfectly made up eyelids. Then she glared at me. "He's not insane. He's brilliant. All of the great minds are misunderstood." She glanced back at Miles who had pulled himself to his feet and was brushing himself off, totally immune to Demi's adoration.

"Darling?" she asked in a silky voice. "Shall I kill her for you?"

"Hmm?" Miles finally looked up and acknowledged her with a dismissive glance. "No, I rather want her alive. I told you, your part is done. I merely needed access to the grounds. You can go now."

Demi's expression was one of hurt before it twisted into rage. She turned back to me, her lips twisting into a snarl. "This is all because of you, mutt. Like you're worth obsessing over. I'm over it."

And with that, she lunged.

Her hands closed around my neck before I could block her. I wasn't used to fighting other people. Wolves didn't pose the same threat, what with the lack of opposable thumbs. I struggled with her, and when I couldn't pry her hands free, I yanked and sent us tumbling. It was enough to loosen her grip but we still rolled and clawed at each other.

She was animalistic in her approach, regardless of her human form; like a feral cat. It was all I could do to keep up with her. She clawed and swiped and I felt the sting of blood being drawn across my cheek. We rolled some more, and I managed to land on top, pinning her. I'd lost my stake at some point in our tussle so I used both hands to put all my weight against her, pinning her at the shoulders and trying to hold her still. She was craning her neck towards my arm and showing her teeth. When I realized what she was trying to do, I swung out and connected with her jaw.

"You're trying to bite me?" I demanded.

Demi didn't answer. I'd hit her hard enough to subdue her for the moment. I took advantage of that and picked her head up and slammed it down on the rock floor beneath. Her eyes rolled back in her head and her body went slack. I let go and her head lolled to one side. She was clearly unconscious, but something in me snapped. I needed to fight. It wasn't enough to silence a stupid high school girl. I needed to rip into something – to flex my muscles and feel nothing but the thrill of winning a battle.

I jumped up and took off across the cavern, towards the fighting still going on. Cambria and Logan stood back to back, dancing around a couple of Werewolves that were slowly closing the distance. Both of them looked exhausted while the Werewolves looked fresh and full of energy. I wasn't sure how much longer my friends could hold them off.

Beyond them, Cord and Alex were faring a little better. One of the Werewolves, the brown one that Cord had fought with, lay bleeding and still in a heap to one side. The other three were taking turns attacking. All of them moved with a speed that blew my mind, and I was struck at how much faster and stronger these Werewolves were, compared to any other I'd met. We needed backup.

"Logan, call Kane!" I yelled.

"On it," he yelled back, not taking his eyes off his attacker.

I headed for them, realizing they needed the most help, but Miles' voice called me back.

"Last chance, Tara. Come with me now or George won't make it."

I froze, furious with myself for getting distracted and leaving George alone. I turned and saw that Miles had George in a tight grip, with one arm around his neck, while the other held a syringe filled with some milky fluid, poised at the vein in George's neck.

"No!" I yelled, running at Miles and barreling into him, knocking us all to the ground.

I rolled to my knees, pushing George aside, and put all my weight into holding Miles still. Miles said something to me, but I couldn't hear it over the rushing sound in my ears. I pulled back and sank my fist into his cheek, relishing the sound of bone cracking as his head snapped to one side. He didn't try to talk again, but I kept my fists moving anyway.

"Tara!"

The sound of George's voice calling my name was what finally got my attention. My hands stilled, and I stared down at the blood that ran from Miles' nose and mouth before turning to face George. He looked at me with a stricken expression, and I stared back, trying to figure out the reason. He held something up, and my eyes landed on the syringe in his hand.

It was empty.

I slid away from Miles and went to George.

"Did it –? I mean, did he –?" I stopped. I couldn't say it.

George brought his hand to his neck. I saw a tiny trickle of blood running down into his shirt. The hole was nothing more than a pin prick, but it terrified me more than any other wound I could've imagined.

"Yeah, he got me." George's words came out a little high pitched; like he wasn't sure how bad it was.

Behind me, Miles groaned. I hesitated, wanting to help George but unsure how – or if it was already too late.

"What did you do to him?" I hissed, scooting back towards Miles and shaking him. He was somewhere between conscious and not, but he managed to look pleased with himself, even through all the blood on his face.

"I made him more than he was," Miles whispered.

"That stuff in the needle…that will make him like them?" I nodded toward the Werewolves across the cavern.

Miles shook his head. "Not quite. I told you, the humans didn't take to it." Miles broke off and spat blood out of his mouth.

"What's going to happen to him?" I demanded.

"He's going to become more than human but less than Werewolf." Miles grinned and a tiny laugh escaped him.

I stared at Miles, trying to make sense of what he was saying, but he was being cryptic – as usual. All I knew was that this was bad. George was going to change into some sort of Werewolf, and if Miles was right, it wouldn't be a good kind of change.

Vaguely, I became aware of the shouts of others. Kane must've arrived. I assumed he'd brought a good number of Hunters with him, based on the shrieks and howls of the remaining Werewolves. Still, I continued to stare down at Miles in a silent panic.

I felt a hand close around mine. I jerked, but it was only George. He'd scooted closer, and I knew he'd heard what Miles said, but he didn't ask questions; just quietly held my hand and sat.

Across the cavern, the fighting was breaking up. The Werewolves were finally down, thanks to Kane and his reinforcements. They weren't all dead but they were subdued – our side had clearly won – finally. Cord and Alex were backing off, their help no longer needed. I knew they'd head this way any second, and then my chance to figure out how to fix this would be gone.

"They'll never let him survive it anyway," Miles said.

He was looking across the cavern, but I knew who he meant. He was right. None of the Hunters would allow this once they found out. A human, being changed into a Werewolf? Hybrids were bad enough, as far as they were concerned. This would be something else, totally.

I squeezed my eyes shut and resisted the urge to take Miles by the throat and apply pressure. He was done, anyway. Without Demi or his hybrid entourage – not to mention a broken nose and possibly jaw – he wasn't getting away.

I could see Cord and Alex walking this way; Cord's eyes blazed with unrestrained fury.

I turned back to Miles. "How long does he have?" I hissed.

"Another moon, maybe two," said Miles.

"How do I fix it?"

"There is no cure, if that's what you mean. But if you want to make him whole, give him Hunter blood. Maybe it'll be enough to retain his humanity."

I didn't answer. Alex and Cord were too close. Alex crouched down across from Miles and stared at me.

"Are you okay?" he asked.

I nodded.

"What about him?" Alex gestured to George, and I made a snap decision.

"He's fine," I said. "Miles, not so much."

Alex turned his attention to Miles' bloody face and grunted. I felt relieved to have the focus off George. I didn't want to lie to Alex, but I couldn't take the chance of the wrong Hunters finding out. It would only put George in more danger. I squeezed George's hand, hoping he caught my meaning and kept his mouth shut. Out of the corner of my eye, I saw him slide the syringe into his pocket, and I knew he'd understood.

"What should we do with him?" I asked, gesturing to Miles.

He was sitting now, but had otherwise made no move to get up. Cord stood a few feet away, and if looks could kill, Miles would be nothing but ashes. Alex glanced toward Kane and considered it.

"Kane's still rounding things up over there," said Alex. He looked down at Miles. "Get up."

Miles didn't move or give any indication that he'd heard Alex. Cord stepped forward and sank her foot into Miles' rib cage. Miles came to life, then, turning toward Cord and snarling. She pulled her boot back, prepared to lodge another kick, but Miles rolled out of reach, and got to his feet, looking a lot more okay than he had seconds ago. He glared at Cord for a split second and then, without warning, launched himself at me.

I wasn't ready for it, and we both went flying. I landed with a thud that stole my breath, and for a second, all I could do was gag and gasp for air. Miles had his arms around me, holding me still, and he leaned down until his lips were almost touching my ear. When he spoke, hot breath blew across my cheek. I recoiled, but Miles held firm.

"My mission cannot die. Astor De'Luca has the answers. Find him," he whispered.

Then his body jerked violently against me and everything went slack. His hands lost their hold; his eyes glazed over. His head slumped against my shoulder and he became deadweight. Hands came down and yanked his body off mine, and I stared up into Cord's burning eyes. She was panting and staring at Miles with the most twisted expression I'd ever seen.

I looked at Miles, a sinking feeling in my stomach. He was on his side and his expression was blank. A heavy stake protruded from his back, right behind his heart. Steady streams of blood were already coating his shirt.

"Cord?"

She didn't respond to my voice.

Then Alex and George were there, both looking a little shocked, and I let them help me up. We all stared down at Miles.

"Everybody okay?"

The sound of Kane's voice brought us all back. He frowned at Miles' body and then looked back and forth between our faces. Logan came up behind him, looking concerned and exhausted. Cambria followed but her expression was something different. She was wide eyed and transfixed on Miles' ashen face.

"We're fine," Alex answered.

"What happened?" Kane asked.

I glanced over at Cord and saw the look of open hate she wore as she stared down at Miles' body.

"He attacked Tara," Alex said. "Cord stopped him." I didn't miss the confusion in his tone, as if he was trying to understand what had happened.

Either Kane didn't notice or didn't care. He glanced at Cord, who was still as a statue, and nodded once. "A clean kill. That's my girl," he said. Then he turned on his heel and began shouting out orders to the Hunters that scurried over the room.

Cambria inched closer. She was still staring down at Miles and shaking her head side to side in some pattern of shock.

"What is it?" I asked.

"I don't believe it. I mean, I knew it the moment I saw him. But..." She looked over to where Demi was being roused awake. "He played me, but her... he was honest with her and she was okay with that."

"What are you talking about? You knew Miles?"

Cambria met my eyes and blinked. "That," she said, pointing a finger at Miles' body, "is Phillipe. My ex."

I looked back and forth between her and Miles while that sunk in. Then I looked back at Demi, all of it finally clicking into place.

Demi was standing, with help. She had a Hunter clinging to each elbow, helping her make her way towards the trail that would lead her out of the cave and back to school. Our eyes met across the room, and I held her gaze, hoping she could read exactly what I thought of her in my expression. She didn't even blink at my hostility. Just before she turned the corner and disappeared, she winked.

CHAPTER THIRTY-THREE

The dim lighting didn't help the pressure behind my eyes. It felt like the culmination of an entire semester of stress; a heavy ball of pain had finally burst inside my skull and I couldn't get past the pounding. I was in the infirmary, halfway between awake and pretending to be asleep, thankful it was three in the morning. If anyone had spoken to me then, I would've ripped their head off to stop the blaring noise before it reached my eardrum.

In the bed next to me, behind the half closed hospital-issued curtain, George slept. They'd kept him here for observation not because they knew about the injection, but because he was a human; a weakling who would probably collapse into shock the moment the drama dissipated.

I'd stayed because I was a nervous wreck that any moment, George was going to morph into a flesh-eating monster like Miles had said. If it came to that, I'd make sure my flesh was first, and pray Miles wasn't lying when he said Hunter blood would be the cure. But so far, George was himself. He was soaking in all the attention, too. Between Cambria, Cord, and my mother–who'd arrived after dinner, along with Grandma–George was getting the royal treatment.

I was okay with it. It kept my mother occupied and the room too crowded for her to really let loose on me.

So far.

I had no doubt it was coming.

Voices drifted back from the office and the door was wrenched opened, the rusty hinges amplifying the pounding in my skull. I cringed against the pain in my head caused by the bass in the speaker's voice and tried to pry my eyes open to identify the footsteps that approached. I managed to squint out into the darkened room but it did little good. The curtain that surrounded my bed was pulled shut enough that I couldn't see around it.

The voices came closer.

"Put them here," said the man whose voice echoed in my skull like a drum beat. Through the migraine, I recognized him. It was Kane. "And cover them up." There was a pause while he waited for someone to obey him and then he said, "No, all the way over their heads. We don't want anyone to recognize them. Or see the restraints."

"Won't it look suspicious?" came a woman's voice. The nurse who'd checked us in. She sounded even more mousy and nervous than when I'd met her earlier. Kane probably had a way of bringing that out in people.

"We'll pull the curtains around them. No one will notice, and if they do, your patients will appear asleep," said Kane.

"But –"

"It's the best we can do until we figure this out," he snapped.

"O–okay," she stammered.

Approaching footsteps sounded on the linoleum. "Sir?" It was a female's voice but overly deep. A mental picture of Betty popped into my head. "You wanted to see me?"

"How are the wards coming?" Kane asked, confirming my suspicions.

"Slow, sir. I'm not as good at this as Vera – I mean, Ms. Gallagher."

"Well, work faster. We don't need any more of these getting in," he said. "Or more importantly, any unwanted information getting out, until we have it under control."

"Yes, sir," Betty said. "Are those the survivors from the cave?"

"Yes. There were only these two." Kane sighed, but it sounded more impatient and aggravated than sad. "There were a few more but they managed to slip away. And if these two are any indication, this is a long way from over."

"Is it true then?" Betty asked. "I wasn't there, but I heard… I mean – are they really–?"

Kane cut her off. "Mr. and Mrs. Lexington? That information is highly classified until I say otherwise, do you understand?"

"Yes, but they're…" Betty trailed off, her voice a mixture of disbelief and awe.

"Some sort of hybrid," Kane finished for her. He sounded grim. "It shouldn't be possible, but here they are. CHAS is going to have their hands full with this mess."

No one responded, and I heard the sound of another arrival.

"Professor Kane? We've got a situation." It was Alex.

I froze, the pounding in my head momentarily forgotten as I held my breath and listened.

"What is it?" Kane asked.

"Intruders at the main gate. A pack of them, sir, and some are familiar faces. The students won't fight their own people."

"They're not our people anymore," Kane growled.

"Either way, this isn't going to end well unless you get out there," Alex said.

"Fine. I'm going. Betty, you're with me. See what wards you can construct while we're there." Footsteps started and then stopped again. "Harriet, I trust you can keep our patients… quiet until I return?"

"Yes, Jonah, I can do that," she said, her exhaustion coming through in her tone. She obviously didn't like what was being asked of her.

"Is there a problem?" Kane demanded, his tone harsh and impatient.

"Well, I'm not sure we should–"

"I don't have time for this," Kane interrupted, his voice rising.

"Jonah, please. You'll wake the others," the nurse said.

"I'll stay with them," Alex said.

"I can't spare a fighter right now," said Kane.

"You'll have plenty of manpower at the front, if you can get them to fight," Alex said.

Kane sighed. "Fine, but keep your earpiece on. I'll call if I need you."

"Yes, sir."

The footsteps receded, and the door creaked closed. The throbbing in my head lessened some once they left, and I tried to make sense of what I'd heard. Victoria's parents were alive, lying in bed somewhere in this room. And they were… hybrids?

The curtain in front of me fluttered as it was pulled aside. I tensed. I had no time to move or react before a face appeared from the other side. I let out the breath that had caught in my throat and forced the adrenaline away.

"Alex," I said.

His eyes narrowed. "I thought you'd be asleep. How much of that did you hear?" I didn't answer. "That's what I figured," he muttered. He stepped into the small space and came closer. "You can't tell anyone about them."

"By them, do you mean Victoria's parents or the Hunter–hybrids as a whole?"

Alex sighed. "Yes. I mean, all of it. At least not until we figure out how to deal with them."

I raised a brow and winced at the throbbing it caused. "We?"

Alex shrugged. "The school, CHAS, the Hunter community."

"And you're back to being a part of that?"

"I never stopped being a part of that," he said. His words were gentle, but his expression was serious. "Just because I helped you with Miles and kept it from Kane for a few days doesn't make me a traitor to my own kind. It doesn't mean I've turned my back on my purpose."

I scowled. It sounded so childish when he put it that way. Of course he hadn't turned his back on anyone. "I know that, I meant –"

"And to prove that I'm not taking sides, and that I can be your friend AND be true to my Hunter side, I'll tell you something you don't know. Something that I'm not supposed to share."

"What?"

"Remember that pack of rogue Werewolves that attacked us in the woods near Luray? The ones that killed Miles' errand boy?"

I nodded. How could I forget?

"Well, after everything went down at the cave today I told Kane about them, and he sent some guys up there to take a look and the entire pack of them were hybrids."

"What? Hunters?"

Alex shook his head. "Not Hunters. Humans."

I stared back at him, wide eyed. "But how…?" I remembered Miles saying that humans didn't take to the serum very well, so he'd used Hunters instead. It made sense when I thought of the wolf that had pinned me. He'd been so violent, so intent on killing… there was no humanity there like there was in other Weres.

"I don't know," Alex said. "But I know they had it out for you, for some reason. I'm telling you this because I think you might still be in danger, and I think you deserve to know."

I nodded, still processing everything; still connecting all the dots.

"Even on school grounds, I want you to be careful. Betty's skill with wards isn't entirely solid yet."

"Yeah, be careful, don't get dead. I get it," I said, waving a hand. My head was cramping again. I leaned back and shut my eyes.

"How are you feeling?" I could hear the frown in Alex's voice even with my eyes closed.

"Nasty headache," I said through gritted teeth.

Alex didn't answer. I cracked an eye open and found him leaning over me, frowning in concentration.

"What?" I said.

"I don't know. You feel different."

"This again? I can't deal with this right now. My head hurts."

"Interesting…" He leaned closer again and our eyes locked.

I felt a shudder go through me, and the pain cleared enough that I felt my muscles tense in excited anticipation. I stared up at him, feeling warm and shaky all at the same time. He stared back at me, his dark eyes burning into mine for what felt like forever.

"I might've lied," he said finally. It was a whisper, gruff and low, and I could feel his breath on my face. He didn't pull away but he didn't come closer, either.

"About what?" I breathed.

"About staying away from you. About letting you go. And about my ability to do either one."

"Oh." I blinked up at him, trying to think of something else to say, but my brain was foggy.

"You'd kiss me back right now if I kissed you," he said, and I tried to decide whether to even attempt a denial. "But then you'd remember him and you'd feel bad for it."

His face clouded, and I dropped my eyes from his, already feeling guilty at the reminder. His hand came up and brushed hair away from my face, his fingertips barely grazing my skin and leaving a trail of tingles in their wake.

"When you won't feel guilty anymore, I'll kiss you again." He eased back, looking down over me with an expression that said he was actually enjoying my speechlessness. "Get some sleep," he said. Then he turned and slipped out.

CHAPTER THIRTY-FOUR

The sound of a door being yanked on its hinges raked across the nerves behind my eyeballs, and I tensed and grit my teeth so hard my jaw hurt. Before I could form a complaint, even to myself, the goose bumps began. Voices sounded in the outer office and got louder before the sound of hurrying feet cut off the words. I looked around for a weapon, trying to ignore the pain in my head, but I came up empty. Unless a bedpan counted. Probably not.

Then the curtain surrounding my bed was being viciously ripped aside. I blinked into the dim fluorescent lighting and a halo of auburn hair came into focus.

Wes was at my side before I could move.

He grabbed me and pulled me up into his arms, holding me tight against his chest and burying his face in my hair.

"Hey," I mumbled.

My voice was muffled against the leather of his jacket, but I didn't care. I closed my eyes and inhaled the scent of leather and woods. An ache that I'd never even realized was there dissolved into relief.

We stayed like that until someone cleared their throat. I jerked away, remembering the goose bumps. Two pairs of eyes stared back at me from the foot of the bed.

"Jack, Fee, you came." I beamed at them, and they smiled back and came closer.

"Of course we came, honey. How are you feeling? I was worried when they said you were in the infirmary," Fee said. She came and put a hand on my forehead, a motherly gesture. Warmth flowed from her hand to my skin, and the headache dialed back into something bearable.

"Oh, I'm fine," I said, sighing at the small relief from the headache. "I stayed to keep an eye on George."

"And how is he?" she asked.

"Seems okay. A few bruises but nothing serious. They kept him overnight for observation." I glanced at Wes again, who was staring at me with an intent expression, like he was trying to memorize the sight of me. I squeezed his hand and he squeezed back.

"But you're sure you're okay?" Fee asked, her brows pulling together in concern. Her eyes scanned my body and she frowned.

"Other than a massive headache, yes," I said.

"Ahh. I knew there was something. I'll take care of it." She came closer and laid her hand across my forehead again. She bent down close to me, whispering a string of words that were too low and quick for me to understand. Then she fished in her bag and handed me a small vial of clear liquid. "Drink this. It'll clear you right up."

I took it gratefully, trying not to remember how gross her potions tasted. "Thanks."

She nodded. "I'm going to go speak with the nurse and see if there's anything I can do for George," she said. "I would've already asked, but someone wasn't very nice on his way in and I didn't get a chance." She sent Wes an accusatory glare.

He shrugged. "She wasn't going to let us in until morning."

Fee rolled her eyes. "You catch more flies with honey, ever heard that?"

He shrugged. "I don't like flies. They're annoying." He grinned. "I'd rather catch hell."

Fee shook her head. "Obviously."

She disappeared around the curtain, and I pulled the lid off the vial and braced myself before downing the medicine all in one swallow. I made a face and shuddered, but I could feel the medicine warming inside me as it traveled to my stomach and spread. Already, the pain in my head was receding. In another moment, it was gone. I sighed.

Jack took Fee's place on the empty side of my bed and looked down at me. He leaned heavily on a polished cane, but otherwise, he looked good. His beard had grown out and he looked more like the bear I imagined he was.

He grinned. "You went off and had all the fun without us."

"It's boring here," I said. "And they don't yell at me nearly as much as you do. Had to find something else to pass the time."

He grinned wider. "I knew it. Hunters are going soft."

"He's really dead, though, right?" Wes said. He wasn't smiling. He looked worried.

"He's really dead," I said.

"Vera said it was Cord who finished him," said Wes. His lips pressed together in a thin line, and I couldn't tell if he was pleased with the news or not.

"That's right," I said, and left it at that.

Remembering those last few seconds with Cord still made me uncomfortable. The look in her eyes, the level of violence, was disturbing. Not that I had any real sympathy for Miles, but part of me felt like Cord had been a little too hasty with killing him. He could've just as easily been pulled aside and restrained. I'd yet to find a minute alone to confront her about it but I fully planned on it, very soon.

"Ah, you're only jealous it wasn't you, kid. Wipe the sourpuss look off your face," Jack said. He slapped Wes on the shoulder and it seemed to pull Wes out of it because he smiled and swatted at Jack.

"I'm not the only one jealous of missing the action, old man," Wes said.

"Damn straight. Next time, I'll be in it, I can guarantee you that." There was a serious promise in Jack's eyes, and I didn't doubt him for a second. He wouldn't be kept out of the fighting for much longer, not by anyone. And I was glad for it, because it meant he was alive.

"If we don't take a year to get here, that might be possible," said Wes.

Jack frowned, and I realized it really had taken them a lot longer to get here than it should have.

"What took you guys so long anyway?" I asked. Jack and Wes exchanged a look that I didn't like. "What?" I demanded.

Wes spoke up. "You know Miles found a way to create Werewolves, right?" I nodded. "He failed to mention he left a pack of them outside the front gates of the school."

My eyes widened. "Were you attacked?"

"No. Detained," he said in a flat voice.

Even Jack looked pissed, and I realized what they meant. "They didn't think you guys were part of them? But Vera would've vouched for you."

"Vera was a little busy with Miles' body and other arrangements. They conveniently couldn't get a hold of her right away," said Wes.

"Thought I was going to have to put those kids in their place," Jack muttered.

He looked annoyed and dangerous, but I wondered how well he really would've done against a group of Hunters, with his injuries. I was glad it hadn't come to that.

"Did they hurt you?" I asked, looking at Wes again.

He shook his head. "No, but only because they thought we were one of Miles' people. They were on orders to detain, not kill, so they could bring them in. Apparently, he found a way to turn Hunters into Werewolves, creating some sort of hybrids. Some of them were recognized as the alumni that have gone missing."

"He said he'd found a way to turn Hunters." I was reminded of the shocked gasps from Alex and the others when the Werewolves had walked into the cavern. They must've recognized some of them… like Victoria's parents, maybe? I remembered what I'd overhead from Kane earlier in the night. I opened my mouth to tell them but I was interrupted.

"Tara?" George's sleepy voice came from the other side of the curtain and then he was pulling it aside, rubbing his face. He blinked when he saw that I had company and then his eyes narrowed as he realized who it was.

"Hello, George," said Wes. He nodded stiffly, which was about all I could hope for at this point.

George gave some sort of grunt and nodded back, looking fully awake now. "Wes, right? What are you doing here? Do you go here, too?"

George had asked me a lot of questions when everything had quieted down, but I'd really only answered the ones I had to. Like the fact that no, he wasn't crazy; those were people turning into wolves. And no, I wasn't one of them; I was a Hunter, which led to a whole new round of explanations needed. Cord hadn't looked very happy that I'd spilled everything; neither had Alex, for that matter, but there was really no better option. George had been infected and on the off chance it led to a monster version of himself, he needed to know that Werewolves existed. But none of my explaining had covered Wes, so George was guessing right now.

"No, I don't go here," was all Wes said.

George raised an eyebrow at him. Jack cut in and held out his hand across the bed to George.

"I'm Jack," he said.

George took Jack's massive hand in his and they shook.

"George."

"Nice to meet you, George. Thanks for being there for Tara today."

That seemed to be all George needed to hear to make up his mind because he smiled, and I felt some of his tension dissolve. "Anytime. Tara's a really special girl."

Wes' hand tightened on mine.

"That, she is." Jack was smiling and glancing between Wes and George, and I could see he was enjoying this way more than he should.

Thankfully, Fee came back and poked her head around the curtain.

"Oh, George, you're awake," she said. She came into the little room and held out her hand for him to shake. "I'm Fee, Jack's wife. It's nice to meet you."

"Nice to meet you, too, ma'am," George said, taking her hand.

"Oh, listen to you. A boy with manners," she said, poking an elbow at Wes, who grumbled. George grinned wider. "The nurse says you escaped with minor injuries, but I want to make sure you're feeling okay. Can we talk for a minute, in your room?" Fee asked.

"Sure..." George glanced from her to me. I nodded, letting him know it was okay to go with her, and they disappeared behind the curtain.

I could hear Fee asking him to show her his bruises and scrapes and then offering him a vial of something to drink. When they were done, George returned looking like he'd chugged a pot of coffee.

"Wow, I feel amazing," he said. He looked at Fee in open awe. "What was in that stuff?"

"The usual healing ingredients," she said, waving a dismissive hand. "Hawk's eyes, lizard guts, dragon tongue." George gaped at her, and she laughed. "I'm kidding. There's ginseng and some vitamins and herbs. It's more about the words spoken over the liquid than anything else. It heightens their power over your body."

George nodded, pretending to understand everything she'd said, and still looking completely taken with Fee.

Jack cleared his throat and hobbled closer to her. "Well, I'm tired, and since I'm off Wood Point's Most Wanted list, maybe we could get a room," he said, wiggling an eyebrow at Fee.

She swatted his arm. "All right, Vera said to come see her when we were ready to get some rest. Let's go old man." Fee turned to me. "We'll see you in the morning, Tara. Try to get some rest." Her eyes flickered to Wes. "All of you."

They left and George stood around awkwardly, scratching the back of his head. "I'm going to uh, go see if the nurse has anything to eat," he said, scooting around the curtain and leaving me alone with Wes.

He sank onto the bed beside me and reached out his hand, letting his finger trail the scratch on my face. When his hand fell away I caught it in my own.

I felt restless, all of a sudden. I needed to move. "Can we take a walk?" I asked.

"Now?" He glanced at the window, even though it was too glazed over to tell what time of day it might be. "It's not even dawn."

"I need to stretch my legs."

He shrugged. "Why not?"

He helped me to my feet, and I pulled my boots on. We crept past the nurse's station without being seen. I was here of my own free will, but I wasn't sure how pleased she would be to see me leaving with a Werewolf, in the middle of the night.

We didn't speak again until we were far away from Griffin Hall, under the cover of thick woods.

"I'm glad you're okay," said Wes, pulling me to a stop under a wide oak whose branches were just beginning to bud. "I was worried."

In the filtered moonlight, I could see his expression. Worry lines etched across his forehead and his jaw looked tense. I ran my hand over the roughness of his cheek.

"I'm glad you're here," I said.

"Where else would I be? I wish I could've gotten here sooner." He frowned; an expression that reminded me of Jack.

"I'm glad it's over," I said. The frown deepened. "What?"

"When I was being held by security earlier, I heard them talking. They know that Miles found a way to turn those Hunters. They're forming search parties to hunt them down and kill them."

"But… why? They aren't necessarily evil. Miles was making them work for him, but what if they chose to be good?"

Wes shook his head. "Sounds like they aren't going to give them the choice. They don't like that it was possible in the first place and they're going to eliminate them before it gets out of control."

"But some of them were kids, like us. I saw them."

"I know."

"I can't believe this. I thought they were detaining them, trying to capture them, like Victoria's parents."

"Victoria's parents?" Wes' brows crinkled in confusion.

I filled him in on what I'd over heard from Kane. "He was talking about how CHAS was going to have their hands full trying to figure out how to deal with all of it," I finished.

"Maybe the order came from CHAS."

"You really think CHAS would order its own people killed?" I asked. Even as I said the words, I knew the answer. If it meant stopping a Werewolf, the answer would always be "yes." Wes didn't answer and I knew he thought the same thing. "We have to stop it," I said.

Wes' eyebrow shot up. "Right. You and me. No problem. How exactly do you plan on doing that?"

I sighed. "I don't know. But we have to try. What if we find them first? If they pledge allegiance to The Cause, doesn't that make them off limits for CHAS?"

"Yes…It does." he said, and I could see the wheels turning. "That could work. But it would mean…."

"You would have to leave again," I finished. I leaned back against the tree, my good mood fading.

"If I want to find them before Kane's people do, then yes."

I sighed. "I should come with you."

"Tara –"

I kicked at a tree root. "I didn't say I would. I said I should."

"School will be out in a few more weeks. You'll be home for the summer."

"You think you'll be back by then?"

He cocked his head to the side. "I don't know. Do you want me to be back by then?"

"Of course I do."

He leaned forward, clearly not satisfied with my simple answer. His eyes were sharp and searching. "Where do we stand?"

"I know things have been… complicated since I've been here. I still care about you, and I still want to be with you, but I need you to be honest with me. And I need you to have confidence that I can handle myself."

"And you need me to stay away from you on a full moon?" His expression softened. There was even a hint of humor.

"I don't know. We'll figure it out. Maybe I'll invest in a lunar calendar or something."

We both smiled.

"I missed you," he whispered, leaning down until we were nose to nose.

"I know. I wish you didn't have to go away again. But you have to. We have to try and help those people."

"Miles really left a mess behind."

"Do you think Jack will go for it? Tracking them all down, I mean."

"I need to talk to him about it, but yeah. Jack would want to help save them. Especially if Fee lets him come, too."

"At least you're being a hybrid will come in handy for once."

Wes smiled. "True. I'll need help, though. I'd probably take Cord with me."

I rolled my eyes. "Oh, darn. I'm heartbroken."

He laughed. "I'm proud of you for lasting this long." Then he turned serious. "How is she? Dealing with Miles again had to be rough on her."

"You could say that. She seemed pretty shaken up." I paused, trying to decide how much to tell. But it was Wes, and I could tell him anything. "She kind of freaked out. I mean, I know she was trying to protect me, but I'm not convinced killing him was actually necessary. Alex was right there. And Miles wasn't trying to kill me. He was–" I stopped. I forgot that I still hadn't said anything about George.

"He was what?"

"I don't know. He mentioned a name. Astor De'Luca. He said I should contact him about the hybrids. I think he might know a way to help George."

"Why does George need help?" Wes' eyes narrowed, and I could tell he didn't like where this was going.

"Miles injected him with something. He said it would make George a Werewolf but it would be a different version. A monster. He said it was because the humans didn't take to the serum like Hunters did, and if I want to save him, I should give him my blood."

"Do you believe him?"

"I think so. He was way too proud of this whole project to lie about the results. He wanted the world to know what he'd created."

"Have you told anyone?"

"No way. The Hunters here would kill him if they knew."

"What are you going to do?"

"I don't know. I explained as much as I could to George, but I'm stuck here. I can't be there for him when he gets home. What if he–what if he hurts someone?"

"We can't exactly lock him up."

"And we can't tell anyone."

Wes sighed. "I can have Fee keep an eye on him."

"You think she'll do it?"

"Yeah, she'll do it." He frowned. "You're going to have to figure something out when you get back for the summer, though."

"I know. I will. You should talk to Cord, make sure she's okay."

"I will."

He leaned down, letting his lips brush mine but not applying any real pressure. I felt all of the tension drain away. I brought my arms up and laced my fingers together behind his head.

He leaned closer and pressed his lips firmly to mine, and for a while, I let myself get lost in kissing him. I let myself forget about all of the stress of the last few weeks; the hybrids, Miles dying, and the violence I'd seen in Cord. I forgot about George and the possibility that he could become a Werewolf. I forgot about the fact that Vera was dying, and having visions of me, and that someday, I'd have to choose between two opposing political futures.

For a few blissful moments, none of that mattered. Because I had Wes.

I was so lost in the kiss that I didn't even notice the goose bumps, or that they weren't raising out of some physical reaction to Wes' roaming hands on my body.

Wes noticed. I felt him stiffen and knew that the feeling was a warning.

A Werewolf.

Probably more than one, if my body's reaction was any indication. Wes turned around, scanning the trees and blocking my body with his.

"Do you see anything?" I whispered.

Wes shook his head.

From somewhere within the trees, a growl went up. Then another. And another. They echoed off each other so it sounded like dozens of voices, or just one. Movement caught my eye. To my left, a wolf appeared, moving slowly like one would with cornered prey. Wes was shaking, and I knew it wouldn't be long before he shifted. I inched further away, around the side of the tree.

"Two for the price of one," the wolf snarled.

Even in the dim light, I saw that its fur was caked in mud. And its eyes were yellow. Exactly like the Werewolf Alex had killed the day I'd gone to meet Miles.

"What do you want?" Wes demanded. His voice shook with the control of staying human this long. He shed his jacket and let it fall to the ground beside him.

"The girl. But we'll take you, too."

The wolf snarled and other voices joined in. One by one, more wolves stepped clear of the trees. My eyes widened as I counted them. There were already eight of them. And more were coming.

"Tara, stay back. I can't–I have to change." Wes struggled to speak.

"Do it," I whispered.

As soon as I'd spoken, his form shimmered and twisted and fabric was torn away as his human form was replaced by that of a massive, russet-colored wolf.

The moment he changed, the other Werewolf charged. Half a dozen others followed at his heels, and all I could see was fur. I was momentarily forgotten in the chaos, which was fine by me. I dropped to my knees and felt around with my hands, careful to keep my eyes on the battle in front of me. My hands closed on twigs and broken branches, all of them skinny and weak. I tossed them away and crawled further out, still feeling with my hands. My fingers closed around a thicker branch and I almost cried out with relief. I had a weapon. I got to my feet and ran towards the small crowd of Werewolves with the stake raised and ready.

Fear – for Wes and myself – threatened to paralyze me, but I couldn't let it. There wasn't time. I shoved aside all thought and emotion; I let go of anything human that would hold me back and let instinct take over as I charged into the fray.

Werewolves were thrown aside as I worked my way towards the center. They came back, teeth snapping, when they realized it was me yanking on them. I shoved them away again with my fists and feet, wading further in.

I had to find Wes.

Growls echoed around me, but I shut them out. A Werewolf came at me, saliva dripping from its jowls. I waited until it was within arm's reach and shot out with my stake. I felt it pierce the Were's flesh and shoved again, until the Werewolf's eyes bulged and its tongue went slack. It fell to the ground, already being trampled by its pack mates as the next attacker took its place.

A harsh growl went up, and I turned. I caught sight of Wes, his teeth buried in the neck of the muddy Werewolf. He yanked and pulled on the Werewolf, sending them zigzagging away from the crowd of bodies I was now in the middle of.

A gray wolf lunged at me from my right, thinking I wasn't paying attention. I brought my hand up and my head around at the same time and smashed my fist into its nose. Blood poured out of its nostrils and it yelped, falling away and shaking its head. Another Were came at me as the first fell away. Instead of baring its teeth and lunging for my throat, the way most of them did, it fell away at the last moment and slashed my calf with its claws.

I felt my jeans rip and the sting of breaking skin, and I brought my fist around and smashed it into the Were's ribs. It fell away and I glanced over at Wes again.

He and the muddy wolf circled each other. Patches of flesh hung loose around the muddy wolf's neck and blood dripped from the wounds, leaving thick puddles. It didn't seem to faze the wolf, though. If anything, it looked more determined. Wes circled around and caught me watching him.

Our eyes met and held for a split second, and I could see he was as worried for me as I was for him.

"Tara, look out!" Wes growled a warning but there was no need.

I felt the Werewolf approaching me from behind and stuck my leg out in a backwards kick like Professor Flaherty had taught us. It went down with a yelp.

Wes was still watching me and not paying enough attention to the danger in front of him. The muddy wolf took advantage of the moment and made its move. It lunged forward and locked its teeth around Wes' throat, throwing him to the ground with a jerk.

"No!" I yelled, running towards them.

Wes struggled against the wolf's hold but he wasn't getting up, and he hadn't pulled free. Out of the numbness inside me, anger boiled to the surface.

My body shook as I ran. I was too hot.

Boiling lava seared my veins.

It felt like I was burning alive, from the inside out.

I didn't bother with the deep breaths or anything else to try and calm down. None of that mattered. Neither did the anger, or whatever waited for me on the other side of it. All that mattered was Wes.

I reached the muddy wolf and extended my hands, grabbing fistfuls of fur. I yanked him back with a strength that should've surprised me. But I was too far gone on the anger to feel anything but satisfaction as I felt his jaw loosen and break free of its hold on Wes. I lifted the muddy wolf off the ground and tossed it aside like it weighed nothing.

I bent over Wes. "Are you okay?" My voice sounded foreign to my own ears.

Wes – still a wolf – blinked up at me. Bloody holes marred the fur on his neck where teeth had penetrated. I tried not to look at them, but my eyes kept getting pulled back.

"I'm fine," he said, finally.

I nodded. My entire body felt like it was being pulled in different directions. I wanted to stay, to make sure Wes really was okay. But another part of me – a much bigger part – needed to finish the fight.

"I'll be back. Don't move." I rose and turned back to the remaining Werewolves. Wes didn't argue, which let me know how hurt he was.

The heat in my body rose another level.

I looked at the muddy wolf, lying in a heap on the ground, and something inside me snapped.

What happened after was a blur. Time unaccounted for. Like the day on the rooftop, when I'd spaced out.

Only this time, when the haze cleared, I stood amidst bodies. A couple of them were human but most were Werewolves.

And all of them were dead.

I blinked, somehow thinking if I did it enough, the bodies would disappear and I'd be back in the clinic with Wes.

"Tara?"

I whirled at the sound of my name.

On edge. Ready for another fight.

For a second, I didn't even recognize the voice. And then it was like reality clicked back into place.

"Wes," I said. I let relief wash over me that he was okay. And then I realized he was still a wolf. "Are you okay?" I took a step toward him.

He cocked his head to the side. "I'm fine. I'll heal faster this way. Plus… no clothes."

I nodded, sure I should be feeling something more than I was right now.

"Are you okay?" he asked.

"Of course. I didn't get bit. You did."

"Right, but you…" He seemed at a loss. He was still looking at me that way, his head cocked to one side, like he couldn't figure me out.

"What?"

"You killed them all," he said. "How did you do that? I've never seen…" He didn't seem to know how to explain.

I tried to remember but came up blank. I shrugged. "I was protecting you. You were hurt."

"Tara." He took a step toward me. "You killed them all. Even the ones who tried to leave. You chased them down and killed them. Then you came back and killed the injured ones. The ones who couldn't get up or fight any more."

I stared at him, trying to remember something, anything, of what he was saying.

"I don't remember that," I said. My voice sounded small. I looked around at all of the bodies.

"And you smell." He took another step towards me. "The whole time you were fighting, you smelled… different." He was close enough to touch now, but I didn't move. I couldn't. I knew what he was going to say.

"What did I smell like?" I whispered.

His caramel eyes met mine. I could see my reflection in them. "Like a wolf."

ABOUT THE AUTHOR

Heather Hildenbrand lives in coastal Virginia where she writes paranormal and fantasy romance with lots of kissing & killing. Her most frequent hobbies are cuddling with her 100-pound goldendoodle, riding country roads on the back of her husband's motorcycle, and avoiding killer slugs.

You can find out more about Heather and her books at www.heatherhildenbrand.com.

www.ingramcontent.com/pod-product-compliance
Lightning Source LLC
Chambersburg PA
CBHW020247030826
48979CB00030B/2648/J

* 9 7 8 1 9 6 1 4 5 5 2 7 6 *